Praise for Chris Manby

'A fast track fun romance full of monkey business'
Daily Mail on *Girl Meets Ape*

'The perfect antidote to the cold winter weather . . . light-hearted romp of sun, sea, sand and sex . . . This merry novel should blow away the winter blues'
Hello on *Seven Sunny Days*

'Engaging and humorous'
OK Magazine on *Seven Sunny Days*

'Very funny, hugely feel-good and the perfect antidote for anyone who worries that the only career ladder they've achieved is a run in their tights'
Fiona Walker on *Lizzie Jordan's Secret Life*

'It's a great idea for a plot, and Manby's writing more than does it justice'
Marie Claire on *Getting Personal*

'A funny first novel . . . that's more realistic than *Friends*, cleaner than *The Young Ones* and not as frightening as *Shallow Grave*'
Daily Mail on *Flatmates*

About the author

Chris Manby is the author of eight romantic comedy novels for Hodder and Stoughton. She is also editor/contributor to the *Girls' Night In* and *Girls' Night Out/Boy's Night In* anthologies, which have so far raised more than £600,000 for the children's charity War Child, and topped book charts all over the world. Chris grew up in Gloucester but now lives in London and Los Angeles. She is working on her second screenplay.

CHRIS MANBY

Girl Meets Ape

HODDER

Copyright © 2004 by Chris Manby

First published in Great Britain in 2004 by Hodder & Stoughton
A division of Hodder Headline

The right of Chris Manby to be identified as the
Author of the Work has been asserted by her in accordance
with the Copyright, Designs and Patents Act 1988.

A Hodder paperback

A CIP catalogue record for this title
is available from the British Library

ISBN 0 340 89846 1

Typeset in 9/11pt Plantin Light by
Hewer Text UK Ltd, Edinburgh

Printed and bound in Great Britain by
Mackays of Chatham Ltd, Chatham, Kent

Hodder Headline's policy is to use papers that are natural, renewable
and recyclable products and made from wood grown in sustainable
forests. The logging and manufacturing processes are expected to
conform to the environmental regulations of the country of origin.

Hodder & Stoughton Ltd
A division of Hodder Headline
338 Euston Road
London NW1 3BH

For the real Jennifer Niederhauser

I

'Oh, I'm the king of the swingers . . .' sang the man in the monkey suit.

'And he certainly is!' laughed Dahlia. 'Would you look at the lunchbox on that!'

By this point, the gorilla-gram was already down to a fetching red thong. He kept the gorilla mask on, though, much to the girls' disappointment.

'Everything off!' Dahlia screamed at him. 'Come on! They paid for everything! You did pay for everything off, didn't you?' Dahlia asked Jennifer Niederhauser, her chief bridesmaid and coordinator of the hen night.

'I promised your fiancé I would keep you out of trouble,' said Jennifer in earnest. 'But yes, Dahlia, we paid for *everything* off.'

'Woo-hoo!' whooped Dahlia. 'Then shake that banana, baby!'

She shimmied into the centre of the crowd of hen-night revellers that surrounded the stripper and mimed something lewd with a banana of her own. The stripper handed her a bottle of baby oil and invited her to rub some on his pecs. Dahlia was in heaven. Jennifer was secretly relieved.

Jennifer hadn't expected much from the local kiss-o-gram company. Certainly not the buffed and toned body that gyrated on the dance floor with Dahlia now. She definitely hadn't seen the likes of this man in the sleepy little town of Tincastle before. The men who had frequented Cinderella's on a Friday night while Jennifer was growing up there were either fat-free weeds or the kind of guys who were proud of having beer bellies that made you wonder when the baby was due. This stripper-gram could have been a model.

Or maybe not. He still hadn't taken his mask off. It was too much to hope that he might have a face to match that physique.

Perhaps it was even worse than the hairy ape muzzle that covered it.

Dahlia was still dancing round him to the strains of the Rolling Stones' 'Satisfaction'.

'I can't get no . . .' she sang with a growl.

The stripper's body was slick with baby oil now and Dahlia was looking pretty sticky too. Jennifer wanted to cover her eyes when Dahlia ran her hand down the middle of the stripper's chest, lingering for a moment over his tidy abdominal muscles, then carrying right on down towards that skimpy red excuse for a pair of underpants. It had been way too long since Jennifer had run her own hands over a man's body. But she would *never* run her hands over one that had been paid for! She stepped a little further back out of the way.

It hadn't actually been Jennifer's idea to get a stripper at all. In fact, when Dahlia asked her if she would care to be chief brides-maid at her wedding to Henry, Jennifer had wanted to say no. No. No way! There's something distinctly undignified about a twenty-seven-year-old woman in a bridesmaid's dress. (To be honest, Jennifer thought there was something distinctly undigni-fied about a woman over the age of twenty-five dressed in bridal white as well.) But Dahlia had promised that Jennifer would be able to choose her own outfit. And they had been friends since they were tiny, hadn't they? Since their first day at primary school, Dahlia reminded her. Again and again and again.

Jennifer caved in. There were worse things in life than wearing a hideous dress for one whole day for your very best friend. And at least if she arranged the hen night, Jennifer thought, there would be no late night in a horrible sweaty club to endure. She envisaged instead a quiet evening in a classy restaurant. Some-thing akin to a nice American bridal shower, such as those she had attended while on an exchange placement at the University of San Diego. She'd choose somewhere that did modern Italian food, where Dahlia's old friends and new workmates could meet and mingle over Caesar salad and tuna carpaccio and a nice big glass of chilled Chardonnay (for those who drank, which Jennifer didn't). The most raucous moment would come when Dahlia unwrapped the presents the girls would bring her. Someone would inevitably have brought along a 'funny' sex toy. Just so long as Jennifer didn't have to touch it . . .

She attempted to get the evening going via e-mail, sending a mass mailing outlining her sedate hen-night plans to all the names Dahlia had given her. The dissension had been instantaneous. Four of Dahlia's workmates wrote back a joint petition, copying in everyone else on the list of course, saying, 'Are you joking? This is *Dahlia's* hen night we're talking about. Dahlia Wilde can't have her last night of freedom in a *restaurant*!'

They lobbied hard for a nightclub. Dahlia would want it that way, was what they said. They informed Jennifer that they had already had a whip-round in the office to pay for the stripper. Because there had to be a stripper, didn't there? What was a hen night without a live naked man? Karen and Briony would happily take charge of the trip to Ann Summers to get everyone's hen-night *accessories* . . .

Within three e-mails, the arrangements were completely out of Jennifer's hands. Karen and Briony had taken control. And that was how Jennifer came to end up in Cinderella's nightclub, wearing a plastic silver tiara and a cerise feather boa that clashed hideously with her favourite red Diane Von Furstenburg wrap dress, while a gang of other girls in tiaras cheered Dahlia on as, dressed as a naughty nun with L plates, she poured baby oil down the front of a thong worn by a stripper masquerading as a gorilla.

It was Jennifer's idea of hell.

While the other girls bayed for the stripper's body, Jennifer hovered at the edge of the dance floor like a non-swimmer with no armbands at the edge of a deep, deep pool.

'Come on, girl!' Dahlia shouted back to her after a while. 'Help me out here!'

It didn't matter whether she wanted to or not. Dahlia grabbed Jennifer by the wrist and pulled her into the centre of the circle. She slapped the baby-oil bottle into Jennifer's hand and invited her to do the stripper's other side. Jennifer was paralysed with embarrassment.

'I can't . . . I don't . . .' she stuttered. 'I'd really rather not . . .'

'Go on, gorgeous,' the gorilla-gram whispered. 'Don't be shy.'

3

At least, that's what Jennifer thought he said. It was quite hard to hear through the rubber mouth of the mask. But whatever he said, it didn't help her overcome her reluctance. Jennifer held the bottle of baby oil gingerly, trying not to get it all over her hands, and resisted by digging her heels in like a donkey when the stripper tried to pull her closer still.

The rest of the girls in the hen party started to clap in time to the music.

'Get 'em off! Get 'em off! Get 'em off,' they chanted. A bunch of drunken women is far scarier than a crowd of football hooligans, Jennifer thought not for the first time that evening.

'Mask or pants?' teased Dahlia.

'Both!' was the unanimous reply.

'Let's do this together,' Dahlia suggested to her bridesmaid.

'I don't want to,' said Jennifer, taking another step back. 'He's got baby oil all over him and this was quite an expensive dress and it might get all over me and I don't know if dry-cleaning gets baby oil out of silk jersey and—'

Too late. Without warning, the gorilla-gram leapt towards Jennifer, wrapped his arm around her waist and lifted her bodily off her feet. She let out a squeal of horror for herself and the dress, but he wouldn't let her go. Jennifer kicked her legs in mid-air like King Kong's Fay Wray dangling from the giant monster's arms at the top of a hundred-storey building.

'You do the mask!' Dahlia shouted above the music. At the same time the far from virginal bride-to-be ripped off the red thong with unseemly expertise.

'Wha-hey!' Dahlia waved the thong above her head like a trophy and the crowd of girls erupted with delight at the sight of their man in all his glory.

King of the Swingers he was indeed! When she stopped whooping to look at it, even Dahlia was momentarily dumbstruck by the beauty of the package she'd just unwrapped. Jennifer was simply open-mouthed with awe from her extremely close-up point of view.

'Get it off! Get it off!' The crowd hadn't finished with the stripper yet. These girls had seen a thousand penises between them (though not many had been quite so magnificent). What they really wanted to see now was what lay beneath the fierce rubber mask he still wore.

'Ug, ug, ug,' grunted the stripper, sticking closely to his role. He wasn't taking that mask off without a fight. With Jennifer tucked under his arm, the stripper careened around the circle like a frighteningly real ape.

'Put me down!' Jennifer protested. 'Put me down!'

He had her over his shoulder now. She pummelled her fists against his muscular back to no effect whatsoever. She tried slapping instead but stopped abruptly when he growled through his rubber canine teeth, 'That feels quite nice.'

'Get his mask off!' Dahlia instructed loudly from the sidelines. 'Get his mask off!'

'Get him to put me down first!'

The gorilla-gram wouldn't do that.

Jennifer was almost in tears. This kind of thing always happened. Specifically, this kind of thing always happened *to her*. Strippers are like cats which make a bee-line for the person with the allergies. They always pick on the shy girl in the audience. They have an instinct for it. They always get the one most easily embarrassed to rub lotion all over their bodies and simulate sex with exotic fruit.

'If you don't put me down I'll bite you!' Jennifer warned.

'I'd like that, too,' said the stripper with a growl.

'Get his mask off!' Dahlia shrieked again. 'Oh, for goodness' sake. Do I have to do everything myself?'

While the stripper whirled around with Jennifer still hanging over his shoulder like a rag doll, Dahlia jumped on to his other side like a tenacious little dog. Surprised by the attack from this five-foot-tall nun in a mini-skirt, the stripper released his prisoner into a crumpled heap on the dance floor. Dahlia leapt on his back and, grabbing the bottom of the rubber gorilla mask in both hands, ripped it upwards, nearly taking the poor bloke's nose off as she did so.

'I got him!' Dahlia was triumphant.

'Ow!' The stripper stumbled backwards, rubbing his newly denuded face.

'Why, Mr Jones, you're lovely!' Dahlia sighed dramatically

when she saw the delicious chocolate eyes beneath his curly brown hair. 'Isn't he lovely, girls?'

The hen party agreed.

The music ended.

'That's all, folks!' the stripper said, retrieving his mask from Dahlia's grasp and flourishing it at his fans as he took a courtly bow. The hens whooped and whistled.

'Have a wonderful wedding,' he kissed Dahlia on the cheek. 'And if you ever want to get married, just give me a shout,' was what he said to Jennifer with a wink. And a pinch to her bottom. He kissed her, too. On the side of the mouth. He would have got her full on the lips but she had already turned her head away in anger and was considering whether she ought to give the man another slap. A proper one this time. Right across his smug ape face.

'I need to talk to you about my dry-cleaning!' she shouted after him as he made a break for the gents' holding the mask protectively over his family jewels. 'This dress cost more than two hundred pounds, you know. I'm going to call your company and demand that they pay for this! You'd better hope they've got good insurance.'

The stripper didn't hear her. The music was too loud.

'Thank you, sweetheart!' Dahlia threw her arms around Jennifer's neck, ignoring her thunderous expression. 'This has been the best hen night ever! I was so worried we were going to end up somewhere dull, eating salad and carpaccio. But this has been a proper send-off. You really are the best, best bridesmaid a girl could ever have. You are my best, best, best, *best* friend,' she added. 'Did I tell you that?'

'Only five times this evening.'

Dahlia was very drunk.

'Where did you find that bloke?' she asked. 'Wasn't he amazing?'

'He was an idiot,' said Jennifer decisively. 'Look what he did to my dress.' The slinky red jersey was stained dark burgundy where the baby oil had soaked right through. 'I am going to get him to bloody well pay for this.'

'Oh, come on,' said Dahlia. 'It's a horrible dress anyway. Red doesn't suit you, you know.'

Jennifer opened her mouth to complain but Dahlia wasn't about to listen.

'Ah-ah-ah! I don't want to hear it. This is my hen night, Jennifer! Get into the party spirit. You're too uptight. That's why you haven't got a man . . . I thought you liked chimpanzees anyway.'

'He was supposed to be a gorilla,' Jennifer pointed out.

'Never mind,' said Dahlia. 'All monkeys to me . . .'

'They're *apes*. It was an ape that ruined my dress.'

'I'll get my rich new husband to buy you a new one.'

'Thanks.'

'There's lots of romantic potential in here,' Dahlia continued. She cast her eye around the dance floor. The local men who had been intimidated into the shadows by the gorgeous stripper were venturing back out into the disco lights again now. 'I will find you a boyfriend tonight,' Dahlia told her best friend. 'Otherwise you'll have to cop off with the best man next week.'

'That does not bear thinking about,' said Jennifer, as an image of a leering Craig Gascott, best man in name only, pushed the irritating ape boy from the front of her furious mind.

'How about that one?' asked Dahlia, pointing at a bloke who was showing his friends how he could rest a pint glass on top of his paunch without spilling a drop.

'Nice,' Jennifer's voice was dripping with sarcasm. 'Isn't it time to go home yet?'

She glanced involuntarily in the direction of the men's room. The stripper emerged in his day clothes just as she did so, looking almost better in his jeans and a soft grey sweater than he had done out of them. He seemed to be in a hurry. But Jennifer was certain he tried to catch her eye as he passed. In fact, she thought he might have winked at her again. The cheek of it. If Dahlia hadn't been hanging on to her arm, Jennifer would have stormed across that nightclub and had another go at him about the state of her outfit. Her Diane Von Furstenburg dress from San Diego! It was like losing a favourite dog . . .

'OK,' said Dahlia. 'You have to chat up the pint-glass bloke or down a vodka and red bull in one.'

'You know I don't drink,' said Jennifer irritably.

'Then you have to dance with the fat boy!' said Dahlia with glee.

'It's three minutes to two,' said DJ Sloppy, the local spin-doctor. 'Time for one last song before you reprobates go home to your mothers. Let's make it a slow one, shall we? Take your partners for the last chance dance . . . Move closer . . .'

Dahlia raised her eyebrows in the direction of the paunchy stranger. He took it as his cue to come and join them.

'This is my friend Jennifer,' said Dahlia, as she joined her friend and the stranger hand to hand. 'She fancies you.'

'No,' said Jennifer. 'Actually, I don't. And I'm not dancing tonight!'

Too late. The stranger wrapped his arms around her and pressed her hard against his belly.

'Dahlia!' Jennifer shrieked. 'Get him off me!'

But Dahlia was already bumping hips with the fat boy's friend. The fat boy started to nuzzle at Jennifer's neck. Mustering all of her strength, she broke free from his embrace and walloped him across the cheek with the flat of her hand. Fat boy stumbled backwards and landed on a woman who turned out to be his girlfriend.

'You bastard!' The girlfriend set about him with her handbag. 'Who was that girl you was dancing with? I can't take my eyes off you for a second. Take that,' she thumped him with her fake Kate Spade. 'And that, you tosser. And that.'

Time to make a sharp exit, thought Jennifer.

8

2

On the other side of town, Nessa O'Neill of Prowdes Animal Sanctuary was also having a very late night. This wasn't such an unusual state of affairs for her, however. When you work with animals, you can't expect to keep terribly human hours. Nessa knew that only too well. She would tell all her new recruits that working with animals is like having a baby stuck perpetually at six months old in your care. You can't tell them that you haven't had enough sleep when they demand your attention in the middle of the night. And they can't tell you exactly where it is that hurts and what is making them cry.

That night, Nessa had been called from her soft warm bed to tend to Hermione, the Vietnamese pot-bellied pig. Hermione and her companion, Harry Porker, had been delivered to the sanctuary a month previously. Their owner had bought them as darling little piglets, presents for his demanding children (he felt guilty because of the divorce). He was unaware that the tiny black bundles wouldn't be half so cute in a year and that his children wouldn't be half so interested in caring for them either.

Hermione and her piggy husband were too big for the stupid bloke's garden now. They were expensive to feed and impossible to contain. They had escaped on more than one occasion and dug up a neighbour's flower beds in search of roots. So he had to get rid of them. Nessa agreed to take them in. Nessa had *never* turned a homeless animal away from her sanctuary, whether it was a pig or a dog or a one-legged hedgehog. She was extremely proud of that record.

What she didn't know at the time was that Hermione was already pregnant with her first litter of piglets. Now Hermione was in labour, making noises the like of which you would expect to hear in a slaughterhouse, not this five-star pig hotel. Nessa gritted her teeth and tried to soothe Hermione by stroking her head while the sanctuary's vet, Harrison Arnold, took control of proceedings at the other end. Harry Porker squealed in sympathy from his side of the pen.

'You got her into this mess,' Nessa reminded him.

'Here comes the first one,' said Harrison. Nessa closed her eyes as a little pale piglet slithered out on to the straw, glistening with afterbirth in the flickering light of a bulb that needed changing.

'Is it breathing?' Nessa still couldn't bear to look.

'Oh, yes. It's breathing all right,' said Harrison, as the new arrival immediately let out a squeal of its own to add a high-pitched harmony to the cacophony. Hermione had already woken some of the pigs' sanctuary neighbours with her racket. In the background, a donkey brayed in annoyance at being woken up, an old dog howled in agreement, a chimpanzee gave a curious hoot.

Half an hour later, Prowdes' pot-bellied pig population had swelled by three hundred per cent. Hermione grunted with contentment as the six healthy piglets suckled. Harry Porker gazed over the low fence between them, proud as any human dad. But Nessa, glad as she was to see the charming family tableau in her shed, could only think of her overdraft.

'You should go back to bed. Get some beauty sleep.'

Nessa felt a gentle hand on her shoulder as she looked down upon Prowdes' Family Pig. It was Guy Gibson, head keeper at the sanctuary, one of her most trusted employees and lately a very valuable friend. Guy was in charge of the sanctuary's primates, but could be relied upon to turn his hand to pig husbandry in an emergency and that night, with the keeper who usually looked after the traditional farm animals on holiday, Nessa wasn't sure she could cope.

'I came as quickly as I could,' said Guy.

'Thank you, Guy. I'm very grateful you could make it. Hermione seemed to be having trouble and I wasn't sure Harrison would get here in time. Were you at a party?' Nessa asked. 'It sounded like I was interrupting a good night out.'

'Not exactly,' Guy grimaced. 'How many piglets did she have?'

'Six,' said Nessa. 'Six more mouths to feed. God knows how we're going to pay for them.'

'I've told you to stop worrying about that,' Guy said firmly. 'We're going to get a big grant for the chimpanzee project now we've got that university boffin on board. Everything will be OK before you know it. You might even be able to give me a raise,' he added cheekily.

Nessa stood up on tiptoes in her wellingtons and rumpled Guy's curly brown hair.

'If you were just thirty years older,' she sighed.

Guy smiled. He folded a tired and crumpled Nessa into his arms for a hug. Nessa breathed in the smell of his old jumper gratefully. Though he was young enough to be her son, there was something about capable Guy Gibson that Nessa found very reassuring. When Guy said that everything was going to be OK, Nessa could almost believe it.

3

Outside its natural habitat, Prowdes Animal Sanctuary was one of the best places a wild animal could hope to spend its days. The sanctuary was situated on forty acres of prime Devon farmland, just outside the little town of Tincastle, surrounding a beautiful seventeenth-century house that had been home to the O'Neill family for four generations. It had been home to an altogether smarter family before that, but in 1875, Charles Edward Prowde had lost the house and its farmland to Gillon Michael O'Neill in a poker game.

Gillon O'Neill was a horse-breeder from the west coast of Ireland. He was legendary in racing circles, able to turn just about any old nag into a Derby champion. Lame horses *danced* for Gillon O'Neill. His magic touch with animals had been passed down through the years to his great-granddaughter, Nessa.

These days, Nessa was widely regarded as one of Britain's most dedicated conservationists but once upon a time her unconventional image had made her something of a joke in the conservation world. A velvet cape accessorised with a diamante pin and wellingtons was a favourite ensemble of hers whether she was meeting local dignitaries or mucking out the donkeys. Before the birth of Prowdes Animal Sanctuary, the former debutante spent her life throwing herself into adventures and good causes with the enthusiasm of a Labrador puppy after a chocolate drop. Aged seventeen, she had run away from boarding school to Italy and studied painting under the auspices of an artist thirty years her senior who became her very first lover. In her early twenties, she dumped the old man for his nephew and went to Morocco in search of perfect light. Aged twenty-three, she drove across the Sahara with a couple of Frenchmen she had met just two nights before while smoking hashish in a Moroccan bar (dressed as a man, of course). After the Sahara, she trekked all the way down to South Africa, narrowly escaping kidnapping in the Congo by painting a tribal leader's portrait in the style of van Gogh.

After Africa came South America. Polo with the gauchos in Argentina. In Alaska she lived with the Inuit and chewed seal skin to make leather boots. In Australia she learned how to shear sheep. She learned to dive, to fly and to sail. She had more lovers than she cared to remember. Or *could* remember, if the truth be told. Only recently, she had been introduced to one of her former flames at a charity ball, failing quite spectacularly to recall that the shabby bald chap standing in front of her with the slightly green expression on his face was once a raven-haired Oxford undergrad who swore he'd throw himself off Magdalen bell tower if she didn't marry him after his finals. (She had refused. He compromised by throwing himself off Magdalen Bridge rather than the bell tower but he still broke both his ankles and gained a limp for life.)

In brief, Nessa O'Neill was not a girl to be taken seriously. The entire world was littered with the evidence of her short-lived passions. Broken-hearted boys were the least of it. There was the half-restored mural on the walls of a small sixteenth-century church in Tuscany. The half-retiled hammam in Marrakesh. The burnt-out Land Rover buried in a sand dune somewhere near Namibia's Skeleton Coast. It was a good job for Nessa O'Neill that Charlie Macintosh and his friends had been passing in their own Land Rover that day. It wasn't such great news for Charlie's fiancée back in Chelsea.

Nessa O'Neill had the attention span of a gnat. Which is why no one expected her to remember she had brought home a stray dog from Greece by the time it finished its stay in British quarantine. Much less did they expect her to go straight back to Crete and bring home four more to keep the first dog company. She inherited Prowdes rather suddenly after that (her father died of a heart attack just before her thirty-fifth birthday) and moved her collection of stray dogs into the old stable block. The first British stray arrived a day later, left tied to the gates of the house with a piece of old string, attached to which was a note that said, 'I know you'll look after him.'

By the end of her first year as Lady of the Manor, Nessa's pack of lost and lonely animals had swelled by four more dogs, two cats and a three-legged badger. Then came the baby deer someone had found in their back garden. A fox that had been hit by a car. A dray horse earmarked for the glue factory (which subsequently lived another eighteen years). Nessa's nickname in the village was Mrs Noah long before she brought her first chimpanzee home.

It happened five years after Nessa accidentally opened her sanctuary. She was taking a rare break from the animals, holiday-ing in southern Spain with her latest flame, a dashing film-maker called Fernando Martin, while her first full-time employee, Eddy Hamilton, held the fort at home. A photographer approached Nessa outside a beach bar where she was taking morning coffee and asked whether she wanted to have her photograph taken with his 'little girl'. Nessa was intrigued and then horrified when she discovered what a hairy little girl the photographer had.

The eighteen-month-old chimpanzee was called Virginia. The V pronounced like a B in the photographer's exotic accent. Virginia lolled in Nessa's arms when she held her, clearly knocked out by some sedative drug to stop her misbehaving or complain-ing as she was passed from tourist to tourist like a beanbag. Nessa didn't know much about chimpanzees at the time but she knew enough about young animals to guess that this one was in a very poor state indeed.

Virginia was small and light and her limbs hung limply from her tiny frame. Pulling back the blanket the chimpanzee was wrapped in, Nessa saw patches of dry grey skin where Virginia's hair had been rubbed away by baby clothes that were too tight. When the infant ape eventually opened her eyes, they seemed unfocused and confused.

'I love her like my little girl,' the photographer insisted when Nessa tackled him in clumsy Spanish about the state of Virginia's health. The photographer's real daughter stood behind him shyly, just six or seven years old herself. She carried a heavy box of photograph albums and print samples around her neck. Too heavy for such a small child.

Nessa would have taken both the chimpanzee *and* the girl back to Prowdes if she could have done. She suspected that the photographer might have let the girl go for perhaps twice the five hundred pounds in cash Nessa paid for the chimp that afternoon.

'What are we going to do with that bloody thing?' asked Fernando when she showed him the results of her latest accidental shopping trip.

'I'm going to take her back to Prowdes.'

'But you don't know anything about chimpanzees,' Fernando lamented. 'You've got too many dogs and badgers and donkeys as it is. You're a crazy lady, Nessa. You've gone *insane.*' It was a refrain that was to become all too familiar.

And perhaps it was true. Perhaps Nessa really had gone mad. Could she really offer Virginia a better life than the photographer had? Nessa knew as much about chimps as he did . . . Which was nothing.

Virginia couldn't come to England right away, so Nessa found herself staying in Spain for another three months, reading every chimpanzee book she could lay her hands on, while, with the help of a local vet, she nursed Virginia back to a level of fitness that would make it safe for her to travel and face the quarantine at the other end of her journey. Over time, Nessa grew confident that caring for Virginia would be no more difficult than caring for her dogs. But one afternoon, while Nessa dozed in the garden of Fernando's magnificent villa, Virginia proved how much cleverer than a dog she really was.

Pepita was a good-natured young mongrel, who belonged to Fernando's housekeeper. The scruffy dog seemed to know that Virginia required special care. She never nipped her new chimpanzee housemate, though Virginia was always happy to pull Pepita's tail if the dog got dangerously close.

That day, Virginia was playing with one of Pepita's chewed-up toys. When the dog came to investigate, Virginia held the rubber ball up to Pepita's nose. Pepita wagged her tail, sensing the start of a game. Virginia drew back her arm as if to throw the ball. Pepita crouched down, ready to spring off in pursuit. Virginia swung her arm forward like a fielder aiming for a wicket. Pepita hared away in the direction of the ball's trajectory. Except that the ball wasn't following any trajectory . . . While Pepita raced the full length of the garden and skidded to an uncontrolled and uncomfortable stop against the fence, Virginia examined the red ball she still held in her hand.

Nessa watched from her deckchair with curiosity. Perhaps Virginia had just forgotten to let go. But the infant ape's open-mouthed play-grin suggested otherwise; that she had *deliberately* sent Pepita bounding off after a handful of thin air. At that moment, Nessa made a commitment to the chimpanzee child in her care. This was no simple creature that would be content with enough food and a warm place to sleep, like the donkeys and the dogs. Virginia's new home would have to be so much more than the usual safari park.

Twenty years after that amazing afternoon, Prowdes was home to almost thirty chimpanzees. Arriving back in England with Virginia, Nessa set about transforming the beautiful country manor into a miniature African state. She designed enclosures far bigger than any she had seen at already established zoos, taking advice from academics and conservation specialists who had worked with chimpanzees in the wild.

It was an expensive business. Chimpanzees take a lot of containing. Ditches had to be dug and twelve-foot-high fences topped off with revolving barrels erected around the land that was to become the main enclosure. An adult chimpanzee can easily jump eight feet. The barrels would make it all but impossible to climb over.

Nessa quickly used up most of her cash. But she couldn't turn any chimp away. Absolutely not. And as soon as news about Prowdes' fantastic new facilities leaked out, the chimps started to arrive by the truckload as other do-gooders brought them back from Spain or foolish people who had raised chimps as pets realised that if a human teenager is difficult, a chimpanzee teen is far worse. Fortunately there were other assets about the house to be made liquid. A small horse painting by Stubbs was the first casualty, swapped with a local farmer for a consignment of hay when Nessa found herself momentarily embarrassed while waiting for the next chunk of cash from her trust.

Within a couple of years, the beautiful rooms at Prowdes were almost empty as Nessa liquidated anything that could be moved to complete her chimpanzee haven. These days a last remaining Queen Anne chair flanked an Ikea desk in Nessa's office. The walls were bare of heirloom paintings, though you could see where they had once hung from bright patches on the faded yellow walls. Nessa didn't mind too much about the pictures – after all, the family portraits were of the Prowde family, not the O'Neills.

And in the grounds of the house, in gardens once landscaped by a designer to rival Capability Brown, a state-of-the-art ape habitat had been created. The troop of chimps roamed a site of ten acres. Two decades since Nessa rescued her from a brief life as a photographic model, Virginia was top female in Prowdes' artificial troop. She was a mother now. Her eldest son, Victor, known more frequently as Big Ears, was the first baby chimp to be born at Prowdes.

It was his arrival which finally forced Nessa to make Prowdes a registered charity. Members of the public had offered donations in the past. Now Nessa's chimp family had grown so large she could no longer keep the place afloat with her inheritance. She had to open up the grounds of her house to the public and take on extra staff. She added a tea room and a gift shop. Nessa was amazed and disappointed by the number of visitors who spent more time in the gift shop choosing between pink acrylic lemurs made in Taiwan than looking at the real, live animals who swung from the trees outside.

Animals like Modimo and Badimo. Modimo and Badimo were chimpanzee twins, now almost three years old. Their mother, Priscilla, had been badly abused as a captive infant. She was clueless as to how she should care for her babies and they'd had to be removed from her possession in the main enclosure to be hand-reared for their own safety. They were named after a two-headed god from Zimbabwe, whose magical names were to be uttered only by shamans, prophets and children. According to legend, any adult daring to name-drop Modimo or Badimo would become a child trapped in a grown-up's body.

It didn't much matter. Apart from the fact that you pretty much had to be a child at heart to want to work at Prowdes in the first place, nobody called the twins by their full names anyway, preferring to refer to them as Mad and Bad. As with human twins, their keepers found it easiest to distinguish between Mad and Bad by dressing them in different colours. They were too small to go naked all year round in the changeable English weather. Volunteers had donated a variety of children's clothes to keep them warm, including a selection of kid-sized football strips. Bad wore Manchester United colours. Mad, quite by chance, was Chelsea.

Then there was Achilles. If you could tear yourself away from the chimpanzee-shaped tablemats and coasters in the gift shop, you'd never see a more impressive ape.

Achilles was the father of Virginia's son, Big Ears, and alpha male of the artificial family group Nessa had created. He arrived at Prowdes from a bankrupt safari park in the north of England in the late 1980s, along with two rather ragged-looking donkeys, who had carried children around the park's funfair. One of the donkeys died distressingly soon after beginning his child-free retirement in Nessa's gentle care. The other was still living in the old stable block, company to a llama imported into Britain by an imaginative entrepreneur who envisioned himself flooding the British textile market with llama wool. (The creative businessman gave up shortly after Daisy, as the llama was called, kicked him in the head while he was examining her feet and he spent two days in hospital with concussion.)

When Achilles arrived at Prowdes, the chimpanzee troop already numbered eleven. They were a pretty shabby bunch of animals then, mostly rescued from similar circumstances to those in which Nessa had found Virginia. Mostly young. Mostly a little on the small side through poor nutrition. Nobody was sure how old Achilles was, but he was probably reaching the end of puberty. And he was big. Almost five feet tall when he stood on his back legs, with an arm span of about the same length, and easily weighing a hundred and fifty pounds. One hundred and fifty pounds of pure solid muscle. The keepers at the safari park where he had been raised had at least taken good care of his nutritional needs. Achilles seemed the perfect name for him. He was a proud chimp. And, as it turned out, quite a warrior.

As with all new arrivals to the sanctuary, once it was established that he was free from infectious diseases after a period in quarantine, Achilles was introduced to his new family in a very gradual fashion. At first, he was housed in a holding pen within the main enclosure, allowed out into his own yard for just a couple of hours a day so that he could see the other chimps through wire and they could have a good look at him without getting close enough for a bite. When it seemed that all the chimps were happy to have the new boy around, Achilles was allowed out for real.

That was on a Monday morning. He spent that day sitting a little way to the side of Virginia and her chimpanzee acolytes, working out who was really in charge, who could be an ally, who would need to be subdued. He was as careful as any politician, observing but not interacting just yet, knowing that a wrong move at such an early stage could jeopardise his whole campaign.

A young male called Sacha was the first to feel the sharp end of Achilles' agenda. Sacha was minding his own business, rolling an empty banana skin between his lips, when Achilles bounded towards him and reared up on his back legs to display, puffing out his hair so that he appeared twice as broad as he really was. Sacha stared at Achilles in bewilderment as the new chimp gave a piercing 'wah-bark'. Sacha had never seen such behaviour in earnest before. But he quickly learned that Achilles wasn't messing around.

Achilles hammered home his message by jumping on Sacha's back when the smaller chimp finally bowed down in submission. Barking and screaming, Virginia flew towards Achilles in Sacha's defence but soon suffered the same humiliating fate. None of the other chimps were brave enough to make much of a fuss after that.

Achilles' coup was a distant memory now. The young warlord had grown into an impressive emperor. These days he very rarely had to display at the other chimps to remind them who was in charge. Any insurrection on the part of younger males was soon put down by Virginia and the other high-ranking females who backed Achilles absolutely, just as high-ranking females rally round an alpha male in the wild. Achilles swaggered around the enclosure like an old-style East End gangster. The females and infants adored him. He was even getting a little fat, which seemed symbolic of his sense of security. Brutal though he could be, one couldn't help but admire him. Because it wasn't just his size that had raised him to his position of leadership. Achilles was intelligent, too.

Too intelligent to keep finding joy in the same old surroundings, perhaps? It started to occur to Nessa that no matter how wonderful she made her sanctuary, it would never be quite wonderful enough. Did Achilles feel, while living at Prowdes, as Nessa might have done if forced to live in a hotel for the rest of her life? It might have been wonderful to spend month after month at the Ritz but, in the end, it would never be home. Not really.

On her visits to the main chimp enclosure to deliver fruit to her troop, Nessa became increasingly watchful for signs of unhappiness in her chimpanzee family. She wanted to know what Achilles was thinking when he gazed out over the ditch and beyond the wire, contemplatively stripping the leaves from one of the few plants that had managed to get a toehold on the somewhat barren clump of land where he lived (the chimps had quickly stripped every tree within the enclosure bare). Was he remembering another place? No one knew where Achilles had come from. The safari park had bought him from a very dodgy supplier who couldn't say whether the infant ape had been captive-born or taken from the wild.

Nessa became obsessed with the idea that when Achilles sat by the edge of the enclosure and looked out across the pale green fields in the direction of the Devonshire coastline, he was thinking of a way to cross the ocean. He was remembering a childhood in the African forest, riding through the treetops on his devoted mother's back. What could she do to make Achilles' life closer to what he might have experienced in Africa? Or perhaps to even make it possible to take him back there?

On a visit to a conservation conference, Nessa heard a young zoologist talk about a troop of domesticated chimpanzees from a sanctuary in Eastern Europe that had been released into the wild in West Africa. It had been a difficult process. Some of the chimpanzees had been made so un-chimp-like by their time in captivity that they literally had to be taught to behave like animals again. The young zoologist raised a few laughs as she described how she spent three months in the forest with her charges, acting as a temporary alpha male. At times it had seemed as though the project wouldn't work. Day after day, the chimps refused to hunt and forage for themselves, preferring to track their way back to the last place they had seen the supply van. But, eventually, the zoologist sensed that her chimps had become independent. On her most recent visit to check up on them, she had discovered that one of the young females was pregnant. They were looking forward to a rare instance of a once-captive chimpanzee giving birth in the wild.

That conference set Nessa's imagination alight. And now that she knew it was possible, nothing could stop her from taking her chimps back to Africa. It might take months. It might take years. It would definitely take a lot of money. But one day Achilles would find himself looking out over Africa for real, not Devon. Nessa was determined. Though she didn't know where to start. That was why she had hired 'the boffin'.

4

'Jennifer Niederhauser. My name is Dr Jennifer Niederhauser.'
Jennifer held out her hand to shake the hand of a new imaginary
colleague. She smiled broadly. Her reflection in the dressing-table
mirror smiled back an equally enthusiastic grin before it collapsed
into a mask of tiredness again.

What a stressful weekend! Jennifer calculated she hadn't had
more than six hours' sleep since Friday evening. That weekend
had seen Dahlia get married. Friday night had been devoted to
calming the bride's nerves, sitting up until four in the morning to
reassure her that her husband-to-be *would* turn up for the
ceremony. Of course he would. There was no way on earth he
would have found out that Dahlia had lusted after the gorilla-
gram and decided to call the wedding off as a result of her mental
infidelity.

'Lusting after strippers doesn't count,' Jennifer concluded.

'What about that bloke I kissed in the taxi rank afterwards?'
Dahlia worried.

'Tongues?' asked Jennifer.

'No.'

'It was your hen night. You're excused.'

Saturday had been taken up by the wedding itself. Hairdres-
sers' appointments at seven. Seven in the morning! Insanity,
thought Jennifer. The wedding wasn't until three in the afternoon!
But Malcolm Twist's salon, 'Hedley Twist', was the most popular
in Tincastle (actually it was the only salon in Tincastle apart from
the one with the sun-faded pictures of eighties' 'Studio Line' ads
in the window) and he had four different brides and their brides-
maids to do before lunch.

'You are my favourite bride, though,' Malcolm confided to
Dahlia as he tied an apron over her clothes.

Then why did he give her a hairstyle that looked like a cross between a cottage loaf and a pineapple, Jennifer couldn't help but wonder. Meanwhile, Malcolm's young assistant turned her own straight blonde hair into something resembling an untidy croissant.

Bakery-related hairdos notwithstanding, the wedding went without a hitch. Henry did turn up on time (with the unspeakable Craig Gascott in tow). Nobody forgot the rings. And everyone who needed to say 'I do' did so at the appropriate moment.

After that to Buckstaff Manor, the recently renovated hotel and conference centre on the outskirts of the town where all four of that day's Tincastle brides were having their wedding receptions. They had followed each other round the manicured gardens having their pictures taken sitting on the same wrought-iron loveseats and in front of the same reproduction classical statues. It all got rather confusing. Several of Dahlia and Henry's guests accidentally ended up in the new Mr and Mrs Taylor's group photo.

Fortunately Dahlia's father had booked the best room at the manor for their meal. The Vista Room. The one with the huge windows that overlooked the sea. The champagne flowed ceaselessly and when the time came to make the speeches, the crowd was feeling very receptive indeed. Even Jennifer (who had merely sipped at half a glass of fizz for sociability's sake) couldn't help but find herself chuckling at Craig Gascott's seemingly endless supply of jokes involving the groom and a female sheep.

They partied until three in the morning before retiring to rooms in the hotel which had been block-booked since the previous February. They were up early the next morning for a champagne breakfast (orange juice for Jennifer this time) and to wish the bride and groom 'Bon Voyage' as they left for their honeymoon in the Maldives. Dahlia threw the bouquet for the single girls in the wedding party. Jennifer was in the ladies' room at the time. Not that she believed in such ridiculous superstition . . .

Jennifer spent the rest of the day doing the dutiful chief bridesmaid bit, ensuring that guests from out of town saw the very best of Tincastle – the town where she had grown up that had recently become her home again. She endured a lunch with three

23

of Dahlia's aunties, who all wanted to know why she wasn't being made a decent woman of herself rather than hear about her brand new doctorate. Then it was back to the cottage to prepare for Monday morning. Jennifer's own big day. Her first day at work.

Just three months before, Jennifer had been up in Scotland, putting the finishing touches to her PhD thesis. It was titled '*Primate culture: differences in goal-directed tool use between chimpanzee troops in Liberia and the Gabon*'. It was a dry title for what was actually a pretty fascinating subject but the important thing was that it had impressed her tutor enough to ensure that Jennifer got those precious letters after her name.

Those three letters were the culmination of almost two and half decades of study (if you counted school as well). They were Jennifer's reward for endless nights spent studying and revising in her bedroom while Dahlia was out on the town sifting through the available blokes until she found a husband to worry about the career bit for her. There had been moments when Jennifer wondered whether it had been worth it – all that studying when she could have been having fun – but the morning she received a new chequebook in which all the cheques were printed with her new title was one of the proudest moments of her life. She went straight into town and bought a five-pack of cotton knickers at Marks and Spencer, just for the pleasure of flashing her new status via cheque guarantee card. It was extremely disappointing when the salesgirl didn't comment.

'I always knew you'd be a doctor of something one day,' said Dahlia.

Jennifer had always known, too. At school, she had been nicknamed the Professor. She was the brightest girl in her class by far. In fact, she was the brightest in her school. It didn't make her popular, though. Except at test time, when everyone would clamour to sit in a desk behind or to the side of her so that they might get a sneaky look at her answers.

But there soon came a point when nobody cared whether they could beat Jennifer in a maths test anyway. The other girls discovered boys and were suddenly grateful that they didn't have Jennifer's swotty, stand-offish and frankly rather weird reputation. Though she was arguably one of the prettiest girls in her class as well as the brightest, Jennifer didn't get her first kiss until she was sixteen and that was only because David Cross was on a dare. Jennifer's seriousness was reflected in her face so that when people looked at her they saw only the bookish frown rather than the beautiful eyes beneath it.

Jennifer became so used to being considered unattractively swotty that by the time she was eighteen it didn't occur to her that anyone would *ever* fancy her at all. Not even when she got to Oxford University, where she was suddenly surrounded by people who had been unattractively swotty at school in exactly the same way. They all considered themselves to be perfectly fanciable now. Only Jennifer Niederhauser continued to act as though her zoology books were her only possible source of satisfaction.

In fact, to Dahlia's disbelief, Jennifer found that a life of books and quiet libraries really *was* quite incredibly satisfying. She didn't feel as though she was missing out when she found herself in a library on Friday and Saturday nights. Those few dates she had been on were pretty disappointing. Even her fellow Oxford undergraduates seemed a little bit too dim for our budding intellectual giant.

But then everything changed.

At the beginning of Jennifer's third and final year at Oxford, she met Dr Timothy Lauder.

Newly qualified Dr Lauder was a primate specialist, just arrived from four years' postgraduate study at Edinburgh University and a summer spent tracking pygmy chimpanzees, or bonobos as they are otherwise called, in the forests of West Africa. He took over supervision of Jennifer's animal behaviour tutorials. Her previous tutor, Dr Grange (known as Dr Strange to most of his students), had left under a cloud at the end of Trinity term.

Jennifer had known how to handle Dr Grange (he wasn't terribly interested in girls anyway) but as if by a magical curse the articulate, intelligent student suddenly developed a stutter when faced by the young man who replaced him. Dr Grange had been old and slightly stinky. Dr Lauder was just four years older than Jennifer. He had hair the colour of straw and eyes with irises so blue they looked as though they had been cut from the sky with a hole punch. At the beginning of their first tutorial together, he greeted her with a smile that suggested he had never been so happy to see anyone in his life . . .

Jennifer found it impossible to say the words 'sexual selection' in Dr Lauder's presence without precipitating a violent coughing fit. After a couple of weeks, Dr Lauder started to take the precaution of having a glass of water ready for her arrival at three o'clock every Tuesday afternoon. Then, one day, he commented on the floral dress she was wearing.

'You're looking very . . . flowery,' was all he said.

Next thing Jennifer saw was the flickering strip light on the ceiling of his office. His simple sort-of compliment had sent her into a faint.

It might have been the most embarrassing moment of her life ever, but when Jennifer looked up into Dr Lauder's eyes as he checked her dilated pupils for signs of concussion, she realised that his concern went beyond that of a tutor fearing that his tutee had sustained a mortal injury on his time. He offered her his hand to help her to her feet. Jennifer wobbled again at the touch of his warm palm to her elbow. Eventually, however, she revived enough to accept a medicinal coffee in the zoology department canteen.

Over coffee, tutor and tutee finally got talking about things other than Jennifer's essays and, later that week, when Dr Lauder caught the Oxford Express bus that ran from outside college to London to see his own heroine, Jane Goodall, give a talk on her chimpanzees in Gombe, he took Jennifer along with him.

They had their first kiss in the back of the coach on their way back to Oxford. It was wonderful. Jennifer felt as though she had never been kissed before. And that day, the two great fiery passions of Jennifer's life were ignited. Dr Timothy Lauder. And chimpanzees.

'Oh, Dr Lauder,' Jennifer murmured when he kissed her.

'Jennifer, call me Timothy. Please.'

Inspired by Jane Goodall's lecture and Timothy's enthusiasm, Jennifer made primate body language the subject of her final-year dissertation, with special emphasis on the pygmy chimp, or bonobo, the sexually promiscuous ape that was Timothy's area of expertise. Unlike the common chimp, which settles disputes with violent displays of strength, the smaller bonobo chimps make love not war, cementing their social hierarchy with indiscriminate sexual encounters.

They made fascinating subjects. Not that Jennifer needed an excuse to spend all her time in Timothy's office any longer. In this man she had at last discovered what the fuss was all about. He was never boring. His intellectual prowess astounded her. No one knew more about animal behaviour than he did. And no one behaved more like an animal with Jennifer in the bedroom. She was surprised at herself when she was with him. Surprised in a good way that made her cheeks pink all day long. She even caught herself singing along to a Celine Dion song and believing it.

Jennifer sailed through her final exams that summer and began the search for a graduate placement to study for her PhD in the autumn. She applied for positions somewhat half-heartedly, secretly expecting that Timothy would find a place for her. In his department. At Oxford. They hadn't spent a single night apart since that trip back from London on the bus. Their relationship was the greatest Oxbridge love story since Sylvia Plath and Ted Hughes, Jennifer told Dahlia in an e-mail. Conveniently forgetting how that one turned out . . .

Jennifer's face was wreathed with smiles when Timothy finally told her that he had found her the *perfect* placement. But the smiles evaporated like the contrail of the jet plane that would take her there when he told her where it was.

'It's in Edinburgh,' he said. 'With my old tutor, Dr Carl Buzzell. He was very impressed by your dissertation. It's an incredible opportunity for you. What that man doesn't know about chimpanzees—'

'Edinburgh? But Edinburgh is so far away,' Jennifer protested.

'We'll see each other every weekend,' Timothy promised her. 'It's important that you study with the right minds. I want you to become a great thinker, Jennifer. Like me. We have the rest of our lives to be together after you've got that doctorate.'

During an emergency phone call late that night, Dahlia reluctantly agreed with Timothy's assertion that it wasn't entirely a bad idea for Jennifer to study with such a genius. 'It's disappointing he didn't find room for you on his own research staff,' she admitted. 'But absence does make the heart grow fonder, Jenny. You've been in each other's pockets since you got together. You're letting him get much too used to you. Spending some time apart will give him a chance to realise what he could lose if he doesn't propose to you right away.'

Dahlia was all about getting the ring. She had just started seeing Henry Nichols and was applying every Rule in the book to make sure that he was the One whether he liked it or not.

Jennifer sniffed in unhappy agreement with Dahlia's supportive prognosis. At least there was the summer. There were still two and a half long hot months before the start of the next academic year. Two and a half months they could spend together. And they did.

Jennifer and Timothy had a wonderful six weeks tracking chimps through the forest in the Gabon for real. During the day, they traversed dozens of miles, working hard to keep up with the troop they were following. At night they slept under the stars, curled around each other on the ground beneath the trees in which the apes nested overhead. Jennifer had never been so happy.

'I love you,' she told him.

'I know.'

At the end of the summer Jennifer moved out of Timothy's little house in Oxford's Jericho, took the coach to Heathrow Airport and from there a plane up to Edinburgh. She felt like Persephone, stepping from light into darkness when she arrived at Edinburgh airport. Oxford had been sunny that morning. In Edinburgh, rain clouds glowered over the grey-green landscape like a meteorological manifestation of her mood. The stern grey-stone city on the hill seemed a very strange place to continue her chimpanzee education, doubly chilly as it was without her lover to wrap his arms around her. But she had to be brave. This was a temporary hard patch on the road to her ultimate bliss.

*　　*　　*

Absence makes the heart grow fonder, Dahlia had promised. Timothy had even said the very same words himself as he waved her off on the coach. And at first, it seemed that Dahlia was right. There were phone calls, text messages, e-mails by the dozen. The communication from her beloved was frequent and affectionate and peppered with 'I love you'.

But Jennifer was soon to discover that 'Absence Makes the Fond Heart Wander' was closer to the truth. Two months into Jennifer's first year in Edinburgh, Timothy started to make excuses on those weekends when he was supposed to travel north and asked Jennifer to postpone a couple of her visits to Oxford, too.

'I am working so hard,' he told her. 'I'm on the verge of a breakthrough with this research. I don't want to interrupt the flow.'

'I understand, darling,' she assured him.

But in the end, after four weekend visits in a row had been cancelled, even Jennifer could be understanding no longer. She missed her lover. So she made the fatal mistake.

She surprised him.

Jennifer arrived at his Oxford office one drizzly Friday afternoon with a red rose between her teeth and her best underwear beneath her raincoat. And caught Dr Timothy Lauder behaving like an animal with some other girl . . .

29

5

So, Dr Lauder proved himself to be as promiscuous as the bonobos he had made his life's work. He was unworthy of Jennifer's attention. Fortunately, the same was not true of the chimpanzees. And Timothy had at least done his ex-girlfriend one real favour. Dr Carl Buzzell *was* a fabulous teacher who fostered his new graduate student's enthusiasm like a father encouraging a favourite child.

There were field trips to Africa, including one to a new sanctuary near Jane Goodall's famous Gombe. There were primate research conferences all over the world. Berlin, Cape Town, San Diego. Jennifer was given the opportunity to spend an academic year in San Diego. The California sunshine went a long way towards making life look better.

Jennifer had quickly decided the best way to get over Timothy was to throw herself into her work. Work would take her mind off the pain. Relationships were nothing but trouble. That was clear now. Other people were unpredictable and inevitably let you down. Work was different. If she put half as much effort into her work as she had done into loving her faithless boyfriend, she would have lasting renown and satisfaction that no hormonally crazed, overgrown schoolboy could ever take away with his careless infidelity.

The position at Prowdes was advertised on the Internet, via a website that acted as a noticeboard for chimpanzee conservationists all over the world. Jennifer was immediately intrigued.

Growing up around Tincastle, she had visited the sanctuary many times with her parents. As an academic, she had become rather snobby about what she regarded as the sanctuary's amateur efforts to rehabilitate the chimps Nessa had rescued over the past twenty years. Jennifer couldn't help but regard the sanctuary as rather better suited to the rescued donkeys which comprised most of its inmates back in the 1970s. After all, Nessa O'Neill wasn't a qualified naturalist, just a bored rich woman with time on her hands. Now, however, as a newly qualified PhD, Jennifer saw the chance to make her mark.

Project Africa was what Nessa called her plan to release some of her captive chimpanzees into the wild. Rehabilitation on such a grand scale was an area of conservation that particularly interested Jennifer and she had plenty of ideas about how it could be done. She stayed up all night to prepare her application for the position of project leader. Nessa was thrilled to receive Jennifer's carefully written proposal, explaining the different ways in which it might be possible to start the chimpanzees' 're-education' before taking them to a release spot. Essentially, how it might be possible to make the chimps more 'wild' while they remained in captivity by altering their diets, forcing them to forage and breaking down their dependency on their human keepers. Jennifer also had the contacts Nessa didn't in the worldwide primatology community to find that perfect release site.

Jennifer took the train down to Tincastle a couple of days later for an interview, not knowing at the time that Nessa was prepared to beg the young woman to come and join them. Jennifer's face-to-face delivery of her plans impressed Nessa even more than her proposal document had done. The Sanctuary's trustees were awed by her confidence and poise. Jennifer had the job.

It was strange to be returning to Tincastle after so much time in the north. Since leaving school, Jennifer had done her best to stay away from the place, choosing university courses at colleges a considerable distance from home and travelling during the holidays.

To the holidaymakers who poured into the small town each summer, Tincastle was idyllic. To a teenager who had always lived there, Tincastle was like a pretty prison colony. There was nothing to do when the summer season ended and the crazy golf course closed down. Absolutely nothing. And if you made your own entertainment, as teenagers will, there was always someone who would find out and tell your mother.

But things would be different now. Jennifer was twenty-seven, after all. She no longer had to worry if Mrs Winterson or Mr Green saw her coming out of the off-licence with a two-litre bottle of cider hidden under her coat. Not that Jennifer had ever tried to buy alcohol under age. And her parents were no longer in town to hear any gossip anyway. They had recently sold their house in Tincastle to move to Germany to care for Jennifer's paternal grandparents. Jennifer's mother was most upset that she could no longer offer her daughter a room in the house she had grown up in. But Jennifer was actually pretty relieved to be spared moving back in with her folks. Instead, she took a lease on a small cottage, not remembering until Dahlia reminded her that the cottage she had taken used to belong to a spinster with three cats whom they called 'The Witch'.

The Witch was long gone now. She had been in her eighties even when Dahlia and Jennifer dared each other to ring her doorbell and run away as they passed her house on the way home from school. After she died, the Witch's cottage had been sold to an affluent young couple from London who intended to use the place as a weekend retreat. But paying two mortgages kept them working in London over the weekends. And when they did find themselves with time off, they were too tired to make the long drive from Clapham for just a couple of nights before the working week rolled round again. Renting the cottage out and using the money left over to jet off to Madrid or Majorca once a month suddenly seemed a much better idea and, as a result, Jennifer was the first person to properly benefit from their *Elle* décor-style renovation of the once dingy little hovel.

When she saw the new Philip Starck bathroom suite, Dahlia agreed that the cottage definitely didn't look as it had done when poor Miss Roberts lived there with her flea-bitten mogs, but she couldn't help teasing. 'I can still feel her spirit in the place. You'll get a tabby by the end of the month, grow hairs on your chin and never marry.'

'Thank you so much,' said Jennifer.

'We're practically neighbours again,' Dahlia smiled. 'I'll be able to see you constantly.'

'And constantly poke your nose into my business,' Jennifer replied. But both she and Dahlia knew that Jennifer was secretly glad to be near her best friend once more. It would make the move back from Edinburgh that much more fun.

Jennifer moved into the cottage two weeks before she was due to start work. She soon discovered that the cottage on Apple Tree Lane wasn't the only part of Tincastle that had undergone a transformation during her nine-year absence. The population had almost doubled and many of the new faces were alternative, creative types. 'Crusties', according to Jennifer's father, who still disapproved of men with long hair. Crusties they may have been, but the new bohemians (who had almost all been to public school, as a matter of fact) brought with them a market for some of the finer things in life. The Spar supermarket now stocked sun-dried tomato ciabatta and virgin olive oil. You could get your chakras realigned in a shop that once sold only knitting patterns and wool.

Jennifer began to feel optimistic about her return to her home town. It had a new image and so did she.

'Dr Jennifer Niederhauser,' she introduced herself to her reflection one more time, before she climbed into her beaten-up Ford Fiesta and drove to the sanctuary to head up Nessa O'Neill's chimpanzee team. That morning, with the sun shining down upon her little red car like a blessing, Jennifer could really believe she was about to become the world's leading expert on the rehabilitation of captive chimpanzees.

6

Unfortunately, the drive into work was to be the best part of the day.

No amount of planning could have prepared Jennifer for the reality of her first morning at Prowdes. No amount of time spent rehearsing her opening speech in her head would have helped her. She had yet to meet most of the people who were to become her staff that morning. The head keeper, Guy Gibson, had been on holiday when Jennifer interviewed for her position as his boss. Jennifer had decided it was important that she impress him in particular.

She knew that Guy Gibson was one of the longest serving staff at the sanctuary. Nessa hadn't said much about him beyond extolling his professionalism and dedication to the chimps. But Jennifer had built up an image of the man. Forty-something. Bearded, as almost all men who worked with animals were in Jennifer's experience. He was probably quite set in his ways. Resentful perhaps, that he hadn't been asked to head up Nessa's new project himself after so many years in her employ. *Mortified* when he discovered that his new boss was going to be a woman. And a pretty bloody young one at that.

Well, Jennifer wasn't going to take any stick because of her sex or her age. She was determined that she would be treated with the respect due to someone of her educational status. She was no bimbo. Even if she did have blonde hair. She'd tied that back in a rather severe ponytail. She wore a suit for this first meeting too. She would establish the hierarchy with her own subtle dominance display. Not quite an alpha male rearing up on to his hind legs and beating his chest but equally effective. She would change into her overalls *after* introductions had been made.

34

'I am Dr Jennifer Niederhauser,' she muttered to herself one more time as she crunched across the gravel from the car park. 'You may not like the way I am going to do things but I am here to tell you that the way I do things is the way to do them right!' Perhaps she wouldn't deliver that line in the Wild West sheriff's accent she had been using in her head but she would make it absolutely clear by the end of this first meeting that she was not a woman to be messed with.

'Jennifer!' said Nessa O'Neill. 'You made it. We're so happy to have you join us at last! Come and meet the team.'

Nessa had assembled the entire staff of Prowdes in her office to meet the university 'boffin' who was going to help put them on the research map and bring in that valuable grant. A row of primate-keepers in dark green overalls regarded their new project leader warily. But Jennifer would not be distracted by the fact that her staff was mostly male and older than her. Or that just ten days earlier her new second-in-command had invited her to rub baby oil on his bottom . . .

Guy Gibson, head keeper and part-time gorilla-gram, kept his eyes firmly on the floor.

7

It was, to use the parlance of the playing field, one hell of a curve ball.

In retrospect, Jennifer would realise that perhaps the right thing would have been to laugh it off. She could have made a joke about 'knowing' Guy quite well already, given him a wink and got everything off to a friendly, jovial start. But, unfortunately, Jennifer chose not to do that. Head muddied by the stress of preparing for that all-important morning, at first she was shocked into silence as the realisation of why his face seemed so familiar clicked into place. The pain of throwing that ruined dress away was still with her. Whatever Dahlia said about it, Jennifer was sure that it was the most flattering garment she had ever owned and there would never be another quite like it.

So instead of acting like an adult and making a joke of the affair, Jennifer decided that it was best to pretend she had never seen Guy before in her life, let alone seen him waggle his crown jewels. When Nessa presented head keeper and project leader to one another, Jennifer met Guy's eye with what she hoped was a neutral sort of gaze and a cursory nod. To Guy and his fellow keepers, neutral seemed downright frosty. He knew only too well that she knew where they'd met before. He could only assume she still wanted to kill him.

So, what might have been the perfect bonding moment became distinctly unfriendly and awkward. And Jennifer followed her chilly introduction with a speech about Project Africa that blew yet more cold air over the warm, welcoming party at Prowdes.

'My name is Dr Niederhauser and I am going to do things differently,' she began.

*   *   *

She certainly did. One of the best things about Prowdes, the employees generally agreed, was the family atmosphere. Staff all called each other by their first names, no matter what their 'rank'. Nessa was just as likely to give you a hug as call you into her office for an official appraisal. It was one of the reasons why Nessa's staff stayed with her for years and years despite the long hours and the low wages they received in return.

With her corporate managerial-style speech, Jennifer was immediately at odds with Prowdes' ramshackle regime. As she delivered her speech, she walked up and down the line of staff gathered to meet her like a general surveying her troops. The embarrassment of meeting Guy again under such different circumstances had triggered a bout of nervousness. And, unlike most people who might stutter and forget what to say, when Jennifer got nervous, she got defensively pompous and said a great deal.

The keepers shared apprehensive glances in her wake and grimaced at her talk of 'strictly applied nutritional plans and observational rotas'. By the time Jennifer finished her opening address, she had certainly succeeded in letting everyone know that she was not to be messed with. But she definitely hadn't made any friends.

Lecture over, the keepers returned to work. Guy headed back to the chimpanzee nursery, where Mad and Bad were growing up in exactly the kind of pampered fashion Jennifer was there to stamp out. He was accompanied by Jo-Jo Potts, head of orang-utans (all one of them), and Snowy Pilkington, deputy head of chimps.

'What do you think then?' Jo-Jo asked Snowy.

'She's a bit bloody fierce, isn't she? Reminds me of Anne Robinson on that game show.'

'You said you *fancied* Anne Robinson the other day,' said Jo-Jo.

'I did not!' said Snowy.

'You did. You're sick! What do you think, chief?' Jo-Jo asked Guy. He had been rather quiet since Jennifer arrived on the scene but didn't think it was a good idea to tell anyone why.

'I'm sure she knows what she's doing,' said Guy, staring at the sheaf of papers Jennifer had given him to peruse while she finalised a few details of her contract with Nessa in the office up at the big house.

'I don't think so,' said Jo-Jo. 'She may have all those letters after her name but everyone knows that you can't reduce chimpanzees to statistics. I can't wait to see her "implement her new regime" with Achilles or Mad and Bad. Or Hector.'

Hector was the sanctuary's solitary male Sumatran orangutan – a rather pitiful creature who spent most days sitting in the back of his enclosure, plucking at what remained of his gingery hair.

'Well, I'm sure she'll be *terrified* when she meets Hector,' said Snowy. Snowy often liked to remind Jo-Jo that his charges were far more dangerous than hers. Jo-Jo's habitual response was to ask him where he'd mislaid his eyebrows. Snowy was so-called because he was preternaturally pale with such fair hair that you could barely see his lashes or his brows.

'All I'm saying is,' Jo-Jo continued, '*Dr Niederhauser* must be mad if she thinks we can suddenly change the way we work to fit in with her stupid theories. All the animals are *individuals*. In fact, I think they're more individual than most of the human men I've met,' she added, with the premature cynicism of a nineteen-year-old who already thought she'd seen it all when it came to the opposite sex. 'And what about all these forms she wants us to fill in? I haven't got enough time to fill in forms. My job is to look after Hector and you know how much attention he demands. That woman is going to get *such* a rude awakening if she expects the way we work to change.'

'Nothing much is going to change,' Guy reassured his colleagues. 'But my suggestion is that we give her a chance and listen to what she's got to say. Not everything here has always worked perfectly. Some of our animals have terrible habits,' he added, thinking of Sacha, the chimpanzee rescued from a life as a bar-room amusement, who would still steal cigarettes whenever he could get his hands on them (which seemed to be often, even though staff were officially banned from smoking on the premises). Luckily, so far Sacha had failed to steal any matches. 'I haven't got a clue where to start with getting these chimps ready to be released into the wild.'

'They'll never be ready,' said Snowy firmly.

Guy ignored him. Snowy had reacted particularly badly to Nessa's announcement that she wanted to return some of the chimps to their natural habitat. Snowy knew that it was the right thing to do, but he was naturally unhappy to think of saying goodbye to some of the animals he had known for over a decade. 'Dr Niederhauser might have some useful suggestions,' Guy concluded.

Jo-Jo and Snowy shared a sceptical glance.

Guy flipped through the pages of Jennifer's inch-thick dissertation and gulped when he chanced upon a single sentence containing six words in a row that he didn't immediately recognise or understand. This was definitely going to be interesting.

'I give her a fortnight,' said Jo-Jo.

'Two weeks,' said Snowy.

8

Two weeks later, Jennifer was beginning to understand the truth in that old adage about never working with children or animals.

She had been bitten three times by Mad and twice by Bad (thank God for tetanus jabs) and narrowly missed having her head ripped off by Achilles when she visited the main enclosure to make an initial assessment of how the chimpanzees there interacted with each other compared to chimps in the wild.

'He'll get used to you,' Guy promised, as they slumped against the wire, panting from having had to run away from the alpha male.

Jennifer vowed never to step into the main enclosure without an electric prod again.

Meanwhile, she was being frozen out in the staff room. The keepers in her staff were just like children! She had warned in her opening address that helping the chimpanzees to have as wild a life as possible would involve some measures that might seem rather harsh at first. The problem was that there had been too much *anthropomorphism* in the Prowdes' regime, she told them at the weekly meeting where Guy, Jo-Jo, Snowy and three part-timers gathered to report on their charges.

Six blank faces looked back at her.

'Come on. Anthropomorphism. You must know what that means. Surely.'

Six heads shook out their no's.

'You have been treating the apes as though they are children,' she said slowly. 'Human children. It isn't right.'

Because the keepers attributed human emotions to their charges, they reacted to Jennifer's suggestions accordingly. Trying to persuade Snowy that Mad and Bad needed to be weaned off relying on human contact and cups of tea and Marmite on toast and be integrated into the troop at the earliest possible opportunity had been particularly difficult.

'They'll get depressed!' he protested.

Snowy had raised those chimps from babyhood. From two days old they had been in his care. He had treated those chimpanzees as though they were his own children. In fact, while they still needed to be fed every couple of hours day and night, Mad and Bad had lived *as* Snowy's children, in his own house, tucked up in a cot in the corner of the bedroom he shared with his wife. Fortunately for Snowy, his wife had been thrilled by her hairy foster sons. Two years into their marriage, she had been getting rather broody. A few months spent with Mad and Bad in the house was good practice for motherhood. And just enough good practice to convince her that she would wait another year or five.

But as a result, Snowy was unusually attached to his charges and the idea of sending them to the main chimpanzee enclosure, where Achilles ruled in true African dictator style, was too much for him.

'They're still too young,' he said.

'They're just the right age,' Jennifer assured him. 'Achilles is far less likely to be aggressive towards them while they are still so small and don't represent a real threat to his status. One of the female chimps or a juvenile male will adopt them and make sure they're taken care of. It always happens. The longer you rear these chimps like children, Snowy, the longer it will take for them to adjust back to being chimpanzees. And they need to be chimps to be successfully reintroduced into the wild some day. You do want them to have the chance to be wild that their mother never had, don't you?'

Of course Snowy did. Objectively he knew that was absolutely the right thing for his chimpanzee charges. But it was hard to convince his heart that the time had come to let them leave the nursery and his tender care to take their chances with the adults. Mad and Bad clung to him more tightly than ever, as though they knew what Jennifer was suggesting when she stood in their cage with her clipboard, barking orders.

'No more tea and Marmite in the mornings from now on.'

*   *   *

At least Snowy could be reasoned with. That was more than could be said for Jo-Jo Potts. Jo-Jo was the youngest member of the Prowdes staff and there was no doubt in Jennifer's mind that she acted like the baby. Though Jo-Jo was nominally 'head of orang-utans' most of her day was spent helping out in the chimpanzee enclosures, where she reported to Snowy and Guy and now Jennifer as well. Not that you would have guessed Jennifer was Jo-Jo's boss from the way she reacted to even the most simple requests.

'Jo-Jo, could you please put those bananas in the refrigerator?' elicited much huffing and dragging of feet. Asking Jo-Jo to muck out a cage might precipitate a full-blown tantrum.

'Why do I always have to do *everything*?' Jo-Jo would shout. She was every inch the teenager. One minute so worldly wise and cynical you might have thought she'd lived through ninety years. Next minute so hot-headed it was all you could do not to laugh at how easy it was to offend her.

Well, Jennifer tried her best to cut Jo-Jo some slack. After all, she couldn't be sure that she hadn't been a nightmare teen once herself. But what Jennifer couldn't abide was laziness and there were moments when Jo-Jo was very lazy indeed. The big problem was that laziness in an environment like an animal sanctuary could be dangerous. Such as when Jo-Jo let enclosure doors slam shut behind her instead of pushing them to and making sure that they were properly closed and locked before she carried on with whatever she was doing.

On several occasions Jennifer had walked past Hector's enclosure to find the door wide open. It had a tricky catch. If you tried to slam it, one time in every ten it wouldn't shut at all. Fortunately for Jo-Jo, Hector was just about Prowdes' laziest inmate. He wasn't interested in being outside his enclosure as long as he had food to eat and a stick to dig in the dirt with and so far he had never escaped.

'But that's beside the point,' Jennifer reminded Jo-Jo on an all-too-regular basis. 'What if a visitor goes into the enclosure and tries to touch Hector? What if he were to bite them? What if the next time you slammed a gate and it didn't shut behind you, it was the gate to the main chimpanzee enclosure?'

'The chimp enclosure has a double-safety gate. They still couldn't get out,' said Jo-Jo, ever the smart alec.

'We don't need lazy people at Prowdes,' said Jennifer coldly. 'Next time I find Hector's gate open, I will give you a written warning. You'll get two written warnings before a dismissal.'

Jo-Jo was momentarily dumbstruck.

Whatever he thought of her strict new regime in private, Guy did his best to back Jennifer up. Though she had hardly made efforts to cement their relationship from her side. Six weeks into her time at Prowdes, they still hadn't spoken about the very first time they met. Their conversations were purely professional. Guy even found himself calling her Dr Niederhauser when he contacted her on the walkie-talkies they used about the place, though she had told him more than once he could call her by her first name.

Guy tried to be enthusiastic about the forms Jennifer needed him to fill out for her research too. After all, it was Jennifer who was going to persuade some swanky university somewhere to give Prowdes a big fat grant for all this paperwork on her findings in connection with the rehabilitation of domesticated chimps. It was a grant that would enable the realisation of Nessa's African dream and one that could save the sanctuary from closing altogether. Though she brought as much sunshine to the place as a hurricane, Guy realised that Jennifer's presence was probably a very necessary pain.

Because money was definitely too tight to mention up at the big house. While Jennifer wrote complicated grant proposals and waited to hear whether this or that fund was interested in supporting her research at the project, Nessa was secretly dipping into the extremely small salary she paid herself to buy extra food for the chimps. Her own cupboards were bare. And nobody on the staff but Guy knew.

Another miserable British summer had seen the number of visitors to the sanctuary drop by almost half the previous year. Added to the terrible weather, regulations to stop the spread of foot-and-mouth disease through the countryside had left those members of the public who would risk getting caught in the rain confused as to whether they were actually allowed to visit the animals at all. Nessa had had to let many of her part-time weekend staff go. She simply couldn't afford to keep them on. Guy had secretly arranged to take a cut in his wages until the worst had passed.

'I can't ask you to do that,' Nessa had insisted.

'I know last summer was just a blip,' Guy told her as confidently as he could manage. 'This summer will be better and I want Prowdes to be open to make the most of it. Plus, I have ways of supplementing my income.'

Nessa couldn't persuade him to tell her what they were. 'Gigolo?' she guessed.

'I don't think anyone would pay for my services as an escort,' Guy smiled in reply.

Nessa forced herself to smile back. Though she felt as if she was working as an escort herself. Things had gotten so bad that she was having to allow the Major to take her out to dinner three times a week just so that she could eat too.

Nessa felt terrible about that. It wasn't as though she had had many scruples about allowing men to pay for her supper in the past. The way she saw it, the sparkling company she provided in return for two courses and half a bottle of wine was more than equal exchange. But the Major wasn't like most men Nessa had found herself tangling with before. She knew that no matter how many times she graced his arm at the local trattoria, the Major would never expect her to provide a physical return on his investment. (It would probably have killed him anyway. At seventy-nine years old, he was twenty years her senior.) No, the Major was thoroughly *safe in taxis*. He was chivalrous and sweet and kind. And in all probability absolutely bonkers.

The Major had wandered into Prowdes three years earlier, around the time Modimo and Badimo were born, muttering something about Africa and demanding to be taken on 'the tour'. Nobody had ever seen the Major before. But he walked around the sanctuary with such calm authority that Nessa felt strangely compelled to abandon her plans for the afternoon and give him a tour of her project herself.

44

He was an upright sort of man. Impeccably dressed in a jacket and tie despite the heat of that August afternoon. Nessa wasn't surprised to discover that he had enjoyed a long career in the military. As they walked, he told her his life story in a booming voice made for shouting across battlefields. He had been one of the lucky men to survive the evacuations from Dunkirk during World War Two. After that, he was posted to Africa. So far so credible. But he also claimed to have been injured in a jungle battle, left for dead by his comrades and rescued from death's door by chimpanzees.

Nessa was standing with the Major, looking into the main chimpanzee enclosure with him when he told her.

'Chimpanzees saved my life,' he said quite matter-of-factly. 'You know,' he added, pointing to Virginia, who at that moment had a bottom like a big pink balloon as she came into oestrus. 'The female who found me looked very much like that one there.'

'Really?' said Nessa. What else was she supposed to say?

'Oh yes,' the Major continued. 'I called her the Matron.'

It was an amazing story. According to the Major, the Matron's face was the first he saw when he came round from his spell of unconsciousness in the jungle. He didn't know how long he had been unconscious. Maybe hours. Maybe days. But when he awoke, the forest around him was quiet. No gun shots. No human voices. Just the gentle rustling of leaves as the Matron prepared a leaf sponge to clean his wounds.

'I sat up pretty bloody sharpish and looked for my gun!' the Major exclaimed.

But his gun was gone.

'Madam,' said the Major to Nessa. 'I have never been so scared in my life. A bloody great chimpanzee was examining my ankle and my bloody gun was nowhere to be seen. She had teeth like a wolf-hound. Never seen anything like it. I had no idea chimpanzees were so big. I assumed she wanted to eat me. But then she looked at me with those kind brown eyes and I knew that I was safe. As though she realised I was frightened, she reached out the back of her hairy hand and touched my face with it, gentle as you like.'

45

Nessa could imagine the gesture. It was a gesture of appeasement she had often seen Virginia make to Achilles. It was a gesture that never failed to calm him down.

'I had been found by an angel. An animal Florence Nightingale,' the Major continued. 'She was wonderful. Cleaned my wounds, she did, with those leaves and wiped other leaves covered in dew over my mouth to give me moisture. She brought me bananas and nuts she found and nursed me back to health.'

'How long were you in the jungle for?' Nessa humoured him.

'About six months,' said the Major without missing a beat. 'That's how long it seemed anyway. All that time the Matron stayed with me. Cared for me better than my wife did back in Surrey. It was as though that damn chimpanzee had fallen in love with me. She shared all her food with me. Kept me clean by grooming me. And eventually I was able to walk again. It was a miracle.'

'And then you made your way back to civilisation,' said Nessa.

'Oh no,' said the Major. 'Why would I want to get back to bloody civilisation? All those idiots killing each other at the behest of governments who saw them as less valuable than the shotguns they carried. Madam, they left me without my gun. Left me for dead with no means of defending myself if they were wrong. When I thought about that, I made up my mind to stay in the jungle for ever. I had everything I needed there. The Matron and her family had accepted me. The General, that's what I called the alpha male, saw me as his second-in-command.'

Nessa nodded. 'He did?'

'Oh yes. Six months after my human comrades had left me for dead, I *was* a chimpanzee and a bloody happy one at that.'

'So what happened?'

'Bloody bastards came looking for me,' the Major said through gritted teeth. 'That's what happened. Some local tribesman had seen me swinging through the forest with my friends. I suppose I wasn't too well camouflaged with my big white bottom flashing against the green of the forest canopy. This chap told some British soldiers stationed in his town that he'd seen a *muzungu* in the jungle. A white man. There was a reward for the capture of any enemy soldiers at the time. So they followed him to the place where I was living on the off-chance I was a deserter.'

'And rescued you.'

'Rescued me? Pah! You could hardly call it a rescue. They shot every damn one of my family! The Matron. The General. Little Snowball, the baby chimp with the pale face. Every one of them. Dead in a minute. Bang, bang, bang.' The Major mimed the shots. 'I think they thought the chimps were trying to attack me. I was wrestling with the General when they came across us. But we were just play-fighting, you see. Sparring like I did with the lads back at Sandhurst. They killed every one of them. Every last one.' The Major shook his head. 'Madam, I was a trained killer myself in those days. A soldier. I probably would have done the same if I had been in their shoes, seeing a man and a monkey wrestling in the trees. I probably would have done the same. But those chimpanzees were my family. I cried for the first and last time in my life that day.'

'That is terrible,' said Nessa.

The Major nodded in agreement. 'It broke my heart.'

'An incredible story,' Nessa told him. Incredible in the true sense of the world.

After that, the Major continued, he spent six months in an army prison for deserting. No one believed his story. They assumed instead that he was a deserter. The men who had left him for dead had hazy recollections of the skirmish that led to his abandonment and couldn't be sure that he hadn't run away first.

The Major gave up telling the chimpanzee story when the army psychiatrist prescribed anti-psychotics. Back in Surrey, his wife did her best to convince him to forget the jungle altogether and concentrate on getting his career back on track. His superiors were willing to give him another chance. He had been a very popular soldier. And until the 'jungle incident', a true professional. A trusted, reliable man. Nobody wanted to lose him from the army. The Major accepted his second chance. He stayed in the army until he retired, finding himself sent everywhere but Africa. He didn't even speak about Africa again. Until his wife died.

'Now I want to buy myself a little piece of jungle,' he ended his story. 'And I'm going to go back there. I want to die in Africa,' said the Major vehemently. 'Because really, when I think about it, Africa is where my heart is. I was never so happy again as I was for those few short months with that family of apes. The Matron was the love of my life.'

'A charming tale,' said Nessa.

'Completely bonkers,' said Guy when she relayed the story to him that night.

But after that first day, when Nessa listened to the Major's African fairy tale, he started to come by every day. At first, he just stood at the perimeter of the chimp enclosure and watched the action inside, lost in his own memories of God only knew what, occasionally calling to the apes behind the fence with uncannily accurate pant-hoots and grunts.

'Perhaps he really did live with chimps,' said Snowy when he heard the Major's 'wah-bark'.

Eventually, the Major became familiar to the staff and they started to invite him to experience the Prowdes Sanctuary animals at closer range than the average visitor. Jo-Jo was only too thrilled to let the Major muck out Hector's enclosure. She had never known an orang-utan with such active bowels. Snowy sometimes let him bottle-feed Mad and Bad, figuring that the chimp twins were still small enough to be relatively safe with a stranger.

Nessa and her staff decided that the Major might be mad but he was harmless. He was just a lonely old man who benefited from being allowed to see the animals every day. Nessa insisted that he didn't have to pay the admission fee any more. In return, the Major insisted that she accompany him to dinner at the trattoria in Tincastle. And now she was having dinner with him three times a week. He had started to call her his 'girlfriend'.

'Who is that old man?' asked Jennifer one evening, when the Major turned up to take Nessa out in his sparkling clean car. The Major had been on holiday for a couple of weeks, visiting an old army pal in Scotland. He had yet to meet the new girl in charge.

'Oh, that's the Major,' said Guy. 'He comes by most days. We let him feed Mad and Bad and muck out Hector's cage some-times.'

'Oh no,' said Jennifer. 'No, no, no. That really won't do at all. Untrained personnel are not to be allowed near the animals, Guy. Why on earth has he been allowed in before? He could be carrying all sorts of infection. Chimps of Mad and Bad's age could be killed by a dose of the flu. Don't you know that?'

'Of course I do,' Guy began. 'But—'

'No buts about it, Guy. I'm afraid you'll have to tell this Major chap to stay outside the wire like everybody else. He can't be allowed in the nursery. And tell Jo-Jo to muck Hector out herself. That's what she's paid for, isn't it?'

Guy duly passed on the news to the Major who immediately went into a stiff-upper-lipped sulk and disappeared from the sanctuary for five days. Nessa had to reassure him that they still wanted him around and that his assistance in the gift shop would be just as valuable as his assistance in the enclosures until Mad and Bad were past the critical age.

'Is it absolutely necessary to be so strict?' Nessa asked Jennifer. 'The Major really is one of us.'

'I'm surprised you even have to ask that,' said Jennifer. 'There have been some severe lapses of hygiene in the sanctuary in the past. It's amazing that we haven't seen more infections. Or even deaths. Jo-Jo in particular has been very slapdash about keeping her animals clean. In fact, I'm going to have a word with her about it right now.'

Nessa winced as she watched Jennifer stride off in the direction of Hector's House, as the orangutan enclosure was called, in honour of a children's television programme that Jo-Jo was too young to remember.

Later that week, Jennifer found orang-utan shit in one of her wellingtons. She told herself that it must have got in there by accident.

9

'What's your new boss like?' Guy's landlady, Arlene, asked him that Saturday night.

'Hard as nails,' said Guy.

'Attractive?'

'Hmmm,' Guy hesitated.

Snowy and Jo-Jo, who were sharing a pint with Guy that night, pulled faces of disgust. Jo-Jo snorted into her cider.

'She's not bad-looking. If you go for the ice-maiden thing,' Guy elaborated.

'And you don't?' Arlene teased.

'I don't think she'd have me if I did.'

'Oh, come on,' said Arlene. 'You could melt any girl's heart.'

'Dr Jennifer Niederhauser obviously doesn't have one,' said Jo-Jo.

Guy Gibson had melted Arlene Grey's heart a long time ago, when he first walked into her pub to enquire about the room for rent. She had actually just decided to rent the room above the Wily Fox to a well-muscled Geordie bloke who was going to be staying in Tincastle while he helped the first of a series of yuppie couples from London restore an old cottage in the town. But Guy soon changed her mind.

She watched him walk across the pub's garden from her office window. It wasn't easy to be undistracted by a six-foot-two hunk with a face like all your favourite film stars squished into one. Arlene's accounts remained unfinished while she waited to see where the good-looking stranger was headed.

Meanwhile, Arlene's six-year-old son, Jamie, was playing all alone on the grass. Jamie fired a shot at Guy from an imaginary gun. Guy immediately threw himself on to the gravel of the car park as though mortally wounded by a real bullet, with no regard for his clothes or the fact that he was a grown man. Jamie was astonished. Then horrified to see the stranger lying motionless on the ground. But when he realised that Guy was just playing, he was delighted. Guy had to play for another ten minutes before Jamie would let him anywhere near the pub.

'I've come about the room,' Guy said to Arlene when Jamie eventually allowed him to pass. 'Is it still available?'

Jamie was grinning from the pub doorway behind his new friend (the six-year-old wasn't allowed to use the front door to the bar while the pub was open).

'I'll have to take references,' said Arlene as professionally as she could. But she already knew that the spare room belonged to Guy. Not many people would have known so instinctively how to play with her son. Even the other kids who lived down the street and had known him since he was tiny generally gave Jamie a wide berth. Jamie Grey wasn't always easy to play with. Because Jamie was profoundly deaf.

Months later, Guy characteristically shook the compliment off when Arlene finally told him what had swayed her decision to let him into her home that day.

'You had such a natural way with my kid.'

'Children and animals,' he said with a shrug. 'They both adore me. Shame the same can't be said for grown-up girls.'

'They must find your gorgeousness intimidating,' said Arlene seriously. It was totally incomprehensible that Guy didn't have a girlfriend.

'Oh, I know I could get laid,' Guy admitted. 'But I'm looking for something special. It's got to be someone who understands how much time I spend with the chimps for a start. How much they mean to me.'

Guy was loading his overalls into the washing machine as he said this.

'And someone without a sense of smell,' Arlene commented as she caught a pungent whiff of ape.

Arlene and Guy's landlord/tenant relationship quickly became a friendship too. Arlene made Guy so welcome at the Wily Fox that he was always happy to help her out with babysitting when the young girls from town let her down. Arlene was so touched that she started to cry the first time Guy signed 'good morning' to Jamie across the breakfast table. Pretty soon, Guy knew more sign language than she did and Arlene often had to ask him what her son was talking about when he came home from his school near Exeter, hands a-blur with news and gossip.

In the early days, Guy often took Jamie with him to the sanctuary at weekends and during school holidays. Jamie had been thrilled to play with Mad and Bad, calling them his little brothers. But Jamie was fourteen now and he wasn't so interested in animals any more.

'The chimps are sad,' he signed.

'You would be, too, if you'd been through some of the things they have,' Guy signed back.

'I don't mean "sad" like unhappy,' Jamie signed with a sigh. 'I mean "sad" like uncool, Guy. Like you are.'

Guy didn't need to babysit for Jamie any more. Arlene was happy to leave her teenage son alone upstairs in the flat now, while she worked downstairs in the bar. Jamie couldn't get into too much trouble tapping away on his computer (mostly trying to get through the parental blocks Arlene used to make sure that he didn't download any porn). But it wasn't long before she needed Guy to do her a favour again.

Arlene was quite a businesswoman. Since her husband left her when Jamie was just a few months old – unable to cope with the fact of his son's deafness – she had kept her little family afloat by increasingly inventive means. Managing the pub gave them a roof over their heads, but to buy all the extras Jamie needed – the state-of-the-art computer, the digital cameras and top-of-the-range colour printers (he wanted to be a photographer when he grew up) – Arlene moonlighted as an interior designer, a shopping consultant and an event planner. There wasn't much need for the former two in Tincastle (though she had managed to persuade the yuppies who bought the Witch's cottage to install a Philip Starck bathroom!). But latterly her event-planning skills had come into their own.

Arlene had noticed that Tincastle was becoming an increasingly popular destination for hen parties. It was cheap, for a start. Dirt cheap. Off-season, a gang of girls could take over an entire hotel for less than twenty quid a head. And it was cheesy, too. There were plenty of 'kiss me quick' hats to be had down on the seafront. And yet, at the same time, Tincastle was one of the loveliest seaside resorts in the country. Hen-night frivolity could be tempered with windswept walks along a beautiful beach to blow away the hangover. Tincastle provided the perfect combination of cheapness, cheesiness and wonderful countryside. All within easy-ish reach of London by train.

Arlene was a very canny marketer. She soon had an arrangement with all the hotel managers in town. When a gang of girls booked in, they would receive a special hen-night information pack, with vouchers for meals at favoured restaurants (including the pub, of course) and details of some *special* services.

It started when one of her barmen, Greg, dressed up as a security guard and did a *Full Monty*-style strip as part of the pub's efforts to raise money for Comic Relief. He was good. Surprisingly good. But while the girls of Tincastle were busy ogling Greg's hitherto unseen muscles, Arlene was seeing pound signs. Three pints later, Greg agreed to let Arlene be his 'manager' and she had him booked to entertain a hen party the following weekend.

Tincastle was full of strapping young men sporting muscles gained through lugging beer barrels (in Greg's case) or working on farms or on fishing boats. And very few of them would turn their nose up at earning a few extra bob. By the end of her first month, Arlene had five boys on her books, sending them as far afield as Exeter and Land's End to take their clothes off. Six months on, Jim, who dressed up as a fireman (he was in fact a fireman in his day job too), often stripped three times on a spare Saturday night.

It was the last thing Guy imagined he would end up doing. Though he was undoubtedly a good-looking bloke, the idea of actually capitalising on his body was total anathema to him. He listened to the stories of Arlene's blossoming business with incredulity. Were there really women out there who would pay that much money to see a fireman take his uniform off?

'You could do it,' Arlene often told her lodger.

Guy would always change the subject.

'Really. I'm serious. You could.'

How could Guy become a male stripper? He was the kind of man who cleared dance floors when he stepped on to them. And not because everyone wanted to watch him get down *à la* John Travolta.

'You don't have to be able to dance,' said Arlene.

'Not going to be a very entertaining strip then, is it?'

'I saw you being *very* entertaining for Jamie the other day.'

Guy couldn't begin to see the connection. 'What on earth are you talking about now?'

'That chimpanzee impression you were doing for him was pretty impressive,' Arlene explained. 'I couldn't stop him chimping round the house for hours after you left for work. He nearly broke his neck swinging off the bloody banister.'

'What has this got to do with me stripping?' asked Guy.

'You could combine your strip with a chimpanzee impression. It'd be incredible. I can see it now. Guy Gibson. The Ape Man.' Arlene blinked out the name with her hands as though it was written in lights on a theatre canopy.

It was the funniest thing Guy had ever heard.

And he wouldn't have done it. Ever. Except that Guy had the softest heart this side of Bambi and when Arlene came to him in tears the following Saturday night, saying that Jim couldn't make his latest appointment as a fireman stripper because he had a real emergency on his hands, Guy stepped into the breach. It took quite a lot of crying on Arlene's part to convince him, but eventually he donned the fireman's suit and waggled his own hose for a gang of girls from the next town.

It was the most awful three minutes of Guy's life. Never had the Rolling Stones' 'Satisfaction' seemed to go on for so long. Jim was almost six feet five and the fireman's trousers were way too big for his stand-in. But the girls weren't too surprised that a man wearing a full fireman's suit couldn't really *dance* in it. And when he started to take the suit off, they didn't really care. They were simply ecstatic to see such a hunk in the buff. Or the nearly buff. Guy flatly refused to take his thong off that first night.

At the end of the evening, Arlene slapped a fifty-pound note into Guy's hand.

'You've come over to the dark side now,' she said.

And that was it.

Prowdes was in trouble. Guy was already thinking about taking a voluntary pay cut to help Nessa out. But he still wanted to save up for a home of his own. And a better car. His old Suzuki jeep was ailing, spluttering like a smoker with emphysema every time he turned the key in the ignition. The prospect of fifty quid, tax-free, for half an hour's extra work was just too tempting.

Arlene bought a gorilla suit from a fancy-dress shop that was clearing out its old stock and a CD of songs from Disney's *Jungle Book*. 'King of the Swingers' seemed an appropriate theme. The very next Saturday, a gang of girls from Plymouth called asking for something really 'different'. Guy the Gorilla-gram was born.

Since then, as news of his super-realistic animal impression spread, Guy had hardly had a Saturday night to himself. That evening was no exception. Arlene called last orders at the bar. Guy looked at his watch. He had half an hour to get to Cinderella's nightclub where he would be expected to turn himself from an ape into a handsome prince on the stroke of midnight. Jo-Jo and Snowy were used to having their friend bail out on them while the night was still young. They knew how he made his extra money but had sworn not to reveal his secret to Nessa.

'Hen party?' Jo-Jo asked.

'Thirtieth birthday,' said Guy.

'They'll eat you alive!' said Jo-Jo.

Snowy failed to laugh. He was still reeling from the fact that the chimpanzee twins were to join the adult troop at the end of the month. Jo-Jo tried to lighten things up further by proposing a toast to Jennifer.

'May she be feeling as miserable as we are tonight!'

'I can't raise my glass to that,' said Guy. 'That's horrible.'

'So is she,' said Jo-Jo.

10

Jennifer was indeed feeling miserable that night. But not for the reasons one might normally expect to be miserable on a Saturday. It wasn't as if she was sitting at home alone, eating her way through a packet of Kettle Chips and wondering why the phone never rang. No, Jennifer was at a dinner party.

'How is the new job going?' Dahlia asked. Since returning from their honeymoon, Henry and Dahlia had been busy styling themselves as the new social axis of Tincastle. At least once a week, Dahlia would cook for their assorted friends. She was having a fit of domesticity and had even learned how to make her own bread. That week it was rosemary focaccia.

'Easy when you know how,' she said smugly when Jennifer breathed her admiration. Dahlia conveniently forgot about the five practice-run burned bread cow-pats in the dustbin.

Jennifer predicted that this new domestic goddess phase would last at most six months but, in the meantime, she was always invited to these 'impromptu' gatherings. As was a spare man from Henry's company in Exeter . . . It seemed any old spare man would do.

That evening's candidate was an auditor called Charlie, who sported a 'fat boy's goatee'. Someone had obviously told him that growing a skinny landing strip of hair on his uppermost chin would distract from the three other chins that dangled beneath like a bag of blancmange.

'He's really quite bright,' said Dahlia hopefully.

Jennifer rolled her eyes. As usual, she spent most of the evening hanging out in the kitchen on the pretence of helping Dahlia with the cooking. It was definitely a pretence. It was almost a point of honour for Jennifer that she couldn't cook. Why should she have to do the domestic thing at all when she was so busy being an intellectual giant, was her excuse.

'Yeah, well, even intellectual giants will get fat if all they ever eat is takeaway Chinese food and Kettle Chips,' said Dahlia, as she put the finishing touches to the cheese plate so that it could be slowly warming its way up to room temperature while they ate pudding. 'You need to take as much care of yourself as you do of those monkeys.' It was as though Jennifer had two mothers. She already suspected that Dahlia phoned her mum for a debrief after each of these dinners.

'*And I had it up my jumper all the bloody time!*' The sound of Charlie's voice burst from the dining room to interrupt them. He was recounting a tale of drama on the high seas in his loud, public school foghorn. Specifically, Charlie was talking about a rough crossing from Southampton to the Isle of Wight during Cowes Week. Jennifer winced.

'I wish you would stop trying to set me up with men from Henry's office,' she whispered to Dahlia. 'It's starting to get a bit embarrassing.'

'Perhaps I should stop wasting my time, go straight to the pet shop and buy you a cat,' Dahlia laughed. 'Or perhaps there's something you're not telling me! You're having a passionate affair with the stripper, aren't you? Please tell me you are. Please. I have to live vicariously through you these days. I'm never going to shag anyone but Henry Nichols ever again. Can you believe it?'

Not quite, thought Jennifer. But of course she didn't say that.

'I am so jealous of you,' Dahlia sighed. 'Of all the jammy luck to end up working with the Marky Mark of the monkey world!'

'Exactly. *Working* being the operative word. We are working together. That is all.'

Dahlia gave a sceptical nod.

'Besides,' Jennifer continued, 'even if we weren't working together, there is the small issue that the man is an idiot. The fact that his body is magnificent does not make up for the fact that he forced it against mine against my will and ruined a very expensive dress in the process. That was practically an assault as far as I'm concerned. Why on earth would I want to be with a man like that? Plus, he's stupid.'

Dahlia raised an eyebrow.

'You should see his reports, Dahlia. I sometimes wonder whether I should suggest that he gets one of the chimpanzees to help him write them. His spelling is atrocious.'

'Being unable to spell doesn't make you a bad person,' Dahlia reminded her gently. Dahlia herself was dyslexic. 'You used to help me get my work done. And as I remember, you used to be quite good at not making me feel stupid when you did.'

'That was different,' said Jennifer. 'You don't know how frustrating it is to work with people like Guy Gibson. All of them. Snowy. Jo-Jo. Everyone at that bloody sanctuary acts as if I hate the animals just because I don't think it's right to treat them like children. They are chimpanzees, Dahlia! Animals! Chimpanzees! They don't benefit from being treated like pets. And that Jo-Jo girl is a total bitch.'

'Ah!' Dahlia pricked up her ears in expectation of some gossip. 'Is *she* shagging the gorilla-gram?'

'I have no idea.' Jennifer paused. 'And I don't care if she is. But she put orang-utan shit into one of my wellington boots.'

Dahlia sniggered into the cream she had been whipping.

'Just because I said she can't give Hector a Mars Bar every morning any more! I mean—'

'Who is Hector and why can't he have the odd Mars Bar?' Dahlia asked.

'Hector is a Sumatran orang-utan,' Jennifer reminded Dahlia for the fifth time. She was beginning to think Dahlia wasn't actually that interested in what she did at Prowdes at all. 'Orangs do not eat milk chocolate in the wild. Why on earth should he eat it in captivity? He'll end up developing diabetes. Snowy gives Mad and Bad a cup of tea and toast and Marmite every morning. Where are they going to get a cup of tea in Liberia?'

'Don't they have tea in Liberia?' Dahlia asked.

'Not for chimpanzees,' Jennifer sighed. Dahlia was almost as exasperating as Jo-Jo. 'Through their soft-heartedness, the staff at Prowdes have created a bunch of neurotic animals with ridiculous human dependencies that will scupper them when they are released into the wild. If they're ever ready to be released. Which I very much doubt they will be. Do you understand what I'm up against now?' Jennifer asked her friend. 'They are undermining my every effort to get those chimps ready for life in Africa with their anthropomorphism.'

'Yeah. Anthropomorphism. That sucks.' Dahlia nodded as though she knew what Jennifer was talking about.

'I have no authority. No one gets the message.'

'Hmmm. Sometimes you just need to try presenting the message a different way,' Dahlia began. 'Now I'm not saying that you're not absolutely right that this Hector chap shouldn't be giving the chimps a cup of tea—'

'Keep up, Dahlia. Hector is an orang-utan. He's not giving anyone any tea.'

'Oh, right. Hector is the *orang-utan* and Snowy is the keeper. I don't know how I'm supposed to remember who's an animal and who isn't when the animals all have human names and the keepers are named after cats. Anyway, what I'm trying to say is, I've known you for over twenty years now and, whether you realise it or not, sometimes you do have a slightly—'

Fortunately for Dahlia, Henry popped his head round the kitchen door before she could finish her sentence and incur her best friend's wrath.

'Hello, Mr Nichols!' she said.

'Hello, Mrs Nichols,' said Henry.

They were still at that sickening stage when they thought it was cute to address each other as Mr and Mrs Nichols *all the time*.

'What are you doing in here, Jenny?'

'It's Jennifer,' Jennifer hissed. She hated to have her name shortened. Only Dahlia had ever got away with it. Henry obviously thought that the privilege would extend to him too now that they were married. But it wouldn't.

'Come back out into the dining room and keep Charlie entertained. Honestly, I line these fantastic blokes up for you and this is all the thanks I get. People will start to think you're a lesbian, you know. Dahlia tells me that you're not even tempted by this Tarzan bloke who works at your sanctuary.'

'For heaven's sake,' said Jennifer. 'You're like born-again Christians, you married people. Do you think it's your duty to convert me to the joys of coupledom before I go to single-girl hell

59

or something? I am perfectly happy as I am. I do not need to be set up with any of your workmates and I certainly do not need to shag one of my colleagues to stop myself from "seizing up" as you so kindly suggested last week, Henry. Everything about my life is fine and dandy right now. In fact, I am extremely pleased to be young, free and single.'

'Not so young these days,' Henry muttered dangerously.

'Still young enough to kick you in the nuts. Thank you very much, Henry. Thanks for dinner, Dahlia. I'm not going to stay for pudding.'

'What? But it's your favourite!'

'Stop acting like my mother! And bread and butter pudding is not my favourite. Never has been.'

Jennifer retrieved her coat from the back of the kitchen door and waved goodbye.

Mr and Mrs Nichols shared a complicit glance. 'Oooooh. Touched on a raw nerve there,' said Henry.

'I think she fancies that bloke at work but he isn't putting out,' concluded Dahlia.

Jennifer might ordinarily have been a little nervous, walking back through the dark streets of Tincastle to her cottage, but that night she was ready for anyone who might try to ambush her on the way home. Like Devon's answer to Lara Croft, she was a bundle of pure irritation, ready to lash out at anyone who crossed her. Dahlia and Henry had been driving her crazy for years with their match-making efforts but right then work was a far bigger worry.

Jennifer had expected some resistance to her plans for the chimps from her new colleagues at Prowdes, but nothing like the amount she had been receiving. It was as though Nessa and Jennifer were the only people at the sanctuary who wanted the chimps to go back to the wild. Certain members of staff even seemed to be doing their best to prevent that from ever happening. It was getting harder and harder for Jennifer to remain enthusiastic about her job. It was hopeless. Jennifer had attached herself to the worst bunch of losers in the primatology community. She was increasingly beginning to think that she had accidentally joined a circus instead of a sanctuary.

Getting home to the cottage, she slammed the door shut behind her and switched on the television. At least leaving Dahlia's dinner party early meant that Jennifer was home in time to watch a repeat episode from David Attenborough's series on mammals for the BBC. That night's segment was the one on chimps. Perfect. Jennifer could watch how it should be done.

She made herself a cup of herbal tea, got out the emergency packet of fig rolls she kept on the highest shelf in the cupboard, and sat down to watch the programme. She never got bored of David Attenborough. Attenborough had been one of her heroes since childhood. If only she could meet a man like him, she might be persuaded to give love another whirl. There weren't many men so charismatic in the animal conservation world, that was for sure. Not Snowy Pilkington, picking his nose and eating it like he was one of the chimps himself. Not Ernie the part-time chimp-keeper who could belch the National Anthem. Not even Guy Gibson. Jennifer wasn't into beauty without brains.

'I'm here in the forests of Gombe . . .'

Attenborough's soothing voice soon made Jennifer forget about the orang-utan shit in her wellington boots.

II

There's no such thing as a regular weekend for people who work with animals. On Sunday morning, Jennifer got out of bed at six o'clock and made her bleary-eyed way to the sanctuary on auto-pilot. At least she wasn't hung-over, like Snowy and Jo-Jo, who had never been able to adjust their mindset so that Saturday wasn't always a party night whether or not they had to work the following day. They were both sporting sunspecs as they shuffled about the staff room that Sunday. It was as though Quentin Tarantino circa *Reservoir Dogs* had been put in charge of dressing the team.

Jennifer made herself a cup of herbal tea without getting involved in their conversation. Rather, without Snowy and Jo-Jo involving her in their conversation. Then she holed herself up in her office and made a start on that week's admin work while Puccini's *Tosca* played on her CD player. *Tosca* was her favourite but not even *Tosca* could cheer her up that morning. Not even the bit where Tosca throws herself to her death.

A fax had arrived during the night from a contact in Liberia, telling her that much as he would like to be able to offer the Prowdes' chimps a haven in the forest there, he was unable to promise anything while there was the possibility that he might have to flee the country to save his own life at any moment. It was a problem that Nessa seemed unable to grasp. Even if Jennifer felt the chimps were ready to be moved, it wasn't just a question of turning up in Africa and letting them loose. The best natural habitats were shrinking year on year as natural disasters forced humans into chimpanzee terri-tory in search of food, development demanded that acres of forest were cut down for roads or pasture, and civil wars raged.

Jennifer turned the CD player off with an angry punch to the on/off key. Her melancholy mood was morphing into irritation now. The last thing she needed was to hear Jo-Jo's terrified voice pipe up over the sanctuary intercom.

'Ape on the loose,' she shouted. 'Ape on the loose!'

The ape in question was Hector, of course. He was nowhere to be seen. Jo-Jo was already in tears in front of the empty orang-utan enclosure by the time Jennifer arrived.

'How long has he been gone?' Jennifer asked brusquely.

'I don't know,' Jo-Jo sniffed. 'Maybe ten minutes. But he might have been gone for an hour. I've been mucking out the chimp nursery for at least that long.'

'Has nobody seen him?'

'Nobody's seen him *at all*,' Jo-Jo wailed.

Every keeper was on the hunt. They started with the obvious places. Hector was an elderly orang. Not fast on his feet like the chimps. He couldn't have gone that far even if he had been gone for an hour. Snowy kept saying as much in an attempt to reassure his young friend. They searched the trees directly around his enclosure first. The food bins were an obvious destination for an orang-utan on a diet, too, but the bins in the shed next to the orang enclosure were untouched.

Unfortunately, for once it had been so dry for the past few weeks that there weren't even any clear tracks to follow. Calling Hector's name got no response. Neither did waving bananas to tempt him out of hiding.

While the other keepers systematically swept through the sanctuary in search of their runaway, Jo-Jo sat on the ground against the wire to Hector's enclosure with her head in her hands and sobbed great snorting sobs.

'Crying isn't going to help us find him,' Jennifer snapped.

'He can't have got far,' said Snowy again.

'He might have done,' said Jo-Jo doomily. 'What if he got out on the road and got knocked over?'

'Has anyone checked the road outside the sanctuary?' Guy asked quietly. 'Though if someone had knocked over an orang-utan, I'm sure they would have let us know.'

'What . . . what if he's been kidnapped!' Jo-Jo wailed then. 'Someone might have taken him home to be their pet.'

'Would you want that stinking creature as a pet?' Guy said reasonably.

Jo-Jo looked at him with hurt in her eyes. Stinky or not, she loved her solitary charge. 'I just want him to be safe,' she said.

But the search continued fruitlessly. On those few occasions when apes had escaped before, they had been pretty easy to track from the trail of destruction they wreaked on their way to freedom. Sacha and Virginia had once made it over the main chimpanzee enclosure fence by using a loose plank from one of their climbing frames as a makeshift ladder. Amazingly, the plank was long enough that the chimps were able to simply tumble over the barrels at the top.

'At least this proves that chimpanzees are capable of goal-directed tool use,' Nessa had quipped when the keepers realised what had happened.

Once outside, Sacha and Virginia had gone on a wrecking spree, pulling up the neatly planted flower beds, swinging from signs until they broke, breaking the wing mirrors off a Porsche in the visitors' car park . . . They were finally cornered on the roof of the keepers' restroom. For two hours the keepers tried to persuade them to come down with a combination of threats, bananas and Mars Bars. In the end, it fell to Harrison and his tranquilliser darts to get the runaways down. After that, Nessa and Guy had to have a serious review of the type of playthings that went into the main chimp enclosure. Anything that could be pulled up and used as a bridge or a ladder was out. The wooden climbing frame was replaced by a combination of ropes and rubber tyres strung from two very sturdy metal poles sunk deep into concrete moorings. Even then, Virginia was caught attempting to get over the wire by standing on top of a tyre she had managed to untie. It gave the keepers hours of fun to watch her trying to stand on the upright tyre like a clown trying to balance on a unicycle . . .

But that day Hector had left no trail.

'Where would he have gone?' Nessa asked. 'Where are his favourite places?'

'His bed? He never even goes to the far side of his enclosure.' Jo-Jo was baffled.

Eight forty. It was getting close to opening time. If Hector wasn't tracked down and contained within the next twenty minutes, the sanctuary would have to remain closed to visitors until he was found. They couldn't risk having a child be the first to come across their runaway. Soppy as he was around Jo-Jo, the staff had no idea how Hector would react if anyone else tried to touch him, particularly someone smaller than he was.

'Tell Marjorie not to open the ticket booth just yet,' Nessa said resignedly. 'I don't suppose we've got a queue of people waiting to come in but we'd better stay closed just in case . . .'

Snowy duly headed off to relay the message. But before he could get to Marjorie, Marjorie came running out of the ticket booth screaming as though the devil was on her tail.

'There's a man under the ticket desk!' she shrieked. 'He put his hand right up my skirt!'

The keepers regarded Marjorie in shock and horror. Not just because she was seventy-seven years old and occasionally wore such big bloomers that you could see them hanging beneath her hemline.

'Marjorie, calm down,' said Nessa. 'Tell us exactly what happened.'

'I was just setting up the cash box. I felt this hand upon my ankle. It went all the way up to my knee! Covered in ginger hair, it was. Must be that man from the bakery. He's always trying to flirt with me when I'm in there buying my buns.'

'Hector,' said Guy.

Jo-Jo and Snowy took off in the direction of the ticket office at once.

And sure enough, there he was. Sitting beneath the cash desk, working his way through a box full of Mars Bars (the ticket office sold tuck to those visitors who couldn't wait to get to the gift shop).

'Hector!' Jo-Jo hollered.

The ginger ape ducked back into the shadows at the sound of his keeper's voice, but his brief taste of freedom was over.

Half an hour later, Hector was safely back in his enclosure and the sanctuary was open for business again. In the past, a successful conclusion to an escape had been celebrated as such with cups of tea, pats on the back and extra biscuits all round. But that was under the old regime. While the keepers made bawdy jokes about Marjorie and her brush with a real animal, Jennifer remained stony-faced. She stood behind Jo-Jo and watched her like a headmistress watching a pupil scrub graffiti off a wall while the youngest keeper closed and double-locked the gate to Hector's enclosure. Then Jennifer announced that there would be an emergency staff meeting to debrief as soon as the sanctuary closed for the day at five o'clock.

'I've got to get home,' said Snowy. 'My wife's mother is coming over. She'll kill me if I don't get back in time to help her tidy up.'

'Non-attendance at this meeting will be viewed very dimly,' Jennifer said.

Snowy looked to Nessa but Nessa could only shrug. 'Dr Niederhauser is in charge of the chimpanzee project,' Nessa reminded her staff. 'I think it best if all primate-keepers attend.'

Jo-Jo looked at Nessa appealingly but Nessa had employed Jennifer on the basis that she would have sole control of the primate projects at Prowdes and thus felt honour-bound to let Jennifer deal with this latest escape in her own way.

So at five past five, as the last of the visitors' cars left the car park, the keepers – including the part-timers, Ernie, Jack and David – gathered in Jennifer's office. Jo-Jo slunk in behind everyone else and stayed near the door as though she knew she might have to make a quick escape. Her face was pale beneath her pixie short brown hair. Suddenly, she looked every bit the inexperienced teenager she really was. Snowy gave a subtle squeeze of reassurance to her shoulder.

'Jo-Jo,' Jennifer went straight to what she believed to be the root cause of the problem, 'we have had more than one conversation about the importance of making sure that enclosures are properly shut and on the last occasion I think we both agreed that another lapse in security would merit a written warning.'

Jo-Jo was white with fear.

'You did leave the enclosure open again, didn't you?'

Jo-Jo's bottom lip wobbled.

'Didn't you?'

66

Guy and Snowy both coughed at once.

'What is it?' Jennifer asked in irritation.

'Dr Niederhauser,' said Guy. 'Jo-Jo didn't leave Hector's enclosure open. But I think I might have done.'

'No, he didn't,' said Snowy. 'I did. I should have the written warning, seeing as it is definitely my fault.'

'I don't think so, Snowy. I might have accidentally left it open after I went in there to have a look at that blocked drain,' said Ernie, who hadn't even been at work that morning. He'd arrived with the second shift at twelve.

'I definitely did it,' said Guy.

'No, I did,' said Snowy.

'It was me,' Ernie insisted. 'I'm always leaving doors unlocked. It's my age, you see. I'm getting forgetful.'

Only Jo-Jo was quiet.

'Jo-Jo,' Jennifer gave her a chance to confess.

'If anyone deserves a written warning it's me,' Guy continued.

'Give me one,' Snowy and Ernie chimed in with him.

'What is this?' Jennifer interrupted with a shout. 'Are we re-enacting *Spartacus* or what?' She referred to the moment in the Kirk Douglas gladiator film when all the captured slaves claim to be Spartacus to save their hero from death.

'All we're saying is that none of us can be entirely sure who left the enclosure open,' said Guy. 'We've all been in there this morning.'

'Why? Why were any of you in the orang-utan enclosure except Jo-Jo?' Jennifer asked.

'Change of scene,' said Guy with a smile.

His winning smile. The smile he used when trying to get a big tip while stripping for a hen party.

Jennifer shook her head. But she knew she was defeated.

'Well, in that case, this warning goes for *all* of you,' she said at last. 'We were lucky today. The worst that happened was that Hector ate a few Mars Bars he shouldn't have had and Marjorie got a bit of a shock . . .'

'Best shock she's had in years,' said Ernie.

Jennifer shot him her look.

'But if one of our animals bites a visitor, then the whole

sanctuary will pay for it. The council doesn't need much of an excuse to close us down. Enclosure gates must be properly closed and *locked* with padlocks. We've got to be more vigilant. All of us,' she added, but she was looking directly at Jo-Jo as she said it. 'That's all.'

The keepers filed out of her office, leaving Jennifer alone to write up a report of that morning's escape in the Health and Safety log book. As she meticulously documented the incident, Jennifer felt her jaw tighten. She wasn't angry with Jo-Jo any more. She was angry with Guy now. He had deliberately undermined her by pretending that the escape could really have been anyone's fault but Jo-Jo's. How had Jennifer let that happen? Guy had essentially *flirted* Jo-Jo out of jail.

From her office window, Jennifer could see him now, chasing Jo-Jo across the lawn with a pitchfork full of dirty straw as the keepers tidied the sanctuary in preparation for the night. Jo-Jo squealed as Guy cornered her by the back of the chimp nursery. Then he looked back in the direction of Jennifer's office, as though he could feel her eyes upon him. Seeming suddenly embarrassed, Guy lowered the pitchfork and let Jo-Jo escape. He smiled, half to himself, half in the direction of the shadowy figure at Jennifer's window. Jennifer didn't smile in return. She dropped her eyes back to her report.

One more month. That was all she was prepared to give it. If Jennifer didn't feel as though she was making progress with Project Africa and her colleagues at Prowdes in that time, she was going.

12

But Jennifer didn't have long to feel angry. A few days later an altogether more important matter than the *Spartacus* moment at the staff meeting was occupying everybody's attention. Jennifer had just arrived at the sanctuary and was walking across the car park to her office when her walkie-talkie sprang to life.

It was Nessa.

'Darling,' she said, 'I know you've just got in but I need you to march straight back to the car park, get into the van and go down to the customs and excise people in Plymouth at once. I've already called Harrison the vet. He's going to meet you there. Take Guy and Snowy and a transportation cage. We're going to have a new visitor.'

Excepting the surprising twin birth of Mad and Bad, the chimpanzee population at Prowdes had not grown at all for almost five years. Far fewer chimps needed rescuing in Europe these days. Thank goodness. The British holidaymakers, who once made up most of the Spanish beach photographers' clientele on the Costa Del Sol, were getting much too savvy about conservation thanks to the likes of Rolf Harris and his animal rescue shows. Nobody wanted to be photographed with an endangered species any more. The beach photographers were more likely to get a punch in the face for mistreating animals than a commission.

It wasn't just the traditionally animal-loving Brits who were disgusted by the photographers' trade either. The Germans, the French, the Italians and even the Spanish themselves, who not so long ago seemed to think nothing of throwing a goat off the top of a church in celebration, were getting equally uncomfortable about the exploitation of exotic animals.

Meanwhile, fewer people were keeping chimps as pets. The

practice had been illegal in many countries for quite some time. Elsewhere, stories of the reality of chimp husbandry had put the remaining idiots off the idea. Even by three years old, a chimpanzee is strong enough to do serious damage to a fully grown man. Who wants a pet you have every reason to live in fear of? And so the trade in infant chimpanzees began to dwindle.

Which was why Nessa was surprised to get a call from customs that early summer morning to tell her that they thought they had found a chimpanzee. It was on a boat they had boarded on suspicion of drug smuggling.

'What do you mean, you "think" it's a chimp?' Nessa asked. 'It either is or it isn't.'

'We're not sure,' said the customs officer who spoke to her. 'My colleague opened the door, saw the *whatever-it-is* and promptly shut the door again. He was terrified. He's having a cup of tea with lots of sugar in it as we speak. He didn't get a proper look. But he thinks it was a chimp. Or maybe a gorilla. It was pretty big, he said. And I can't risk sending anyone in to investigate more closely without an expert on hand. Can you help us?'

Nessa immediately called Harrison Arnold and arranged for him to meet Guy, Snowy and Jennifer at the docks with his tranquilliser darts and a blowpipe.

'A blowpipe?' said the customs officer warily. 'Does he have to get the animal by traditional African means or what?'

Nessa laughed. It was much more prosaic than that. Harrison always used a blowpipe rather than a gun to tranquillise the animals at Prowdes when any of them needed to be sedated for examination. It had taken him some practice to become a good shot with the thing but it was worth it. Unlike a gun, the blowpipe made no noise, which meant that if you didn't manage to hit the animal you wanted to sedate first time, you wouldn't have frightened it out of range with the bang of a gun going off. It was an important consideration. A frightened chimpanzee is every bit as terrifying as a cornered tiger.

Not that the animal they were on their way to see that day would have far to run.

Guy and Snowy abandoned their plans for the morning and loaded up the transportation cage at once, leaving Jo-Jo to prepare the empty enclosure next to Mad and Bad's cage as a temporary quarantine. Jennifer sat between Guy and Snowy in the front of the transit van. The news that they were expecting a new arrival had momentarily taken her mind off Jo-Jo's insurrection but it hadn't particularly cheered her up.

'I can't believe we've got to take another chimp,' she said. 'It will disturb the stability of the group.'

'Prowdes has never turned an animal in need away,' Snowy reminded her.

In the office, Nessa took a deep breath, picked up the phone, and prepared to remind her bank manager of the same.

By the time the Prowdes' team arrived at the docks, Harrison was already preparing his blowpipe. The yacht was surrounded by armed guards, just in case what the customs officer thought was a chimp was in fact a small but very hairy man who might emerge from his cabin toting a loaded machine gun. A doctor had been called for the same reason, in case a human being rather than a chimp got a tranquilliser dart in the bum. It was impossible to find out before opening the door. The cabin in which the chimp/hairy man was contained had no exterior window and its occupant had made no sound since his discovery to give the officers a clue. Animal? Vegetable? Dead or alive?

'He might be dead,' said the officer who had raised the alarm. 'He didn't look particularly lively and the smell was bloody awful.'

'Where's the boat come from?' Harrison asked.

'We've been watching it since it left Southern Spain.'

'Spain!' Harrison exhaled. 'Who would want to bring a chimp that far on a boat this size?'

Snowy and Guy prepared the cage and carried it on board the yacht.

'Who on earth would keep any animal on a boat like this anyway?' Snowy asked. The yacht was beautiful. It was clearly expensive and well loved. The smooth teak boards on the deck shone like the floors in a ballroom. Having seen what Mad and Bad did to his house even as infants without proper teeth, Snowy wouldn't have wanted to let a chimpanzee anywhere near such luxury.

'You ready?' Guy asked Harrison. When it came to sedating and containing chimps, they had worked as a team many times before.

Harrison nodded and covered his eyes with shatterproof glasses. The customs officer had also insisted that he wear a bullet-proof vest. The plan was to open the door just a little way and try to get a dart in the animal through the gap.

'I hope he's a good shot,' said one of the customs officers.

'The best,' said Guy, remembering how Harrison had taken down Achilles one afternoon the previous year. The alpha male had an infected cut to his foot and was refusing to let anyone near enough to look at it. The pain of the infection had made Achilles pretty bloody irritable. When Guy and Harrison appeared in the enclosure with placatory bananas, Achilles flew at his keeper in a rage. Harrison had got a dart in the chimp's neck just in time. Achilles froze in mid-leap as the tranquilliser took immediate effect and slumped to the ground, teeth still bared, within a foot of their feet. Guy almost asked for a tranquilliser himself after the shock of that close encounter.

'On my signal,' said Harrison now. 'Open the door, count two and slam the door shut again after I've let out the shot.'

Guy took the door handle.

'One, two . . .!'

There was a little hollow popping sound as Harrison puffed into one end of the pipe and the dart flew out of the other. But there wasn't even a squeak of protest from his target. Man or chimp, the creature behind the door didn't even have time to stand up before the tranquilliser hit him.

As it happened, Guy and Harrison need not have worried too much about getting to the animal behind the door in safety. The chimp – it definitely was a chimp – was tethered by a large dog-leash around his neck to a post in the middle of the cabin. It was a young male. Probably about five or six years old, Guy guessed from his height. Still a child in chimpanzee terms. Not many people knew that in the wild a chimpanzee will hang around its

72

mother until it is well into its teens, sometimes even continuing to suckle until it is at least the size of this poor sea-faring ape.

One of the customs officers quickly cut through the rope. Guy and Snowy hoisted the chimp's limp body out of the little cabin and laid him out on the deck so that Harrison, and Jennifer could get a closer look at him.

'He's in a pretty bad way,' Harrison sighed as he checked the dilation of the animal's pupils with a torch. 'Dehydrated.' And the collar the chimp had been wearing had obviously been fitted when the animal was much younger and smaller. The skin around his neck was rubbed raw and showed signs of infection.

'I'll get him on antibiotics to clear that up right away,' Harrison told Jennifer. 'And I should have the blood test results back pretty quickly.' He was taking a syringe-full of the chimpanzee's blood as he spoke. 'No bones broken as far as I can tell.'

Harrison's mobile phone chirruped to let him know he had a text message.

'Uh-oh. One of my giraffes at the Teignton zoo has gone into labour. I'm going to have to go. Guy, you know the procedure, don't you? I'll check back with you as soon as I've sorted this new baby out.'

Guy nodded. Being one of the few vets in the south of England qualified to deal with large African mammals made Harrison a very busy man. Giraffe births in captivity were almost always a nightmare. Giraffes like to give birth standing up and it's a long way for a baby giraffe to drop, from mother to the concrete floor of an enclosure. Harrison was already on the phone, instructing the giraffe's keepers to make sure the baby had plenty of straw to fall on to, as he raced back to his car.

'What? Where's he going?' Jennifer fussed.

'We can deal with this,' Guy assured her.

Guy and Snowy tenderly arranged the new chimpanzee in the bottom of the transportation cage that they had made more comfortable with blankets donated by the little old ladies of Tincastle.

Jennifer signed papers to confirm that she had taken possession of the property of Her Majesty's Customs and Excise. And then they were on their way back to Prowdes, hoping that Jo-Jo would have properly cleaned out the quarantine cage before they got back.

'What shall we call him?' asked Snowy as they started the drive. 'How about Eric? He looks like an Eric to me.' Snowy had been lobbying to have at least one chimp called Eric since he started working at Prowdes almost a decade before. Eric Idle of *Monty Python* fame was his hero.

'No. Not Eric. Besides, you know the tradition,' said Guy. He nodded in Jennifer's direction. 'This is Dr Niederhauser's first pick-up. She gets to choose his name. What'll it be, Doctor?'

'I don't know,' she stammered, taken by surprise at Guy's suggestion. Since the disciplinary meeting, Jennifer had felt even more of an outsider than before. On the drive down to Plymouth, she felt like a prison guard accompanying two prisoners, barely included in the conversation. Guy's insistence that she choose the new chimp's name was like an invitation to rejoin the gang. 'I've never really thought about it before.'

'You can't think about it in advance,' Guy laughed. 'Chimpanzees are as individual as humans. You can't choose a name without knowing anything about them or seeing them first. But he's definitely not an Eric,' Guy added for Snowy's benefit. 'Too intelligent-looking for that.'

'Well,' said Jennifer thoughtfully. 'It sounds as though he has come a great distance by sea. Perhaps he should be named after one of the great sailors.'

'Hornblower!' piped up Snowy. His wife had a crush on Ioan Gruffud. Snowy didn't mind too much as long as he got to watch some quality naval costume drama as a result.

'No. How can you call a chimpanzee Hornblower? Nelson?' suggested Guy. 'Christopher Columbus? Wasn't he Spanish? That would be appropriate.'

'Ulysses,' said Jennifer.

'Uly-what?' said Snowy.

'Ulysses, like the hero in the myth.'

The two men looked at each other as they considered the exotic new moniker.

'I think that suits him very well,' said Guy at last.

'Still looks like an Eric to me,' Snowy grumbled.

'He is not an Eric.' Guy shared a smile with Jennifer. And for a moment, it actually felt as though one day soon they might be friends.

13

It was to be a day of surprises at Prowdes. While Nessa waited for her staff to return from the docks with their precious new chimpanzee cargo, she took a deep breath and made a few of those phone calls she had been dreading for weeks. The first was to her accountant, Mr Nelson, who confirmed the bad news she had been hoping wasn't true. Nessa's rose-tinted specs had only been serving to make Prowdes' financial situation look more red. Especially since Jennifer had just informed her that they had missed the boat for applying to many academic funds that year. The second call was to her bank manager, to see if he could do anything about it.

Nessa had hoped that by telling Mr Knowles that another chimp was on its way to Prowdes that very minute, she might tug on his heart-strings and extract a few more pounds, another extension to her incredible elasticated overdraft. Instead he said abruptly, 'You're going to have to start turning animals away, Nessa. I really can't help you any longer.' Nessa put the phone down in tears. Slammed it down. Probably not the best idea to slam the phone down on your bank manager.

She immediately set about composing a suitably grovelling apology and prepared to hit redial and deliver it. But the phone rang before she could press the button. Nessa's stomach took an express-lift trip to her mouth. She crossed her fingers and screwed her eyes shut. Then she opened one ever so slightly to read the caller ID display. Was Mr Knowles calling back to say he was closing the Prowdes' account altogether as a result of Nessa's rudeness?

It wasn't Mr Knowles.

Nessa was shaking as she put down the phone again half an hour later. Had she been made the victim of a hoax? Or had a complete stranger really just offered her the means to save her beloved sanctuary in the most spectacular way? She looked at the details she had scribbled on a post-it note while the stranger talked.

'Somebody pinch me,' Nessa murmured to herself.

The caller had been one Faith O'Connell from Animal House Entertainment. She was a television producer, she said. And as the name of her company suggested, she specialised in making documentary programmes about wildlife. Nessa might have seen one of her shows, called *Head in the Clouds*, about the life of a baby giraffe called Shorty born in a Scottish zoo. It had been enormously popular. They were about to make another show, following up on the young giraffe's progress during its first year. They had recently completed a series on a family of Kalahari meerkats living in the same zoo too – the community-minded little critters were always a crowd pleaser, Faith laughed. And now she wanted to film some chimpanzees.

'We've heard about Project Africa,' said Faith.

That was a surprise to Nessa. The only paper that had covered the project at all was the *Tincastle Herald*, hardly a national.

'We want to see your chimps at the sanctuary. Hear how they came to be with you. Find out how you integrate them into an artificial troop. And follow their progress when you release them into the wild. We want to make the public aware of how modern chimpanzee conservation works. And I hope we can make it worth your while,' Faith O'Connell added smoothly.

'It might not be appropriate,' said Nessa, though every part of her wanted to squeal 'yes' at once. 'I'd have to ask Dr Niederhauser. I run the sanctuary but she has sole responsibility for the apes.'

'Then perhaps my assistant producer and I could come and see you both. Have a proper meeting before you dismiss the idea out of hand? How about that? I have to be honest with you and say that you're not the only sanctuary we're looking at in any case. We're also considering Howletts and Monkey World.'

'Of course,' said Nessa, when she heard the names of her two main rivals.

77

'Shall we go ahead and book that meeting?'

The producer suggested a date. Nessa scribbled it down in her diary. The only other appointment she had that month was D-Day with Mr Knowles of Barclays.

'I have a feeling that this could be the start of a wonderful working relationship,' said Faith O'Connell confidently. 'It could be a great opportunity to spread your conservation message to the general public.'

'It's certainly given me food for thought,' said Nessa. And food for the chimps? She hoped so.

The sanctuary's transit van pulled into the car park right outside Nessa's window while she was considering Faith O'Connell's surprising offer. She put down the pen she had been chewing and went out to greet her team.

'What have we got?' she asked as Guy threw open the back doors of the van to show her.

'Young male. Probably about five or six,' Jennifer explained. 'Doesn't seem to be too much wrong with him apart from that nasty welt around his neck where his collar was too tight.'

Nessa bit her lip as she tenderly parted the fur on the animal's neck and looked at the wound beneath. It was as though she could feel the pain herself. 'Better get him into the quarantine block before he wakes up and starts to take a dislike to us,' she said. 'What have you called him?'

'I think he's an Eric,' said Snowy quickly.

'Ulysses,' said Guy. 'We've already named him Ulysses.'

'Very noble,' Nessa agreed.

Jennifer wheeled a trolley up to the van. Snowy and Guy eased the cage out on to it, careful not to disturb their cargo too much.

Ulysses had slept for most of the journey, but was just beginning to come round from the tranquilliser now. He blinked his eyes open momentarily and looked up into Nessa's as she peered in at him through the mesh. Her eyes crinkled upwards at the edges in a smile. Kind and brown.

'Welcome to Prowdes, Ulysses,' said Nessa.

14

It was decided that the new chimpanzee should be kept under observation all night that first night. Guy volunteered at once to put in the overtime. Snowy was under strict orders to spend that evening at home (it was his wedding anniversary) and Jo-Jo was just too inexperienced to be left alone in charge. Jennifer argued that she should do the watch instead. It had come down to the toss of a coin. Guy won. Or lost. Depending on how you viewed the prospect of a night in a deckchair spent watching a slumbering chimp.

But Guy wanted to be there when Ulysses finally shook off the sedative and realised he wasn't on the boat any more. He had already prepared a selection of guaranteed chimp favourites and put them in the cage with the sleeping ape. Mad and Bad had watched curiously as their new neighbour was wheeled in. Mad, living up to his name, had done a little bit of chest beating and puffing out his hair, an alpha male in miniature.

'You are a quarter of his size, Mad,' Snowy had warned him before he left for the night. 'You'll be grateful for the bars in between you when he wakes up and hears you making such a fuss.'

Bad had settled for poking a finger out through the bars of the high-ceiling enclosure he shared with Mad, in an attempt to touch the stranger's hairy back. He couldn't reach. In any case, there was a floor-to-ceiling glass screen between the twins' cage and the one that held Ulysses. Until the results of the blood tests came through, Ulysses would be allowed no physical contact whatsoever with the other chimps. Though he looked healthy enough, apart from the fact that he was a little undernourished, Ulysses might have been carrying anything. They still didn't know where he had come from. Was he wild-born? Or had he been born in a lab? Where had he been living before he took his far from pleasurable boat trip?

Guy knew there were sanctuaries in the United States whose entire chimp populations had HIV – or SIV, for Simian Immunodeficiency Virus, as the condition is known in apes. They had been infected in laboratories, for use in AIDS drug tests. The big joke, if you could find it remotely funny, was that none of the chimps went on to develop AIDS or its simian equivalent after all. They were useless when it came to researching the effects of drugs intended for use on human beings because they simply didn't react like humans to certain diseases. They couldn't be released into the wild again, however, because they could pass the HIV virus on by biting some hapless stranger.

Guy prayed that Ulysses would be given the all-clear. Warnings had been circulated in the conservation world that there were some chimps, liberated from laboratories by animal rights activists in ignorance of their infective status, being raised as pets. Ulysses had no laboratory tattoo, but there was a little rip in the top of one of his ears which might indicate that he had once sported a laboratory tag.

'Where have you come from, eh?' Guy murmured as Ulysses slept. 'What could you tell us?' He touched the rip in Ulysses' ear affectionately. Just thinking about the way some of the chimpanzees at Prowdes had come to be there could make the tears prickle at the back of Guy's eyes. The cruelty they had endured should have been an embarrassment to the entire human race. Sometimes Guy wanted to give up his citizenship of humanity out of shame. Sometimes, such as at that moment, he was simply grateful for the chance to help.

Guy Gibson's parents Don and Elaine weren't to know how the choice of name they made for their youngest son would influence his life. They chose 'Guy' because it was the name of a much-loved uncle on Elaine's side of the family. Gibson was simply Don's surname. They weren't to know that by the time Guy got to junior school, children's television show *Blue Peter* would have made London Zoo's Guy the Gorilla the most famous primate on the planet. Sharing a first name with the majestic old silverback was enough to get Guy pelted with banana skins at break-time. It was just a matter of time before 'Gibson' became 'Gibbon' and the correct response to any mention of Guy's name at school (even when the register was being called in the morning) was a primate grunt and much scratching of armpits. All meant affectionately, of course. Some of Guy's oldest friends still greeted him with some pretty impressive chimp-style 'pant-hoots' when he walked into the pub back in his home town near Manchester.

But in his final year at junior school, Guy found himself in Miss Blaine's form. Miss Blaine was a teacher in real 'old school' style who didn't take too kindly to the way her new class of ten-year-olds exploded into raucous jungle noises halfway through calling the register each morning. With the strange logic of so many teachers, she decided to punish Guy for their racket – though, of course, he was the only one who *wasn't* making any noise. She set him a project on the great apes, to be written during the half-term holiday, and warned the rest of the form that anyone making noises like a 'monkey' during registration the following morning would have to join Guy in the library.

What Miss Blaine didn't know was that Guy's punishment would be quite literally life-changing. Annoyed as he was to be spending his precious half-term in a damp-smelling corner of the reference library, Guy couldn't help but be interested by the things he was reading. As a result, Guy Gibson's project on the great apes was the best piece of work Miss Blaine had seen from a ten-year-old in all her years as a teacher. At the end-of-year prize-giving ceremony, Guy was given a special award for 'effort'. The prize was a hard-backed copy of Jane Goodall's biography. An ape enthusiast was born.

Elaine Gibson still had a photograph of her son receiving that prize on the mantelpiece of her tidy house. There were times when Guy wondered whether that was the last time he had truly made her proud. His time as the best boy in school had been disappointingly brief. At secondary school he hung out with the wrong crowd and by the time most lads his age were smoking Marlboro Lights behind the bike shed, he was already smoking dope. He was expelled when the head boy – who wasn't half so subtle about his habit – was caught smoking in the sixth-form toilets and grassed Guy up as his supplier to escape a harsher penalty himself. Guy had to leave without taking his A levels. No other school in town would take him. University was suddenly out of the question. The idea that he might one day become a great naturalist like Sir David Attenborough fast became a distant dream.

Ten years after being expelled from school, Guy found himself working in a factory, packing sausages. Working with animals, but hardly in the way he'd envisaged it. The crunch came when he attended a leaving party for one of his fellow sausage-packers. Jimmy had been at the factory for almost forty years. Ever since he arrived there because he thought it would be an easy way to earn money for a couple of months while he decided what he really wanted to do . . . While they raised a glass to Jimmy's escape, Guy saw his whole life flash in front of his eyes. His future life. And it was sausages all the way.

He handed in his notice that night. His boss was at the pub with them. Guy wrote out his letter of resignation on the back of a beer mat and knew at once that he had done the right thing when his hitherto super-macho boss burst into tears at the thought of never being able to do the same. Back at home, Guy got out a map of Europe and a drawing pin. Perhaps he would go to Venice and become a gondolier. He could be a life-guard in the south of France. He could spend the summer picking grapes in the Champagne region. Harvesting strawberries in Spain. Anything was better than packing cold pork sausages in Britain's frozen north. He would see where the pin landed and take a chance.

Though Guy's hand hovered tantalisingly close to the Mediterranean for a couple of seconds, the pin eventually landed in Devon. In Tincastle. 'Zoo' was written in tiny red letters on the map next to the town Guy had never heard of. When Guy found out that the 'zoo' was in fact a sanctuary with a large community of apes, his mind was made up. He left the north of England the following weekend and on Monday morning he knocked on Nessa's door and asked her for a job.

Not many zoos would have taken on someone with as few qualifications as Guy Gibson had then, but Nessa could see beyond bits of paper. Passion was more important than exam results. And Guy had passion for primates. Nessa could tell he was telling the truth when he told her that he'd never really had much interest in anything else. After the interview, she took Guy into the chimpanzee nursery. At the time, the only chimp in there was Big Ears, who had been temporarily separated from his parents because he seemed to be losing weight.

Guy was certain that he had blown the interview. Nessa had seemed friendly enough but Eddy Hamilton, who was head keeper back in those days, hadn't seemed quite so impressed.

'Well, Guy—' Nessa drew breath. Guy thought he knew what was coming. The position was too senior for someone with no experience of working with animals, no qualifications . . .

Nessa was holding Big Ears in her arms. Big Ears wasn't the prettiest of chimp children. It seemed as though he already had the ears that would fit his grown-up head, hence his name. Big Ears had wrapped his legs around Nessa's waist, leaving his hands free to play with the string of bright-coloured beads around her neck. But his attention was distracted by the suddenly serious look on Nessa's face. She bit her lip. She was looking towards Guy with an expression of regret.

Big Ears turned to look at Guy too. Then he stretched out both his arms and, suddenly catching hold of the front of Guy's jumper, pulled himself free from Nessa's hug and wrapped himself around the cuddly stranger instead.

All this time, Guy's gaze was still fixed on Nessa's face, waiting for her to finish her sentence. It was almost as though he hadn't noticed Big Ears's sudden switch of affection. Nessa's regretful expression was replaced by a relieved sort of smile.

'Well, Big Ears has given his vote,' Nessa said.

Guy started the very next week.

Eddy had been a little harder to convince. 'Typical woman,' he said of Nessa's decision to give Guy the job because Big Ears liked him.

Fortunately, Eddy Hamilton soon ate his words. Guy proved himself to be a very capable keeper. He studied part-time to get his City and Guilds qualification, coming top of his class in the exams. And when Eddy retired, he had no hesitation in recommending that Guy take his place.

But Guy never forgot the way Big Ears changed his life with a cuddle. Big Ears was a chimpanzee teenager these days, as awkward as any human equivalent. But when Guy let himself into the main enclosure with a food delivery, Big Ears was always there to greet him with a pant-hoot and sometimes, when he was sure no one else was looking, a plasticine-lipped chimp kiss.

On the other side of the nursery, Mad was finding it difficult to settle. He had grown used to being left alone to sleep on a nest of straw with his brother every night. But now that Guy was around, he wanted to play. Mad climbed halfway up the bars of his cage and rattled them like the King Kong he thought he was, directing his play-grin at his keeper.

'Will you be quiet?' Guy asked the little ape.

Mad rattled harder, causing Bad to look up too, wondering why the fuss.

'All right then.' Guy sighed like a young mother who has promised herself that baby won't sleep in the big bed any more but eventually caves in again through sleep deprivation and an inability to resist that plaintive cry. Guy opened Mad and Bad's cage and stepped inside. Both small apes immediately hurled themselves on to his body like satellites drawn irresistibly towards a docking station. Guy swirled a blanket around on the floor to make a chimpanzee-style sleeping nest for three. From the safety of Guy's big body, Mad and Bad watched the stranger in the cage next door all night. Guy fell asleep.

15

Back in her warm bed in the Witch's cottage, Jennifer lay wide awake. Guy had insisted that he didn't need her to stay overnight in the quarantine unit too. No point both of them being uncomfortable. He promised he would call if anything requiring her attention should arise during the night and Jennifer had duly set the telephone on the table beside her bed, so that she wouldn't sleep through the ringing. But the fact was, that night she didn't think she would get any sleep anyway. Her mind was racing. Ulysses was the first chimp admitted to the sanctuary under Jennifer's supervision and she wanted to make sure that everything went without a hitch. Would Guy really let her know if something went awry? Every time she closed her eyes, a new worst-case scenario would pop into her brain as though a malevolent cinematographer was projecting it on to the inside of her eyelids.

She got up to fetch a glass of water but soon found herself putting on her jeans over her pyjamas. If she couldn't sleep, then she might as well be awake in the quarantine unit with the new chimpanzee.

It was two o'clock in the morning when she turned her little red car into the car park at Prowdes.

The quarantine unit was silent as Jennifer approached. She opened the door as quietly as she could, but not quite quietly enough for Mad and Bad. Mad immediately let out a scream of warning. Bad followed suit. He always followed his brother, just as he had been born seven minutes later.

'What? What?'

Guy struggled upright from his place on the straw. Both chimps clung to his head for safety.

'It's just me,' said Jennifer. 'No need to panic. It's Jennifer.'

'Doctor Niederhauser,' said Guy automatically.

'I'm *definitely* Jennifer at this time of the morning,' she told him. She moved into the puddle of weak yellow light emitted by the night light. 'Have you been sleeping on the floor in there with the twins?' she asked.

'Must have dropped off. I'm sorry.'

'You don't have to be sorry,' said Jennifer. 'It doesn't look very comfortable, that's all.'

'It isn't,' said Guy.

'How's Ulysses?' she asked. 'Anything happened?'

'Not a peep,' said Guy. And indeed Ulysses hadn't moved since Jennifer arrived either. Guy carried Mad and Bad out into the corridor and joined Jennifer at the glass to Ulysses' enclosure. The blanket under which the ape had hidden himself stirred ever so slightly. Guy and Jennifer exhaled simultaneously. In relief.

'He's still alive,' said Jennifer.

'Of course,' said Guy with a confidence he didn't really feel. It had happened before. Seemingly healthy chimps dropped dead within hours of arrival at their new home, perhaps reacting badly to the tranquilliser. 'He's in pretty good shape compared to some of the other chimps we've had through here. You should have seen Mad and Bad's mum. She didn't have a hair on her body when she arrived. She plucked it all out. Her owners raised her in their house like a child until she got too big. Then they stuck her in a kennel in the garden with a rope around her neck. And then she got depressed.'

Jennifer nodded sadly.

'I wonder what this little guy had to go through before he got here,' she said.

Just then, Mad reached out from the safety of Guy's shoulders and gave Jennifer's ponytail a hard tug.

'Ow! Even the animals here hate my guts,' she exclaimed. But she quickly composed herself, blinking back the tears before they could start. Even though she could have passed them off as shock at the pain of Mad's attack rather than sadness. Even though that's what they were . . . 'You can go home now, if you like,' she told Guy. 'I'll take over. You get some proper sleep.'

'That's what you were supposed to be doing.'

'I can't sleep.'

'Stuff on your mind?'

'Too much caffeine,' Jennifer lied. 'Give me the twins. I'll put them back to bed.'

'No. I'm staying,' said Guy firmly. He moved towards the kettle with the twins still attached to his body like a pair of hairy growths. 'I don't want to offend you, but I know Mad and Bad won't settle if you're here and I'm not. And if they don't settle, then the new boy might not feel brave enough to come out from under his blanket. Another coffee?' Guy asked. 'Oh no, I forgot. You don't drink anything with caffeine in, do you?' Guy turned away to spare Jennifer as she blushed at his easy uncovering of her lie. 'Herbal tea?'

'Yes, please,' said Jennifer meekly.

Half an hour later, the twins were settled back in their nest and Jennifer and Guy sat side by side, facing Ulysses, on the deck-chairs that comprised the only human seating in the nursery/quarantine block. Outside, the wind was picking up, whipping through the palm trees that Nessa had planted all over the sanctuary. They grew surprisingly well down in Devon where the Gulf Stream warmed the wind that blew in from the sea.

The night light bathed the nursery in candle-light yellow. Jennifer and Guy had subconsciously positioned their chairs inside the pale circle of illumination as though huddling close to a fire for warmth. It was the kind of light that made you want to tell stories. But Jennifer was determined not to let any of her story out that night, so she kept self-consciously quiet.

Guy felt compelled to break the silence.

'So,' he asked, 'how are you finding Tincastle?'

'Same as it ever was,' said Jennifer. 'I grew up here.'

'I didn't know.'

'I didn't tell you.' She paused. 'You're not from around here originally, are you?'

Guy laughed. 'Does my accent give it away?'

'How did you end up here?'

'I stuck a pin in a map,' he said.

'No. Really?'

'Yes, really.' Guy told her the sausage factory story.

'And you didn't give yourself another go with the pin?' Jennifer asked when he had finished.

'That would have been trying to cheat fate,' Guy replied. 'Especially when I found out about Prowdes. It felt like I'd found my place in the world.'

'That's nice,' said Jennifer.

'It's completely unique.'

'You can say that again,' Jennifer muttered. 'What do you think of this TV show idea?' she asked Guy then. Nessa had told them about it that afternoon as they unloaded Ulysses from his travelling cage.

'Well, we could certainly use the money,' said Guy. 'But I don't know how happy I am about the idea of having cameras in here. You've seen how some of the chimps react to a change in routine.'

Without thinking Jennifer looked at the scar on her index finger, testimony to how badly Mad reacted to a change in his care.

'It's a real Hobson's choice,' Jennifer agreed. 'It will almost certainly be disruptive. But the money makes it pretty hard to say no. Especially since I've managed to bring absolutely no cash to this place for my research so far.'

'Next year,' said Guy.

Jennifer shrugged gratefully at his optimism. She wished she could feel it.

'Who knows if we'll have the opportunity to turn it down anyway,' Guy concluded. 'We're up against Monkey World.' He followed the mention of that other primate sanctuary with the appropriate Prowdes' staff response, which was to pretend to spit on to the floor.

Jennifer forced a smile.

'You haven't got the hang of it yet, have you?' Guy said. 'Monkey World,' he repeated.

'I hate spitting,' Jennifer replied.

'Sorry.'

'I guess I'll never be able to be properly part of the gang,' Jennifer said then. She meant it to sound light but it didn't quite come out that way.

'It takes a long time to win people's trust,' Guy told her. 'We've done things a certain way here for years. People don't like change. They're like the chimps.'

'All the changes I've been trying to implement are supposed to make life easier.' Jennifer was automatically defensive.

They resumed their silent vigil of Ulysses.

'I don't just make this stuff up, you know,' said Jennifer suddenly. 'All the things I've been asking you to do. I'm working to a very careful plan designed to have the chimps living in the wild again within the not too distant future. It's based on the findings of some of the most important researchers in the primatology community. Their findings work.'

Guy nodded. 'I understand.'

'Do you really, Guy? Sometimes I don't think you do. Sometimes, you seem to be more determined to work against me than any of the others. Why did you pretend that it was you who left Hector's cage open instead of Jo-Jo?'

'Because it might have been me,' said Guy simply.

'We both know that's not true.'

Guy shrugged this time.

'It doesn't make my job any easier,' said Jennifer. 'It just gives Jo-Jo the impression that she can carry on as she always has done and someone else will bail her out.'

'She's only nineteen,' said Guy.

'Old enough to know better.'

'Do you think you were? At that age? I mean, everyone who ever lives past fifteen thinks they know it all before they hit twenty, but looking back now, you must be able to see that you made some mistakes yourself. Jo-Jo didn't leave the cage open out of spite or to upset you. It was careless but careless isn't the same as malicious.'

'Sometimes you have to punish carelessness to make people take their responsibilities more seriously,' said Jennifer.

'With written warnings?'

'If that's what it takes.'

Guy sighed. 'This is a chimpanzee sanctuary, not the headquarters of some big corporation. This place limps on because we have always been more like a family than a firm. Everyone helps each other out. Caring for these animals isn't our job, it's our lives. Jo-Jo earns less for a sixty-hour week at Prowdes than she could earn on a paper round. But she is passionate about Hector and the chimps and that is what makes her lucky to have her job and Prowdes lucky to have her here.' Guy looked directly into Jennifer's eyes. 'Jo-Jo just needs your patience and respect. If you treat her like an adult she'll be far more likely to act like one. Most of all she needs your respect.'

Jennifer felt her forehead crease into a frown. She didn't know how to reply.

'I'm sorry.' Guy dropped his gaze. 'What do I know? You're the one with all the qualifications.'

'I am,' said Jennifer simply.

'But we're all working towards the same end. I'm not just here because I couldn't do anything else. Neither are Jo-Jo and Snowy and Ernie and Jack and David. I would give my life to see these chimps returned safely to the wild.' Guy underlined his speech by holding his fist to his heart. 'I know that they would too.'

Silence again.

'Another cup of tea?' said Guy eventually.

'Yes,' said Jennifer. 'That would be lovely.'

Thank God for tea, diluter of social awkwardness, they both thought, as Guy got up to boil the kettle.

16

When Snowy arrived for the early shift in the chimp nursery next morning, he was astonished to find Guy and Jennifer both asleep in deckchairs in front of the quarantine pen. Guy's head was slumped on his chest. Jennifer had her head back and her mouth wide open. She was snoring like a Harry Porker. Together in their deckchairs, they looked like a couple who had been married for forty years, sitting on the seafront at Brighton, dozing off a big lunch of fish and chips.

Snowy didn't know what to do. If Guy had been asleep alone, Snowy would have just grabbed him by the shoulder and shaken him awake. But he didn't think Dr Niederhauser would appreciate the same rough treatment, so instead he tried a subtle cough. Then a less subtle cough. And a thoroughly unsubtle one. When that didn't work, he opened the door to Mad and Bad's cage and let them out into the corridor while he made their breakfast. Mad and Bad had no qualms about waking their sleeping keepers with high-pitched shrieks of excitement and, in Mad's case, by vaulting on to Jennifer's lap and pulling her hair.

'Morning,' said Snowy.

'What?' said Guy. 'Where am I?'

'Ugh,' said Jennifer, wiping the dribble from her chin and wishing she hadn't come out in her pyjama top after all. She knew at once that she had probably been snoring. 'Have I been asleep?'

'Not for very long, I'm sure,' said Snowy. 'Not seeing as how you were meant to be keeping an eye on the new chimp and all,' he added. Jennifer could tell he was enjoying this rare chance to poke fun at her. 'How is Eric anyway?'

'It's Ulysses,' said Jennifer and Guy simultaneously.

'Jinx,' they both replied. Again at once.

Snowy raised his eyebrows at Guy.

Guy ignored the gesture and immediately set to work, carrying the empty tea mugs to the sink and swilling them out.

'Ulysses is fine,' said Jennifer. 'He's obviously decided that he wants a bit of peace and quiet. Hardly surprising, really.'

Snowy joined Jennifer in front of Ulysses' cage and they both peered at the figure beneath the blankets.

'Raaaarrrk!' said Mad. He was hanging from Snowy's neck.

The blanket moved as Ulysses pulled it a little more tightly around him.

'There,' said Jennifer. 'Still alive.'

'Hasn't eaten anything,' Snowy observed.

'We'll start worrying about that when he hasn't eaten for a couple of days,' said Jennifer brusquely. She was back into boss mode. 'I don't think I'd feel like eating much after a week at sea. Would you?'

'Perhaps he'd like a Mars Bar,' said Jo-Jo provocatively. She had come into the nursery block in search of a cuppa. Hector was still on a Mars Bar ban.

Jennifer turned towards her.

'Been having a pyjama party?' Jo-Jo commented.

'Let me know when Harrison arrives,' said Jennifer, ignoring Jo-Jo's comment. 'I'll be in my office.' She left at a trot.

Jo-Jo waited until the door had slammed shut behind Jennifer before she let out an exclamation of amusement. 'What on earth was she wearing? That was a pyjama top, right? She was wearing her pyjamas. Tell me I didn't imagine it.'

'I found them both asleep in the deckchairs,' said Snowy, jerking his thumb towards Guy.

'Guy!' Jo-Jo shrieked. 'What's that about? What has been going on?'

'We were just keeping an eye on Ulysses,' Guy insisted.

'It all looked very cosy,' Snowy teased.

'There was nothing cosy about it.'

'Their chairs were side by side. Her head was on his shoulder,' Snowy continued with actions.

'We were just watching the chimps. She dropped off She's been working really hard. And then, well, I must have dropped off too.

Her head was *not* on my shoulder,' Guy said vehemently, before he added, 'Was it?'

Snowy and Jo-Jo howled with laughter at that.

'There's nothing funny about it . . .'

But Snowy and Jo-Jo thought it was hilarious. Snowy mimed a passionate kiss on the back of his hand.

'Jesus, you two,' Guy sighed. 'Will you just grow up? She's my boss. She's your boss! Give me a shout on the walkie-talkie when Harrison arrives. I'm going out to get some air.'

'Guy and Jennifer, sitting in a tree . . .' Jo-Jo sang. Snowy chimed in.

'K-I-S-S-I-N-G.'

'Immature!' Guy shouted back over his shoulder.

His colleagues' laughter followed Guy all the way to the main chimp enclosure.

Jennifer made sure her eyes were glued firmly to the papers on her desk as he passed her office window on his way.

As soon as he had finished checking on the giraffe baby he had rushed off to deliver halfway through Ulysses' rescue, Harrison drove straight to Prowdes to give the new chimp another check-up. The good news was that Ulysses' blood tests had revealed nothing sinister. Nothing that would have forced Harrison to euthanise the little ape. Nessa was delighted. The old lady who made the chimpanzee-shaped coasters on sale in the gift shop was immediately set to work making a new name plate for the quarantine cage with Ulysses' name painted upon it.

And there was other good news that morning, too. Faith O'Connell, the television producer who had called Nessa with the suggestion of a show, suddenly found herself with spare time to visit the sanctuary at once rather than waiting for the following week. Everyone was set to work making the place look tidy. At least as tidy as it was possible for a place where two tonnes of animal dung were produced every day to be.

Jo-Jo and Snowy were amazed and amused to see Jennifer mucking in.

'What is wrong with her?' Snowy mused out loud.

'Guy must have done something to put a smile on her face,' Jo-

Jo decided. 'Did she really have her head on his shoulder when you found them asleep together?'

The moment had already taken on such mythological proportions that Snowy was almost convinced of it by now.

'I'm not sure,' he said. 'I think I saw her move her head from his shoulder as I came in.'

'Do you think she fancies him?' Jo-Jo asked

'Jo-Jo!' Before Snowy could give his opinion, Jennifer interrupted them. 'I wonder if you could have another quick go over Hector's cage. He seems to have an upset stomach.'

'Shit,' said Jo-Jo.

'Literally,' Jennifer responded.

Jennifer handed Jo-Jo a mop.

None of the staff at Prowdes had ever met a television producer before. They'd met the odd journalist from the local paper – the *Tincastle Herald* often ran stories on the animals in a quiet news week. But they had never met a real producer from the capital city with the power to put them on television screens in every home in the land. As such, they were rather disappointed when Faith O'Connell arrived in a taxi from the train station, with her assistant, Helen, in tow. She looked so, well, so ordinary in her jeans and jumper with her short brown hair brushed back from her face. She wasn't even wearing sunglasses on her head.

But she looked friendly. And she was definitely a professional. Faith had already prepared a presentation on her lap-top to help Nessa and her team decide whether or not they wanted their fifteen minutes of fame right now. Bullet points outlined the advantages of letting the cameras in. Every question Nessa had, Faith answered with confidence and aplomb.

'So, that's it then,' said Nessa, when she'd finished. 'We'd be happy to have you here.'

Faith closed the lid on her lap-top and smiled. 'Well, it isn't quite that easy. As I explained on the phone, I've been looking at a couple of other zoos with primate projects as well. Howletts are doing some very interesting work with gorillas and Monkey World – well, you know how good Monkey World is . . .' The assembled Prowdes members fought the urge to mime some spitting. 'Now that we've established that you would like to be involved in principle, we still have to ascertain whether or not there's a real story here. The ideal thing would be to be able to focus on one animal in particular and follow him throughout the whole process from rescue to release.'

'Oh, there's a real story,' Jo-Jo blurted. 'We had a new chimp arrive yesterday morning. You could focus the series around him.'

'A new chimp?' Faith cocked her head in a gesture of interest.

'Rescued from a drug-runner's boat by Customs and Excise,' Jo-Jo elaborated.

'Jo-Jo,' said Nessa, 'I don't know if we're allowed to talk about that.'

'Can I see him?' Faith asked. 'I won't tell anybody if you don't.'

Nessa, Guy and the others looked to Jennifer. Nessa had promised that Jennifer would have the final word on which animals could be featured.

'Of course you can see Ulysses,' said Jennifer.

There was a collective sigh of relief.

Nessa gave Faith and Helen the tour of the entire sanctuary, including the quarantine enclosure. Unfortunately, there wasn't much to see there. Following Harrison's investigative prodding that morning, Ulysses had retreated back beneath the blanket. But Mad and Bad were only too happy to make up for Ulysses' reticence. Nessa gasped when Mad pulled Helen's hair. Fortunately, she decided to believe it was a compliment when Snowy quickly told her that Mad only pulled the hair of people he took a fancy to.

'He pulls Dr Niederhauser's hair all the time,' Snowy elaborated.

Jennifer hid her mangled finger in her pocket in a subconscious gesture designed to support the lie.

From the nursery to the orang-utan enclosure, where Hector was contemplatively chewing on an old piece of rubber tyre, perhaps remembering his all-too-brief taste of freedom.

'Do something funny, Hec,' Jo-Jo urged him.

Hector scratched his anus and sniffed his finger.

The television girls winced.

'He's really very amusing sometimes,' Jo-Jo insisted. 'I've seen him run right across the enclosure doing somersaults all the way like an Olympic gymnast.'

'We're not expecting the animals we film to do tricks,' Faith assured her.

'That's a good job,' Snowy hissed in Jo-Jo's ear as Faith and Helen were moved along to the main chimp enclosure. 'Because I've never heard such bollocks in my life. Hector doing somersaults. My arse.'

As they neared the main chimpanzee enclosure, the little tour group were stopped in their tracks by an enormous 'wah-bark' of aggression.

'Oh my God.' Helen clutched on to her boss's arm. 'What on earth was that?'

'I expect it was one of the big males,' said Nessa authoritatively. 'That kind of shout usually signals that someone isn't too happy about something. Achilles is our alpha male. He makes a sound like that if he feels as though one of the other chimps is threatening his position.'

'Pretty scary sound,' said Faith.

'Chimps can be pretty scary animals.'

But it wasn't one of the chimps at all.

As they turned the corner, Nessa put her hand up to her eyes in disbelief as the Major called through the wire to the chimps. This time they saw him make the unearthly sound.

'Who is *that*?' asked Helen.

'Major,' called Nessa, 'are you tormenting my chimpanzees?'

'Nessa!' The Major waved his bamboo stick, last remnant of his days in Africa. 'Just having a bit of fun with my friend Achilles here. Who are these lovely young ladies?' He waited to be introduced to Faith and Helen. 'I come and see the chimps every day,' he said. 'Used to be allowed in with them until the regime around here changed,' he added in a stage whisper. 'That doctor woman thinks it's too dangerous for someone who isn't properly trained. But what I don't know about chimpanzees . . . I lived with chimpanzees in the jungle for half a bloody year,' he continued.

'You did?' asked Faith.

Nessa could only roll her eyes and make a cutting gesture with her finger across her throat.

'Saved my life, a chimpanzee. I was fighting with my regiment in the Congo, y'see—'

'Oh look!' Nessa tried to change the subject. 'There's Virginia. Prowdes' first ever chimp. Rescued from a Spanish beach photographer twenty years ago.'

Faith and Helen dutifully put their noses to the wire and looked at Prowdes' alpha female as she delicately picked through the fur on Achilles' back in search of juicy ticks. The tour continued. Guy helpfully called the Major across to look at Ulysses and he didn't get a chance to finish his story. Faith hadn't forgotten it, though.

'Now he's an extraordinary man,' she said. 'Do you think he's telling the truth? About his time with the chimpanzees?'

'It's not impossible,' Nessa conceded. 'But slightly unlikely.'

'Could add a bit of humour to a show being shot here,' Helen commented. Faith agreed.

Helen made a quick note on her clipboard.

'Nessa, I have to be honest with you,' Faith said then. 'The other ape projects we've been discussing this programme with have very strong stories too. But I also have to say that Prowdes has been my favourite project so far. There's a family feel about this place. The staff are just as interesting as the animals,' she added with a glance back over her shoulder towards the Major. 'And when you're filming a programme like this, the people involved are just as important as the animals in making the show a success.'

'We certainly need the money,' Nessa said quietly.

'I'm going to do my best to get it for you. I'm going to put Prowdes forward as my number-one choice.'

'When will we know?'

'I've got a big meeting with my bosses this afternoon to choose the project we're going to follow and then it's just a matter of getting the right presenter on board. After that, we'll have contracts out to everybody as fast as the lawyer's secretary can type them. We're aiming to air this show before Christmas. That

97

doesn't give us much time. We would need to start filming by the end of the month. Six weeks here, say, then a couple of months editing the footage together.'

'Can I ask who you think is going to be the presenter?'

Faith smiled a confidential smile. She had explained that the show would have to have a professional presenter, to make it more coherent. 'It's supposed to be top secret. But we're talking to . . .' She reeled off the names of a few people that Nessa hadn't heard of. She hadn't actually watched any TV since the previous Christmas, when she swapped her old black-and-white set for a bale of straw. Still, Nessa nodded knowledgeably, not wanting to appear entirely ignorant of current affairs in the media world.

'We're aiming for something a little bit different,' Faith continued. 'We want a more heavyweight presenter than usual. Not just someone who loves animals but someone who truly understands them. In my ideal world' – Faith paused for effect – 'I would like to get . . .' Faith whispered a name into Nessa's ear.

Nessa beamed. Now that was a name she had heard of. She thought she had seen that chap present a paper on bonobos at the last Ape Conservation Society meeting she had attended. She remembered how impressed she had been by the young man. He was clearly dedicated to his subject. His paper had been thoughtful and thought-provoking. And, bloody hell, he was as handsome as a matinee idol to boot.

'It's a long shot,' Faith sighed. 'So I'd be grateful if you kept it quiet. Please don't tell any of your staff. If it leaked out to the press that he was going to present the show and then it turned out that he wasn't able to do it after all, it could be pretty embarrassing for us.'

'I understand,' said Nessa. 'My lips are sealed.'

'Thank you for meeting us at such short notice,' said Faith as she shook Nessa's hand. 'You're doing some wonderful work.'

It was wonderful work. But it was often hard work, too. While Nessa concluded her chat with Faith O'Connell and waved her and Helen off again in their taxi, Guy, Snowy, Jo-Jo and Jennifer lined up along Ulysses' cage and regarded the chimpanzee inside with something approaching despair.

The fruit which Guy had left in the cage that morning was still uneaten. They had hoped that the chimpanzee would try something while there were no humans around to observe him and while Mad and Bad were playing in their outdoor enclosure and not barking at him from their side of the glass divide. But Ulysses had not touched so much as a grape. And if Ulysses hadn't eaten any of the bananas in particular, then he hadn't got any of the antibiotics and vitamin tablets that Jennifer had hidden inside them. That morning, Harrison had given Ulysses a jab, but he didn't want to have to inject him every day. Hiding tablets inside soft fruit such as grapes and bananas was usually the best way to dose up an ape.

'Any more ideas?' Jennifer asked.

'Why are you asking us?' said Jo-Jo. 'You're the expert.'

'And I'm expert enough to know when I'm beaten,' Jennifer replied.

'It isn't urgent,' said Guy. 'Not yet. He's only been here for twenty-four hours. They're often like this when they first arrive. Too confused and worried to eat. It's just a matter of building up trust.'

At the sound of Guy's voice, Ulysses unwound his blanket just a little, like a coy Indian girl peeping out from behind the folds of her sari veil.

'You'll learn to trust me, won't you?' Guy whispered.

'Well, I've got to go and feed Hector,' said Jo-Jo. 'He's one ape I don't have to worry about starving.'

'You're sticking to the diet sheet I gave you?' asked Jennifer.

'Yessir,' Jo-Jo saluted. Hector's regime had become strictly calorie-controlled. 'I hope Prowdes' insurance will cover a false arm when Hector rips one of mine off because I haven't got a Mars Bar to placate him with.'

Jo-Jo flounced out.

'I can't say anything right to her,' Jennifer sighed.

Snowy shrugged. Guy shot him a look.

'PMS,' he said to excuse Jo-Jo's behaviour. 'I meant that as a joke, of course,' he added, just in case Jennifer didn't find that funny. 'Some of us are going to the Wily Fox later tonight. Why don't you come? Jo-Jo will be there.'

Jennifer shook her head. 'I need to catch up on some sleep,' she said. 'I'll see you both tomorrow.'

'What do you want to go inviting her to the pub for?' Snowy asked when Jennifer had gone back to her office.

'For heaven's sake, Snowy. Why the hell shouldn't she come along?'

'Because she's the boss. And a cow.'

'She isn't that bad,' said Guy. 'She's just got a brusque manner. When you get to know her—'

'Like you did.'

'I just think it's time you and Jo-Jo tried to make her feel more welcome.'

'Make who feel more welcome?' Jo-Jo asked. She had left Hector's vitamin supplements on the kitchen shelf and popped back to fetch them.

'He thinks we should invite the Witch to come to the pub with us.'

'What? His new girlfriend?' Jo-Jo sneered.

Guy looked from Jo-Jo to Snowy sadly. 'The only way to help this place survive is for all of us to work as a team,' he told them. 'I don't want to be part of the bitching any more. When you're ready to invite Jennifer to the pub, then I'll see you there as well. Until then, you can count me out.' Then Guy walked out of the nursery too, leaving Snowy and Jo-Jo open-mouthed with shock.

17

That night, Nessa joined the Major for dinner at the trattoria. They ate the usual. Nessa had the daily risotto and a salad. The Major had spaghetti carbonara and Julia, the proprietor's wife, made sure that he had extra ham in his portion.

'It's a wonder you haven't keeled over and died of a heart attack,' said Nessa, watching the Major pile Parmesan cheese on top of his already fat-laden supper.

'Don't you start with that healthy eating nonsense again,' he told her. 'A man's got to keep his strength up. I'll outlive the lot of you,' he added, when Guido tried to wrestle the cheese bowl from his grasp so that the restaurant's only other customers that night – a couple who were clearly on their first date (you could tell by how polite they were being to each other) – might have some too.

'Bloody exciting stuff this television programme,' the Major said when he had finally had his fill of fat and carbohydrates. 'Be damn good for the sanctuary.'

'Perhaps,' said Nessa. 'I'm still not totally convinced. If they do choose us, then our money problems will be solved for a while. But what if they make us look bad?'

'How could they possibly make Prowdes look bad?' asked the Major. 'You're running the best damn sanctuary in the land and don't you forget it.'

Nessa smiled gratefully. But lately something hadn't felt quite right. The atmosphere at Prowdes wasn't so jolly as it had been in the past and Nessa thought it might have something to do with the new girl.

Jennifer had been the most outstanding candidate of the people who applied for her job. There was no doubt about that. But she just didn't seem to be fitting in. Her academic skills and her knowledge of chimpanzees simply weren't matched by her ability to deal with people. She was too harsh. Too self-contained. Jo-Jo was an idiot girl sometimes, for sure, but, like a mother, Nessa knew that the best way to treat the essentially good-natured teen was by offering a carrot, not waving a stick.

What Prowdes needed was some kind of team-building experience that would break down the barriers Jennifer seemed to have erected around herself. In the old days, Nessa would have had some kind of party. But lately she hadn't felt much like partying. Or been able to afford it.

Nessa subconsciously tensed her jaw as she thought about the television programme again. She was unable to eat, stomach churning with a mixture of excitement and pre-emptive disappointment as she considered the far more likely possibility that the production company would be wowed by the less ramshackle facilities at one of Prowdes' sanctuary rivals.

Without an injection of cash (and it seemed increasingly unlikely that either of Jennifer's two outstanding grant proposals would turn up trumps – chimpanzees just weren't that year's academic fashion), Nessa and her accountant had worked out that at current rates of visitor attendance, the sanctuary could limp on for another five months. After that, the future looked bleak indeed. Nessa had wept when Mr Nelson put forward the alternatives. Cutting staff numbers to the bare minimum. Selling the house to a property developer and moving Prowdes to a smaller plot of land. Sending some of the animals to other zoos. Nessa shuddered at the thought of that. She would not let one of her animals be placed in the care of people she didn't know. Not one ragged old donkey or cantankerous goat from the children's zoo she had created in the former stables. Certainly not any of her chimpanzees. Not unless they were on their way to Africa.

How was it possible that it had come to this? It just didn't seem fair that Nessa's passion and dedication over all those years could really come to nothing in the end. A bunch of homeless, hopeless animals, suddenly made homeless all over again.

Tears pricked at the back of her eyes.

Please, Nessa whispered to a God she didn't really believe in, let them choose us.

'You look worried,' the Major observed.

'I am worried,' Nessa admitted.

The sound of a mobile phone interrupted her reverie.

'Bloody young people,' the Major grumbled, staring straight at the courting couple. 'This is a restaurant. We're supposed to be relaxing and enjoying our food in a civilised atmosphere. Why don't they turn those damn things off when they come in?'

Nessa nodded absently. And then she realised that the courting couple were staring back across at the table she shared with the Major with equal annoyance. It was a couple of moments before she realised that the telephone was ringing out from *her* handbag.

She snatched up her bag, cheeks ablaze.

'Sorry! Sorry!' she apologised to everyone in the restaurant, the couple, the Major, the staff. 'I wouldn't normally have my phone on. But I had better get this. You know. What if it's about Ulysses?' she added to the Major. Nessa headed for the car park.

'An urgent call,' the Major explained to the courting couple. 'She does some very valuable conservation work, you know. This could be *very* important.'

And it was. Nessa didn't recognise the number that appeared on the display screen of her phone.

'Nessa!' said Faith O'Connell brightly. 'I'm so glad I caught you. Not in the middle of dinner, I hope.'

'Of course not,' Nessa lied.

'I thought you would want to know right away. We've just finished our meeting . . .'

The line crackled for a second, then went dead.

'No,' Nessa shook her phone as though that might improve the signal. Right there and then, she vowed never to sign another petition against erecting mobile-phone masts in their area of outstanding natural beauty.

'What's going on?' The Major and Guido watched from the restaurant window. 'She's lost the signal,' suggested Guido.

They watched Nessa jump as the phone rang right in her ear.

'Nessa,' said Faith O'Connell breathlessly. 'Sorry about that. Just went through a tunnel. Now, how far did I get before you lost me?'

'You said you'd had your meeting,' said Nessa.

'Yes!' said Faith. 'It went on for ever . . .'

And so is this moment, thought Nessa.

'You wouldn't believe how long it takes to get a decision out of some people. For every extra person who has a say, you can double the time it will take to come to a conclusion . . .'

Crackle, went the phone again.

'What did they decide?' asked Nessa desperately.

'We'd like to film at Prowdes, of course. If you'll have us!' Crackle.

'Did you say what I thought you just said?'

Another loud crackle.

'We'd like to film at Prowdes.'

'You want to film here?'

'We're all very, very pleased,' said Faith quickly, as though she was trying to get everything out before her phone cut out again. 'You were always my number-one choice!'

Click. She was gone.

'Thank you,' said Nessa quietly. 'Thank you.'

Nessa turned off her phone and stood for a minute, as though trying to take it all in. She closed her eyes and felt the cool sea-breeze on her face. To the Major and Guido, watching from inside, it was impossible to tell what had been said.

In the restaurant car park, Nessa punched the air.

'Thank God,' said Guido, as they watched Nessa skip around from one foot to another like an excited child. 'It is the TV people. I'm sure of it. Have we got any cold champagne?' he asked one of the waiters.

'I'm on the case,' the waiter replied.

Guido and the Major scrambled back to their places so that Nessa wouldn't know they had been spying.

'We've got the show,' Nessa flung open the door and shouted across the room.

A waiter emerged with champagne.

The Major jumped up from his chair and set aside all formality to give Nessa a big, bear-sized hug. Guido popped the cork out of the bottle and managed to get a direct hit on a lampshade. He poured glasses of fizz for the celebrants, the staff and the courting couple. Nessa and the Major set off around the restaurant in a polka. The courting boy chanced placing a kiss on his blushing date's cheek while they were caught up in such excitement. Guido was already trying to work out how a small Italian restaurant might be able to appear in a series about chimps.

'We're saved,' Nessa laughed. Then she burst into happy tears.

18

What better excuse for a party! Nessa gathered all her staff for a meeting first thing the following morning and told them the good news and, furthermore, that when the sanctuary closed to the public that evening, attendance at a celebratory party would be mandatory.

At five o'clock in the afternoon, Guy and Snowy carried trestle tables out of the sanctuary's café on to the front lawn of the main house. The sun, thank goodness, was, shining. Nessa covered the tables with the last remaining tablecloths from what had once been a magnificent collection of linen, kept pristine by her extremely house-proud mother. Guido and his wife had kindly agreed to do the catering. Nessa was relieved. Otherwise it might have been peanut butter sandwiches for twenty.

Guest of honour, the Major, arrived at six o'clock on the dot, wearing a pale cream linen suit set off with a bright red tie. Snowy had dressed Mad and Bad in their Sunday-best football strip and they joined the human beings – chimp-keepers, donkey-handlers, gift-shop workers, the lot – at the table when all the members of the public visiting the sanctuary that day had gone home.

Just like human children, Mad and Bad started the party on their very best behaviour. Mad even offered his ever-so-slightly smaller brother a bit of one of his bananas. The humans at the table had a variety of Italian antipasti to eat. And Guido's special cocktails to drink.

'Non-alcoholic?' asked Jennifer.

'Of course,' Guido shrugged.

'Shame,' said Jo-Jo. 'That's hardly in the party spirit.'

'Never a good idea to mix chimpanzees and vodka,' Nessa reminded her. Nessa had never forgotten an afternoon almost twenty years earlier when she was sitting in the garden with young

Virginia and had dozed off, leaving the chimp to help herself from a pitcher of Pimms. The clean-up operation after Virginia's drunken rampage took days.

But it was still warm and everybody was so thirsty that the punch disappeared by the pint, alcoholic or not. When the first round of pitchers had been drained, Jo-Jo volunteered to take them into the keepers' kitchen and make another batch. Guido shouted the recipe and left her to it.

'Thoughtful girl,' said the Major, as Jo-Jo wandered off to prepare more drinks.

'Yes,' said Nessa. 'She's doing very well here. I'm extremely proud of her.'

Jo-Jo was Nessa's protégée. She was young. Only just turned nineteen. She'd left school with no qualifications, giving a lie to the *Daily Mail*'s annual complaint that exams were almost impossible to fail these days. But Nessa knew that it wasn't that Jo-Jo was unintelligent. She just needed to be kept focused. Her love for the animals was very real and passionate. Hector had thrived under her care (it was hard to believe it, but the shabby old ape had once looked even more threadbare). And Jo-Jo reminded Nessa just a little bit of the girl she had once been herself. Headstrong, adventurous, sometimes slightly silly. But ultimately good-hearted.

Unfortunately, Jo-Jo was about to let her slightly silly part come to the fore.

Though Jennifer insisted, when pressed by Guy and Nessa, that the incident had been forgotten, Jo-Jo was still smarting from the way Jennifer had launched into her after Hector's daring escape. It was great to know that Guy, Snowy and even Ernie cared enough about her to take her punishment and save her from getting the sack, but that thought hadn't lessened the sting of Jo-Jo's embarrassment. For the past forty-eight hours, Jo-Jo had been imagining increasingly inventive ways to get her own back on her new boss. But how to do it? She'd already done the old orang-utan shit in the wellies trick. Besides, Jo-Jo wanted Dr Up-Her-Own-Arse Niederhauser to be *embarrassed*, not just annoyed. She acted like she had never made a mistake in her life. She was always so horribly in control.

At the back of the refrigerator in the chimp-keepers' kitchen were two big bottles of vodka. They had been prizes at a raffle held at the sanctuary's annual summer fair the previous year. The holder of green ticket 356 hadn't bothered to claim them on the day. And so they were placed in the keepers' kitchen for safe keeping. Almost a year later, it was clear that Mr Green Ticket was never going to show up but the staff at Prowdes were all too polite to sneak the bottles home.

Now, however, Jo-Jo thought she had found the perfect use for them. She started to concoct the punch according to Guido's recipe. Orange juice, apple juice, cranberry juice. All had been stored in the fridge to keep them nice and cool while the party was in progress outside. Jo-Jo tasted the mixture as she went. Then she tasted it with about an egg-cup full of vodka from one of the raffle prize bottles. The taint of alcohol didn't register at all. Another egg-cup full. Jo-Jo still couldn't taste it. And another. Jo-Jo continued to doctor one of the pitchers of punch until she had used almost a whole bottle of vodka. At this point she had a mild panic. Was the alcohol really undetectable or was it just that she had become desensitised?

Jo-Jo chopped up an orange, an apple and a cucumber and added slices to each jug as a garnish that she hoped would distract from any taint. As she chopped she came up with a plan. If anyone complained about the taste of the punch from the doctored pitcher, she would suggest that they could perhaps taste the washing-up liquid she had used when she rinsed the jugs out. Yes. That was a good one. Jo-Jo prepared to rejoin the party and wait for the fun to really begin.

Teetotal Jennifer's glass was the first Jo-Jo offered to replenish.

19

At seven o'clock, the tea party was still going strong. The atmosphere was very festive as everyone at the sanctuary looked forward to their first fifteen minutes of fame.

'They will be featuring the piglets, won't they?' asked Sheryl, who cared for Hermione and Harry Porker. 'At least in passing.'

Nessa wondered whether the production company would bring along a hair and make-up team to make her ready for the cameras every morning. Guido's wife, Julia, teased Guy that he would become a big star and have his face plastered over the bedroom walls of teenage girls all over the country.

'What about me?' Snowy asked.

'You'll be the thinking girl's crumpet,' said Nessa comfortingly.

'Yeah. Because it takes a really good imagination to imagine what's fanciable about you, Snowy!' chipped in Jo-Jo. The rest of the gang roared with laughter, sending Mad and Bad into chimpy hysterics as well.

'How do you feel about being recognised in the supermarket, Dr Niederhauser?' the Major asked Jennifer, when the hysterics subsided for a moment as the human guests and chimpanzees alike concentrated instead on the cake Julia had just produced from the back of her mobile catering company van.

Jennifer shrugged. 'I'm not quite sure. Do you think we will be?'

'Of course we will. This is going to be huge!' said Jo-Jo, appearing at Jennifer's shoulder with a jug in each hand. 'More punch?'

'I don't see why not.' Jennifer held out her glass for a third refill. She was feeling surprisingly thirsty. Perhaps the antipasti were too salty for her.

'A toast to us all,' Nessa announced then. 'To the survival of

Prowdes and to my wonderful, wonderful staff who have helped the sanctuary get this far without having to close down. I really couldn't have done it without you. I adore you all. Each and every single one of you. I love you!' Nessa blew actorly kisses to each of the people sitting at the table that evening. The Major raised a cheer. Mad and Bad shrieked excitedly.

'Hip! Hip!'

'Hooray!' the party-goers shouted.

Jennifer put her hand to her ear to block out the sound of Mad hooting directly into it.

Maybe it was just the heat. It had been a surprisingly hot day for June. Or maybe she was coming down with something. Jennifer surreptitiously put her hand up to her cheek to feel her temperature. She felt as though she was starting to burn up. Her nose was itching. And from time to time, even her eyesight was beginning to seem blurred.

'Excuse me,' she said as she got up from the table. Not that anyone really noticed her leaving. Tired of behaving themselves properly, Mad and Bad were rapidly reducing the gathering to a real chimps' tea party. The first banana-shaped missile of the food fight had been thrown. Now Bad was standing in the middle of the celebratory cake (Julia had baked a cake in the shape of a television screen and iced a chimpanzee face on to it), pulling off pieces of icing, alternately stuffing them into his mouth and lobbing them at his brother, who screamed from a place of safety on Snowy's lap. The Major was delighted, even when a piece of icing caught him right between the eyes.

Jennifer walked slowly and quietly across the gardens to the prefabricated hut that was her office. Every step seemed to take her in a slightly different direction. At one point, she bumped against one of the tall pine trees that lined the path. She ricocheted off that tree and into another one on the other side of the footway, grazing the hand that she put out to steady herself on the rough bark of the tree trunk.

'Ow.' Jennifer looked at her palm but was surprised to discover that it didn't really hurt. A few spots of blood appeared on her pale skin like tiny ruby beads. She just licked them away and continued her stagger. Though no matter how many steps she took, the office didn't seem to be getting much closer.

When eventually she made it, Jennifer let herself straight into the bathroom and ran cold water over both her hands in a pretty hopeless attempt to cool down. Then she bolted the door and sat down on the loo without lifting the seat. She leaned her head against the wall to stop the room from moving around her. It really was most peculiar. If she didn't know better, Jennifer might have said she was drunk.

Back at the long table, Jo-Jo was grinning inanely. She'd divided most of the spiked punch between her boss and herself. A seasoned regular at the Wily Fox, Jo-Jo could hold a pint or four no problem, but when Bad got her between the eyes with a blini loaded with smoked salmon and cream cheese, she fell off her chair in a giggling heap and found that she was unable to get back up again.

'Are you OK?' Nessa asked Jo-Jo meaningfully as she helped her back on to her seat.

'I'm just fabulous,' said Jo-Jo.

'If I didn't know that you haven't been drinking,' Nessa continued, 'I might think you were drunk.'

'Why on earth would you drink I was thunk?' Jo-Jo asked.

'Jo-Jo,' said Nessa sternly, 'what did you put in that punch?'

'Nothing,' Jo-Jo insisted.

Unable to believe her youngest employee, Nessa took a sniff at what remained in the bottom of the jug. She certainly couldn't smell anything.

'Well, except a little bit of vodka perhaps,' Jo-Jo admitted suddenly. 'Just one bottle though.'

'A bottle!' Nessa exclaimed. Her exclamation immediately drew everyone's attention away from the chimpanzee antics.

'That's hardly anything!'

'It's a huge amount of alcohol for someone who never touches a drop. No wonder Dr Niederhauser fell over on her way back to the office. You got her drunk. You stupid girl!' Nessa shook Jo-Jo by the arm. 'You stupid, stupid girl. People here have got to drive home.'

'I only gave it to her and me,' said Jo-Jo in a feeble defence.

'I would have had some,' Snowy interrupted.

'Snowy,' said Nessa in a warning tones, 'you shouldn't encourage her. Jo-Jo, you're going to have some apologising to do. You'd better hope Dr Niederhauser isn't being sick over there in her office.'

'I just thought it would make things more lively,' said Jo-Jo, who was sobering up fast now that she realised Nessa wasn't getting the joke. 'Make it more of a party, you know.'

'I'll check on Jennifer,' said Guy.

'Good idea. I'd better go with you,' said Nessa. 'God knows what kind of state she might be in.'

They expected the worst when they found Jennifer's office empty but the door to the adjoining bathroom locked. Knocking wouldn't rouse her.

'She might have passed out,' said Nessa worriedly.

She made Guy lift her up on to the sill outside the little bathroom window so that she could get a look at the carnage inside. Jennifer was in there all right. She was sitting on the toilet seat, lid down and overalls safely buttoned up, thank goodness, with her head resting on the small handbasin.

'Is she breathing?' Guy asked.

'I don't know,' said Nessa. 'I can't see. She's got her face down away from me.'

But then, conveniently, Jennifer shifted in her sleep and let out an enormous snorting snore as her head lolled backwards.

'She's breathing,' Nessa confirmed. 'Oh, goodness, Guy. What are we going to do? How can we get her out?'

'We could just leave her to sleep it off?' Guy suggested.

'But what if she's sick in her sleep?' Nessa asked, immediately thinking the worst. 'She might choke. We've got to get her out of there. Could we pick the lock?'

They couldn't. Because there was no keyhole. The bathroom door was fastened with a simple bolt on the inside and there was no way to slide the bolt open from outside the door. They couldn't break the door in either, since Jennifer was leaning heavily against it now that she had moved her head from the basin. If they couldn't persuade her to move out of the way first, then breaking the door down might cause her an injury.

'Hand me a stick,' said Nessa, who was perched precariously on the windowsill again. Guy duly found her a spindly branch from one of the nearby trees. Nessa inserted it carefully through the narrow open portion of the window and gave Jennifer a poke in the shoulder. Jennifer stirred, groaned in annoyance even, but she still didn't wake up.

'Oh, why did she have to lock herself in there?' said Nessa agitatedly. 'Jennifer,' she called. 'Jennifer,' she said, half shouting. She chanced another poke with the stick. It had an effect. But not the one they wanted. As though she was unconsciously trying to move out of the way of the thing that was interrupting her drunken dreams, Jennifer slid off the toilet seat to sit on the floor between toilet and basin, jamming herself more firmly against the door as she did so and thus making the option of breaking the door down without hurting her even more remote.

'We should just wait until she wakes up,' Guy suggested again.

'No,' said Nessa. 'Absolutely not. I can't leave her there like that. I wouldn't leave any of you there like that. We've got to get her out. I could climb through the window.'

Guy didn't have to say anything. Even as she thought it, Nessa glanced down at her own girth and realised how stupid that particular suggestion had been. She might have been able to do it once, but middle age had definitely caught up with her lately. Mostly around the middle.

'Come down from there before you fall down.' Guy helped his boss down from the windowsill.

'Could you get through that window?' Nessa asked him.

'Perhaps when I was five or six,' Guy replied. These days he might have been slim enough around the waist but his shoulders were definitely too broad.

By now, all the other guests at the party had drifted across the lawn to find out what was going on.

'This is all your fault,' Nessa reminded Jo-Jo. Jo-Jo was already crying.

'Leave her to sleep it off,' almost everyone suggested. Except Guido, who had seen plenty of drunks in his time. He took a restaurateur's point of view. You really couldn't be too careful. Didn't want someone choking to death on your premises, he pointed out doomily. Might raise your insurance charges.

'You have to get her out,' he said.

'None of us will fit through the window,' said Nessa. Even Sheryl, Prowdes' smallest staff member, feared that she might get stuck halfway through thanks to her very British arse.

Snowy was trying to get a look in at Jennifer now. At a whole foot and three inches taller than Nessa, he didn't need a leg up on to the sill. Mad was sitting on his shoulders like a human toddler. As Snowy peered in through the window, Mad detached himself from his keeper and climbed in through the gap.

'Snowy! Grab him!' Nessa shouted, spotting that Mad was escaping before he did.

Too late. Snowy made an ineffectual snatch at Mad's ankle as the chimp let himself inside and jumped down on to the closed toilet seat. Mad instantly set about trying to wake Jennifer in his usual way, giving her a hefty tug on the plaits.

'Great. Now we've got a drunk *and* a chimp stuck in the bathroom,' Nessa sighed.

'I'm sorry,' Jo-Jo wailed.

'You should be,' Nessa told her. 'I don't believe this. Snowy, how many times has Jennifer told you you've got to keep that chimp on a lead when he's outside the nursery.'

'I'm not putting my chimps on leads,' Snowy protested. 'They always do as they're told. Usually . . .'

'Well, tell him to come back out of there.'

Easier said than done. Mad soon got bored of trying to rouse the comatose zoologist but discovered to his annoyance that he couldn't get a grip on the shiny tiled wall of the bathroom that would enable him to climb back out again.

'We'll have to call the fire brigade,' said the Major.

'Yes,' said Nessa. 'Good idea.'

'No,' said Guido. 'Bad idea.'

'No?' Nessa repeated.

'What if this gets into the local paper? You don't want a scandal before the television company even gets here. You haven't signed any contracts yet . . .'

'What about the safety of my staff member?'

Mad shrieked in annoyance. His angry face appeared briefly at the window before he slid back down the tiles again.

'Mad, calm down!' Snowy called to him. Outside on the lawn, Bad was getting agitated too.

'I can't believe she's sleeping through this,' Guy commented.

'Perhaps she's in a coma!' said Nessa. 'Oh my God, oh my God, oh my God.'

'Don't panic,' said Snowy. 'Things could be worse . . .'

Indeed they could. Just as Snowy said that, Bad performed an acrobatic leap from his shoulders and slipped in through the bathroom window to join his brother like a ferret down a hole after a rabbit.

'Snowy!' Nessa cried. 'You've done it again!'

From inside the bathroom came the unmistakable sound of two chimps wrestling. Still no noise from Jennifer. Outside on the lawn, a chorus of accusations and apologies. Jo-Jo threw up into a flower bed. The Major began to dial the fire brigade on his brick-sized mobile phone. Guido wrestled it from him. Guy had his hands full trying to stop Nessa from killing Snowy. Everyone was too busy to hear the bathroom door click open.

'It's Mad!' said Julia, Guido's wife.

'I know,' said Sheryl, the petite pig-keeper. 'What good is all this shouting going to do?'

'No. It's Mad,' Julia repeated. 'Right there.'

20

Julia pointed towards the window of Jennifer's main office. And sure enough, there was Mad the chimpanzee, no longer in the bathroom but sitting on the sleeping doctor's desk, stuffing one piece of paper into his mouth and jumping up and down on what had once been a very neat pile of notes.

Bad was in the office too, opening and closing the drawers in Jennifer's filing cabinet like a secretary gone berserk, pulling out files by the dozen and flinging them over his shoulder in Mad's general direction.

'What are they doing in there?' Snowy asked, voicing the question that everyone wanted to ask.

Somehow, while everyone outside argued about the best way to rescue them, Mad and Bad had escaped from the locked bathroom. But who had unlocked the bolt?

The humans rushed inside to find Jennifer now snoring with her head on the toilet seat. While Snowy and Jo-Jo tried to contain the twins, Nessa and Guy looked in astonishment at the bolt on the inside of the bathroom door. It hadn't been broken off. Just opened in the conventional way.

'Do you think Mad could have done it?' Guy asked.

'He hasn't got the patience. But Bad perhaps . . . No,' Nessa concluded. 'It just isn't possible. Jennifer must have unlocked the door herself.'

But if Jennifer had been the architect of the chimps' escape, she must have done it in her sleep.

Guy lifted his boss gently from her place on the floor.

'So much for Tincastle girls being able to take their drink,' he joked as he wrapped one of her arms around his neck and tucked his shoulder under her armpit to better help her walk out of there.

Jennifer managed to put her weight on her feet without crumbling, but she still didn't open her eyes. Instead, she wrapped her other arm around Guy's neck too, so that they were face to face like dancers. 'Mmmmm,' she said dreamily, her mouth close to the head keeper's. 'Timothy.' Guy and Nessa shared a smile.

'I wonder who *Timothy* is?' Guy asked.

'A lucky man, eh, Guy?' Nessa teased.

Guy backed Jennifer up to her swivel chair and manoeuvred her into the safety of a sitting position. Snowy finally wrestled the twins back out on to the lawn. Julia appeared with a cup of strong coffee and waved it under the sleeping girl's nose in a further attempt to revive her. Jennifer snored on.

'Probably best if she doesn't wake up until we've had time to sort this mess out anyway,' said Nessa. Jennifer's files were sprinkled about the office like confetti and those that weren't torn into tiny pieces were covered in chimpanzee slobber.

'This could take a while,' said the Major, as he lifted a pile of papers from the floor and discovered another chimpanzee present beneath it.

'Shit,' said Jo-Jo.

'Literally,' Nessa and Guy chimed.

'Well, I think we know who's going to be cleaning this lot up,' said Nessa. Jo-Jo slunk away in the direction of the cupboard where the cleaning products were kept.

Nessa, Guy, Julia and the Major made a semi-circle around Jennifer where she snored on her swivel chair. At first they regarded her seriously, but pretty soon Nessa was chewing at her lip to suppress a smile. Julia put her hand up to her mouth to conceal a giggle. Then Jennifer let out a snore like a hippopotamus and the struggle to contain the hilarity was over.

'This isn't funny,' said Nessa between snorts. 'It really isn't funny at all.' She wiped her eyes. 'Will you drive her home?' she asked Guy.

'Of course,' he said. 'I should be going anyway.'

'Got a date with some lovely young lady?' the Major asked.

'Sort of,' said Guy.

A hen party in Exeter was expecting Guy the Gorilla at midnight.

* * *

At least Guy would be able to give up the night job again when the production fee came in, he consoled himself as he prepared to load Jennifer into the back of his car. Providing there was enough money left to reinstate his normal wages after all the essential repair work was done. The roof to the quarantine building had been patched with polythene a dozen times that year. It probably wouldn't last another winter.

Talking of the quarantine block, Guy had one last chore to do before he could drive Jennifer home.

Since the little chimp had arrived at the sanctuary three days previously, Ulysses and his blanket had become inseparable. When Guy poked his head around the door to the quarantine unit now, he could make out a blanket-covered lump in the far corner of the cage. It tried to make itself a little smaller as he stepped into the room.

'Hello there, sailor,' said Guy in a quiet voice. 'How are you feeling this evening? You missed all the fun,' he added, crouching down to see if making himself smaller too might instil more confidence in the ape. Ulysses stayed firmly under cover.

Guy looked at the big metal bowl of fruit he had placed in the cage that lunchtime. It remained untouched. 'Still not hungry?' he asked. 'You know, I really wish you would at least try one of these bananas. They're really rather good.' Guy stepped inside the cage to refill the water bowl.

'I've got to drive Dr Niederhauser home,' he said conversationally. 'And then it's off to the next job. Did I tell you that I dress up as a chimp to earn extra money in my spare time? I think my chimp impression is getting pretty good. What do you think of this?' Guy gave a little hoot of greeting of the kind wild chimps made when returning to their camp after a foraging expedition. The blanket moved ever so slightly. 'No good? Ah well. I'll keep practising. Now, you better eat some of these bananas before I come back again because getting your vitamins this way is far preferable to getting them delivered up your bum via one of Harrison's enemas. You have been warned. Night-night, sailor.'

Guy closed the cage behind him. But he paused at the door just long enough on his way out to see a hairy hand emerge from beneath the blanket and reach for the big metal fruit bowl. His heart swelled with feeling for the little chimp, who was probably as scared and bewildered as any six-year-old human child would be.

'Good lad,' he whispered. 'See you tomorrow.'

21

'Please don't throw up,' Guy entreated his sleeping passenger before he started the drive back to her house. Guy knew very well where Jennifer lived. Tincastle certainly wasn't a big town and the arrival of the gorgeous young blonde at the Witch's cottage had been big news in the Wily Fox before Jennifer started work at Prowdes and quickly earned herself a reputation for being as stuck-up as she was beautiful.

Guy sometimes walked past Jennifer's house on his way from the Fox to the cliff path he liked to take on his day off. Once or twice, he had thought about knocking on her door, asking whether she would like to come along for the walk too, but he never did.

Guy had never met a woman like Jennifer. He had never met a woman so young and yet so focused. The problem was, her focus seemed to make her so inflexible. There was no room for playfulness in Jennifer's brand of conservation. And it seemed there was no room for revision of first impressions either. Was it possible that she would ever start to see him as a capable, trustworthy colleague, rather than the imbecile stripper who had ruined her dress? He hoped so. In any case, he thought, as he pulled the car up to her front gate and set about carrying her dead weight into the house, he felt that they must be pretty even after this.

Jennifer had slept through the whole thing. Being loaded into the car, driven home and unloaded at the other end. When she didn't respond to Guy's questions about the whereabouts of her house keys, he took a deep breath and dived into her bag in search of them. They dangled, appropriately, from a fluffy chimpanzee key-chain.

Inside, the house was neat but sparse. Guy was used to Arlene's home, where every empty surface or wall space was covered in knick-knacks and family photographs. The fridge in Arlene's kitchen was covered in lewd postcards sent from all around the world by pub regulars, attached by magnets shaped like fruit, bread rolls and the more important parts of naked men's anatomy. Jennifer's was pristine by comparison, plain white, but for a neatly printed list of important phone numbers fastened by a plain black magnetic dot.

Guy carried Jennifer through into the sitting room. It was equally Spartan. A plain glass vase on the mantelpiece held no flowers (in fact it had never been used). The coffee table sported a neat pile of scientific journals, lined up so that their edges were parallel to the table edge. Even the cushions on the sofa were arranged with military-style precision, one small cushion balanced on its end like a diamond against each big cushion. Ah well, thought Guy. He was about to ruin that.

Still holding on to Jennifer with one arm, he arranged the cushions like a pillow at one end of the sofa and dropped her gently on to them. Jennifer sighed happily in her sleep. It really was astonishing just how deeply asleep she was. Guy covered her over with her coat. She didn't look terribly comfy but he wasn't about to venture into the bedroom for more pillows or a blanket. He decided he would fetch her a glass of water, though, for when she woke up with terrible dehydration, as she inevitably would.

While he was looking through the kitchen cupboards for the place where the glasses were kept in sparkling, straight lines, Guy heard a groan.

'Where are you taking me?' Jennifer asked the empty sitting room.

Guy hurried back to her side with the water and perched on the coffee table to reassure her and answer her questions as she came round.

'Where am I?' She flailed about with her arms as she started to wake up. 'Guy,' she said. Her eyes swam about his face as she tried to focus. 'Guy Gibson? Is that you? What are you doing here?'

'I drove you home,' he said. 'You had a bit too much to drink.'

'But I don't drink,' said Jennifer simply.

'I know,' said Guy. 'It showed.'

Jennifer attempted to haul herself upright but soon sank back down into the cushiony sofa as though her bones had melted.

'Did they send me home from the party early?' she asked in a little girl voice.

'The party had pretty much finished by the time we left,' Guy assured her.

'I bet it wasn't,' Jennifer slurred. 'I bet they were just waiting for me to leave so they could start the real fun. That's what happened, isn't it? You can tell me the truth.'

'Don't be silly,' said Guy.

'I'm not being silly. I know it's true. They waited for me to go home. They all hate me, don't they? All of them.'

'I don't know what you're talking about. I think you should get some sleep. Drink some of this first.' Guy pressed the water glass to Jennifer's lips. She took a slurp.

'You hate me, don't you?' she said then.

'No,' Guy insisted. 'Of course I don't.' It was hard to resist the urge to laugh at his Snow Queen boss suddenly rambling like a teenager who had never touched liquor before.

'I haven't made any friends at the sanctuary, have I? Nobody likes me and everybody wishes I wasn't there. They waited until I went home to start the party and you probably just want to leave me here and get back and join your friends and carry on having a good time.'

Guy shook his head. 'Nobody hates you and I have no doubt that the party really is over. I'm certainly not going back because . . .' Guy hesitated. 'Well, because I've got something else to do tonight.'

'Are you going to take your clothes off?' Jennifer asked. 'All of them?'

Guy gulped. She had asked that question in a way that could only be described as flirtatious, lowered eyes all faux-coy. 'Well,' he said. 'Some of them.'

'My friend thinks you've got a lovely body,' Jennifer hiccuped. 'Ooops. I shouldn't have said that, should I? You're the boss.'

'No,' Guy corrected her. 'You're the boss. But thank you anyway.'

'What for?' Jennifer had already forgotten. She seemed to be having a hard time persuading her eyes to go in the same direction. 'You like me, don't you, Guy?' She pulled herself upright again.

'Yes. I like you. I've already told you that.'

'How much do you like me? Why do you like me?'

Guy scratched his head subconsciously.

'You can't say, can you?' Jennifer pouted. 'Because you don't really like me at all. Oh God, I hate working at Prowdes,' she suddenly sobbed. 'I hate working in Tincastle. I don't know why I'm here. I'm a waste of space and nobody wants me. I hate my life.'

'No, you don't,' said Guy. 'You've just had a bit too much to drink. The world looks ugly through the bottom of a glass. That's what my mum always used to say. Just get some sleep and when you wake up in the morning, everything will be better again, I promise.' He touched her arm to reassure her, but pulled his hand away again as soon as he realised he was touching the boss.

'But you do like me?' said Jennifer one more time.

'I do like you,' Guy said solemnly.

'How much? Tell me how much you like me.'

Guy looked into the water glass.

'Tell me,' Jennifer persisted. 'Tell me now.'

'Don't make me say something stupid,' Guy muttered towards the carpet.

Jennifer's eyes flickered shut.

'Jennifer? Jennifer?'

She responded with a snore.

It was getting late. Guy needed to leave at once if he wasn't going to miss his rendezvous with the hen party. With Jennifer falling asleep again like that, Guy thought it would be a good idea to leave a note for her to read when she woke up. He had no doubt that she wouldn't remember a word of their drunken conversation and decided that a note would reassure her that nothing sinister had happened.

'Hope you feel OK,' he scribbled on a post-it he found by the telephone. 'No need to feel ashamed of yourself!'

That was a good note, wasn't it? Brief. Jokey. Comforting. Guy almost signed off with a kiss, but remembered halfway through the first down stroke that he was leaving a note for his boss, not for Arlene, and instead had to make the aborted kiss into a weird downward flourish that made it look as though he had had a sudden twitch while writing. Then he put the note beneath another glass of water so that it wouldn't get blown away in the breeze from the window and left to entertain the wild and crazy hens of Exeter with his baby oil and bananas.

He really didn't feel much like doing his Guy the Gorilla routine that night but as though he had been born to the stage, Guy set aside his usual reservations, stepped out into the spotlight once more in an Exeter nightclub and had the crowd in the palm of his hand by the time he finished his first loping circuit of the dance floor.

In fact, that night's performance was pretty damn stellar and when Guy emerged from the men's room in his day clothes, a queue of women were waiting to press their phone numbers into his hand.

'You scared the life out of me,' that evening's bride-to-be admitted. 'I couldn't believe there was a man inside that monkey suit. You were so realistic. I thought you were a real chimpanzee.'

Guy thanked her for her compliments and pointed out that he was actually supposed to be a gorilla.

'A realistic gorilla then,' the bride-to-be amended. 'Wasn't he realistic?' she canvassed her drunken friends.

'I think you look better out of your monkey suit,' said another member of the hen party. 'You can carry me off into the jungle any time you like.'

'Are you single?' one of the girls asked.

Guy merely smiled enigmatically. It was the best way to deal with that question, he had discovered.

'Can I buy you a drink?' said a little round red-head.

'Let *me* buy you a drink,' said her taller bottle-blonde friend.

'Thanks, but I've got to go,' Guy insisted.

'Going home to your girlfriend?' the bride-to-be asked.

Guy shook his head.

'Not going home to your *boyfriend*?' the bottle blonde asked.

Guy laughed. 'Oh God,' said the blonde. 'Isn't it always the way! All the best-looking ones are gay. I knew it. He's too lovely for womankind!'

Guy made a swift exit, car keys already in his hand for the fastest possible escape. He had been followed out to the car by particularly persistent girls before. This time, he was lucky. He made it out alone.

Safely in his car, he turned on the engine and sat with his hands on the steering wheel. It was half past twelve. And Jennifer was still on Guy's mind. But by the time he got back to Tincastle, it would be too late to drop by and see if she was OK, wouldn't it? But what if she had been sick in her sleep or something like that? Far better to risk disturbing her sleep than risk finding her dead in the morning. He should check on her. Guy hesitated in the car park, engine still running.

As he sat there, one of the hen-party girls staggered out and vomited all over her shoes. Her friend followed to look after her.

'Hey! It's the monkey boy!' the sick girl shouted, upon seeing Guy in his car. 'You waiting for me, sweetheart? Well, here I am!'

Guy quickly reversed out of his parking space and exited the car park. By the time he got back to Tincastle, he would make a decision about whether or not to disturb Jennifer's sleep.

22

By the time Jennifer woke up, it was dark outside. She woke suddenly, emerging from her heavy drunken dream sleep like a diver bursting through the surface of the water, gasping to fill empty lungs. Sitting up abruptly, she flailed out an arm at an imaginary dream assailant and sent the glass of water that Guy had set down on the coffee table flying.

'Get off me!' she shouted, as she chopped at empty air. 'What? What?'

Recovering slowly, Jennifer propped herself up on the cushions and looked about the sitting room as though it was an entirely alien scene to her. Though her head was still woozy (in fact, she was still slightly drunk) it was immediately clear that some important piece of her day was missing. She had been at the tea party to celebrate the TV company's decision to film at Prowdes and now she was at home. She had fallen asleep on the sofa but she still had her shoes on. She *never* wore her shoes indoors (cream carpets were not a terribly practical choice for a girl whose shoes were inevitably covered in chimp shit). The inside of her mouth felt like the newspaper at the bottom of an old cat's litter tray.

And then she found the note.

It was sticking to the wet coffee table like a communion wafer sticks to your tongue. The writing had been mostly obliterated by the water Jennifer had knocked all over it. In fact, all she could really make out was the end of the last sentence: '. . . feel ashamed of yourself! Guy'. And after his name, something that must have been a kiss before the note got soaked.

Jennifer's mouth dropped open slightly as she read the note again. '. . . feel ashamed of yourself!' Why should she feel ashamed of herself? The exclamation point after those four words seemed to say more than any of them. And the kiss. Oh God.

Jennifer lifted her coat off her body somewhat gingerly to inspect her state of dress.

Everything she was wearing was still fastened shut. All buttons done up. Her shirt was still tucked into her jeans.

But maybe Guy had dressed her again before he left? She must have been drunk. But how? The punch at the party was non-alcoholic. Had someone spiked it? Fragments of the evening glittered in her mind for mere seconds like dolphins cresting the waves before diving back under an endless grey sea. She had a brief recollection of having her nose against Guy's neck. As she rubbed at her eyes now, she thought perhaps she could even smell him on her hands. That lovely sandalwood smell that wafted out of the keepers' shower when Guy had been in there . . .

And he had carried her into the room, hadn't he? She remembered that, too. She had her arms around him. His face had been close to hers as he laid her down on the cushions. Then nothing. At least she could remember nothing. But that didn't mean that nothing had happened . . . Oh God. Jennifer looked around the room for clues with a sense of rising panic.

Then the phone rang.

'Jennifer! You picked up at last. I've been phoning all evening. You're always at home on a Friday night. Where have you been? What have you been up to?'

It was Dahlia. That woman had a sixth sense for potential gossip.

'I don't know,' was Jennifer's disarmingly honest reply.

'What do you mean, you don't know what you've been up to?' Dahlia asked. 'I was ringing you up to tell you the news about Mary Rickard, but this sounds much more interesting. Spill.'

'Tell me about Mary,' said Jennifer. Anything to change the subject, though Dahlia's inane gossip usually bored her senseless. Jennifer had been known to turn the television on the minute Dahlia called, set the sound to mute and read a film via teletext while Dahlia was in full 'he said/she said' flow.

'Well, she got engaged to the *other* brother. But that's boring.

We all knew that was going to happen in the end. I want to know what happened to you. Are you OK? You don't sound too well.'

'I don't feel too well.'

'In what way?'

'I think I might have been poisoned.'

'Poisoned!' Dahlia exclaimed.

'Made drunk,' Jennifer clarified, before Dahlia got it into her head that there was an arsenic killer on the loose.

'But you don't drink.'

'Exactly. I think someone must have spiked my drinks. At the sanctuary. We were having a tea party to celebrate getting the television programme.'

'You got the television programme!' Dahlia exclaimed. 'Honestly, you never tell me anything important . . . But that's brilliant news. Do you think you can get me into the Baftas?'

'What?'

'When you're up for the best wildlife programme award . . .' Dahlia explained.

'Dahlia, they haven't even started filming yet. I might not even be in it.'

'Not if you continue to wear your hair like Heidi's spinster auntie,' Dahlia agreed (she was constantly trying to persuade her friend to try something other than a ponytail or plaits). 'But I can fix that. What happened at that party, for God's sake?'

'I'm not sure. I remember talking to the Major about the TV show. I remember Nessa giving a toast to us all. I remember the chimp twins starting a food fight. Then . . .'

'Then?' asked Dahlia eagerly.

'I don't know. All I can remember is having my nose in Guy's neck. Then I woke up on the sofa and found a note.'

'What did it say?'

'Feel ashamed of yourself . . .' Jennifer intoned.

'Feel ashamed of yourself? Is that all?'

'Well, I don't think that was *all* originally but the note got covered in water when I knocked over a glass that someone put on the coffee table and I can't read what the rest of it says.'

'Do you know who wrote it?'

'Yes. It was Guy. He signed it. With a kiss.'

A dramatic intake of breath at Dahlia's end of the phone. 'Guy the Gorilla-gram?'

'The very same.'

'Guy the Gorilla-gram came into your home?'

'Well, he left a note. What do you think it means?'

'Oh, darling,' said Dahlia, pausing to convey that she was considering the matter carefully. 'You really are so silly. It means that you definitely did something you should feel ashamed of, of course!'

'Oh God,' Jennifer groaned. 'I had a feeling you'd say that.'

Dahlia laughed her most tinkling laugh. If she hadn't had the phone in one hand, she would have clapped with delight. 'This is fabulous,' she said. 'I wonder if you did it.'

'Dahlia!'

'Oh no. Silly me. Of course you'd know if you did it. With a thing that size! My God. Imagine if you had slept through that. What a waste—'

'This isn't funny,' Jennifer interrupted. 'I may have done something stupid in front of one of my staff. Or even *with* one of my staff.'

'Well, there's only one way to find out,' Dahlia told her.

'How's that?' asked Jennifer.

'Ask him. And if you did,' Dahlia continued, 'I for one will be very glad indeed. You've been without sex for way too long. You probably qualify as a born-again virgin. How long is it now? Eighteen months. Two years?'

'Five years,' Jennifer said quietly. Irritably.

Silence at the other end of the phone. Then a choking noise. Very few things could shock the former Ms Wilde, but Jennifer had just managed it.

'Did you just say five years?' she asked eventually.

'Five years and six months. Almost to the day,' said Jennifer.

'That means . . .' Dahlia made a mental calculation. 'No. It can't be.'

'That the last person I had sex with was Timothy Lauder. Yes.'

'What? You mean you didn't even do it with that computer programmer you met at Fiona and Jeremy's wedding? The boss-eyed one you went upstairs with.'

'Not even him.'

'Well, he told everybody you did.'

'You really know how to make a girl feel better. I didn't even go upstairs *with* that man. I went to the loo and he followed.'

'Jennifer, this is terrible. If someone stops you in the street tomorrow and asks who was the last person you shagged, you'll have to tell them it was Timothy Lauder.'

'I'll have to tell them to mind their own business.'

'And that means he is still part of your life,' Dahlia continued. 'He's still *ongoing*.'

'He's not *ongoing*.'

'Oh yes he is. No wonder you can't find yourself a boyfriend. If you tell any man you've gone five years without sex it's bound to freak him out.'

'Dahlia, I don't habitually discuss when I last had sex with anyone, let alone a man on a first date.'

'You don't have to say it. You just ooze it. You're oozing celibacy. I should have guessed.'

'I'm not listening to you any more,' said Jennifer firmly. 'I am going to put the phone down on you now. I want you to know that I am not hanging up on you. I am just saying "goodbye" and putting down the phone. Goodbye.'

Jennifer put down the phone.

Dahlia called back at once.

'What?'

'I was just giving you some friendly advice.'

'Well, don't.'

'Actually, Henry said the bit about you not having sex for so long being what makes you give out anti-man vibes. But that was when we thought you'd only gone without sex since the computer programmer.'

'I'm still not feeling any better. Why don't you just say sorry?'

'Oh.'

Jennifer knew at once that she had scored a direct hit.

'Look, I'm sorry too,' she said softly. 'It's just that this is a rather difficult moment for me. I've never had a blackout before.'

'Beg to differ. What about my twenty-first birthday party . . .'

'OK. So I had a blackout then too. But this is just horrible. I don't know what I did and I really can't bear to ask.'

'I can think of a question you could ask yourself right now that might make you feel a great deal better.'

'What? What is it?'

'Aren't you secretly just a little bit pleased at the thought that Guy Gibson might have *wanted* to take advantage of you in your state of inebriation?'

23

When Dahlia finally decided that she had had enough of teasing Jennifer for the evening and put the phone down, Jennifer got up from the sofa and made her way unsteadily to the kitchen to get another glass of water. She felt disgusting. This was why she had pretty much given up drinking after an unfortunate evening with a bottle of Vermouth during Freshers' Week at Oxford. Right now, Jennifer's mouth felt as though it was full of pencil sharpenings and she was starting to get a headache like someone was tightening a metal band around her temples. Someone particularly mean.

'Yuk.' She downed half a litre of Evian straight from the fridge. Even drinking water felt like punishment. This was why she didn't get drunk. That and the fact that whenever she did get drunk, she inevitably said something stupid.

Jennifer sat down at the kitchen table and once again tried to piece the evening back together from the moment the tea party started until the moment Guy put her key in the door for her because she was too tipsy to do it herself. Had she said anything stupid?

Another sudden lucid flash. Jennifer saw Guy sitting on the edge of her coffee table, hands crossed nervously in his lap, face golden in the light from her standard lamp.

'Don't make me say something stupid,' he said.

Don't make me say something stupid? What did that mean?

If she hadn't been his boss, Jennifer would have known exactly what that meant. It was a sentence loaded with romantic intention. Oh God. During her conversation with Dahlia, Jennifer had pretty much convinced herself that nothing physical had transpired between her and her colleague. But all the evidence was suggesting that she had definitely been flirting with him. Guy Gibson. A member of her staff. What was wrong with her?

Was anything wrong with her?

In the early morning gloom of her kitchen, Jennifer remembered what Dahlia had said when she confirmed that Timothy was still the last person she had slept with.

'You haven't slept with anybody since you split up with Timothy Lauder?'

'No.'

'Do you think he's been living the life of a monk?' Dahlia had asked. 'No.' She'd answered the question for her. 'So why have you?'

'It just hasn't felt right to sleep with anyone else.'

'Jennifer!' Dahlia only ever used her best friend's full name when she was exasperated. 'You have been acting like the widow of some heroic World War One soldier. And Timothy Lauder was far from being a hero. You don't have to keep a sacred flame burning for a man who tried to use an animal behaviour "paradigm" to excuse the fact that he couldn't keep his dick in his pants while you weren't there to watch him. *Paradigm*. Huh.' (Dahlia had been snorting about that on and off for five years. In one of his post-infidelity e-mails to Jennifer, Timothy had actually tried to explain to her that sex for him was like sex between the bonobos. It was all about the smooth running of the social hierarchy, not love. He only *loved* Jennifer. 'So he was just "smoothing things over" that undergraduate,' Dahlia had laughed cruelly.)

'I'm not keeping a sacred flame burning for Timothy Lauder,' Jennifer had said this evening. 'I never even think about the man any more.'

'Yeah, right.'

'Yeah. *Right!*' Jennifer had exclaimed.

At the time she and Timothy broke up, Jennifer's girlfriends were surprised and faintly *awed* by the way she handled the split. Not for Jennifer the traditional three weeks spent huddled beneath a duvet, crying her eyes dry and subsisting on nothing but chocolate, Chardonnay and Marlboro Lights. That terrible afternoon, Jennifer simply took the train straight back up to Edinburgh, locked herself in her office and wrote fifteen thousand words on the manner in which chimpanzee mothers in Gabon teach their offspring to crack kola nuts, before collapsing into bed at 4 a.m.

She didn't even let Dahlia know what had happened until some three days later. And then it was only because Dahlia had called to impart some juicy gossip about another girl they both knew.

'So,' Dahlia said at the end of forty minutes' worth of slander about Mary Rickard (this was when she was going out with the first brother). 'How's life with you?'

'I broke up with Timothy,' Jennifer said flatly.

Dahlia shrieked as though she had been poked in the eye. 'You didn't tell me! I can't believe you didn't call me the minute it happened! Are you OK?' Dahlia asked. 'Do you want me to come up there and look after you? I can get a train to Edinburgh this afternoon. I'm packing my bags right now.'

'No. I am fine,' Jennifer said. 'Absolutely fine.' And she really believed she was.

You see, Jennifer approached the whole thing intellectually. She decided she had to treat Timothy as though he were a drug to which she had become carelessly addicted. She had to go cold turkey, cutting him out absolutely and all at once. So the letters were shredded. The e-mails were erased. Once the hard evidence of the whole affair had been consigned to the real bin and the recycle bin on her lap-top, Jennifer set about dealing with the softer drive of her mind. To clear that, she decided she would apply classic Pavlovian psychology, as studied for the animal behaviour model of her undergraduate degree. She slipped a thick elastic band around her wrist and pinged it every time she thought of her ex-lover in the hope that the physically painful association would discourage her mind from wandering in his direction after too long.

It was hard. But Jennifer didn't waver. Not once did she pick up a telephone and dial Timothy's number only to put the receiver down before he picked up. Not once did she put pen to paper and pour out her heart in a vitriolic yet truly desperate letter she would never dare to post. Not once did she eat a whole family-sized bar of Dairy Milk then make herself sick with overeating and self-loathing. All her energy was diverted into her chimpanzee research. And eventually, Jennifer began even to forget what Timothy looked like. Her memories of him faded like old photographs left out in the sun.

'You're going about this all wrong,' Dahlia said at the time, when Jennifer refused to make a voodoo doll of her ex or even flush a piece of paper with his name scribbled on it down the toilet. 'You think you're being all grown-up and mature. You think you're not allowing this to get to you. But I think you are in *denial*.' Dahlia prodded her best friend in the chest. 'You've got to let the emotion out to get proper *closure*.'

Closure. Jennifer snorted. What a horrid, women's magazine sort of word.

'Because if you don't get closure,' Dahlia continued, 'trust me when I say that, one day, the emotions that you think you're dealing with so neatly now are going to come back and bite you on the arse.'

'Dahlia,' Jennifer said. 'You're *so* ridiculous.'

Now the closure issue had raised its ugly head again. 'You need to have sex with someone else quickly,' had been Dahlia's considered advice this evening. 'You have attached too much importance to that bloody primatologist because he's the last man you had sex with.'

'I haven't attached any importance to him at all. *I don't even think about him!*' Jennifer had said a little more loudly.

'I mean,' Dahlia ignored her, 'I can't even remember who I was seeing five years ago. I'm sure if I passed the poor bloke in the street, I wouldn't even recognise him, much less cry myself to sleep over him night after night.'

'You had just started seeing Henry five years ago,' Jennifer had pointed out.

'Oh gosh. So I had.' Dahlia had at least had the grace to blush. 'But what I'm saying still stands. It was a long time ago. If you and Timothy hadn't split up when you did, you would be sick to death of him by now. You'd be fantasising about the postman every time lovely Timmy tried to hump you. You'd be just about due for a great big five-and-a-half-year itch. Perspective. That's what you need. And it's very hard to get perspective without comparison. You're a scientist. You're always telling me you wouldn't base a new theory on the results of just one test. So why are you basing your future love life on the results of one disastrous affair that happened *all those years ago*?'

'I am not.'

'Oh, wake up. You've been living in a man-free bubble just in case Timothy comes back to you.'

'That's rubbish. I just haven't met anyone interesting. Where do people meet interesting people these days?'

'Internet dating?' Dahlia had suggested.

'That's too weird.'

'Says the scientist who has been so busy with her graphs that she hasn't had a shag in five years.'

Jennifer had pulled a face. 'But it's still so . . . so artificial. How do normal people meet each other?'

'In a bar. In a club. At *work*.' Dahlia had said this with meaning.

'Oh no,' Jennifer had said, cottoning on to Dahlia's implication immediately. 'No way.'

'Oh come on. He's gorgeous. And you work at Prowdes Animal Sanctuary, not in the head office of Price Waterhouse Coopers. What damage could a little *monkey*-ing around possibly do to your career?'

'Just because I work in a somewhat unprofessional environment doesn't mean that I shouldn't act the consummate professional at all times,' Jennifer had protested. 'Besides, he probably doesn't fancy me.'

'He fancied you enough on my hen night.'

'Dahlia, that was a long time ago.'

It was a long time ago, wasn't it, Jennifer reflected in her kitchen that night. And yet?

'He fancied you enough to make sure you got home safely . . .'

Don't make me say something stupid.

Jennifer could see his face as he said it. A half-smile. Jennifer may have been much more adept at reading non-verbal signals in chimpanzees than in human beings but even she knew that, at that moment, Guy had been looking at her not as his boss but as a woman he might want to get to know better in a very different context.

Though she was alone with no one to watch her, Jennifer felt the heat rise in her cheeks. Because the thing was, she realised then, she wished that Guy Gibson had said *something stupid*. During the course of that evening, perhaps even during the course of the past two months, Guy had been slowly metamorphosing in her mind. He might be hopeless at remembering to fill out her all-important observation forms. He might not know how to spell 'antibiotic' or understand the meaning of 'anthropomorphism' but there was something about him, something dedicated and serious about the animals, that made those little niggles suddenly assume their real size. Very little.

Jennifer touched her hand to her cheek, where Guy had kissed her 'goodnight' for ever so slightly too long.

Perhaps Dahlia was right. For once. Since finding Timothy shagging that undergraduate, Jennifer had been in a holding pattern. She had made a decision that day that she would never allow herself to be in a position where she could be so horribly hurt again. It had seemed like the only way to deal with the situation at the time. But where had that decision really got her?

She was lonely. That was the truth of it. If you stayed out of the game to avoid the pitfalls then you were no longer eligible for the prizes either. Going without the pain meant going without the pleasure. She was twenty-seven years old and she had only ever slept with one man in her life. (She realised that wasn't necessarily a bad thing. On her more thoughtful days, Dahlia often bemoaned the fact that there were men in the world she wouldn't even recognise on the street in broad daylight who had seen the little strawberry tattooed on her buttock. At least Jennifer would never know that slightly shameful feeling.) But it wasn't as if Timothy was sitting in Oxford right now, watching his tears drop into a pint of Guinness as he thought the same thing.

Thinking about Guy just then, Jennifer had felt a flicker of something she hadn't experienced in a very long time. She had felt a rush of liquid heat through her limbs that made her worry she was about to go into meltdown. It took her a moment to remember that this puddling feeling inside was the beginning of lust and not the ebola virus liquefying her internal organs.

Perhaps Dahlia was right. Perhaps Guy Gibson was the man she had been looking for. Perhaps it didn't matter if he didn't have all the letters after his name. Perhaps it didn't matter that he couldn't tell Bach from Beethoven.

Sitting at her kitchen table, with the water-spoiled note in her hand, Jennifer experienced nothing short of a reawakening. It was as though someone had turned a power supply back on and a body that had been in storage was suddenly in full operation again. Why hadn't she noticed that he smelled so good before (actually, it was because Guy rarely wore aftershave to work – some of the animals objected)?

It was time to lay the ghost of Timothy Lauder to rest by laying another man over the top of him. At least there would be no nasty surprises when Guy took his trousers off.

Perhaps it was time to get back on that *donkey*, as Dahlia had so crudely put it.

24

When Guy got back to the Wily Fox after thrilling the hens of Devon with his incredible gorilla-gram routine, Arlene was still up. The pub had been closed for three hours but she was busy doing paperwork, ordering more Pilsner and peanuts for the week ahead. She looked knackered.

'How did it go?' she asked, forcing a friendly smile onto her tired face. 'You're back a bit later than I expected.'

Guy didn't tell her that once he got back to Tincastle from Exeter, he had spent a further twenty minutes driving up and down the street where Jennifer lived, slowing down each time he drew near the cottage, only to speed up again and drive on past when the more realistic/pessimistic part of his brain reminded him that she was his boss, she probably wouldn't appreciate a visit after midnight and she thought he was stupid.

'Well, we had a fantastic night here,' said Arlene, pronouncing the adjective with heavy sarcasm. 'Joanne didn't turn up.' Joanne the barmaid was famous for failing to turn up for work when she and her boyfriend had a row, an occurrence which was becoming increasingly regular as Joanne pushed her reluctant beau for more commitment. 'Greg cut his thumb open on a broken bottle and had to go home early. Then the soda pump broke so I ended up having to give out bottled Coke instead of Coke from the tap. That will have wiped out half my profits for the week.'

'Tomorrow will be a better day,' said Guy.

'I don't know,' said Arlene gloomily. 'Do you think Jamie will have aged ten years and turned from a teenager to a decent human being by morning? I nearly threw him out of the house today. He thinks I don't recognise half the swearwords he signs at me. When he came down to breakfast, he signed "Hello, you old bitch." I could have bloody knocked his head off.'

'Are you sure that's what he said?' Guy asked.

'I'm sure,' said Arlene flatly. 'I don't know what's happened to him. He's turned from the sweetest little boy in the world into a monster overnight. Less than a year ago, I was the person he loved most in the whole world. I couldn't do anything wrong in his eyes. Now he acts like I'm some kind of oppressive dictator. Just because I said he couldn't go out last night. It was a school night. He's only fourteen for heaven's sake. I didn't think he would get like this for at least another three years.'

'They're teenagers by the time they're ten these days,' said Guy. He'd seen plenty of the awkward in-betweeners trailing after their parents round the sanctuary. Too old to get excited about the animals any more (or at least too old to want to be seen to be getting excited about something) yet still way too young to go off on their own.

'I can't help thinking it's my fault,' said Arlene. 'He wouldn't be like this if I'd been stricter with him when he was growing up. But first there was his dad leaving. And then there's his deafness. I guess I wanted to make up for the things he didn't have. Do you know what the stupid woman at the hairdresser's said to me the other day? She said, "At least you won't have to worry about him playing loud music when he's a teenager." I nearly clocked her one as well.'

Guy couldn't help smiling. His smile sparked one off in Arlene too. Guy knew that dealing with a deaf teen had its own set of unique problems. The biggest of which for Guy was that Jamie had taken to spending hours on end in the bathroom, showering until all the hot water was gone and the boiler shuddered dangerously in the cupboard under the stairs as it strained to keep up with consumption. There was no point hammering on the door. So Guy had come up with the ingenious measure of turning off the water supply when Jamie overstayed his bathroom slot.

'Guy,' said Arlene, 'do you think you could talk to him?'

Guy nodded. 'I'll have a go. He can come and help out at the sanctuary one night after school.'

'If you can get him away from his computer.'

'I'll offer him a tenner. We need some help getting the place tidy for the TV people.'

'How did your party go?' Arlene suddenly remembered.

'It all ended rather badly.' Guy told her about Jennifer, the spiked punch and the locked bathroom door. 'I drove her home and put her on the sofa.'

'And just left her there?' Arlene raised her eyebrows.

'I think she was over the worst. But what was I supposed to do? She's my boss. I couldn't exactly tuck her up in bed.'

'You like her, don't you?' Arlene said with a nod.

Guy didn't respond.

'Oh dear.'

'Oh dear indeed,' Guy said after a while.

'There's no reason why you shouldn't ask her out.'

'What?'

'Ask her out.'

'She's my boss.'

'There's no law against it. And if a cat can look at a queen, you can certainly ask your boss if she fancies a drink.'

'But what if she says no?'

'She says no. You carry on the same old frosty relationship you've been having. But . . .' Arlene paused. 'I am willing to bet that the reason why your relationship has been so frosty is because she's as confused about you as you have been about her.'

Guy looked sceptical.

'Trust me,' said Arlene. 'I'm a woman. I've lived through this a thousand times since I was old enough to know that the world is split into girls and boys. It happens in the school playground. When a girl thinks she might be in love with a boy, the first thing she does is ignore him, try to pretend that she isn't interested. Boys only drop spiders down the collars of the girls they secretly like best.'

Guy nodded in recognition. 'I put chewing gum in my favourite girl's hair.'

'There you go. There's a very thin line between love and hate and that shows in the way we act towards people. If she's acting like a bitch, then she probably thinks you're the hottest thing in Tincastle. Guaranteed. Well,' Arlene concluded, 'you don't have that much competition.'

Guy playfully cuffed his landlady round the ear.

'Give it a go,' Arlene said seriously. 'You have nothing to lose. If she isn't interested, then I'm sure that she will be just as happy to pretend you never asked as you will be. And if she is interested . . .'

'She won't be interested—' Guy began.

'Have a bit more self-confidence, please. You just took your clothes off in front of a bunch of women you'd never met before in your life.'

'That was different.'

'Well, this Dr Niederhauser must be very different. I don't think I've ever seen you quite so agitated by a woman before. I hope she deserves it.'

'I think she does,' said Guy.

'Then ask her out. Ask her to come to the Wily Fox for a drink. I want to get a proper look at her. Check her over.'

'The last thing I need is for you to get a proper look at her.'

Arlene pulled a face that suggested Guy was spoiling her fun.

'But you know what, perhaps I will invite her for a drink. I mean, I can make that sound as though it isn't a date, can't I? I can ask her to come for a drink to discuss the animals. Ulysses, for example. We need to have a proper talk about him.'

'Coward,' Arlene tutted.

'Sensible,' said Guy. 'I'm going to bed. Next time Jamie and I cross on our way to the bathroom, I'll ask him to come over to Prowdes. But I really don't think you need to worry about him. He's a good kid at heart. This is just a phase he's going through. It'll last at most' – Guy counted on his fingers – 'another twenty years.'

Arlene groaned and rested her forehead on the table in front of her. 'I can't bear it.'

'Goodnight,' said Guy.

'Ask her tomorrow!' Arlene called after him as he climbed the stairs to bed. 'Before you chicken out. She's a very lucky girl.'

The following morning, both Guy and Jennifer were awake long before their respective alarm clocks trilled the ugly electronic reveille.

Jennifer had woken periodically throughout the night, desperate to go to the loo and head aching through dehydration. When she woke for the fifth time at six o'clock, to the sound of a noisy wood pigeon bellowing the dawn chorus in her back garden, she abandoned all hope of getting any more sleep and instead put the kettle on for the first cup of nettle tea of the day.

Meanwhile, in the colourful kitchen of the Wily Fox, Guy went for coffee and a breakfast of a bread roll filled with hard yellow cheese that had been sitting under a plastic cover on the bar all the previous day. It tasted as disgusting as it looked.

Jennifer jumped into her car just as Guy was getting into his rusty jeep outside the pub. Half a mile outside the sanctuary, they found themselves travelling in convoy. Jennifer chanced a little wave at him via her rear-view mirror. They parked side by side in the car park. Guy got out of his car first. Seeing Jennifer struggling to lift up a pile of serious-looking books and papers she had been conveying to the sanctuary on the passenger seat, Guy stepped up to open her door for her.

Jennifer slid out of the driver's seat in the best finishing-school manner she could manage. She dropped half her books on the ground as she did so. As she and Guy both bent to pick the books up, they cracked heads.

'Guy . . .'

'Jennifer . . .'

A pregnant pause.

'I just wanted to say . . .' they both started.

Their coffee advert moment had arrived.

25

It was one of those times when the air is heavy with possibility, like the scent of honeysuckle on a warm summer's evening. If you believe in the stars then they are definitely aligned and you know that whatever you want to ask for can be yours.

Guy and Jennifer straightened up, both holding on to the books, Guy not quite letting them go and Jennifer not quite taking them from him, in that classic gesture that lets everyone who sees it know that the two people involved really want to be holding hands rather than whatever it is between them and they should be left well alone until they have said what needs to be said and preferably arranged a time and place to say some more. Their body language read like a Mills and Boon novel for anyone who cared to look hard enough. Jennifer's heart was fluttering so fast as she and Guy held the books like a bridge, that she barely noticed Jo-Jo slinking up to them.

Jo-Jo had been awake all night, dreading the time when she would have to face Dr Niederhauser and apologise for spiking the punch. She had arrived at the sanctuary early, steeling herself up to get the grovelling out of the way as quickly as possible, watching the car park for the arrival of the little red Ford like a peasant awaiting an invading army. Nessa had warned her that Jennifer alone had the power to decide what Jo-Jo's punishment would be. Snowy had intimated that there would be no *Spartacus* moment this time. She had better make an appointment at the job centre.

'Dr Niederhauser,' Jo-Jo began, 'I want to say sorry about the punch.'

'Oh, that doesn't matter,' said Jennifer. 'You were just trying to liven things up. I feel absolutely fine this morning.'

Guy's mouth curled up at the edges in a smile.

Jo-Jo stared at her boss in confusion.

'But . . . I . . . I thought . . .' Jo-Jo tried again.

'Have you checked the post yet this morning?' Guy asked her to give her the opportunity to quit while she was ahead. Jo-Jo took it. Leaving Guy and Jennifer still standing there, books between them.

'About last night,' said Jennifer eventually. The three most dreaded little words in the English language. 'I think I might have embarrassed myself.'

'You didn't embarrass yourself at all,' said Guy.

'I was drunk.'

'You make a charming drunk.'

'I find that very hard to believe.'

Slowly, Jennifer started to take the books into her possession. She looked down at the gravel. Seeing his chance begin to recede, Guy breathed deep, found the bottom of his well of courage and said, 'Perhaps you'd like to be a charming drunk again some time this week?'

'What?' Jennifer's brow creased momentarily. Had he said the wrong thing?

'I mean, perhaps you'd like to come for a drink,' Guy tried again. 'To discuss the chimps,' he added quickly. 'Ulysses. Ulysses in particular. I think we need to talk about his progress.'

'Oh. OK,' Jennifer said overly cheerily. 'Yes. That would be nice.'

Guy found himself grinning as her answer flooded him with relief.

'When?' Jennifer asked.

'How about tonight?'

'I think I can do that.'

'Great.'

'Where?'

'Er . . .' Guy hadn't thought that far ahead and his mind was momentarily blanking on venues. It couldn't be the Wily Fox. The thought of Arlene and the rest of the bar staff lining up to gawp was not a particularly pleasant one. 'The Boat House?' he suggested. It was the only other pub Guy could think of. The Wily Fox regulars had beaten the Boat House in a pub quiz the previous week. It wasn't difficult. The Boat House regulars failed in the 1980s' pop round. Hardly surprising since most of them were well into their eighties. Jennifer looked surprised at Guy's suggestion. She didn't go out much, but she went out enough to know that no one ever went to the Boat House. No one without a free bus pass. But she didn't comment.

'OK,' she said. 'I'll meet you there. Eight o'clock.'

'Great.' Guy finally relinquished his hold on the books. 'Great! Better get to work.'

'Yes,' Jennifer agreed.

They both set off in the direction of the staff room, then, strangely embarrassed by the fact that they were walking in the same direction after their small yet momentous conversation, they both stopped, at the same time, and turned towards the big house.

'Just got to see Nessa,' they both said at once.

'You go first,' said Guy.

'OK,' said Jennifer. 'I'll, er, I'll see you later.'

She set off towards the big house at a trot, almost twisting her ankle in a dip in the path that had once held a puddle. She recovered herself quickly and broke into a run, as though that was what she had been intending to do all along and her trip was in fact just a change in pace. She needn't have worried. Guy wasn't watching. He was equally busy tripping down the path in the opposite direction, feeling goofier than little Jamie faced with the sixth-form girl he had a crush on.

26

Guy's first job that day was to check in on Ulysses. Or Blanket, as the young chimp had come to be nicknamed by Snowy and Jo-Jo, in honour of the fact that he still refused to be parted from the grey rug they had wrapped him in to carry him from the boat that had been his prison.

'Not after Michael Jackson's youngest,' Jo-Jo was quick to point out.

Ulysses was a peculiar chimp, Guy decided. He had met many chimpanzees since he started his job at Prowdes and he knew that they all had distinct personalities and that they were far more intelligent than the average human being gave them credit for, but Ulysses had surprised even him. There was something so very serious about the way in which Ulysses watched him as he went about his business in the quarantine unit. He studied Guy with such close attention and with such a thoughtful look in his eyes that Guy half expected the chimp to open his mouth and say, 'You don't want to do it like that. You want to do it like this,' when Guy made a cup of tea or swept the floor or filled up a water bowl. It wasn't like being watched by a chimpanzee at all. It was like being watched by a human child of the same age. A precocious one at that.

'Where did you come from?' Guy asked Ulysses in a whisper as he replenished the chimp's food bowl that morning. Guy had read in the newspaper that the boat on which Ulysses was found had been traced to a notorious gang wanted not just for drug-smuggling, but for a variety of impressively daring robberies along the coast of the Mediterranean. They specialised in stealing jewellery, paintings and antiques to order. They had been linked to thefts from some of the most opulent and well-guarded homes in southern Europe. Their members frequently boasted about their exploits and yet there just hadn't been enough evidence to convict them for anything. No fingerprints. At least, no fingerprints that ever matched any of the gang . . .

'What on earth did they want with you?' Guy wondered aloud to his chimpanzee friend. 'Ah well, I think you're better off with us. Who knows? You might even end up back in Africa.'

Jennifer had been busy making an assessment of which chimps might be suitable for release. Some were too old. Some were too disabled. Like poor Matilda, who lost a foot to an infection caused by a chain that had been wrapped too tightly around her ankle when she was kept as a kind of guard dog by a gold wholesaler in Egypt prior to her rescue. Some were just too 'fucked up' to use Jo-Jo's phrase. The twins' mother, Priscilla, counted among those.

Ulysses might be an ideal candidate. He was young. He was strong. He was recovering well from the infection around his neck.

But was he psychologically strong enough to cope with real chimpanzee life? Guy thought Ulysses seemed unusually shy of Mad and Bad, who shouldn't really have presented any kind of threat to a chimp of Ulysses' size. Perhaps he had never seen another chimp before. Guy had read reports of chimps raised in captivity who didn't recognise other members of their species when they were introduced to them. The captive chimps were convinced that they were human and were as frightened of other chimpanzees as a human child might be.

Guy sank down on to his haunches so that he was face to face with Ulysses through the wire of his pen. He studied the chimpanzee's face while Ulysses appeared to do the same to him. Just as human beings' faces come to reflect the expressions they habitually pull and thus are pretty good indicators of personality, Guy thought chimps' faces reflected their inner selves too. For example, Mad's eyes were generally wide open and mischievous, reflecting the amount of time he spent pulling an open-mouthed play-grin while joyfully thumping his brother. Ulysses' face bore a mixture of two expressions. Worry and benevolence. His brow was typically low over his eyes in a frown, but the set of his mouth was friendly and relaxed. Guy hoped that Ulysses could perceive the same friendliness in his face.

'We'll look after you here,' he murmured. 'Nothing bad will happen to you now, I promise.'

'Who are you talking to?'

It was Jo-Jo.

Guy stood up. 'Just Ulysses.'

'You mean Blanket.'

'I'm not calling him Blanket,' said Guy.

'What on earth did you say to the Snow Queen?' Jo-Jo asked. 'I thought she was going to rip my head off about the spiked punch. Is she going to have a proper go at me later?'

'I don't think so.'

'I can't believe that's all she's going to say on the subject.'

'Maybe she's got more of a sense of humour than you think.'

'And maybe I've got a blue arse like a macaque in heat underneath my overalls . . . What are you doing tonight?' Jo-Jo asked. 'Me and Snowy thought we would get a drink in the Fox after work. His missus is on a hen night tonight so he's coming out to play.'

Guy hesitated. An embarrassing heat suddenly flushed his cheeks. 'I can't.'

'Have you got a date?'

'No. But I am going out for a drink. I'm going to the Boat House.'

'That old man's pub?'

'With Jennifer.'

Jo-Jo whooped. 'Ohmigod! Just wait till I tell Snowy! You're going on a date with the Snow Queen!'

'It's not a date. We're going to talk about Ulysses. That's all.'

'You can do that in the Wily Fox with us. We work at Prowdes too.'

Guy squirmed under Jo-Jo's direct gaze.

'Not tonight. This is high-level stuff.'

'It's a date. It's a date. It's a date,' Jo-Jo chanted. 'Guy Gibson, you are totally dropped from our gang.'

27

'It's not a date.' Jennifer followed the same line of defence when Dahlia called to invite her to dinner that evening.

'Henry!' Dahlia held her hand over the phone receiver but shouted so that Jennifer could hear every word. 'Jennifer can't come over tonight. She's got a date.'

'I have not got a date. We're going to talk about the chimpanzees. We're colleagues.'

'Then if it isn't a date,' Dahlia retorted, 'you should cancel and come over here instead. Henry has lined up the most amazing single bloke. His name is Charlie and—'

'He's got a fat boy's goatee and a voice like a foghorn. You've already tried that one with me. And I have to go to this meeting.'

'Date,' Dahlia corrected.

'Whatever,' said Jennifer in exasperation.

'What are you going to wear?'

'It doesn't matter. This isn't a date.' Jennifer paused. 'Dahlia, you know when you said that my green shirt is better than the pink one because it makes my eyes "pop out"? What exactly did you mean?'

'Date, date, date, date, date,' Dahlia chanted.

With just half an hour to go before he was meant to meet Jennifer at the Boat House, Guy hadn't even managed to get into the bathroom. The great clouds of steam escaping from beneath the bathroom door into the hall told him that Jamie must have been showering for a good twenty minutes already.

'Hurry up!' Guy shouted through the bathroom door at his landlady's son. 'You're not the only person in this house who smells, you know.' Guy hammered on the door before he remembered how useless that gesture was too. He went downstairs into the kitchen and turned the stop-cock closed. Seconds later, Jamie emerged from the bathroom in a cloud of steam, shampoo bubbles still decorating his hair like a curly white wig.

'What's happened to the f-ing water?' he signed.

'Language,' Guy signed back with a stern look on his face. 'What happened to the water was me. You look lovely, Jamie. Any chance I could have a shower now that you've drained the English Channel to have yours?'

Jamie grudgingly agreed to be finished in under two minutes if Guy turned the water back on so that he could rinse his hair.

'And if you come into the sanctuary after it closes tomorrow,' Guy continued to add conditions while he had Jamie in such a weak bargaining position, covered in soap and getting cold.

'What for?' Jamie asked.

'Help me clean up.'

'How much?'

'A tenner.'

Jamie shrugged in what he probably hoped was a nonchalant 'take it or leave it' manner. But Guy knew that the lad was already mentally spending the cash.

'I'll come for two hours,' Jamie signed.

'Then I'll turn the water back on,' said Guy.

'Why are you getting yourself tarted up anyway?' Guy asked as Jamie emerged from the bathroom for the second time, not two minutes but twelve minutes later, face red as a chimp's bottom where he had been squeezing his spots. 'Got a date?'

'No,' Jamie signed. He was just getting himself spruced up for another evening spent hanging out on the corner in front of the pub with his mates. 'Have you?'

'Of course not,' signed Guy. 'I'm going to meet my boss to talk about the new chimp.'

'Then why are you so worried about making yourself look pretty all of a sudden?' Jamie asked. 'And why are you blushing?'

'I am not blushing.'

'You so are. You fancy that woman at work, don't you? Mum told me.'

'Your mum doesn't know what she's talking about.'

'Tell me about it,' Jamie signed with a sigh.

'I will,' said Guy. 'Tomorrow. I'll see you at the sanctuary at five. Now get out of the way.'

Guy wrestled Jamie out of the bathroom doorway and closed himself in there. He wasn't blushing, was he? Guy peered closely at his face in the mirror. He needed a shave. Did he have time to bother? Should he bother? After all, he was only going to meet a work colleague. This wasn't a date.

In the Witch's cottage, Jennifer held up first one polo shirt and then another to her face as she stood in front of her own bathroom mirror. The pink one was her favourite, but Dahlia still maintained that the green one was more flattering with her complexion. Pink. Green. Pink. Green. Jennifer couldn't see much difference herself. How did the green one make her eyes 'pop out'? That didn't actually sound like such a plus point . . .

She looked at the clock. Seven thirty. She didn't have time to continue to ponder exactly what eyes 'popping out' meant. Jennifer put the pink shirt on. Then she took it off and pulled on the green one. Then the pink one again. The clock ticked forward to seven forty-five.

Green. Jennifer smoothed the shirt down over her waist. Then half laughed at her reflection. Why was she so worried how she looked when most days Guy saw her in a sludge-green overall anyway? Besides, they weren't even going on a date . . .

28

But if it wasn't a date, it bloody well felt like one. Jennifer's stomach rumbled loudly as she walked into the pub and scanned the tables for her new friend. Guy stood up as she approached him, suddenly finding manners that he certainly didn't employ in the staff room at Prowdes.

And then there were the compliments.

'You look lovely,' he said.

Jennifer blushed crimson and immediately fumbled in her bag for the book on chimpanzee husbandry she had promised Guy she would lend him to get the focus back on work.

'I think you'll find this useful,' she said.

'Yes. Thank you,' said Guy. 'I'll read it at once. Like a drink?'

Jennifer ordered mineral water to avoid any repetition of last night's debacle. Guy ordered half a pint and managed to spill most of it when he was setting the glass down on the table. Jennifer was similarly cack-handed, opening a bag of peanuts so that the contents scattered all over the floor. Each seemed so nervous it was as though that evening was the very first time they had ever met.

'Ulysses,' said Jennifer eventually, when she and Guy had finished gathering up stray peanuts. 'What are we going to do about him?'

'What indeed?' asked Guy.

'Assuming he's not about to get hauled off to be used as evidence in some trial, I'd like to introduce him to the main troop as quickly as possible. But he's at that awkward age,' she said. 'It might not be that easy. He's not so small that we can rely on one of the others to take him under their wing. And yet he's not quite big enough to hold his own against some of the more aggressive adults. What are your thoughts?'

'I wouldn't like to put him in any danger. I haven't met any chimp quite like him.'

'When I was in San Diego,' Jennifer began, 'we found that a good way to rehabilitate chimps of Ulysses' age was to pair them up with even younger chimps.'

'What was it like in San Diego?' Guy asked.

'Fantastic,' Jennifer sighed.

'I wish I'd gone to university,' said Guy. 'I read in the newspaper today that a boffin has just discovered that the difference in DNA between chimps and human beings is less than 0.1 per cent.'

'Yeah. They might have to reclassify chimps as human beings at this rate,' said Jennifer. 'They're closer to us than they are to gorillas or orangs. I used to love that statistic that man shares 99 per cent of his DNA with a banana,' she added.

'Snowy shares 100 per cent of his DNA with a banana,' said Guy.

Jennifer giggled and after that the conversation flowed a great deal more easily. Guy filled Jennifer in on life at Prowdes before she got there. He had her crying with laughter as he described an incident with a female orang called Helena, brought to the sanctuary in the hope that she might mate with Hector, that had instead developed a crush on Snowy and practically kidnapped the keeper when he went into their enclosure one afternoon. 'She had him backed up against the far fence and wouldn't let us anywhere near him for hours. Poor Snowy. He never was very good at telling girls no. That's basically how he got married.'

'Oh no!' Jennifer cried.

Hector never did get his oats. Helena was returned to the zoo she had come from the day after Snowy's close shave with the amorous ape.

'Tell me more,' said Jennifer in delight. 'Have any of the Prowdes inmates ever developed an unrequited crush on you?'

'Well, none of the female staff have,' he said, becoming shy all over again.

And then (all of a sudden it seemed, though they had in fact continued to banter for another two hours) the barman was calling last orders. The Boat House regulars were shuffling out into the car park on their walking sticks. Jennifer and Guy followed them out there and stood by her car to say their good-byes.

A gentle wind was blowing in from the sea. It lifted Jennifer's hair from behind her ear so that it covered her eyes. Guy reached out and pushed it back out of the way. His hand hesitated at the side of her face and she knew he was going to kiss her.

Jennifer felt so excited and nervous she wasn't sure she could stand up for long enough for Guy to get to her lips. She was relieved when he took the tops of her arms in his hands to pull her nearer. She kept her eyes open until their faces were so close together she had to go cross-eyed to focus on him.

'Is this OK?' Guy murmured softly.

'I think so,' said Jennifer. Their mouths were almost touching. She could feel the gentle percussion of his breath on her lips when he talked. Jennifer brought her own lips together in a tight little bud. Guy took a deep breath and . . .

'Hallelujah!'

An electronic version of the 'Hallelujah' chorus had the car-park kissers springing apart as though they had been caught by the teacher.

Then the tinny tones of another mobile phone trilled out 'The King of the Swingers'.

'What? Aaaaagh.' Guy dived for his pocket.

Simultaneously, Jennifer snatched her own mobile phone from her bag.

'Hello,' they answered their phones urgently, turning away from each other for privacy. 'Who is it?'

Jennifer's caller was Nessa and Guy's was the Major. Both were ringing to convey the same message.

'There's been a terrible fight in the chimpanzee enclosure,' said Nessa. 'Achilles went crazy. Do you think you could come here at once?'

Harrison the vet was already on his way but he would need Guy's help to get the injured chimp out of danger. Jennifer should be there too, experienced as she was in recognising the danger signals of a chimpanzee about to charge. Nessa sounded desperate. The Major was obviously trying not to panic. Guy and

Jennifer finished their calls and turned back to face one another. No time to kiss now.

'I'll drive,' Jennifer announced. They climbed into her car and headed for the sanctuary at top speed.

When Guy and Jennifer arrived at Prowdes, Harrison's car was already in the car park.

The sanctuary was quiet. Jennifer and Guy started off walking but unconsciously quickened their pace as they passed enclosure after enclosure of sleeping animals en route to the main chimpanzee habitat. It was clear that this was where the action was. Nessa and the Major stood by the wire with Harrison, who was on his knees by a body Jennifer couldn't identify.

As she saw Jennifer and Guy approach, Nessa tried a weak smile. But she was white-faced with worry.

'What happened?' Guy asked.

'It's Sacha,' Nessa motioned towards the chimpanzee on the ground. 'We heard the commotion while I was saying goodnight to the Major in the car park. We found Sacha by the gate when we got here.' Nessa loudly sniffed back a tear.

'Is he going to be all right?' Jennifer asked Harrison.

Harrison nodded. 'Yeah. It looks far worse than it is. I had to dart him so we could go in and pick him up. I couldn't properly see whether he'd broken any bones and I didn't want to risk freaking him out by causing him any more pain when we moved him.'

'It was a good job he was so near the gate,' the Major commented. He was still slightly out of breath from his exertions. His smart linen suit was covered in chimpanzee blood. 'It seems as though tempers are still running rather high in there.'

Nessa had turned on the enclosure floodlights. The other chimpanzees were mostly gathered around the climbing structure in the middle. The higher-ranking apes were right at the centre, close to Achilles, who was brandishing a tyre like a gladiator brandishing a shield. His hair was still puffed out and occasionally he gave a loud bark, which he accompanied by bashing his tyre against a metal pole.

'What's been going on?' Jennifer asked.

'I think Virginia is coming into oestrus,' Nessa told her. 'That always makes Achilles a bit insecure. And Sacha here must have got just a bit too close to Achilles' missus.'

'Achilles really did this,' said Jennifer sadly.

'Probably not just Achilles,' said Harrison. 'Though Achilles probably started it. It looks as though Sacha had more than one attacker.'

'Poor old Sacha,' said Nessa. 'He's never really fitted in. Not since Achilles arrived. He was Virginia's favourite until then but once she stopped defending him, he quickly slipped down the ranks. It was just a matter of time before they turned on him like this.'

Jennifer shuddered at the idea of the chimp in front of her now being ostracised and beaten. Despite her in-depth knowledge about chimpanzee culture and politics, she still hated to be reminded quite how dangerous they could be to each other. 'What can we do about Achilles' aggression?' she asked.

'Have him sent to charm school,' said Harrison with a sigh. 'I don't know. You could have him castrated. That might work.'

'No!' Nessa said at once. 'We can't do that. He's our best breeding male.'

'He can hardly go back to Africa without his balls,' added the Major. 'Sorry, Nessa.'

'I don't think he's being unusually aggressive,' Harrison concluded. 'Most of the time, the troop works pretty well. You've got to expect the odd skirmish. They're chimpanzees, after all, not angora bunnies. Okey-doke,' he said, standing up and brushing his hands together as though he had just fixed a puncture on a car. 'I think we're ready to roll. Let's get him to the sick bay, shall we?'

Guy took the other end of the stretcher and they carried Sacha off.

Nessa, Jennifer and the Major remained by the wire, watching Achilles display for his troop like a general mustering his forces.

'It breaks my heart when they act like this,' said Nessa. 'Even after all this time working with chimpanzees, it always takes me by surprise when they turn against each other. When they act in such a war-like, such a very *human*, manner really.'

Jennifer nodded.

'But I suppose I should be glad,' Nessa continued, 'that Achilles hasn't been turned into some big soft hairy pet by his time here. He needs to be able to defend himself against wild chimps if we're ever going to take him back to Africa, doesn't he?'

Jennifer nodded again.

'How are you?' Nessa asked then, turning to face Jennifer full on. 'I feel as though you have rather been thrown to the wolves since you arrived here,' she continued. 'I haven't had as much time to look after you as I hoped to have. The party fiasco . . .'

'Don't even mention it,' said Jennifer sincerely.

'And before that there were so many things to worry about with the financial situation. But that's all sorted now with the television show, thank goodness. We'll be able to get on with planning a better future for our chimps. Tell me, Jennifer, how have you been finding life here at Prowdes? Now that we've got a bit of money again, what do you need to help you do your job here? New computer? I'm terribly sorry about the mess Mad made of your old one. Do you need more research materials? Just let me know what you want.'

'I've got everything I need,' said Jennifer.

'Oh, poor Sacha,' Nessa sighed again. 'Ah well,' she squeezed Jennifer's arm. 'I'm sure he'll be all right. Things can only get better!' She gave a big, beaming 'buck up the troops' smile. 'I'm so glad you're here with us at Prowdes. I hope you know that, Dr N.'

'You're a wonderful young lady,' the Major added. 'We know you're going to get our chimps back to the jungle.'

Jennifer walked back to the big house with Nessa and the Major, each of them linking an arm through one of hers so that they looked like Dorothy and friends hitting the yellow brick road. As they walked, Jennifer felt tears itching at her eyes. It wasn't just because of what had happened to poor Sacha. In a strange way, they were tears of happiness. Because for the first time in a very long time, Jennifer felt as though she might have found her place in the world. Exasperating as her first two months at Prowdes had been, through that evening with Guy, and through Nessa and the Major's kind words, Jennifer suddenly knew that her contribution had been noticed and appreciated. She suddenly realised just how much she had come to love this crazy, disorganised place, the animals who lived there and the staff she worked alongside. She was a real part of the team at last.

'And you know what,' she told her new friends. 'I feel lucky.'

29

Not that lucky.

While Jennifer set about Project Africa with renewed enthusiasm, Faith O'Connell was also hard at work in the stark windowless offices of Animal House Entertainment in London's glamorous Shepherd's Bush.

Late in the afternoon, at about the same time as Jennifer was joining the other keepers in the hay-bale horseplay for the first time since her arrival at Prowdes and then making shy arrangements to meet Guy at the pub again the following evening, Faith was shuttling across the capital in a taxi, en route to a meeting that might make her career as a television producer. And ruin Dr Jennifer Niederhauser's life.

Prowdes had definitely been chosen over Howletts and Monkey World as the primate project the Animal House cameras would be following that summer. Faith was confident that she had made the right choice as she stepped out of the cab and walked into the offices of Taylor Green, the talent agency, for the meeting that would determine the final piece of the puzzle, the programme's presenter. The man who would guarantee the ratings to make Faith's chimpanzee show a success.

Timothy Lauder looked every inch the nascent television star when he walked into the meeting at his agent's swanky office on Haymarket. Faith was impressed to see that he looked even better in grey Armani slacks and a cashmere sloppy joe than he did in the jungle fatigues he wore in the promotional tape she had watched so avidly. He still had a slight tan from the last few months spent tracking chimps for a BBC series on African wildlife which was already being touted as that autumn's sure-fire prime-time hit. His sun-bleached hair was still slightly long and wonderfully ruffleable.

As he kissed both his agent, Felicity Taylor, and Faith 'hello' with perfect 'med-ja' air kisses, Timothy Lauder reflected briefly on how far he had come from his days in his first dingy little office in the zoology department at Oxford. These days he had a far more glamorous office in a sixteenth-century building overlooking the beautiful front quad of St Francis Hall, as befitted his status as a senior fellow of the college. It was panelled in dark wood and a real fire crackled in the grate during the winter. If Timothy were that kind of man, he might have said that the energy of his predecessors and scientific heroes emanated from the walls, pushing him on to greater academic achievements. But Timothy Lauder wasn't that kind of man.

Faith's production company had been thrilled by how photogenic the Oxford office was. If he agreed to front their programme about this chimpanzee rehabilitation project in Devon, then part of the deal was that Timothy would do links and deliver a few closing words of wisdom at the end of each segment from his Oxford room. The American networks would love that. A bit of old country charm. And it was important to Timothy that he impress the Americans too. A lecture tour of the American universities was a lucrative proposition.

Dr Timothy Lauder's career was definitely on the rise. Just that day, a journalist from one of the big Sunday newspapers had telephoned to ask him to comment on the news that his appearance as presenter on a nature series for a children's cable channel had been a factor in a 300 per cent rise in the number of female students applying to read biology at Oxford.

'As long as they're all pretty blonde girls, I'm delighted,' he laughed. 'But joking aside,' he added in his most serious 'devoted to academia' voice, 'I feel very privileged to have been able to inspire so many bright young minds to consider biology as a career. At a time when applications to read sciences are falling as a whole across the British university system, it is vital that we engage the interest of our young people in any way we can. Many of these kids don't even seem to think that science is an option. If television is the medium that works best in reminding them of just how rewarding the study of science can be, then the government should be coercing the BBC to spend more of the licence fee payers' money on programmes exploring natural history. We need more natural history shows.'

Faith O'Connell was certainly working on it.

Specifically, she had been working on setting up a vehicle for Timothy Lauder for months. Getting him as a presenter had been the first objective for the show, before they even decided which animals they were going to be watching. Faith knew that Timothy's BBC series would send his career into orbit and have everyone in the industry making offers. Indeed that was the case. There had been many very good offers. Timothy's agent, Felicity, found a new one on her desk every morning. But Faith knew that Timothy was about to take hers when she heard Felicity's assistant shout, just outside the office door, 'Is that champagne cold enough yet?'

Ten minutes later, the very same champagne – only Veuve Clicquot but vintage – was on Felicity's desk and the three of them were toasting a deal well done.

'There really was no other offer that interested us quite so much,' Felicity confirmed.

'Brilliant. We start filming as soon as possible,' said Faith.

'Can't wait,' said Timothy. 'I think we're going to have a lot of fun working together, you and I.'

He fixed her with his famous smile. The smile that had made a thousand cable-viewing teenage girls apply to read biology at St Francis Hall, Oxford. Was he flirting with her, Faith wondered. She tried her best not to drop her gaze from his, thus letting him know she was flattered and slightly discombobulated by the attention.

'Tell me one more time,' he asked. 'Who is actually heading up the project at Prowdes? It might be a good idea for me to liaise with him before we go down there to start shooting. Get a handle on what he's been doing so far. Where he's coming from, if you know what I—'

'It's a her,' Faith interrupted. 'The coordinator of the project is a woman. She got her PhD quite recently. Did her post-graduate study up in Edinburgh and an exchange placement in San Diego.'

'San Diego. That sounds good. What's her name?'

'Jennifer something,' Faith said. 'Needenhouse. I think that's how you pronounce it. Do you know of her?'

Timothy paused and looked up and away as though he were leafing through a little black book of chimpanzee experts in his brain. A smile flickered at the corner of his mouth then disappeared.

'Nope,' he said eventually. Decisively. 'Jennifer Needenhouse? I don't think I do. Any more of that champers, Felicity?'

'All gone,' said the agent, tipping the empty bottle upside down in its make-shift ice bucket – a real plastic bucket that normally lived under the sink in the agency's tiny kitchen.

'Then we must take Faith for another glass at the Ritz at once.'

'I'd love to, but I've got another meeting,' said Felicity apologetically. 'My less successful clients need me to look after them too.'

'Never mind. In that case,' said Timothy, fixing his new producer with that look again, 'I guess it's just you and me. Shall we go?'

He helped Faith into her butter-soft suede jacket and offered her his arm as he guided her out of the office and into the lift.

Like a lamb to the slaughter, thought Felicity as she watched Faith go. A lamb to the slaughter. She would have to have a word with him about it one day. Timothy needed to know whose affections he could afford to play with and which relationships were best left on a purely professional footing. Faith O'Connell definitely fell into the latter category. She was one of the best in her industry. She had the ear of every important network boss. And nothing could stall a promising television career faster than a high-flying woman producer scorned.

30

Jamie had considered skipping that afternoon's rendezvous with Guy at the sanctuary, but the news that Prowdes was going to be the subject of a television programme about the chimpanzees had suddenly made the sanctuary a far cooler place to hang out than the fountain in the middle of Tincastle. So much so that when Jamie told his mates that he had to skip a trip to the chippy to get to Prowdes on time, several of them volunteered to come with him.

Jamie sent a text message to Guy's mobile phone asking whether he could bring some friends along too. And at five o'clock, four teenagers from Jamie's school arrived to help tidy up a day's worth of mess. Guy and Nessa quickly set them to work sweeping through the gardens with big black bin bags, picking up litter for the price of a couple of Mars Bars and a promise that, yes, when the TV cameras arrived, the eager helpers would be allowed to visit the sanctuary for free to appear in any crowd scenes.

When the litter sweep was over, Jamie popped his head round the door of the chimpanzee nursery to tell Guy that he was going back into town with his mates, to eat chips and hang out by the fountain again.

'Oh no you're not,' Guy signed.

'But the litter's all picked up now. Just give me my tenner. I'll see you later on.'

'Jamie, this isn't about the litter and you know it. I wanted to get you on your own. To talk to you about how you're getting on. At school and that.'

'I'm getting on fine,' Jamie signed with a frown.

'Then I can't blame problems at school for the fact that you're being so rude to your mother?'

'What are you on about? I haven't been rude to her.'

'Hello, you old bitch,' Guy signed like a pro.

Jamie's face dropped. 'I didn't think she could understand me.'

Guy raised an eyebrow. 'Are you coming in or not?'

Jamie signed 'see you later' to his friends, then reluctantly stepped inside the nursery complex properly and let the door shut behind him.

'She was very upset,' Guy continued. 'Especially when you tried to tell her that she'd misread what you signed because she hasn't learned enough signs because she doesn't care if she can communicate with you or not.'

'I said I was sorry.'

'Sorry, you old bitch, wasn't it?'

Jamie let his chin drop on to his chest. He sat down on one of the deckchairs. Mad and Bad shrieked to be allowed out of their cage to join their long-lost friend, remembering happy afternoons spent wrestling with Jamie on the lawn in front of their block, but Jamie kept his back turned towards them.

'Do you want to tell me about it?' Guy signed.

'She just doesn't get it. She's making my life a misery. Everyone else is allowed out on a school night so why not me?'

'Who's everyone?' Guy asked.

'Jake, Owen, Kerry,' Jamie reeled off the names. Or rather the symbols that had come to represent his friends' names in his own private lexicon. Rather than laboriously spell out each name letter by letter, he made signs that described their physical attributes. So Jake was 'broken glasses', though it was three years since he had turned up at school with a pair of National Health Service frames held together with a sticking plaster. Owen was 'scar face' for the pale white stripe across his pink chin. He rather liked that moniker. It made him sound hard. Though the scar in question was the result of tripping over his own shoelaces as a four-year-old, rather than any bad-assed brawling. Kerry was 'curly blonde'. Or 'curvy blonde' to the boys, now that puberty had well and truly set in.

Guy smiled as Jamie explained that all three of his friends were allowed out on week-nights and until midnight at weekends. What Jamie failed to take into consideration was the fact that they were all at least two years older than him. Travelling all the way to Exeter for school meant that he didn't have a wide choice of schoolmates to hang out with in Tincastle outside school hours. Jake, Owen and Kerry were the only other deaf kids within easy reach.

'If I can't stay out later, they're going to stop wanting to hang out with me and then I'll have no mates at all,' Jamie concluded.

Guy sympathised.

'I bet they understand that you can't stay out as late as they can,' he tried.

Jamie shrugged and looked away.

'Where's the new chimp?' he asked eventually.

'There.' Guy pointed towards the lump of blanket in the quarantine cage. 'He doesn't seem too excited to be here.'

'Not the only one,' said Jamie.

'Here,' Guy handed Jamie a banana. 'I'm getting everyone who comes in here to see if they can get some kind of interaction going with him.'

Jamie shrugged again but he crouched down low in front of the wire and poked the banana through a gap in the mesh.

'Perhaps he doesn't like bananas,' Jamie signed when Ulysses didn't emerge.

'Perhaps he doesn't like you,' Guy joked. 'After all, you do smell pretty bad.'

Jamie hurled the banana at Guy's head. They wrestled for a moment in front of the cages. When Jamie was really small, Guy had been able to pick him up and throw him over his shoulder, but that was definitely getting harder to do. Mad and Bad enjoyed the spectacle. If the cage door had been open, the twins would have joined in.

Eventually, Guy let Jamie win the fight and they stood panting side by side in front of Ulysses' cage again. The kerfuffle had at least caused Ulysses to peek out from beneath his grey woollen mantle.

'Ugly, isn't he?' signed Jamie when he saw the new chimp's face.

'Don't say things like that in front of him,' Guy joshed. 'Here. Try again.'

Guy picked up another banana. Jamie poked it through the wire and stood up again to watch what happened. It seemed as though hours passed while they watched the little chimp beneath his blanket edge closer and closer to the fruit, shuffling like a kid playing grandmother's footsteps before a hairy hand suddenly darted out from beneath the blanket and Ulysses raced back to his corner with his prize.

Guy and Jamie high-fived each other.

'You've got the magic touch.'

Ulysses kept his gaze on Jamie the whole time he peeled and ate the banana.

'I think he likes you,' Guy signed.

'It's because I understand what it's like to be an outsider,' Jamie replied dramatically.

'I can't ask your mother to let you have a later curfew even if you did persuade a starving chimpanzee to eat.'

'Couldn't you at least try?' Jamie asked.

'If you can persuade Ulysses to eat this,' said Guy, handing Jamie a banana which had been spiked with the chimp's medication.

Jamie took the banana eagerly.

'Come on, sailor-ape,' he signed.

'I don't think he understands British Sign Language,' Guy teased.

'Yeah. Like he understands any human language at all,' Jamie retorted.

Ulysses ventured across to Jamie again, leaving the blanket behind this time. He sat down just close enough to the wire so that he could reach the banana if he stretched out his pointed black fingertips as far as possible. Discovering that he couldn't get a proper grip on the fruit from that distance, he shuffled just an inch closer still and then performed another quick dart and snatch.

'Manners!' Jamie signed. Ulysses' sudden darting forward like that had given him a shock. 'Didn't even say thank you,' Jamie continued.

Then something extraordinary happened.

Afterwards, Jamie and Guy both stared at the ape in front of them, not signing anything to each other as they tried to work out whether they really had just seen what they thought they saw. It was impossible. Absolutely impossible.

Jamie was the first to put his surprise into words.

'That chimp just signed thank you!'

'I thought I was seeing things,' Guy signed back.

'Has he done it before?'

'Not that I've seen. Will he do it again?'

Guy watched intently as Jamie signed 'thank you' at Ulysses again in an attempt to provoke an action replay. He got what he wanted. The little chimp moved his hand close to his mouth and made the downward moving gesture again.

'He's really signing!' Jamie forgot his teenage cool for a moment and jumped up and down on the spot, clapping his hands together with delight.

Ulysses had raised his hairy black hands to chest height and was steepling his fingers as though taking a deep breath before speaking.

'What's he saying now?' Guy asked.

'I don't know. Nothing. Not yet.'

Slowly, Ulysses brought the forefinger of his right hand to his ear.

'I think he's asking whether I can hear anything,' said Jamie.

'Or scratching his ear,' signed Guy. 'He might just be scratching his ear.'

'No. He's signing. Definitely.'

Guy shook his head. 'Not definitely. Maybe it was just random. Let's not get excited.'

'That's not random,' signed Jamie. 'That's hello.'

Guy had heard about chimps that had been taught to sign before but he had never actually seen one. Nessa had bought him a book about the signing chimp projects in America, but upon reading it he had been disappointed. Fierce arguments raged in the scientific community about whether the chimps' actions really had any meaning at all, whether it was possible for them to sign spontaneously, or whether they were always merely copying their keepers.

Ulysses might simply have been copying Jamie. When Guy asked Jamie to stop signing for a moment, Ulysses stopped too. Whatever, Jamie was utterly convinced that the chimpanzee was interacting with him.

'Man, that was awesome. I can't wait to tell the guys at school.' Jamie already had his mobile phone out of his pocket, poised to send a group text. He got as far as typing 'I just met a signing ch' before Guy snatched the phone away. He took Jamie by the shoulders to make sure that they were face to face. He held him there until he was sure that Jamie was going to be properly focused on what he was about to sign, just as he had done when he needed to tell Jamie off as a smaller child.

'What have I done now?' Jamie protested automatically, reverting to the nine-year-old who had just kicked a ball through a window or run out into the road without checking for traffic in both directions.

'Nothing. You haven't done anything,' Guy assured him. 'But you're not going to do anything either. We've got to keep this secret. No one else must know about what you saw today.'

'Why not?'

'Because perhaps we didn't really see him sign. And if we did, perhaps it's best that we wait a while before we let anyone else find out. Because, in case you didn't know, we have a television crew arriving here at Prowdes in less than a week and if they find out that Ulysses might be able to sign, the whole thing will turn into a freak show. I don't want him to be hounded any more than he already is going to be when the cameras arrive.'

Jamie shrugged.

'I'm serious, Jamie. Do you promise?'

'I promise,' Jamie solemnly signed. Then he added, 'For twenty quid. On top of the tenner you already owe me.'

'You are a nasty little piece of work sometimes,' said Guy. But he duly handed the notes over.

When Jamie was gone, Guy went back to Ulysses' enclosure and stared at the peculiar chimp once more.

'What else do you know?' he signed.

Ulysses communicated nothing in reply.

31

As she drove into work the following morning, Jennifer sang at the top of her voice. She was thrilled to find that, once again, she and Guy were in convoy as they turned into the little lane that led to the sanctuary. They parked their cars side by side. Guy leapt out of his car so that he could open the door to hers.

'Thank you!' she grinned at him. 'I can't wait for tonight.'

'Me neither,' said Guy. Not least because he wanted to tell her about Ulysses. Far away from the sanctuary, so that no one would overhear him.

'Where shall we go?' Jennifer asked. 'To our local?' she added with the kind of coquettish smile she didn't think she had in her repertoire. But her flirtatiousness was to be cut tragically short.

Nessa popped her head out of the window to her office like a cuckoo clock chiming the hour.

'Thank goodness you're both here!' she said. 'I've been waiting for you for ages.'

'What's happened? Is Sacha OK?' Jennifer and Guy simultaneously assumed the worst.

'Still a bit sore, I expect. But Harrison says he's going to make a complete recovery. No, this is really *good* news . . .' Nessa assured them. 'I got an e-mail from Faith O'Connell at Animal House. It's all terribly exciting. They've chosen the chap who's going to be presenter on our programme. I think you might have heard of him, Jennifer. He's one of the leading lights in the primatology world. And he has the kind of looks to die for, to boot.'

'Can't think who that would be,' said Jennifer. 'Perhaps it's studying apes for so long that makes most primatologists end up looking like them.'

'Oh no. This chap is very handsome. As soon as I got Faith's e-mail, I had him googled!' Nessa was a devoted silver surfer and

170

tapped the names of everyone she ever met into *www.google.com*. 'He's a terribly serious academic. He's a fellow at some college in Oxford. He's written hundreds of books. He's already presented a children's programme about apes on a cable channel and he's got a series coming out on the BBC later this summer. Faith is going to send the tapes over so we can get a proper look at the man.'

'Great. But what's his name?' Guy pressed her.

'Dr Timothy Lauder,' said Nessa.

32

Jennifer woke up to find Nessa and Guy staring down at her where she lay on the gravel.

'Are you OK?' Guy immediately helped her to her feet.

'What happened?'

'We were just standing here talking and you passed out,' said Nessa. 'I knew you had been working too hard and not eating properly. Look at you, Jennifer. You're like a rake. You need to look after yourself more.'

Guy helped Jennifer to a bench. Nessa followed, dispensing more advice on sleep and nutrition as they went.

'You're probably right,' Jennifer agreed listlessly, though in reality she knew damn well that it wasn't skipping her cornflakes that morning that had sent her crashing to the gravel.

'Oh, what can we do with you?' Nessa sighed. 'Would you like to have a nap or something?'

'I think I'd just like to go home,' Jennifer said quietly.

'I'll drive you,' Guy volunteered immediately.

'No,' said Jennifer. 'I think I'd rather drive myself.'

'See you later?' he asked.

Jennifer nodded and walked back to her car.

In fact, Jennifer didn't go straight back to the cottage at all. Instead, she drove her little red car out of Tincastle altogether, across the moors and down towards the sea. She parked her car in a clifftop car park and set out along a path that she had taken many times as a child. Every Sunday morning for almost fifteen years, her father had taken her for a walk while her mother prepared Sunday lunch (which in reality simply involved leaving pans of peas to boil dry while she gossiped on the phone with her best friend).

It was on those walks that Jennifer's father had first fostered her interest in the natural world. Mr Niederhauser had studied biology as an undergraduate. He had done a year's exchange placement from his university in Munich, Germany, to Exeter, which is where he had met Jennifer's mother. When it was decided that they would live in Britain rather than Germany after their marriage, Gerd Niederhauser had thrown himself into learning all about his adopted country. He always had a book in his pocket on those walks and looked up the name of every unfamiliar wild flower that bloomed along that stretch of coast. Soon he could recognise every one and pick out the individual songs of at least a dozen birds that made their home along the sometimes inhospitable north Devon coast. Jennifer learned alongside him.

From the cliff path, Jennifer and her father would pick their way down to a secluded beach and paddle in rock pools, tickling anemones until they pulled in their tentacles in annoyance, trying to prise limpets off the rocks, collecting mussels which Mrs Niederhauser would always graciously accept and then refuse to cook for fear of poisoning her husband and only child. Jennifer was still grateful for her early education. Setting out on her walk that morning, she at least knew the names of each and every flower she carelessly pulled up by the roots in anger as she passed.

'Bloody, buggering Speedwell,' she hissed, as she snatched at the little blue buds.

The tide was in. Seagulls wheeled high above her head calling to one another noisily. It was such a long way down to the sea that sometimes the seagulls hung in the air level with Jennifer's feet. When Jennifer reached the very edge of the cliff, she stared down into the metal-grey water and felt an urge to pitch herself forwards and into it. It would have been so easy to walk out, using the backs of the seagulls as stepping stones to oblivion. Perhaps it was the best solution. She would be swept away in an instant. Dr Timothy Lauder's crashing back into her life would become instantly irrelevant.

Talk about coming down to earth with a bump. It didn't seem possible that such a short time ago, Jennifer had truly been able to say that she had never felt happier, more settled and more optimistic in her life. It was as though at the moment she heard about Timothy's appointment as consultant and presenter on the television programme, someone had swapped her rose-tinted spectacles for dark glasses. Nothing looked as good as it had done before. Not even Guy. Especially Guy . . .

Jennifer's mobile phone beeped. The signal out there on the clifftop was sporadic. Jennifer expected to discover that she had missed a call. But it was a text message. From Guy.

'R U OK?' he asked.

Jennifer sighed. She hated text messages. She hated the re-tarded way that people used single capital letters instead of proper words. It was a symptom of a general dumbing-down in society, she had decided. She could already see the widespread damage it was causing. When Jo-Jo filled out forms about Hector, she occasionally used text speak there, too.

Jennifer looked at the text message and sighed again. But this time, it wasn't because of the spelling. It was because she realised that yet another bubble had burst. Just a few hours previously she had been looking forward to getting to work, looking forward to seeing Guy . . . A few hours previously, this simple text message would have filled her with something approaching girlish excite-ment. But that moment had passed. Just the thought of Timothy Lauder was enough to bring her back from her short trip to cloud-cuckoo-land, a land where it was even desirable that she should get together with a man like Guy Gibson.

What had she been thinking? She must have been drunk. Well, she definitely had been drunk that day of the tea party but . . . It was such a good job that Nessa's phone call about Sacha had interrupted them before they had a chance to kiss. Guy wasn't right for her. No matter how much she found him physically attractive. He was a nice enough man. He was devoted to the animals. Everybody liked him. But there would always be some-thing missing. A cerebral aspect to the relationship that Jennifer just couldn't see existing between her with her PhD and her passion for opera and him with his terrible texts.

The reason why it had taken so long to find Timothy Lauder in the first place and the reason why she hadn't found anyone to replace him in her affections since was because he was unique among men. He was irreplaceable. He had been the perfect combination of everything she admired, and in all probability he still was. He couldn't have changed that much. How on earth would she cope, seeing him again, having everything she had ever wanted so close by and yet no longer hers?

Jennifer deleted Guy's text message from her telephone without replying to it. She continued along the cliff path, hands in pockets, contemplating doomsday. The inevitable moment when she and Timothy Lauder would come face to face again.

But was it inevitable? Jennifer hesitated at the cliff edge. She held out her arms and felt the wind try to lift her off her feet. It would be so easy. And it was the perfect kind of suicide since it didn't have to look deliberate. People would just assume that she had got too close to the edge and lost her balance. She would hate for the bastard to think that she had actually killed herself for him! Given the way that his life had obviously developed since she saw him last, he would probably make a TV documentary about depressed single women on the back of it.

Jennifer sat down in the grass before she really did accidentally tip herself into the abyss. There was no point killing herself that day. She could still resign her job and flee the country after all.

33

'Oh my God, oh my God, oh my God!'

These days Dahlia had given up saying 'hello' when Jennifer picked up the phone.

Within half a day of Nessa receiving the e-mail to confirm that Timothy Lauder had been chosen for the documentary, everyone in Tincastle knew. Nessa told Jo-Jo who told the Major, who told Guido at the trattoria, who told his wife, Julia, who told one of the other mothers at the school when she went to pick up their daughter. Unlike Jennifer, who watched television so infrequently that she didn't even know there was a fifth terrestrial channel in the United Kingdom, plenty of people in town knew exactly who Timothy Lauder was and why they might have good reason to be excited. The news spread faster than the latest nits outbreak at Tincastle junior school. No one needed to wait for Nessa's interview in that evening's edition of the local paper. Except Dahlia, who had been on the road all day in her capacity as a sales rep for a children's wear manufacturer.

Jennifer could tell that Dahlia was peeved.

'I can't believe I had to find out your big news along with all the other nobodies in this village,' she complained.

'Well, I haven't exactly been spreading it.'

'Jennifer, I am your best friend. If you've got a problem you can always come to me. You can call me any time. It doesn't matter if you think I'll be at work. I will always take your call. How are you coping, my dear?'

'I'm fine,' said Jennifer. That familiar refrain.

'I'm on my way.'

Dahlia dropped in on Jennifer on her way home from work. She had taken the precaution of buying a huge bar of milk chocolate at the garage en route.

'Emergency aid,' she said when Jennifer opened the door. Though both of them knew that Dahlia would be eating most of it.

'People come back into our lives for a reason,' Dahlia suggested two cups of tea later. 'Especially if we have unfinished business with them. I think that Timothy is coming back into your life so that you can finally see him for the idiot he is. You've mythologised him over the years.'

Jennifer raised her eyebrows at Dahlia's long word.

'You have this image of a man who isn't really real.'

'I mostly have an image of his bare bottom as he shagged that student,' Jennifer corrected. 'And every time I think about it, I hear the overture from *William Tell*.'

'Well, that must be a psychic drain,' said Dahlia.

'I am not ready for this,' said Jennifer.

'But you should be. You've had five years to get ready,' Dahlia told her smugly. 'If you'd followed my advice and got proper closure . . .'

Jennifer scowled.

'Please spare me the lecture. What can I do now? Just tell me, what can I do?'

'Get highlights, lose thirty pounds, spend three hundred pounds on a dress you won't feel comfortable in to impress him,' Dahlia said sarcastically. 'Relax. Let it happen. Just be yourself.'

Just be yourself. The most useless piece of advice in the English language.

'I'm going to leave my job,' Jennifer announced.

'Are you mad?'

'No. It's the only way to avoid him. It isn't as though I've been having such a great time there anyway. The staff and the animals all hate me. I'm making no progress towards rehabilitating them at all. Why should I hang on in there and give Timothy the pleasure of seeing that I'm failing as a conservationist in the same way I obviously failed as a girlfriend?'

'Do you really think you're failing at your job?'

'I don't know what I'm supposed to be doing,' Jennifer con-

177

fided. 'I mean, where to start? I thought we were supposed to be helping the animals to become more independent with a view to releasing them into the wild some day. But kind-hearted as Nessa is, she really hasn't thought about the logistics of it. You can't just take a load of chimps across to Africa by boat and let them get out on the beach and fend for themselves. Take Sacha. He's one of our males. He was raised in a beach bar in Spain. He used to sit on one of the bar stools, drinking whisky and smoking cigarettes. And he developed one hell of a habit. You can probably imagine. Everybody wanted to see the chimpanzee smoke a cigarette. He was getting through more than forty a day. He doesn't get any cigarettes at all now, but he's still a long way off being anything like the kind of chimps I tracked in the Gabon. He's never had to hunt and forage for food. When he arrived at the sanctuary two years ago, he didn't even know how to make a nest.'

'Why would he?' Dahlia asked. 'He isn't a bird.'

Jennifer just rolled her eyes.

'And then there's the new chimp. Ulysses. I'm completely at my wits' end with that one. I can't seem to get any kind of interaction going with him at all. Timothy would have been able to. He probably *will* be able to. I know exactly what's going to happen, Dahlia. He'll walk into that sanctuary like the bastard son of the great Attenborough himself and be able to accomplish in a week what I have been trying to get done for months. They'll all roll over and let him tickle their tummies. Animals and staff. Jo-Jo won't click her heels in a Nazi salute if Timothy suggests that she tidies up Hector's enclosure before it becomes a health hazard.

'I thought,' Jennifer continued, 'when I took the job at Prowdes, that I would be able to make a difference. But I'm not making a difference. And I can't bear for Timothy to see how I've failed. I'm leaving.'

'Jenny,' Dahlia squeezed her best friend round the shoulders. 'You really don't need to do that. Not because of Timothy Lauder.'

'He's just made me realise how ill-suited I am to sanctuary life. I'm obviously a theorist and I can't put my theories into action. I'm better off sticking to my books. I'm going to hand in my notice tomorrow morning.'

The phone rang.

'Shall I get that for you?' Dahlia asked.

'No,' said Jennifer. 'Let the machine get it instead. I don't want to talk to anybody else tonight. If you don't mind going, Dahlia, I've got a letter of resignation to write.'

What is the most terrifying thing you have ever faced in your life?

Sometimes, the things which we have real reason to be scared of – fire, flood, snakes, lions, tigers, bears, driving through the Wandsworth one-way system in a hire car – turn out to be relatively easy to cope with. It's as though our bodies know what to do when faced by real peril. You see a fire. Your body cranks up the adrenalin and you get yourself and your loved ones away. Your car skids on black ice and goes veering across the road towards the edge of a ravine. Once again, adrenalin comes to the rescue, making time appear to slow down so that you are able to react appropriately, turning into the skid instead of fighting against it, thus saving yourself from death in a ditch.

But there are no primeval tactics to cope with the things that scare the average modern girl. There's no adrenalin rush to rescue you just before you walk out of the ladies' room into that important meeting with a ribbon of loo roll attached to your shoe or your skirt tucked up into your knickers. There's no adrenalin rush to prevent you from buying three pairs of un-suitable shoes in a sale and incurring the wrath of your bank manager. And there's no adrenalin rush to make you heroic in the face of ex-boyfriends.

In her twenty-seven years, Jennifer had faced some things that most people would rate pretty highly on the 'terrifying' scale. She had tracked apes through African countries torn apart by civil war, running the risk that she might encounter not just a *gori*lla but a *guer*rilla armed to the teeth and drunk on the joy of killing. She had been in plenty of face-offs with angry chimpanzees who could have ripped her arms off for fun. She had overcome her fear of snakes after waking up to find that a particularly poisonous one had spent the night with her in her sleeping bag.

On a more prosaic level, she had taken hundreds of exams and presented papers at conferences numbering thousands of people, all of them experts in her field who would be more than happy to tear her research apart if it didn't agree with their own.

She wasn't afraid of physical harm or public speaking. She knew what to do if a chip pan caught fire (and had, in fact, once saved Dahlia's kitchen from burning down by fetching a damp tea towel to throw over the pan when an experiment in deep-frying pineapple rings went wrong).

But that night, Jennifer was scared and she didn't know what to do to make that feeling go except throw away her entire career.

34

Guy didn't have such a great evening either. At nine o'clock he gave up waiting for Jennifer to walk into the bar at the Boat House. He had assumed, when he called her at home at eight o'clock and got no answer, that she must be on her way to meet him. But her house was only ten minutes away by car. An hour was a generous amount of time to wait, even if the whole town was clogged up by farmers moving their sheep from field to field (a less unusual occurrence than one might expect in Devon).

At nine o'clock Guy called Jennifer's home phone again. Once more the answer-machine kicked in with its curt little message. 'You have reached Dr Jennifer Niederhauser. Please speak after the tone.' Guy didn't speak after the tone. He had already left one message that night. Perhaps she had gone to bed early, given that she had obviously been feeling unwell earlier that day. He wished she'd called to let him know.

Instead of going straight home, Guy went back to the sanctuary. He couldn't bear the idea of going to the Wily Fox while the bar was still open and having to face all the bar staff who would want a proper reason why he was back so early. Far better to be at work. When he got there, he found Snowy dozing in the nursery unit. Snowy was supposed to be on duty that night.

'Think I might be coming down with something!' he said in his defence when Guy woke him up.

'Don't worry about it,' said Guy. 'I'll take over here.'

'Hey,' Snowy remembered. 'Aren't you supposed to be . . .'

'Nah. Will you do me a favour and look in on Sacha before you leave?'

'Sure. Are you certain you want to take my shift?'

'You can owe me a favour,' said Guy.

Sacha was fine. As was the goat that was inhabiting the sick-bay cage next to him. Uncle Tom, as the goat was called, had cut his muzzle on a carelessly discarded Coke can.

Guy waited until he heard Snowy's car pull out of the car park before he sat down in the deckchair opposite Ulysses' cage. It was as if Ulysses had been waiting for Snowy to go too, because he wasn't asleep at all. When he was certain that only Guy was out in the corridor, Ulysses moved the blanket from his face again.

Guy felt inexplicably nervous as he signed 'hello'.

No reaction from the chimpanzee.

'There,' Guy said to himself. 'No reaction. I imagined it. You didn't sign at all the other day.'

But then Ulysses sat up. The blanket fell away so that his head and shoulders were completely exposed. And his hands.

Guy felt like a NASA scientist in the moment that followed, waiting for a response to a signal beamed into deepest space. Would there be a reply? Was there anybody out there? It was as though a radio channel had crackled into life. There was possibility in that crackle. But was anything intelligible about to come through?

'Hello,' Ulysses signed back.

'Hello,' Guy signed again.

'Hello,' signed Ulysses.

'Hello,' signed Guy.

'Hello,' Ulysses signed more slowly this time. It was almost as though he wondered why the keeper kept repeating himself.

'Water?' Guy asked the question out loud as he made the shapes with his hands.

'Water.' Ulysses made the gestures too.

'Water?' Guy asked again.

Ulysses nodded. At least, it seemed like a nod. It was more like the kind of clumsy head-banging lolling of the head that toddlers make when they are learning the nod but find themselves surprised by the weight of their heads when they do. Guy took it as a nod. 'Water,' Guy made the symbol again.

Ulysses repeated the loll-nod.

Guy went to the basin. He filled a bowl. There was no doubt about it. Ulysses was making symbols.

'Cup?' Guy asked, forming the shape with his hands.

'Cup,' Ulysses pointed towards the big striped mug that was actually Guy's own. Jo-Jo had given it to him for his birthday.

'That's my cup,' Guy signed in amusement.

'My cup,' Ulysses repeated.

'Are you just copying me?' Guy asked.

Still, he filled the cup with water and passed it to the ape. Ulysses took the cup by the handle confidently and lifted it to his lips without spilling a drop.

'Pity there's no market for tea-drinking chimps on TV any more,' Guy commented. Ulysses looked at him as if to say, 'I beg your pardon.'

'You know. The PG tips chimps,' Guy explained. 'Oh, why am I telling you that? You're not interested, are you?'

Ulysses handed the cup back to Guy.

'Thank you.'

'Thank you,' Ulysses signed. The signal that had started it all.

'I was going to tell her about you tonight,' Guy said. 'But she didn't turn up at the Boat House. I don't know whether that's because she's not feeling well or because she just didn't feel like turning up to see me. Probably a good job. It was stupid of me to ever think that she was really interested. She's my boss. I'm just one of the keepers. When this Timothy Lauder bloke turns up, she'll probably be all over him. Jo-Jo's been going crazy about the news. She used to watch his programme on kids' TV. There was a picture of him in the paper tonight. He may have all those letters after his name, but I can't help thinking he looks like a bit of a tosser. Still, women like tossers, don't they? Being nice doesn't seem to win you any points when it comes to women,' Guy concluded sadly.

All the time, Ulysses watched as though he was interested in what Guy had to say.

'They like arrogant and they like intelligent,' said Guy. 'I expect Dr Timothy Lauder will be able to work out in half a minute whether you really know how to sign or whether you're just copying everything I do. Yeah, it's a good job Jennifer didn't turn up and I didn't tell her that I think you can understand sign language. She'd only have laughed.'

Guy swilled the chimpanzee slobber off his mug and made himself a cup of tea.

'Sad,' Ulysses signed to his keeper's back. But he meant 'sad' as in unhappy, not as in uncool.

35

Jennifer decided to let Nessa know about her decision first thing in the morning. She got up early to write a letter, outlining her reasons why she felt she needed to move on, without, of course, mentioning Dr Timothy Lauder. Instead she said that, with her lack of practical experience, she didn't feel she could do the sanctuary justice. She even considered not going back to Prowdes at all, just posting the letter and a cheque for half a month's wages unearned. But that would have been too cowardly. The letter was just a formality. Nessa deserved to hear Jennifer's resignation speech face to face.

It was only as Jennifer drove into the car park and saw Guy's jeep there that she remembered where she should have been at eight o'clock the previous evening. She clapped her hand to her forehead in despair. It was all she needed. Another apology to make. Fortunately, Guy seemed just as keen to avoid Jennifer that morning as she was to avoid him. Even Nessa didn't have a minute to see Jennifer until lunchtime.

At the appointed time, Jennifer took herself and her letter of resignation across the lawn to Nessa's office. It was a beautiful day in Devon. The sun had come for breakfast and seemed happy to hang around. Visitor numbers were good (partly because all the news in the local paper about the television programme had reminded people that the sanctuary existed) and with the flower beds in full bloom and happy families lounging on the lawn around picnic baskets, it was hard to imagine that there could be a better place to work in the world.

Nessa beamed widely as Jennifer knocked and entered. She was on the telephone and motioned her 'boffin' to sit down so that she could finish her call.

'That would be fantastic. Of course it's no trouble. How

fortunate for us that you were diverted from the motorway and right past our door! It must be fate!'

The caller said something charming.

'We can't wait to meet you either! In fact, I'd better suggest that you come in the back way to save yourself being mobbed. Everybody is so excited. Just follow the signs to the staff car park and leave your car there. I'll keep an eye out for your arrival. Drive safely down our country lanes!'

She hung up.

'Hello, Jennifer. You'll never guess who's been diverted off the road to Exeter with a spare hour before he has to address the Wildlife Lovers of Devon.'

Nessa didn't have to say the name.

'He's on his way here now.'

'He is?' was all Jennifer could manage.

'Oh, crikey!' Nessa exclaimed as they heard a car crunch on to the gravel. 'He must have been closer than he thought. And here's me without a scrap of make-up!' Nessa dived for the make-up bag she kept in the drawer of her desk and puffed powder all over her nose. 'I'm really sorry about this, darling. Can our important talk wait until after he's gone? Oh wow,' Nessa was at the window now. 'What a fancy car! And, my God, if he isn't even more handsome than he looks on the TV! I've never met a real live television star before. Have you ever met a TV star before?' Nessa asked her surprisingly unexcited colleague. 'Here he comes. How do I look?'

The doorbell on the back door of the main house sounded impossibly loud. Nessa scuttled out into the corridor, leaving Jennifer sitting alone in her bare-walled and echoey office. Jennifer listened to the approach of her former lover as though she was hearing everything that happened through water. His familiar footfall. His voice, so real and yet unreal after so much time. His laugh. 'Bloody roadworks!' The squeaking protest of unoiled hinges as Nessa pushed her office door open.

'I'm afraid you've rather taken us by surprise,' said Nessa.

Understatement of the century, thought Jennifer Niederhauser.

★   ★   ★

186

Keep breathing. Keep breathing. Jennifer chanted this mantra to herself as Timothy walked into the room. She didn't hear the formal introductions Nessa made. The blood was rushing through her ears like floodwater through a sewer, drowning out all sound in the room with the 'th-dump, th-dump' of her heart.

'Dr Jennifer Niederhauser,' said Nessa.

'I think we've met before,' he said.

I think we've met before.

Jennifer shakily put out her hand.

'Jennifer heads up the chimpanzee project here at Prowdes,' Nessa continued happily. 'So I suppose she will be your primary liaison. Anything you want to know about the apes here, just ask Dr Niederhauser. She's just completed her PhD at Edinburgh. Where she worked with . . .'

'Carl Buzzell,' Timothy completed the sentence for her.

Jennifer nodded.

'How did you know?' Nessa asked.

'I'm familiar with his work.'

'Well,' said Nessa, 'I imagine the academic primatology world is pretty small. Shall we have a cup of tea and discuss the programme? Perhaps you could start by giving Dr Lauder an overview of Project Africa, Jennifer. Tell him where we're at.'

Nessa put a call through to Jo-Jo to ask her to come to the office via the tea room and spare no expense on three buns. While Nessa was teasing Jo-Jo, assuring her that it would be well worth her while to complete this little errand, Jennifer and Timothy regarded each other coolly.

I think we've met before.

Well, if he was going to pretend that he hardly knew her, then Jennifer was going to do exactly the same.

'We've got about thirty chimps in the main enclosure,' Jennifer began in a very businesslike fashion. 'Two infants in the nursery and a recently rescued chimp in quarantine. The infants were born here at the sanctuary. They're twins . . .'

'Unusual,' said Timothy.

'That's right. Only twins in captivity in Europe,' Jennifer elaborated. 'They're approaching three years old and we're hoping to reintroduce them to their parents and the rest of the adults pretty soon. I am of the opinion that they'll find it pretty easy to reintegrate . . .'

As she talked about her project, Jennifer felt as though she was having an out-of-body experience. She had no idea how she was managing to keep so calm, to talk about her project so fluently. Prior to this conversation, the last words she had said to Timothy Lauder were the rather less measured 'Fuck you!' Now, here they were, talking like strangers with nothing in common but a mutual interest in chimpanzees. Was he finding this peculiar too? Did he want to grab her by the collar and shout, 'What on earth happened to us?'

'Sounds wonderful,' said Timothy when Jennifer finished her speech. 'I'd love to have a look around.'

'Perhaps Jennifer will show you,' said Nessa.

'I'd love to,' she said. 'But I have a food order to finish before the end of the day. I wonder if you would mind giving Dr Lauder the tour instead?'

'Oh.' Nessa couldn't understand why any woman wouldn't jump at the chance to spend more time with their gorgeous new guest. 'Oh. OK then.'

'I won't take up much of your time,' Timothy said. 'I've got to be in Exeter in a couple of hours. I'm addressing the Wildlife Society.'

'I bet they can't wait to have you. I hope you're prepared for some of the wilder members. One of our team, Guy Gibson, talked to them about the chimpanzees here at Prowdes last year. He barely escaped with his life. They may look like nice old ladies but . . .'

'Thank you for the warning. But I don't think I need to worry. I'm no substitute for David Attenborough. I expect they'll be disappointed.'

'How on earth could they be disappointed?' asked Nessa.

'It's been nice to meet you, Dr Lauder,' Jennifer said to break up the flirt fest. 'Nessa, I'll be in my office if you need me to answer any more questions.'

'I look forward to working with you,' Timothy called after her as she walked out.

'Yes,' Jennifer muttered. She was too busy concentrating on getting across the room without falling over to formulate anything approaching a witty retort. As it was, she somehow managed to get her overall caught on the edge of Nessa's desk. She unhooked herself with a violent jerk, tearing a hole in the thin green fabric that covered her leg and sustaining the knock that would be a big blue bruise by the time she got to the safety of her office.

And as Jennifer was trying to get out, Jo-Jo was trying to get in. The younger girl was carrying a tray loaded with three brimful cups of tea and a selection of sticky buns. Jo-Jo was trying to open the door with her elbow when Jennifer yanked it inwards. Jo-Jo immediately fell backwards into the room, spilling tea all over the place and ending up on top of Jennifer *and* the buns.

'Let me help you!' said Timothy as the two girls struggled to right themselves.

'No,' said Jennifer, quickly getting to her feet before Timothy could so much as graze her elbow with his hand.

Upon realising who her saviour was, Jo-Jo immediately lost control of all her muscles. She was only too happy to let Timothy Lauder tuck his hands beneath her armpits and lift her gently from the floor. While Timothy helped Jo-Jo, Jennifer fled.

'I bet you have women falling for you all the time!' said Nessa. 'This is Jo-Jo.'

'Guh,' said Jo-Jo.

So that was how it happened. It was how it always happened for Jennifer Niederhauser. It seemed that whenever she was facing something she wanted to be particularly well prepared for, fate would find some way to make sure that all her preparation came to naught. Every girl's dream is to meet up with an ex-boyfriend once she's lost half a stone, just had a particularly great haircut and is wearing a wonderful dress with the perfect pair of shoes. No one wants to meet their ex-boyfriend for the first time in five years when they are wearing green overalls and haven't washed their hair in two days.

Back in her office, Jennifer tried to concentrate on the work she had to do. But her mind kept wandering back to the man across the lawn in the big house. She had been given some warning as to

189

how good her ex-lover might look from the photo on a web page she had found while sleeplessly searching the Internet the previous night but, of course, Timothy had looked even better in the flesh. His dress sense had certainly improved. Or his clothes had at least got more expensive. And then there was his presence. Timothy's charm wasn't just for the cameras.

As Jennifer sat at her desk and scribbled a heart on a notepad then scribbled it into a big black cloud when she realised what she was doing, she saw Snowy and Guy troop across the lawn, carrying a chimp twin each. Nessa and Timothy emerged on to the steps of the main house. Introductions were being made. Timothy tickled Mad under the chin. Snowy offered the chimp towards him but Timothy gestured at his soft grey sweater in a way that let it be known he wouldn't appreciate getting ape hair all over it. The sweater was probably cashmere.

Still, it was obvious even from such a distance that Timothy's first meeting with the rest of the Prowdes' team was going very well indeed. Jennifer felt the knot in her stomach tighten even further as she saw Guy tip back his head to laugh at some doubtless hilarious joke her ex-lover had made. Timothy gave Guy a friendly pat on the shoulder. Snowy and Jo-Jo looked at the TV star as though he was the new messiah. Everybody loved him . . .

And indeed, when Jennifer caught up with the keepers in the staff room after Timothy had gone to entertain the wicked ladies of the wildlife club, the talk was all about how down to earth and friendly the big star had been.

'And Nessa said that he thought you and he had met before!' Jo-Jo exclaimed. 'How could you have forgotten that, Dr Niederhauser?'

'How's Sacha getting on?' Jennifer asked Guy to change the subject.

'He's OK. Still a bit sore. But he doesn't seem to have suffered too much from the anaesthetic.'

'Where do you think you met him?' Jo-Jo wasn't about to let Jennifer off the hook.

'I really don't know,' Jennifer snapped. 'Now, Jo-Jo, should you really be in here drinking tea or should you be checking that Hector is happily settled for the night?' Jennifer's tone, combined with Jo-Jo's disbelief that she had got off scot-free after the punch incident, sent her scuttling back to the orang-utan pen at once.

'I think I'll check the heating in the twins' pen,' said Snowy. 'It's been a bit cold today.'

'I'll come with you,' said Guy.

They left Jennifer alone with the kettle and four mugs already containing tea bags and milk that had been waiting for hot water. She had scared everybody away. A big tear plopped into her chimp mug.

36

The telephone rang. Jennifer picked up the receiver. 'Jennifer Niederhauser's office.'

'Jenny,' said the voice at the other end. 'I had *no* idea.'

There was only one person other than Dahlia who had ever called her Jenny and got away with it.

'Yes, well,' said Jennifer. 'Now you know.'

'It was good to see you again,' said Timothy.

'Was it?'

'Yes. It's been a long time. You were looking, er . . . you were looking well.'

Jennifer could see her reflection in her computer screen. She looked far from well. Wild was closer to the word right then. And not in a good way.

'What do you want? How did you get my number?'

'Nessa gave it to me,' Timothy said simplistically. 'She thought we might need to talk again before the show starts. Why? Am I not allowed to call you?'

'It's just . . . just . . . What do you want, Timothy? What can I tell you?'

'I just wanted to talk. To you. Alone. I think we should, don't you?'

'Why?'

'Because we're going to be seeing rather a lot of each other over the next few weeks and I don't think either of us wants it to be awkward.'

'It's not awkward.'

'Jenny, you were so nervous you almost fell over on your way out of Nessa's office. And I've got frostbite all over my face from the looks you were giving me. Look, I think we should meet.'

'What?'

'I think we should meet. Just you and me. Away from Prowdes. And get ourselves properly reacquainted before things start to get strange. How about it?'

'Chuh!' Jennifer snorted.

'Is it better that we just avoid each other for the next couple of months? You know that isn't going to be possible, don't you? Not unless you leave your job.'

Jennifer looked straight at the letter of resignation that still remained on her desk.

'Look, this could be terrible or this could be fine. You get to make the choice.'

'Oh, right.' That was so typical of him, Jennifer fumed inwardly. Now she got to look like the unreasonable one if she refused.

'What are you doing tonight?' he asked.

'Er, I'm . . .' Jennifer hesitated while she tried to come up with something suitably impressive. Timothy saw through her at once.

'You're not doing anything, are you? It's a school night. Look, I was going to drive all the way back to Oxford tonight but the motorway is completely fucked with roadworks. I'm exhausted, I'm hungry and I'm in your vicinity. Let's kill two birds with one stone, get dinner and get this over and done with.'

Jennifer began to protest, but a crackle told her that Timothy's mobile phone had lost reception. He was on his way.

Jennifer began to wonder whether she might have been a real Don Juan in a past life. It was the only possible explanation for her current stinking rotten love-life karma. Why else would she deserve to find herself in this position, forced into a tête-à-tête with the ex-love of her life and no time at all to go shopping in preparation? Or even to go home and wash her hair. She opened the top drawer of her desk and stared into it as though the plastic hairbrush and two emergency scrunchies (the twins were always stealing them from her hair while she was in their enclosure) might somehow metamorphose into a big vanity case bursting with all the girly things she needed to transform herself from a bare-faced zoologist into a vamp. Not that she would have known what to do with the kit if it had appeared. Jennifer had owned just one mascara in the past three years and that had recently rolled beneath the radiator in the bathroom and remained there now that its moment had come, dried up and covered in dust.

Dahlia was an expert at meeting up with ex-boyfriends and turning them from men on her most-hated list into friends. In fact, several of them had attended her wedding to Henry. But Jennifer had no experience of such things, having had just the one boyfriend to be 'exed'. And in any case, she wasn't sure she believed in Dahlia's adage that you could never have too many friends.

Jennifer suddenly realised that she had no idea when Timothy was going to turn up. He hadn't told her how far away he was when he called. Once again, he was closer than she thought. He knocked on the door to her office while she was checking her nostrils for stray hairs in the mirror next to her coat peg.

'You ready?' he asked when she opened the door.

'I've changed my mind,' she said angrily, brushing his hand off her arm. 'I don't want to go for dinner after all.'

'Jennifer, as I said on the phone, I am going to be filming in this goddam shit-hole for at least the next six weeks. Let's get something to eat and sort out how we're going to manage this thing like a pair of adults.'

'How can we do that when only one of us is an adult?' Jennifer spat back.

'I'm glad you've realised quite how childish you are being,' said Timothy, immediately spinning the insult round to face her. 'Come on.' He pulled her up from the chair she had retreated to. He was taller than she remembered. But he smelled exactly the same.

'Eternity for men,' she murmured sadly. 'That brings back memories.'

'Well, you won't have to smell it after today. I think it was agitating those juvenile twins in the football kit.'

'Mad and Bad,' said Jennifer.

'Stupid names.'

'They're actually called Modimo and Badimo,' Jennifer told him. 'After the African gods.'

'Whatever. Where are we going to eat? Is there anywhere round here apart from that dreadful Italian place?'

'That "dreadful Italian place" is the best restaurant in town.'

'Fantastic. I wonder if the Ivy will send food down here by courier. Come on. Let's get in my car and see if we can find a half-decent chicken in a basket in a pub.'

'I haven't said I want to go anywhere with you, yet.'

'Jenny.' Timothy gave her another one of his looks. This was a look that he had yet to use on camera. It was the one he had used whenever she made a stupid point during a tutorial all those years ago. Pitying yet slightly indulgent. 'Take off your disgusting overalls and meet me in the car park in two minutes.'

In the bathroom, trying to unbutton her overalls with shaking fingers, Jennifer pondered her predicament. Unfortunately, the window wasn't big enough to climb through if she wanted to. But what was the point in resisting now? Timothy was right. He was going to be around for the next six weeks whether Jennifer wanted him there or not. If there really was a way to make the whole experience less painful, then she had no choice but to try to work with it.

And it really couldn't get any *worse*, could it? All that time spent strategising with Dahlia about how their first encounter should go – the things she should say, the make-up she should wear – and she had ended up like this. Dressed in overalls, stinking of chimp and feeling faint at the very sight of him.

There was a bang on the bathroom door.

'Hurry up in there. I'm starving. You don't need to get dressed up. It's only me.'

Only me? How could he say that? Only the boy who broke my heart, Jennifer thought.

How different a relationship can appear from both sides of the equation. For Jennifer, this was a moment so momentous she could barely breathe. For him, the distinct impression was that he just wanted someone to keep him company while he ate.

37

Timothy's make-over had extended to his mode of transport. When Jennifer was dating him, back in Oxford, he had yet to get a driving licence. The only wheels he owned then were attached to an extremely rusty bicycle frame that had belonged to Timothy's father when he himself was an undergraduate at St Francis Hall twenty-five years before. These days, Timothy wouldn't be seen dead with a bicycle clip around the bottom of his designer trousers and, as a result, he simply had to get himself a car.

A brand new MGF graced the car park at Prowdes which was more used to battered Land Rover Defenders covered in mud on the outside with chimp shit all over the passenger seats (Mad and Bad frequently took a spin around the sanctuary with Snowy). There would be no chimp shit in Timothy's car, however. Before he would allow her to get inside, Timothy made Jennifer do a twirl so that he could check her bottom for detritus. The same went for her boots.

'Where can we go?' Timothy asked.

Jennifer shrugged.

'Why don't we go to that pub we went to when I came down here to visit you that Christmas?'

Once again, he had taken her breath away with his casual reference to their shared past. Jennifer remembered that Christmas so very well. She remembered how much Timothy had impressed her parents. And her, with a carefully chosen Christmas present. Later, after the break-up, Dahlia had said that she suspected Timothy had solicited help when buying Jennifer the beautiful handbag he gave her that year.

'Men do not know how to buy handbags,' she'd said. 'He probably sent that undergraduate he was shagging out to get it for you.'

The handbag had found its way to Oxfam the following morning.

'What was it called?' Timothy asked. 'That pub.'

'The Green Dragon,' said Jennifer quietly.

They drove for twenty miles until they came to the pub. It was a beautiful seventeenth-century inn, with a thatched roof and a garden that went down to the sea. And that night it was almost deserted. Inside, the spotty young barman flirted with a waitress at the bar. They looked disappointed to be interrupted by actual customers. Until the waitress got a better look at Timothy and realised who he was.

She elbowed her barman boyfriend and they both gawped as Timothy led Jennifer to a corner table by the big fireplace in which a couple of logs were spitting feebly.

'Yes, it is me,' he said when the waitress followed them over with a couple of menus. He already had his pen out of his pocket to sign an autograph. The waitress looked slightly embarrassed as she searched about for something to accept the autograph on and eventually had to settle for the back of a brown sugar sachet.

'Should guarantee us some decent service,' said Timothy as the waitress wandered back to the bar, staring at her sugar sachet in some bemusement. 'Don't know if it will guarantee us some decent food, though,' he complained as he scanned through the menu. 'Was it this bad the last time we were here? This is like the menu that time forgot. They really do have chicken in a basket,' he said in an overly loud voice.

'You know,' said Jennifer, 'I used to work as a waitress in a restaurant in Tincastle. One day, that bloke who played Doctor Who after the one with the curly hair came in. He kept drawing attention to how famous he thought he was by asking to sign autographs on the back of sugar sachets. Four waitresses gobbed in his tomato and basil soup before I took it out to him.'

'I can't help it if people are interested in who I am these days.'

'She wasn't interested,' said Jennifer.

'They gawped at us as we came in!' Timothy insisted.

Jennifer shrugged. She had already chosen from the menu. She was going to have the most expensive thing on it. Though, in reality, she wasn't actually sure that she would be able to eat a bite.

'Chicken in a basket,' she said when the waitress returned to take their order.

Though the pub was empty, the food took so long to arrive that Timothy began to loudly enquire whether the waitress had gone to catch the chicken that Jennifer ordered. While they waited, they filled their time with talk about the sanctuary, steering wide of more personal subjects. Jennifer answered Timothy's questions curtly.

Then, when the food finally arrived, they were occupied with eating and talking about that. The arrival of coffee sent Timothy off on a monologue about how terrible the coffee was in the BBC canteen, which of course segued into a monologue on his brilliant career.

'This show could be big,' he concluded. 'It has all the right elements. Chimps, big houses, mad old aristocrats,' he added, referring to Nessa. 'You've got your work cut out for you with this Project Africa. I certainly didn't expect to see you in a north Devon monkey sanctuary.'

'I didn't expect to ever see you again in my life.'

'You know you broke my heart,' said Timothy.

Jennifer gave her head a startled shake as if to dislodge something from her ears. 'What did you say?' she asked slowly.

'I said, you broke my heart, Jennifer Niederhauser.'

'I broke your heart?' Jennifer exclaimed. 'You were the one who was . . .'

The image of his bouncing bottom returned unbidden again.

Jennifer shook her head, this time to dislodge the image from her brain.

'That was a mistake,' said Timothy in a masterly understatement. 'I was lonely. I'd been working so hard on that conference paper. I was stressed beyond belief. She offered it on a plate. What was I supposed to do?'

'Refuse it,' said Jennifer drily.

Timothy continued regardless. 'You know, ever since that day I've had nightmares about it. I prayed to every god I could think of. If I could just rewind that one day of my life, I said. Go back to breakfast and start again. I'd have cancelled her tutorial. I'd have told her I couldn't teach her any more. When you arrived in your waterproof you'd have found me working on my paper . . .'

'Instead of working on your tutee . . .'

'And we'd still be together today.'

Jennifer looked at him with anguish. 'What are you saying?'

'I couldn't believe the way you cut me out of your life,' he half exclaimed. 'You didn't give me a chance to explain. All those calls that went unanswered. The letters that you didn't reply to.'

'What letters?' asked Jennifer. 'I didn't get any.'

'I sent them to you via your parents. They must have got lost in the post,' said Timothy, not missing a beat. 'But you just turned your back on me, Jenny. You closed your eyes and hardened your heart.'

'What was I supposed to do?'

'Have a little compassion. Some understanding. Some forgiveness?'

'It's hard to forgive someone you love for screwing someone else.'

'Screwing!' Timothy seized upon the word. 'That's all it was, you see. Just screwing.'

Jennifer winced. 'Like bonobos do?' she suggested.

'You could say that. I got rid of her the second you left, you know. I threw her clothes at her and raced out after you as fast as I could.'

Jennifer nodded. But she knew that she had managed to cross the college quadrangle, walk down the high street and get on a bus to the train station without noticing that Timothy was in particularly hot pursuit. Surely he would have caught up with her over that time and distance? He had been proud of his time in the London marathon that year.

'You could have flown up to Edinburgh and waited on my doorstep,' said Jennifer finally. 'I might have thought you were sorry then.'

'How could I have flown up to Edinburgh?' said Timothy throwing his hands in the air in exasperation. 'You know how busy I was.'

'Sometimes we have to alter our priorities to hold on to everything that's important in our lives. I seem to remember you said that to me. When you were advising me to go to Edinburgh in the first place.'

'I did everything I could,' said Timothy. He was getting defensive now. 'You're acting like you're the only one who got hurt when we broke up but, from where I'm sitting, it looks very much to me as though you were looking for an excuse to be rid of me that day.'

'What?'

'That's right, Jenny. That's exactly how it looks. You were probably on your way down to Oxford to tell me it was over and I unwittingly gave you the perfect reason to walk away without explaining and without any guilt.'

'Oh, so you were unwittingly shagging another girl?'

'Will you stop bringing that up?'

'I don't think I brought it up enough. I *crawled* back to Edinburgh that afternoon. I couldn't sleep. I couldn't eat. I thought I was going to die of a broken heart. And your great efforts to make amends, as far as I could tell, amounted to three phone calls explaining that sex for you has as much emotional relevance as sex does to the bonobos you were studying and a couple of e-mails asking if I could post you your Lighthouse Family CD, which, incidentally, I took to a charity shop the very next day. There is no excuse for what you did to me. If you were lonely, you should have called me before I made my surprise visit. I would have been in Oxford in a second. If you were depressed, you should have got a prescription for Prozac. If you wanted to screw someone else, you should have finished with me first. Don't come back into my life now and tell me that I was the one who fucked up . . .'

'God, I love you when you're angry.'

Timothy reached across the table and pulled Jennifer towards him by her forearms. He planted his lips on hers before she could finish her rant.

'This isn't—'

Jennifer meant to say 'this isn't right' but Timothy wasn't going to let her disagree with him again that night. Without taking his mouth off hers, he manoeuvred them both so that they were standing up. He slipped a fifty-pound note inside the bill-fold to cover a bill of less than twenty pounds and, without waiting for change, manhandled Jennifer out towards the car.

Jennifer started to protest again, but Timothy pushed her back against the low roof of his car, bent her backwards across it and carried on kissing her. Jennifer was dimly aware of a camera flash going off in the background. Perhaps the waitress thought she would be able to sell the pitch-black photo to *Hello!*. Then Timothy started to worry that the weight of both their bodies would damage the roof of his car.

'Let's go back to your place,' he whispered hotly in her ear.

'No,' she managed to utter between slurps.

'My place,' Timothy tried instead. 'I've checked into a bed and breakfast in Tincastle.'

'No,' Jennifer gurgled again.

'You want to do it here in the car park?'

'No!' This time, with great effort, Jennifer managed to push him away. 'I don't want to do it with you anywhere. I just want you to drive me home and then leave me alone again.'

'What?' Timothy was confused. He had very quickly become used to the leverage that even a children's cable television series had given him with the girls. Women who would never have looked at him in his incarnation as a bespectacled and bookish professor now couldn't get enough of him. He had been shocked the first time someone asked him to autograph her breast. These days he was shocked if every tenth autograph he signed *wasn't* on someone's mammary. He could have walked down any High Street in England, opened his arms and shouted 'Who wants it?' and had girls from eighteen to eighty lining up to give it to him. But Jennifer was refusing.

'Take me home,' she said again, trying to keep the wobble out of her voice. Her chest was still heaving in true bodice-ripper style. Her tangle with Timothy had raised her heart rate far more effectively than a jog around the block. Her heart was pounding so hard, she wouldn't have been at all surprised if it had flown out of her chest and hit him in the face like a pulsing red custard pie. 'Take me home and we'll pretend this never happened. We cannot do this kind of thing if we're going to be working together.'

'But—' Timothy began.

'No buts,' said Jennifer. He wasn't to know that she was surprising herself as much as she was surprising him with her resistance.

Timothy pressed the button on the key fob gadget that unlocked the car door. Jennifer let herself into the passenger seat. Timothy drove her home obediently, secretly assuming all the way that once they got back to her place, he would be able to change her mind on the pretence of coming in for a coffee that would keep his sleepy person on the road back to his B and B.

'I don't have any coffee,' she told him when they got to the little cottage. 'It gives me an instant headache, remember?'

'Of course I remember,' said Timothy. 'I just thought that you might have got some in for guests.'

'I never have guests,' said Jennifer simply.

'Perhaps you ought to start,' Timothy tried one more time. His hand crept on to her knee and he leaned close to her cheek.

Jennifer got out of the car without kissing him goodbye and walked up to her gate without looking back.

Timothy waited. Jennifer didn't know whether it was because he wanted to make sure she got in safely or because he was still waiting for her to change her mind. But she didn't.

As soon as she got inside, Jennifer leaned her back against the door as though she was the little pig who had managed to escape the big bad wolf. But she couldn't resist peering out through the letter box, just in time to see Timothy thump his fists against the steering wheel of his smart new car in exasperation.

The sight made Jennifer smile for the first time that day.

When she heard his car engine start up again and zoom off down the road, Jennifer touched her fingers to her lips. Timothy had been sporting a touch of designer stubble and her chin was slightly raw where he had given her an impromptu exfoliation.

'Excoriation. That is the proper word for it.'

The phrase popped into Jennifer's mind. Timothy had said it all those years ago, when their fumbling session in the back of the coach on the way to Oxford from London left her with a chin rubbed so raw by his stubble that it started bleeding.

Oh God. It had been exactly the same. So much for her vain hope that she wouldn't fancy him any more. Suddenly Jennifer's body felt alive in a way she hadn't experienced since she was last with that dreadful man. It was as though he alone held the secret to her arousal.

'Bugger, bugger, bugger,' she said.

38

Jennifer phoned Dahlia.

'Do you know what time it is?' Dahlia asked. 'You've woken me up. I've got work in the morning.'

'I'm sorry. I had to call you. Timothy just took me out to dinner. He kissed me.'

'What? What!' Dahlia was immediately awake. 'And you slept with him? You did, didn't you? You're calling to tell me you slept with him and now you want to kill yourself.'

'No. No. I didn't sleep with him,' said Jennifer quickly. 'I told him to stop kissing me and take me home. I didn't even let him come inside for a coffee.'

'Jennifer!' She could hear the admiration in Dahlia's voice. 'I don't believe it.'

'Believe it.'

'How are you feeling?'

'I don't know.' She took a big gasping breath. 'Confused?'

'Tell me all about it. From the beginning. And don't you dare miss anything out.'

Jennifer could hear Henry groaning in the background.

'Oh, shut up,' said Dahlia, hand just about covering the receiver. 'If you don't want to hear it, you can go and sleep in the spare room. Jenny,' Dahlia was back with her full attention, 'tell me everything he said.'

Jennifer recounted her entire day. The sleepless night. The resignation letter. The surprise meeting. The way he had acted as though they'd never met before.

'The bastard,' Dahlia hissed.

Then the phone call. The dinner invitation. Jennifer hadn't known what to do.

'Meeting up seemed like the mature thing,' she said to Dahlia.

'Mm-hm.'

'And he had acted like such an idiot, I felt sure that if I spent even just another fifteen minutes with him, I would be cured of any feelings I still had for him for ever and—'

'So you admit now that you didn't have closure,' Dahlia interrupted.

'Yes, Dahlia. I admit it. But as soon as we got to the restaurant, I felt sure I was going to get it. He signed an autograph for one of the waitresses.'

'Isn't that nice?'

'She didn't even ask for it. And then he complained about the pub and the food and kept on and on about how much better things are in London and telling me about all the posh restaurants he's been to since he started his television career. It was all so big-headed. All the things I used to like about him seemed to have disappeared.'

'Well, that's good.'

'I was ready to tell him exactly what a shit he'd been when he had the cheek to tell me that I'd broken *his* heart!'

Much disgusted tutting from Dahlia at that.

'I couldn't believe I plucked up the courage to do it, but I told him exactly how I had felt. I even told him that I took his Lighthouse Family CD to the charity shop.'

'The one signed by all the band?'

'The very same.'

'And what did he do then?'

'He kissed me!'

The kiss was replayed in detail. Seven times. The drive home. The refusal of coffee. Timothy bashing his fists against the steering wheel in rage.

'And now?'

'And now I feel really awful,' said Jennifer quietly. 'I feel as though my world has been turned upside down again. I feel as though he was probably laughing at me. Just trying to see if he could get me to fall back under his spell.'

'But you didn't,' said Dahlia. 'You know what will happen now, don't you?'

'He'll go off with someone else?'

'No. He'll be all over you. There is nothing a man wants more than a woman who doesn't want him back. Oh, this is so fantastic. I am so *proud* of you. You handled everything absolutely perfectly! Mark my words. There will be flowers before the weekend. I'd better get off the phone now. Henry's been sitting on the landing while we've been having this chat.'

Dahlia hung up, leaving Jennifer sitting in her quiet cottage in deep contemplation of that evening's strange events. The sensible part of her nodded sagely at the thought that she had done the right thing by resisting Timothy's advances but a tiny rebel cell in her heart was more than a little worried that she would never have the chance to resist again.

Dahlia was right about one thing. There were flowers the following day, which was Jennifer's day off from the sanctuary that week. They were delivered to the Witch's cottage while Jennifer was at the supermarket. Her elderly neighbour took them in for her. A dozen beautiful long-stemmed red roses. Half of them were still tightly furled, yet to burst into their fullest bloody glory.

'I couldn't read the card,' said Mrs Greene. 'My glasses are broken.'

'Thanks for looking after them for me,' said Jennifer, ignoring Mrs Greene's hint that she wanted to know who they were from.

Jennifer arranged the roses in the vase that had never been used and immediately the tastefully pale sitting room was transformed by the rude splash of colour. Then she sat on her sofa and looked at the flowers for a very long time. In her hand she held the card. They were from Timothy, of course.

'Me Tarzan, you Jane,' was what he had written.

The four little words made tears spring to Jennifer's eyes at once.

He had remembered. Timothy had remembered the catchphrase of their six weeks in the Gabon all those years ago. The happiest six weeks of Jennifer's life so far. They had been so much in love, she thought then. Happy to be alone together in the jungle as they tracked that chimpanzee troop. That was when she had given Timothy the nickname Tarzan. It was the obvious choice when he swung from a vine that broke beneath his weight and deposited him in a pile of rotting fruit. Timothy didn't seem to mind and after that they always referred to one another as Tarzan and Jane. Timothy would beat his chest. Jennifer would swoon in mock awe.

And he'd remembered. The simple message on the card touched Jennifer far more than the beauty of the expensive flowers themselves. Because he couldn't have written it without thinking of that happier time, could he?

Oh God. What was happening? Was he courting her all over again?

Beneath the message was a phone number. A mobile phone number. And the instruction that Jennifer could use it at any time. Any time at all.

At eleven o'clock that evening, Jennifer held the card in one hand and her telephone in the other. At eleven thirty, she had tapped the number into the keypad but had yet to press 'call'. At eleven forty-five she pressed 'call'.

'Yes.' Timothy sounded sleepy.

'It's Jennifer.'

'Jennifer! You called.'

'Just to say thank you for the flowers. I'm just calling to say thank you for the flowers.'

'Are they beautiful?'

'They are.'

'Just like you,' he murmured.

'Timothy, stop it. I don't know what you want but I want you to stop talking to me like this.'

'I'll never stop talking to you like this. I can't tell you how my heart leapt when I walked into that office at Prowdes and saw you there. I couldn't believe it. I didn't think I'd ever get another chance.'

'You're not getting another chance,' Jennifer pointed out.

'What possible reason do you have to deny me? I realise now how much pain I put you through. I realise that I went about trying to get you back the wrong way. I realise, most importantly, what I lost the day I was unfaithful to you. What *we* lost,' he added. The killer blow. 'Jenny. Janie. Do you remember how much fun we had in the Gabon?'

Jennifer closed her eyes and let his voice wash over her like a warm wave that would ultimately drown her, as he recounted highlights of their time together in the African forest.

'I have never been so happy again since,' was how he concluded.

'Oh, Timothy,' Jennifer moaned. 'Don't do this to me.' A small sane part of her brain tried valiantly to protect her against Timothy's super-romantic onslaught. Five years of recovery was a lot of time to throw away.

'But I have to see you again,' he said. 'When can I see you?'

'I don't know,' she said. But the sane part of her brain was giving up already and she knew that resistance was futile. She definitely would be seeing him again. It was just a matter of choosing a time and venue for her downfall. 'Tomorrow?' she suggested. 'I've got another day off.'

'Wonderful. Meet me in London,' he said. 'Come up on the train. I've got to be there for a meeting with the TV people.'

They agreed to see each other on the steps of the Natural History Museum at two o'clock the following afternoon. It was one of the places they had visited on their first day in London together, when they went to hear Jane Goodall talk. The first time they kissed.

Another sleepless night lay ahead for Jennifer as she made her plans for the rematch. She decided not to tell Dahlia where she was going. She couldn't stand the shrieking. And she also had a feeling that by agreeing to travel up to London, rather than making Timothy drive down to see her in Devon instead, she was in contravention of some kind of girly rule that would determine who had the real power in the relationship from that moment on.

Jennifer took a big fat book on the chimpanzee language experiments of the 1970s and 1980s to read on the train. But though she turned over twenty or so pages during the course of her journey, she wouldn't remember a word. She kept drifting off into a reverie and reading the same paragraph again and again. She was using the card that had come with the roses as a bookmark.

The Exeter train arrived at Paddington Station just before lunchtime. Jennifer took the Circle Line down to South Kensington and was waiting on the steps as instructed at five minutes to two, still kidding herself that she was reading the book as she watched the crowds for signs of her ex. Several times her heart leapt in recognition only to sink back disappointed when she realised she was mistaken. She really would have to get her eyes tested when she got back to Devon. Too much time spent poring over academic papers with very small print . . .

At two fifteen Jennifer started to get a bit twitchy. She wondered if she had the right day. She pulled her mobile phone out of her pocket and checked it roughly every twenty seconds. Perhaps she had somehow managed to switch the ringer off. She had no idea how the damn thing worked.

Eventually, she gave in to her worries and called him.

'Jennifer!' he answered breezily. 'I'm so sorry I'm late. But I'm on my way. In fact, I'm about twenty metres away from you now.'

Jennifer scanned the crowd urgently, but she didn't see him until he was standing right in front of her, mobile phone still pressed to his ear as he said, 'You look so beautiful, I could eat you.'

This time she didn't resist when he pulled her into his arms for a kiss.

39

For propriety's sake, Jennifer and Timothy made a whistle-stop tour of the Natural History Museum, but both knew, as they stood beneath the replica of a blue whale, that neither of them was really interested in reading about baleen plates and sonar. They touched each other like a pair of teenagers stealing precious time out of the teacher's sight on a school trip. Timothy nuzzled the back of Jennifer's neck as they marvelled at the 'Pink Fairy Armadillo' in the mammals hall (yes, there really is such a creature).

'Let's go back to my hotel,' Timothy murmured hotly in her ear.

'I don't know if we should,' Jennifer protested automatically. But she followed him towards the exit with obscene haste.

Animal House Entertainment had booked Timothy a room in the Metropolitan Hotel, a deeply trendy establishment on the edge of Hyde Park where all the rooms were decorated in tasteful neutrals. They started kissing again in the lift up to Timothy's eighth-floor room. Not quite a penthouse suite but still the most luxurious hotel room Jennifer had ever found herself in. Timothy began to unbutton her shirt even as she looked about her new surroundings in awe.

'They must think you're going to be a really big star,' she told him.

'You'd better believe it, baby,' said Timothy as he slipped a hand inside the left cup of her bra.

'Timothy,' Jennifer breathed as he rolled her nipple between his fingers until it started to harden. 'Timothy,' she sighed as he slipped his other hand beneath the waistband of her skirt and sought out the top of her knickers.

They tumbled backwards on to the bed.

'We shouldn't be doing this,' Jennifer murmured one last time.

'Why not?' Timothy asked. 'I'm single. You're single. No one's getting hurt.'

'Yet,' said Jennifer. 'Timothy, I don't want to do this only to have to go through the pain of losing you again.'

'I won't put you through that pain,' said Timothy. 'I promise you.' He murmured this last into her neck. Jennifer felt a delicious chill rush through her body as his lips lit upon a particularly sensitive spot. It was as though her nerve endings were nearer the surface than usual. She hadn't felt like this in . . . Well, actually, since the previous week with Guy in the moment before the kiss that never happened . . . But Jennifer was determined to forget about Guy now.

'Doesn't this feel right to you?' Timothy asked.

'It does,' Jennifer admitted.

It felt completely bloody wonderful. It took her right back to the very first time she and Timothy had tussled on a bed. A single bed in her room at St Francis Hall. How simple things had been back then. There had been no reason to hold back and resist him. No reason to be afraid.

Sod it. Jennifer threw her arms around him and planted her lips on his. Life really was too short and she had gone for far too long without having wild passionate sex. Or any sex at all for that matter. His mouth on her mouth was too delicious. The smell of him in her lungs was too intoxicating. It was as though she had taken a huge snort of some potent illegal substance that had temporarily unhinged her. When Timothy started to fumble with the buttons on the back of her skirt again, she let him carry on.

'I'm wearing my . . .'

'Chastity underwear?' he laughed into her mouth. 'I don't care. You would be irresistible to me in a sack. Besides,' he added, 'it's the inner person that counts.'

Jennifer smiled gratefully. He always said the right thing. Moments later she jumped up, wriggled out of her big pants and kicked them beneath the bed. That was the truth about chastity underwear. It didn't make you keep your clothes *on* at all. In reality, it makes you shed the last few bits extra quickly so that no one would dwell on the greyness of your bra. Now Jennifer stood naked before Timothy again. He was bare to the waist. She pressed her hand against the muscle of his chest as he squeezed her close.

This was every bit as good as she remembered. It was going to be better than she remembered . . .

Four minutes later.

'I can't believe we're back together,' Jennifer murmured into Timothy's chest. He smoothed his hand over her long blonde hair. 'I just can't wait till I tell everyone.'

'Er . . .' Timothy gave a small nervous cough.

'What's the matter?'

'I'm not really sure that's such a good idea.'

Jennifer sat up and looked down into her lover's face as he reclined on the big white pillows with a slightly worried smile.

'What isn't a good idea?'

'Telling people that we're back together,' he explained.

'Why not? You are glad that we're back together as well, aren't you?'

'Of course I am.'

'Then what's the problem with telling everybody about it?'

'Jenny.' Timothy sat up against the pillows and took her by the shoulders, like a father preparing to tell his daughter that her favourite pet hamster is on its way to heaven thanks to next-door's cat. It was a 'soften the blow' sort of gesture. Even Jennifer knew that. 'Things are different now. I'm different. Back in 1997 we were just Jennifer and Timothy. Two young people simply thrilled to have found each other to love in such a difficult, unfriendly world. We didn't have to worry who knew about it. Everybody was as happy for us as we were to be together. But we're not Timothy and Jennifer any more.'

'Well, I'm still Jennifer,' she interrupted. 'Who are you?'

'I'm Dr Timothy Lauder,' he said quite seriously. 'World expert on matters of primate conservation and about to be a prime-time national television personality.' He looked at her as though that should have been explanation in itself.

'I don't get it.'

'What I am trying to say is, it matters who I go out with now. People are interested in my love life.'

'And you don't think I'll live up to the scrutiny?' Jennifer clutched a sheet tightly around her.

'That's not what I'm saying at all. It's because I don't want you to have to *undergo* the scrutiny in the first place that I'm having to take this stand. You don't want to have to run the gauntlet of the paparazzi every time you step outside the cottage, do you?'

'Would it be like that?' Jennifer asked

'Just like Princess Diana.'

'I haven't exactly seen the photographers chasing you down the street,' said Jennifer flatly. 'I don't think we're in imminent danger of a *News of the World* exposé. And even if we were, what would they say? TV personality gets back together with old girlfriend. It's still love, he says. It isn't as though either of us is married or seeing someone else.' Jennifer paused. 'Or is that what you're really trying to say? You're not seeing anyone else, are you?'

Timothy's eyes flickered downwards momentarily. 'Of course not.' He took a big breath.

'Then I don't know what the problem is!'

'Jenny,' Timothy tried another tack, 'I just want to take this slowly. I want us to be able to explore our relationship in private before we put it under the pressure of public scrutiny. You're not the only one who's afraid of getting hurt.'

It hit the mark. Jennifer's expression softened. 'Oh, Timothy. You don't ever have to worry about getting hurt by me.'

He tucked a stray lock of hair back behind her ear. Jennifer grabbed his hand and kissed it from fingertips to wrist.

'I will never hurt you. I swear it.'

Timothy nodded solemnly.

'Shall we have a snooze then?' Jennifer asked. 'The last train for Exeter doesn't leave until eight o'clock.' She pressed her body against his. 'It's just so nice to be able to cuddle up to you again. Shall we spoon?'

To her disappointment, Timothy wriggled out of her embrace. 'Darling, I would like nothing better,' he said, 'but I've got to get ready.'

'What for?'

'I'm having dinner with the production team this evening. To finalise arrangements for the filming and stuff.' He got out of bed as he talked. 'You do understand, don't you, sweetheart? Would you like to have first shower?'

Half an hour later, Jennifer found herself on her way to Paddington Station again. Timothy dialled a taxi on the production company's account. At least she would be back in Exeter before midnight. And she would see Timothy again soon. Really soon. He had promised.

40

As the first day of filming approached, the excitement at Prowdes was starting to build to a level of volcanic pressure. Jo-Jo, who was hitherto rarely seen with brushed hair, suddenly started to wear make-up. The Saturday before filming, she booked herself into Tincastle's best salon for a full head of highlights. Unfortunately, Jo-Jo hadn't learned the golden rule that you should never submit to 'subtle highlights' from a woman whose own hair could best be described as 'stripy'. She came away looking like a badger.

The Major too was taking the possibility of his first national television appearance very seriously. Faith, the producer, had met the Major again on one of her preparatory visits to the sanctuary and been charmed by his old-world manners. The viewers would love him, she said. As a result, Jennifer had been forced to go back on her rule that no civilians were to be allowed into the animal enclosures. The Major became an honorary member of Prowdes' staff.

Not that Jennifer minded too much anyway. The keepers couldn't help noticing that their grumpy old Dr Niederhauser seemed to be extremely chilled out. No one knew what had caused the change in her. It obviously wasn't Guy's attentions. Since the night when she accidentally stood him up, Guy and Jennifer hadn't broached the subject of joint extra-curricular activity again. They were back to being colleagues, pure and simple. Guy hoped that he was hiding his disappointment. Still, he was happy that Jennifer seemed so happy. As was Nessa. For a while she had dreaded every phone call or e-mail from her boffin, expecting Jennifer to quit at any moment. That danger seemed to have passed.

In the fortnight preceding the arrival of the television crew, Jennifer met with Faith O'Connell to discuss the storylines they wanted to follow. Timothy would have been at the meetings too, but he had to fly back out to Africa at the last moment to record some extra links for his BBC series.

'He's a fantastic man,' said Faith when she and Jennifer discussed Timothy's role in the forthcoming show. 'And he's going to be a big star. We're so lucky to have him.'

Jennifer couldn't keep a blush from her face as she considered how lucky she was to have Timothy too. Oh, it was such exquisite agony not to be able to tell anyone. She should have won a Bafta for the surprised expression she managed to muster when Faith said that Timothy had been unexpectedly called out to Africa.

'Has he really?' she said, expertly hiding the fact that Timothy had told her about his sudden trip at the end of a particularly filthy bout of phone sex the night before. 'I'm so looking forward to meeting him again,' she added, thoroughly disingenuously.

It was decided at the production meetings that the television crew would concentrate in particular on the stories of Mad and Bad and Ulysses. Mad and Bad were born for television. Chimpanzee twins are extremely rare and they were at a wonderfully playful and particularly engaging age, only too happy to turn somersaults for the cameras. Jennifer was also very hopeful that Mad and Bad would soon be integrated into the main troop, thus demonstrating the kind of work the team at Prowdes was concerned with.

Ulysses' story was even more interesting to the producers, spanning as it did such a range of emotions. He was still young enough to be cute and the injuries and ill-treatment the poor chimp had sustained at the hands of his previous owners would certainly up the 'aaaah' factor.

Faith was very excited. 'We can follow Ulysses' story from the very beginning,' she said. 'From the moment he was rescued until the moment he joins the other chimps in readiness for release in Africa. The perfect happy ending.'

Jennifer nodded. Just the previous night, she and Timothy had discussed the exact same thing. Jennifer had doubted at first that it would be possible on the television company's timescale but Timothy was optimistic.

'Well,' Guy interrupted, 'that would be nice but I'm sure Dr

Niederhauser has already told you that we can't guarantee that any of the chimps will follow your production schedule exactly.'

The group turned to look at Guy. It was the first time he had spoken in that meeting.

'It isn't simply a matter of waiting for the infected wound on Ulysses' neck to heal and then turfing him out into the main enclosure,' he continued. 'We've got to make sure that he's psychologically ready to make the adjustment to troop living. We don't know anything about his history. We don't know whether he was taken from the wild or captive-born. He might never have lived with other chimpanzees before. He certainly doesn't seem too confident around the twins. If we just throw him into the main enclosure and let him get on with it, we could be putting him in a great deal of danger. The troop already has a well-established hierarchy and if Ulysses is perceived as a threat to the higher-ranking males, he might be attacked. Like Sacha was by Achilles. But Sacha is a fully grown adult. Achilles could kill a juvenile like Ulysses. There have been fatalities through fighting in captive-chimp colonies before.' Guy looked to Jennifer for support.

'He's right,' she said almost grudgingly. 'I won't be able to hurry the progress of any of the animals for the cameras.'

'We know that!' said Faith jovially. 'But the chances are that everything will happen within our timescales anyway. Right?'

'We're going to do our best,' Jennifer replied.

At the end of the day, Jennifer and Guy walked back together from the chimpanzee nursery to the car park.

'Ulysses' neck is pretty much healed now, isn't it?' Jennifer asked.

'It is,' said Guy. 'But I'm not too sure about his progress otherwise. He's very timid.'

'Yes,' Jennifer agreed. 'What do you think we can do about that? To hurry along his integration into the main troop?'

'I don't think we should hurry it along,' Guy said again. 'Jennifer, I was wondering whether you might like to do some-thing this evening? Go to the pub again, perhaps? To talk about Ulysses in more relaxed surroundings.'

Jennifer bit her lip to give the excuse time to form there. Guy felt the liquid in his stomach sloshing from side to side as though he were a washing machine while he waited for her reply.

'Actually,' she lied, 'I'm busy all evening. I said I would go to Exeter to see a friend.'

'Oh. OK then.'

'Can't we talk about Ulysses' progress in the staff room at lunchtime tomorrow?' she asked.

'Of course,' said Guy. 'If you're not too busy. First day of filming tomorrow. I guess it's a good job I'll have the evening to stay in and wash my hair.'

'Yes,' Jennifer nodded.

'I'll see you in the morning,' said Guy. He got into his car.

Jennifer watched him drive away with just a little smidgen of uneasiness. She wondered how long it would be before things were entirely easy between them again. Since Timothy's reappearance on the scene, Guy and Jennifer had barely had a proper conversation. The night Jennifer stood Guy up still hadn't been mentioned at all.

It would be a whole lot simpler if Jennifer could explain to Guy the real reason why she appeared to have blown hot and cold so suddenly. It might make him feel less rejected to know that she had passed up the opportunity of starting something with him to go back to the love of her life.

All those wasted years, Jennifer thought as she got into her own car. If only she had been less stubborn and given Timothy another chance before she marched out of his life like that. How naïve she had been to assume that he was having sex with another woman because he was a hopelessly selfish loser who couldn't keep his dick in his pants. It was so clear to her now that Timothy's infidelity had sprung from a place of loneliness and fear. He had told her so himself. He was so frightened by how much he loved her, he said, that he had sabotaged their relationship to save himself the terrible pain he would feel when Jennifer saw that he wasn't the man she thought he was and started to look elsewhere herself.

'You silly, silly man,' she had kissed him on the forehead when he finished articulating his pain.

'A fool for love,' said Timothy.

41

The television crew arrived the next morning in two white vans
loaded with cameras and sound-recording gear. As agreed, they
set up cameras in the main chimp enclosure to provide a twenty-
four-hour feed from which they could pick out interesting antics.

They would be doing some filming in the nursery too. Guy
watched nervously as the camera operators set up their equip-
ment near Ulysses' pen. Since the night when he and Jamie made
their discovery, Guy had been waiting on tenterhooks for the
moment when someone else would spot the chimp making a sign.
So far it hadn't happened. It was as though Ulysses only bothered
to sign to those humans he thought might be able to understand
him.

'Do something interesting,' said Dave, the cameraman, to the
chimp beneath the blanket. Ulysses didn't move.

'OK,' said Faith when everything was in place. 'Here is the plan.
We're going to be following the story of Ulysses. And as such
we'd like to start at the very beginning, when he arrived from
Spain on that boat.'

'Well, you've missed that,' said Nessa.

'We did,' said Faith. 'Which is why we're going to do a
reconstruction.'

'A reconstruction?'

'Yes. If it's OK with you, I'd like to take the keepers who picked
Ulysses up back down to Plymouth to do a re-enactment so that
we can make it look as though Timothy was there on the day.'

'Is this right?' asked Nessa. 'I thought you were shooting a
factual documentary.'

'We are,' said Faith. 'This is just top and tailing. Unfortunately,
the general public is so *au fait* with cinematic convention these

219

days that even fact-based programmes have to have some kind of story arc.'

'Story arc?' asked Snowy.

'A proper beginning, middle and end,' Faith explained. 'Just like in a fairy tale.'

'But re-enactments,' said Nessa. 'Does this happen often?'

'All the time. How on earth do you think they shoot half those "deep sea" documentaries? The creatures they want to film live at depths where there is no light whatsoever and where the water pressure is so great it would squish a great big camera like an empty can. Likewise all those fantastic shots of mummy fox in the den with her cubs. You don't think the production team goes around digging holes until they find one, do you? It's all set up. Just like filming *EastEnders*. Only the actors are marginally less trouble.'

Nessa looked perturbed. 'It feels like cheating.'

'Everything else we shoot will be 100 per cent genuine, I promise. Just let us work our magic on this piece of the story. We'll make it exactly as it happened.'

'OK,' Nessa agreed.

The sanctuary's van was immediately despatched to the docks with Guy, Snowy and Jennifer on board. The customs team were waiting, albeit next to an entirely different boat. The only player missing from the scene was Ulysses. Faith at least didn't insist that the chimpanzee was dragged back down to the docks as well. It was decided that Guy and Snowy would be filmed carrying out a pile of pillows covered with a blanket. It took a surprisingly long time to get it right.

'Still doesn't look heavy enough,' Faith shouted from behind her monitor. 'Bend your knees a bit more, Snowy. You're carrying a half-grown chimpanzee, not a pile of pillows!'

But Snowy was no actor. And after five extremely unsuccessful takes, Faith sent for a sack of potatoes. A big one.

'Thanks a lot,' Guy hissed. 'This is much heavier than Ulysses was.'

'What do you think of your first piece of stardom?' Nessa asked.

'Agonising,' said Guy as he rubbed at the small of his back.

*   *   *

The real star of the show didn't even turn up until later that afternoon, tanned from five days in West Africa and more deliciously handsome than ever. The TV crew were back at the sanctuary by this time. As media luvvie air kisses were exchanged between presenter and production crew, Jennifer stood at the back of the gawping Prowdes' staff and smiled happily to herself.

'Later,' Timothy mouthed and winked at her as he was led away to film that day's piece to camera. Jennifer watched with Nessa and Jo-Jo.

'Isn't he gorgeous?' said Nessa.

'Not really my type,' Jennifer lied.

'It's been an exciting first day at Prowdes Animal Sanctuary,' Timothy told the camera. 'Early this morning, customs officers in Plymouth boarded a boat they suspected to be carrying drugs only to discover a far more unusual illegal cargo than the usual supplies of cocaine or cannabis. Who knows where Ulysses the chimpanzee started his journey. But he is ending it here at Prowdes in a quarantine cage . . .

'Guy Gibson is head keeper of chimpanzees. Guy, can you tell us what will happen next?'

'Well, Dr Lauder—' Guy began.

'Call him Timothy,' Faith shouted from behind the camera. 'He can call you Timothy, can't he, Timothy?'

Timothy nodded.

'Take it from the top again.'

'I had it perfect there,' Timothy grumbled.

'Sorry,' said Guy.

'You'll get used to it,' Faith assured him. 'Can you just move round to the side a bit so that you're not blocking our view of Timothy? Don't move your hands about so much. Talk slowly and clearly. But not too slowly. And relax!'

Guy looked about as relaxed as a macaque receiving an enema.

'From the top,' said Faith.

'It's been an exciting first day at Prowdes,' Timothy began again.

Jennifer looked forward to an equally exciting night.

*   *   *

While Jennifer and Timothy spent a clandestine evening in each other's arms at the Witch's cottage, Snowy, Jo-Jo and Guy met for a post-mortem at the Wily Fox. They teased Guy about his first speaking part, which had taken six takes to get right. Jo-Jo and Snowy discussed the merits of the television crew. Jo-Jo rather liked Dave the cameraman, with his shaved head and a goatee. While she turned Snowy and Guy puce with her monologue on the merits of facial hair when it came to cunnilingus, the man in question walked into the pub behind her. Snowy spluttered into his beer. Guy mimed that Jo-Jo should shut up.

The entire television crew had come into the Fox, accompanied by Nessa and the Major.

'I told them that this is the best place in town,' Nessa said to Arlene. Arlene sent across a couple of bottles of wine on the house in anticipation of a big boost to future business. The keepers joined Faith and her team to toast a successful first day.

'Such a pity Dr Lauder can't be with us,' the Major commented.

'Yes,' said Faith. 'But he's very tired. He said he needs an early night, having just got back from Africa this morning.'

'Ah, Africa,' the Major sighed. 'Did I ever tell you about the time I spent there, Miss O'Connell?'

'Yes. But it would be very nice to get some of your reminiscences in greater detail on camera,' said Faith.

Guy and Nessa rolled their eyes.

'Where's Jennifer?' Nessa asked Guy during a quiet moment later in the evening.

'Getting her beauty sleep,' suggested Guy.

'Things are, er, OK between you, aren't they?' Nessa probed. 'It's just that it seemed at one point as though you two were getting terribly close. And then . . .' Nessa made a gesture with her hands that suggested something disappearing in a puff of smoke.

Guy smiled into his pint glass.

'You don't need to say anything,' Nessa told him.

'Another toast to Prowdes!' said the Major, saving Guy from imminent embarrassment.

*   *   *

As a cheer was raised in the Wily Fox, Jennifer Niederhauser was doing some celebrating of her own.

She sank back into the pillows after her first orgasm in five and a half years.

'Haven't lost the old touch, eh?' said Timothy. He was extremely proud of himself.

42

It was amazing how quickly the Prowdes' team became used to having the camera crew around. Within a couple of weeks, Jo-Jo could pause in whatever she was doing and explain to the cameras why she was doing it like a seasoned professional. It helped that she was getting increasingly fond of the man behind the camera.

Guy too had become much more relaxed. Snowy still preferred 'action shots' as he called them to talking. It was difficult to get the Major to shut up once he started. The cameras loved Nessa, enlivening the screen with her beautiful exotic clothes like a tropical bird. Even Jennifer was having fun.

She wondered if people watching the programme when it aired in a few months' time would notice the chemistry between her and Timothy as he asked her questions about Project Africa on camera.

'Can you stop flicking your hair around so much?' Faith asked as they were filming Jennifer one afternoon. Jennifer had stopped wearing her hair in a ponytail or plaits. Timothy preferred it loose over her shoulders. But now the thought that she had been flicking it about sent Jennifer crimson. That was unmistakable body language. Timothy gave her a little wink before he wandered across to Faith to talk about the next shot she wanted to get done that day.

Timothy and Faith weren't at the sanctuary every day. For most of the week they were in Oxford and London respectively. Faith had several other television projects to oversee and Timothy's presence was occasionally required by his principal employers at St Francis Hall. It was frustrating for Jennifer. All in all, she and Timothy were managing to spend just one or two nights a week together and even then it was still under hush-hush conditions.

On those nights when he was in Tincastle, Timothy would usually have dinner with the production team at the Wily Fox or at Guido's trattoria, then he would excuse himself for the night. He would tell his dinner companions that he was going back to the bed and breakfast establishment where he was staying but would make a detour via the Witch's cottage, parking his distinctive car in the alley at the back of the house so that no one would spot it.

Sometimes he didn't arrive until almost midnight. Sometimes Jennifer would have been sitting on her sofa, with her best underwear on, since eight o'clock. But she believed him when he told her that the subterfuge was just as hard on him.

'I want to be able to pick you up and kiss you in front of the cameras,' he said.

'I still don't quite understand why you can't.'

About three weeks into their secret affair, Timothy told her why not in much more detail.

'The thing is, sweetness,' he said, 'I've got an awful feeling that Faith O'Connell has a crush on me.'

'She does?'

'I'm afraid so. I've given her no reason whatsoever to think that her feelings are reciprocated, but I'm worried that if you and I suddenly started being lovey-dovey around the place, she might react somewhat unreasonably and sabotage the show in a misplaced act of revenge.'

'What? Why would she do that? *How* would she do that?'

'She seems a very sensible woman on the surface, I know, but underneath she's quite a fragile sort of person just barely holding it together from day to day. She's a brilliant television producer. No doubt about that. But if she gets upset she could turn that brilliance against us. She could use the footage she's shot so far and make it look as though you and I should be on the RSPCA's most-wanted list for animal cruelty.'

'What on earth do you mean?'

'It's all about spin. Think how some of the things you've been doing might look if you weren't also given the chance to explain the rationale behind them. Mad and Bad are bound to get into some distress when they're introduced to the adults for the first time. If you don't get the chance to explain why you're having to separate them from their cups of tea and their Marmite on toast, you could look very cruel indeed.'

Jennifer chewed a hangnail at the corner of her thumb.

'She wouldn't stitch us up like that.'

'I wouldn't bet money against it. I've seen it happen, Jenny. I've seen her fly into incredible tempers in production meetings. I've seen grown men like the guys who operate the cameras actually crying when they come out of her Winnebago. Hell hath no fury like a female producer spurned.'

Jennifer bit the hangnail so hard she drew blood.

'I don't think you should give in to those sorts of tactics,' she said after a moment. 'We're all adults. Faith O'Connell just has to learn to live with the fact that you don't want to be with her and act like the professional she's supposed to be when it comes to making the programme. Nessa only allowed the cameras into the sanctuary at all because Faith promised that her treatment of our work would be entirely sympathetic.'

'Jennifer, don't be so naïve. You know how television works. Horror stories get just as many viewers as happy ones. More, in fact. If we upset Faith O'Connell she will crucify us both. But the real victims will be the chimpanzees . . .' He finished the sentence quietly. Seriously.

'You really mean it, don't you?' Jennifer whispered. 'You really mean that we're going to have to pretend that tonight and all those other nights haven't happened to make sure that the programme shows Prowdes in a favourable light.'

Timothy nodded.

'It's so unfair.'

'It is. But it's only for another three weeks. The filming has to be finished by the beginning of September so they can edit the programme together in time for the winter schedule. You can keep our secret for that long, can't you?' Timothy asked.

'It doesn't look as though I have a choice.'

'It's to protect your own reputation too. You don't want to be known as Dr Timothy Lauder's girlfriend wherever you go. You're a serious conservationist in your own right these days.'

He pinched her cheeks. 'You were always my best and brightest student. My protégée.'

'Was I really?' Jennifer sniffed.

'You know you were. You're going to be the Jane Goodall of your generation. I knew that the first time you walked into my office in that flowery dress you always wore.'

Hearing Timothy say that made Jennifer feel even warmer inside than his caresses had done. She blushed prettily. 'I always wanted you to be impressed by my work,' she said.

'And I am *so* impressed,' said Timothy, tracing a line from her shoulder to the top of the sheet she still clutched tightly around her. 'And I want the whole of the British public to be impressed too, when this show of ours hits the air. The chimpanzee project at Prowdes is doing fabulous work and it's all down to you. Play this my way and your name in the history books is guaranteed.'

'Do you think so?'

'Dr Jennifer Niederhauser, your books will be set texts for every zoology student from Harvard to Hull.'

Jennifer let the sheet drop.

43

Jennifer wasn't the only one holding something back from Faith O'Connell. Ulysses was not quite proving to be the television star that the production team had hoped. In fact, he was rather boring, spending most of his time contemplating the bare walls of his enclosure with the blanket safely to hand.

'Can't you teach him sign language or something?' Faith joked as she reviewed another day's footage without real event.

'Perhaps you shouldn't concentrate on him so much,' Guy suggested. 'I don't think he's ever going to do anything particularly exciting.' Guy had his fingers crossed in his pocket as he said that, imagining Faith's face if Ulysses suddenly chose that moment to sign 'hello'.

'Perhaps,' said Faith.

That afternoon they moved the camera from Ulysses' enclosure to Hector's pen instead. Faith thought it might add a bit of extra interest to contrast the behaviour of the chimps with the orang. Jo-Jo was thrilled. Hector responded in his usual way. By doing nothing . . .

Each night, as the camera crew packed up their gear to go back to the bed and breakfast hotel where they were staying, Jamie would arrive at the sanctuary on his bicycle, ostensibly to help Guy clear up for a bit of extra pocket money. In reality, Jamie was every bit the young scientist, sitting with Ulysses and signing at him non-stop in an attempt to work out just how much the little chimpanzee really knew.

Jamie and Ulysses didn't exactly have very edifying conversations, but Jamie was convinced that Ulysses could understand a lot more than Guy believed possible.

'I don't think he likes it here very much,' signed Jamie. 'I don't think he likes the other chimps.'

'Did you get that from what he signed?' Guy asked.

'No,' Jamie admitted. 'Most of it is just my intuition.'

Guy cuffed Jamie around the head. But he was very relieved that Jamie seemed to be taking an interest in something again, other than hanging round with the gang at the fountain.

'Can I tell anybody about him yet?' Jamie asked.

'No,' said Guy.

'Have you told anybody?'

'No. No I haven't.'

'Not even your boss?' Jamie made kissing motions with his hands.

'Definitely not her.'

'I can't believe she hasn't noticed.'

'He doesn't sign to anybody except you and me.'

Not that Guy thought Jennifer would have noticed if Ulysses had stood up, shook her by the hand and addressed her by name. Jennifer seemed to have lost her focus somewhat. She didn't seem as interested in Ulysses' progress. Didn't seem to have an opinion on it any more. When she came into the nursery now, she came with Timothy Lauder.

Now *he* was a man with plenty of opinions. Including the opinion that it was about time Mad and Bad went to join the grown-ups.

On the appointed morning, Snowy awoke with a sick, empty feeling in his stomach. Even before his brain switched on, and he remembered what day it was, his body was reacting to the loss he would experience before nightfall. Mad and Bad would be joining the main troop that day. Was this how mothers felt when they sent their children off to boarding school, Snowy wondered. He felt as though he was about to walk his children to the edge of a dark forest that he couldn't follow them into. He had tears in his eyes when he arrived at the sanctuary to give his boys their breakfast.

Mad was already hanging on the bars, scrawny arm through a gap in the mesh, pointing towards his favourite Chelsea T-shirt which was folded on a bench within his line of vision.

'Not today,' said Snowy. 'We're doing something different today.'

It had been agreed that the twins would have their breakfast in the nursery while the chimps in the main enclosure ate theirs. Dr Lauder had decided that the best time to take the twins into the transitional cage would be after the bigger chimps had eaten, while they were feeling full and relaxed.

'You'll be able to see them every day,' Nessa reminded him.

'Yes. But . . . It will be different,' said Snowy disconsolately.

'Of course it will be different,' said Jennifer. 'But before long the twins will realise that they are much better off with their own kind. I think you're being rather selfish, Snowy. This isn't about how you feel now. It's about how Mad and Bad will feel in years to come. They'll have so much more fun out there.'

Snowy, Nessa and Jennifer looked in the direction of the main enclosure. A loud wah-bark announced that Achilles wasn't in the best of moods.

'Just a little bit longer,' Snowy pleaded. 'I thought that Mad was a bit sniffly this morning. Maybe he's picked up a cold. If we could just wait to see whether he's in the clear . . .'

Jennifer looked up Mad's nose in search of snot.

'All clear,' she announced. 'He's fine.'

'Come on, boys,' said Snowy. He felt so treacherous as the twins bounded out of their cage and attached themselves one to each hip, as they had done so many times before. They liked their trips around the sanctuary. They were fond of the donkeys and the llama and the angora rabbits in the children's petting zoo. They liked to drop in on Hermione and Harry Porker and the piglets. But whenever they went near the chimp enclosure, they had bristled and squeaked their distress. It was as though they didn't know they were chimps. And adult chimpanzees seemed pretty bloody frightening compared to angora rabbits and pot-bellied pigs.

Snowy hadn't told anybody that he had been disobeying Jennifer's orders. Their daily walks hadn't helped acclimatise the twins to the other chimps because Snowy had started to avoid the chimp enclosure after they passed it one day while Achilles was displaying and both twins wet themselves all over Snowy's overalls. The only apes they had seen close up after that were Hector and Ulysses. Hector hardly cut a terrifying figure as he slowly turned over the dirt in search of interesting stones and Ulysses still seemed to sleep most of the day.

As they neared the main enclosure now, with the TV crew in tow, Snowy began to realise that he might well have been inadvertently cruel by trying to be so kind. He felt both twins' tiny bodies stiffen as he carried them past Hector's enclosure and kept going instead of turning back to see the angora bunnies in the kiddy zoo. Their open-mouthed play-grins morphed into grimaces of fear.

Achilles obviously knew that something was afoot from the number of people gathered by the wire and was showing off accordingly. Achilles' excitement had aroused the females in his harem who were barking in agreement. Snowy felt his stomach lurch as he watched Achilles pick up an old rubber tyre and hurl it in the direction of the wire in a display of his strength. Like every other keeper, Snowy had read enough Jane Goodall to know that a male would often use accessories in a dance of dominance such as this and a small chimp would do just as well as a tyre or a big piece of wood. Achilles picked up the tyre again and in his mind's eye, Snowy saw Mad and Bad's delicate little bodies crash down into the dust when Achilles pitched the rubber ring at his audience.

The twins and their entourage came to a halt outside the gates to the main enclosure and the holding cages. Faith carefully moved Snowy and the twins to the centre of the party.

'Snowy,' said Faith, 'perhaps you'd like to say a few words about what's going on here. What we're doing today.'

Snowy was frozen.

'You're introducing Mad and Bad to the rest of the troop, right?' Timothy prompted. 'They're going to be held in these pens within the enclosure until they're used to the others. Is that what's happening?'

'Just start talking,' said Faith. 'We'll cut anything stupid out.'

Still he said nothing.

'Snowy,' Nessa tried.

'I don't know what we're doing today,' said Snowy suddenly. 'I don't want them to go in there with that . . . that—' He searched for a word to describe Achilles who was currently shaking a fifteen-foot-tall tree as though he was brandishing a feather duster. 'That beast,' he said finally. 'I'm not letting them go in there,' he told Jennifer.

'Come on,' said Jennifer.

'Yes,' said Timothy. 'We haven't got all day.'

'We agreed that this is for the best,' Jennifer elaborated.

'No. I don't believe you,' said Snowy. 'Or him,' he added, pointing at Timothy. 'I especially don't believe him.' Then he set off at a sprint with the babies tucked under his arms. The cameras followed him all the way to the car park, where he climbed into the sanctuary van and sat there with his head in his hands while Mad and Bad made short work of anything that could be pulled off the dashboard.

So, Mad and Bad had one more night in the nursery. But the next morning, they were moved into the halfway-house enclosure inside the bounds of the main enclosure before Snowy even got to the sanctuary. He spent the rest of the day disconsolately watching them through the mesh. The twins were frightened and bewildered and obviously felt betrayed. On the other side of their transitional cage, some of the adult chimps were still displaying aggressively. When Snowy poked a finger through the mesh to tickle Mad, who was sitting closest to him and just about within reach, the little chimp turned his back on his former keeper and friend. Bad did the same. The brothers wrapped their hairy arms around each other instead and kept their eyes averted from the horror of the troop that awaited them.

Guy and Jo-Jo took Snowy to the pub to cheer him up. Jennifer stayed behind. She had assumed she wasn't invited after Jo-Jo sneered, 'God, it must be lovely to be right the whole time,' as she passed Jennifer in the keepers' shower room.

But she was right, wasn't she? It was time for Mad and Bad to leave the nursery. Of course it was going to be a terrifying experience for them. But they were safe in that holding cage. The other chimps might frighten them but they couldn't get close enough to hurt them. Eventually they would be assimilated and when Snowy saw them climbing the trees and playing with the big boys . . . well, he would see how much happier they were.

'We did the right thing, didn't we?' she asked Timothy when they were in bed together later that night.

'Of course we did,' said Timothy. 'Have I ever given you reason not to trust me?'

'Can you stay the night?' Jennifer tried then. 'I really feel like I could use the company.'

'Not tonight, sweetheart,' he said. 'Faith is staying at the same B and B as me this week. Don't want to rouse her suspicions. Just another two weeks to go.'

44

When Timothy left to go back to the bed and breakfast, Jennifer felt more deflated than ever. For once she was glad when Dahlia called for a gossip.

Though Timothy had made her swear that she would keep their affair a secret from everyone, including and especially her best friend with the mouth of a town crier, Jennifer hadn't been able to resist letting Dahlia in on her secret. And Dahlia was being remarkably discreet (she'd only told her husband, who, like most men, wasn't really that interested in another woman's love life anyway. Unless it involved lesbianism).

'He's gone again,' said Jennifer.

'Has he ever stayed the whole night with you since the beginning of this liaison?' Dahlia asked.

'No,' Jennifer admitted. 'But I see his point. We can't risk upsetting Faith O'Connell. It could be dangerous for the sanctuary.'

Dahlia snorted.

'What are you snorting for now?'

'Jenny, dear,' said Dahlia, 'for someone with so many letters after her name, you can be astonishingly gullible. Don't you think it's far more likely that Timothy Lauder is worried about saving his own skin rather than protecting the reputation of the sanctuary? He still spends half the week in Oxford, right?'

'Most of the week,' said Jennifer. 'Well, between Oxford and London. He has to spend a lot of time there, too. His series on chimps for the BBC will be airing halfway through September. There's lots of PR work to do.'

'Do you think it's possible that there's someone else in the city?'

'No,' said Jennifer. 'Nooooo!'

'I think you should ask him. When are you next seeing him?'

'Not for another two days. He's going up to London tomorrow to look over the programmes they've made so far.'

'With Faith O'Connell?'

'With Faith O'Connell,' said Jennifer.

'Oh, Jennifer,' said Dahlia, 'I do hope your man can be trusted.'

'He can.'

'I don't trust him,' said Snowy to the others.

Though Guy, Jo-Jo and Arlene had tried to distract Snowy from the twins' move to the main enclosure with every topic from football to feng shui, the conversation kept coming back to Timothy Lauder.

'The twins weren't ready. Jennifer knew that. She wouldn't have made me put them in with the big chimps. He pushed her. He pushed her to do it so that he could make better television.'

'He wouldn't do that.'

'I wouldn't put it past him.'

'He is a chimpanzee expert,' said Jo-Jo.

'He's read a lot of books. He may have spent a lot of time following chimpanzees through the jungle. But not our chimpanzees. He doesn't know them. I knew those chimps better than I know you and Guy, Jo-Jo. I would have known when they were ready. They weren't ready. They were terrified.'

'Jennifer knows the chimps too,' said Guy, trying hard to bring some balance to the debate. 'I promise you, they were never in danger.'

'Like I said,' Snowy reiterated, 'Jennifer isn't one of us any more.'

'Like she ever really was,' Jo-Jo sniffed.

'She's acting under Timothy Lauder's orders. And all he cares about is making good telly.'

45

The first few episodes of *Chimpanzee Rescue*, as the series was to
be called, were already finished, edited, polished and ready to be
aired. Faith took a tape over to Timothy's room at the Metropolitan Hotel in London the following evening and they watched
episodes one, two and three together over a bottle of wine.

'You look great,' said Faith, when Timothy appeared on the
screen at the end of episode three to explain a little about the way
in which Mad and Bad would be integrated into the main
chimpanzee troop. 'This show is going to make you a huge star.
Not that you're not already pretty damn big,' she added quickly.

'It looks good,' Timothy agreed.

He was having a very good day overall. Preview tapes of his
series on chimpanzees in Africa had been received by the TV
reviewers with great acclaim. Over lunch with Felicity he had
basked in the news of the media coverage he was already guaranteed.

'*TV Quick* are running a big article,' Felicity had told him.
'They're calling you the new Attenborough. As are *Chat* and *TV
Weekly*. Obviously there will be another big piece in *TV Times* to
correspond with the first airing date. Actually, I meant to say, they
are going to want some new photos for that. If it's OK with you, I
thought we could spend the day after the *TV Weekly* awards
doing a photo shoot and interviews. We've had lots of interest
from radio stations up and down the country and, of course,
Richard and Judy have said that they would be delighted to have
you as a guest on their show. Apparently Judy always wanted to
be a naturalist herself.'

'Are you sure she didn't mean "naturist"?' Timothy'd
quipped, remembering a past television award show where Judy
fell out of her dress in front of the nation.

Felicity had laughed appropriately.

And now here was Faith singing his praises too. *Chimpanzee Rescue* was shaping up to be the perfect second step in Timothy's mission to dominate nature programming on the terrestrial channels as well as Discovery.

'Well, it sounds like everything is on track to make this a huge hit,' said Timothy happily.

'Sort of,' said Faith.

'What do you mean, sort of?'

Faith bit her lip. 'I don't know if I can even say this. It sounds a little bit stupid. I know that it makes sense from a television production point of view, but from the point of view of a chimpanzee conservationist, I'm afraid that this is going to sound ridiculous.'

'Faith,' said Timothy, 'I have been teaching Oxford under-graduates for the past six years. I think I've heard just about everything ridiculous there is to hear about chimpanzee conservation. What is the problem?'

Faith closed her eyes and started to spew it out. 'Well, we had a meeting at the office this morning. While you were on your way here. And we showed the tapes we've completed so far to the head of the channel, Ted Gilbert, and I did a little presentation about how the series would pan out from those first three shows. You know, from the early programmes explaining the various chimps' disadvantaged backgrounds and introducing the staff at Prowdes, through the rehabilitation programme until finally we see the chimps ready to leave for their new home.' She had delivered that speech all on one breath and had to stop to take another one.

'Carry on,' said Timothy.

'It would make the perfect series arc. From captivity to free-dom. Or at least, from captivity to a stage where it's clear that the chimps are ready for their freedom. We can do the Africa bit in series two. Ted Gilbert is totally hot to trot for that. But the thing is, it's becoming clear that perhaps we were overly ambitious. It seemed like a gift from the gods when we heard about Ulysses. His rescue from that boat. We didn't think we'd get dramatic footage like that. So we found ourselves concentrating on him. It seemed the obvious thing to do after the way he came into the story. We would focus on one deeply traumatised chimp and follow him until he was swinging about in the trees with his new friends. He became, if you like, our hero.'

'And he's doing very well.'

Faith looked anguished. 'Not quite well enough, I'm afraid. Oh, Timothy, please don't hate me for saying this. I know that you're the chimpanzee expert. You know everything there is to know about apes. But I'm the television producer and what I have on my hands right now is hundreds of hours of footage of the same bloody chimp sitting in the corner of his cage with a blanket over his head occasionally eating a banana. He's no closer to swinging in the trees with the other chimps than he was when I first got there. I do not have footage that adds up to a *happy ending*. And the channel boss is insisting on a happy ending. Our original timescale was that we would have everything we needed on film in a fortnight's time so that the programme could be edited during September and October for airing in November. This series is due to end on Christmas Eve. If it isn't relentlessly feel-good then . . .'

'What?'

Faith put her head down and muttered at top speed, 'They may go with the meerkats and push our chimpanzees back to next year.'

Faith didn't look up. She just waited for Timothy to say something. And it seemed like another mini-series could have been recorded in the time it took for him to respond.

'You must be joking,' he began. 'They're going to go with the meerkats?'

Faith nodded nervously. 'They're thinking about it.'

'What's so great about bloody meerkats?'

'People like them.'

'People like chimpanzees.'

'Not chimpanzees that just sit under a blanket. It could be a crocodile under there for all we get to see.'

'I'm not going to let some idiot channel boss who needs a happy ending put paid to all the hard work I have done for the past four weeks.'

'I know how you must feel, Tim. I've been there for the past four weeks as well. But Ted Gilbert does have absolute power of veto and he has told me in no uncertain terms that we have been allocated the *feel-good* slot and if we don't feel good enough then . . . What can we do? We don't have time to switch the focus on to another individual animal now. And if Ulysses isn't ready to join the other chimps in the main troop then we can hardly force him. I tried to explain to Ted that if Ulysses was released into the enclosure too early then we could actually be putting him in mortal danger from Achilles and the other big males. I personally think that the stuff we've got so far is very interesting viewing and any intelligent viewer will understand that we can't guarantee the rehabilitation will be complete before the end of the series. But Ted Gilbert . . . He's a family man. He's well known for picking the shows that will be a hit with all ages. He judges things on whether or not they'll make his daughter cry and . . . well . . .'

Timothy was staring out of the window, his mouth set in a thin, hard line.

'I know how much those chimpanzees mean to you, Tim,' said Faith. 'I know that the rehabilitation of *one* chimp is just as important to you as a whole television series is to me. I'll go back to Gilbert and tough it out,' she continued, as much to buoy herself up as to placate her star. 'I'll tell him that if he wants a happy ending he'll have to give us more time. But I'll also tell him that I think what we have so far is award-winning stuff. It's real. It's important. It's the truth—'

'I can't wait until next year for this series to come out,' Timothy said suddenly and stridently. Faith was shocked into silence. 'I put off a lot of projects to work on this one, Faith. Once my African series is aired, I have got nothing else on screen until next autumn except for repeats on BBC Choice. I can't afford to be out of the public eye for that long. I'll lose momentum. If this series doesn't air before Christmas, it could completely stall my career. Do you realise how much effort I have put into getting this far?'

'Yes,' Faith began. 'Of course I do but . . .'

'I don't want to be the "new David Attenborough", Faith. I want people to forget that there ever was another naturalist on

TV. When people think about wild animals, I want them to think about Dr Timothy Lauder and no one else. When I was a kid, people thought I was swotty, always reading my books and studying for exams. But I knew exactly where I was going. Cambridge as an undergrad, Edinburgh for my PhD. Oxford. All those bloody months spent tracking chimpanzees through the festering hell that is the African jungle were all building up to this time. I am going to the *TV Weekly* awards next week, Faith. The *TV Weekly* awards. Do you realise what that means? I have been nominated by the public in the category of most popular cable television nature show presenter of the year! I realise that this year I may not get it. The competition is very strong. Attenborough is still hanging on in there after all. But I am damn sure that I will hold that award before I am thirty-three.'

That year he was thirty-two.

'And to make sure that I get another bite at the cherry next year, I need to make sure that the public remember who I am when nomination time comes round again. I need to be beaming into their homes so often that housewives up and down the country know my face better than they know their own husbands'. There is no way that I am going to let my chimpanzees be sidelined for the fucking meerkats because they're not acting "happy" enough.'

'Of course not,' said Faith nervously.

By this time, Timothy was on his feet and thumping his clenched fist on the windowsill as he looked out across Hyde Park.

'And I'll relay all this to Ted Gilbert,' Faith promised. 'I'm sure we can come to some sort of compromise.'

'There will be no compromise,' said Timothy.

Faith had pretty much known he would say that. Her presenters always said that kind of thing before Ted Gilbert saw their careers buried. Last year's 'uncompromising' presenter was already back in his day job at the car showroom. But what Timothy said next, Faith really hadn't expected at all.

'If Ulysses isn't swinging from the trees in that enclosure by the end of next week,' said Timothy Lauder, 'I will take a fucking rifle and shoot him. How's that for a ratings booster?'

46

On her morning rounds of the sanctuary, Nessa had noticed that Big Ears seemed to have acquired a limp overnight. It was a very slight limp but from her lookout on the other side of the fence, Nessa was finding it hard to work out whether the limp was caused by a muscle strain or by a bite or cut on the inside of the chimpanzee's leg where she couldn't see it. Either way, it seemed a good idea to have Harrison check it out before too long.

Harrison arrived as soon as he had finished his early morning visit to the zoo in Teignton. The baby giraffe there was having teething problems. Guy offered to take Harrison out to the chimp enclosure while Jennifer continued to sort through interminable piles of papers in the office.

'So what's it like being a television star?' Harrison asked as he and Guy walked towards the chimps. 'Are you ready for all the screaming girls throwing their knickers at you when you're trying to do your shopping?'

'I don't think any of us needs to worry about that,' said Guy. 'There's going to be only one star of this show.'

'Ulysses?' Harrison asked.

Guy smiled wryly.

'Come on, then. Let's see if we can get a closer look at Big Ears.'

Guy unlocked the first gate and they stepped into the air lock, as the gap between the two fences was called.

'Achilles has been a bit fractious these past few days,' Guy warned the vet. 'Good idea not to turn your back on him. In fact, I wouldn't be at all surprised if Big Ears' limp has something to do with his father. He nearly took a piece out of Snowy the other day. We daren't let the twins out of their cage yet.'

Harrison nodded. Mad and Bad looked at the vet and Guy

mournfully as the human beings walked past their holding pen. Even as Guy spoke about Achilles, he and Harrison could see the alpha male getting slowly to his feet as they approached, puffing out his hair to make him look his very biggest as he did so.

'Probably not a great idea to go introducing him to Ulysses right now then,' Harrison suggested.

'I don't know if that chimp will ever be ready to join the others,' said Guy. 'There's something not quite chimp-ish enough about him.'

Harrison nodded thoughtfully.

'OK. Safe to step out there, I think,' said Harrison. Satisfied that they had seen him at his most impressive when he stood up, Achilles was now sitting down again, contentedly pulling the leaves off a branch while Virginia picked carefully through the thick black hair on his back in search of parasites.

'Where's Big Ears?'

'Over there.' Guy pointed him out. The little chimp was sitting some way off from the others. He was sitting on the floor and almost doubled over as he examined the inside of his own leg, gingerly touching at what must have been the sore spot with his fingers before bringing his fingers up to his face and sniffing them.

'Must be a cut,' said Harrison.

'Do we need to dart him?'

'Big Ears? Maybe not. He's still pretty fond of you, isn't he? Let's see how close we can get.'

They couldn't get anywhere near him. Just as Guy was extending his wrist to Big Ears and hooting in greeting Harrison spotted a worrying development on the other side of the enclosure. Achilles was back on his feet again and moving towards them at speed.

'Shit. Run for it!' Harrison shouted.

It was quite a while before Harrison and Guy stopped panting long enough to be able to speak to one another.

'This is getting ridiculous,' said Harrison.

'Why do you think he's become so much more aggressive of late?'

'I don't know. Could be a reaction to all the changes going on around here. I mean, in the last three months he's had to get used to Jennifer and the television crew going in and out of the enclosure. It's a lot for him to deal with. Apes can be just as insecure as human beings.'

'What can we do about it?'

'Like I keep saying, castration,' Harrison suggested. Only half joking. 'Oh, look, here comes the great doctor.'

Timothy was walking towards them with Faith and Faith's assistant, Helen, who was, as usual, madly scribbling notes. Until she tripped over one of the low white wire fences that protected the flower beds.

'Harrison!' Timothy raised his hand. He didn't acknowledge Guy. The implication was pretty clear. Timothy considered himself to be on a par with the vet. Guy was simply a manual worker.

'How's it going in there?'

'Pretty good,' Harrison lied.

'You been running?' Timothy asked.

'Achilles isn't accepting visitors this morning,' Harrison quipped.

'Well, he's going to have to get used to it. Ulysses is ready to go in there now.'

'You think so?' Harrison asked.

'Yes, I do,' said Timothy.

'It would be a great way to end the series,' said Faith. 'Ulysses joining the others. And we're already in talks about doing another series,' she added excitedly. 'Following the whole troop when they're finally released into the wild.'

'With Dr Lauder here presenting?' said Harrison.

'If we're lucky,' Faith simpered.

Timothy's phone rang.

'Will you excuse me?' he said. He wandered away to take the call from his agent. Faith and Helen hovered nervously by the main enclosure for a while until Faith's phone rang as well and she disappeared after Timothy.

'See you later,' said Helen. She headed off in the direction of the office she and Faith had set up in the big house, scribbling her notes as she went.

'I don't like him,' said Harrison, when all three of their visitors were out of earshot.

'I'll second that,' said Guy.

'They're all the same, these academics. They think they know what they're doing because they've written the book about it. But it's just another example of those who *can't* doing the teaching. His experience of chimpanzees has all been from the far end of a pair of binoculars. Theoretical. And theories can get you into a lot of trouble.'

Guy nodded in agreement.

'Don't let him bully you into releasing any of the smaller chimps into the enclosure before you want to. Especially Ulysses. You know your animals, Guy. You're the best keeper I have ever had the pleasure to work with.'

'Thanks,' said Guy. 'I needed to hear that.'

'Talk to Jennifer,' was Harrison's advice. 'She'll listen to you.'

'Timothy thinks it's time we introduced Ulysses to the rest of the troop,' Jennifer informed Guy when she saw him in the staff room that lunchtime.

'Are you joking?'

'He thinks Ulysses has had long enough to get used to us, now it's time for him to get used to the other chimps. He may be right.'

'He's not right,' said Guy. 'The chimp is a nervous wreck. We've only just persuaded him to eat. Now isn't the time to be compounding his stresses by putting him anywhere near Achilles.'

Jennifer shrugged. 'There's such a thing as being over-cautious . . .'

'It's the wrong time. There are a couple of females coming into season. You know how aggressive that makes our number-one male. Ulysses is too young and too small. If we try to introduce him now, then at best it will be a miserable experience for the little fella and, at worst, it will be fatal.'

'Don't be so pessimistic,' said Jennifer. 'Dr Lauder is one of the most important authorities on chimpanzees in the western world. Perhaps he has noticed something that we haven't. Perhaps Ulysses is just malingering.'

'Malingering?'

'Yes. That's what Timothy thinks.'

'Malingering? Ulysses is a six-year-old chimp, not Snowy or Jo-Jo trying to get out of cleaning up. Talk about anthropomorphism. I'd like to hear Dr Lauder explain why he thinks that.'

'I'm sure he'd love to,' said Jennifer.

Speak of the devil.

Timothy stepped into the staff room.

'Jenny! Ah, Dr Niederhauser,' he corrected himself when he saw that she wasn't alone. 'I was wondering if you might like to go for lunch. To talk about Ulysses.'

Lunch was their new thing. It didn't involve any eating. Just straight back to the Witch's cottage and straight between the sheets when they got there.

'That would be nice,' said Jennifer. 'Can you wait while I finish some calls?'

'Of course.'

'Why don't you come with me to the quarantine unit while you're waiting, Dr Lauder?' Guy suggested. 'I'd like to hear what you think about Ulysses.'

'Are you really going to be that long?' Timothy asked Jennifer, obviously looking for a reason not to go.

'I'll be at least half an hour,' she said.

'Plenty of time,' said Guy.

The two men chatted uncomfortably on their way to see Guy's favourite chimp.

'You've worked here for a long time,' Timothy commented.

'Nearly eight years,' said Guy.

'You must know the chimps pretty well.'

'Exactly,' said Guy. He went straight to the point. 'Which is why I don't think that it would be a good idea to try to introduce Ulysses to the rest of the troop right now.'

Timothy said nothing until they were inside the quarantine unit. Then, he rounded on Guy like Achilles enraged and began, '*You* don't think it would be a good idea? The difference between you and me, Mr Gibson, is one of just three letters. P-H-D.' Timothy prodded Guy in the chest as he spelled out each initial.

'P-H-D. Do you know what that stands for? It stands for ten fucking years studying these animals more closely than you study your girly mags when you go to bed at night. Whatever there is to know about chimpanzees, I know it. Understand me? I wrote the fucking book about it.'

It was true. Timothy had written three books about chimps, in fact.

'When San Diego Zoo want to know what to do with their chimps, it is me they phone up. Not you. Not you, you little *keeper*. You little banana-peeler. You little shit-shoveller. Not you. But me. Me. *Dr* Timothy Lauder. Chimpanzee expert. *Expert* on chimpanzees. So, when I tell you that I think it is time for Ulysses to go back to his own kind, you can rest assured that it really is time. And if you don't start setting up another transitional cage in the main enclosure this afternoon, it will also be time for you to leave this circus and look for another job.'

'I don't remember the day you were appointed to be my boss,' said Guy quietly.

'Sometimes a hierarchy establishes itself quite naturally,' Timothy replied. 'Just like with the chimps. I may not be on the payroll here, but I think you'll find that Dr Niederhauser recognises the scientific basis of what I'm saying and I do believe that she has the power to fire you if I don't.' Timothy folded his arms as if to underline his statement.

Guy didn't bother going into the way things worked at Prowdes. Nobody really had the power to fire anybody except Nessa and she hadn't fired a single employee in all the years Prowdes had been open. But Guy didn't want to start that conversation with Timothy. He didn't want to have to look at his face a moment longer. In case he punched it.

'I'll talk to Dr Niederhauser about Ulysses this afternoon,' he said.

'Good. Then I'll look forward to seeing my suggestions being carried out. Ulysses' cage looks as though it could use a good clean,' said Timothy as he left.

'I heard everything,' said Snowy, emerging from a cubicle both Guy and Timothy had assumed was empty. 'I'm going to go outside and fucking well deck him now!'

Guy held Snowy back. 'Leave it,' he said. 'Leave it.' Guy hung on to Snowy until he felt his friend's muscles relax.

'He'd better not get anywhere near me tonight,' Snowy concluded.

'Tonight?' asked Guy.

'At the party.'

'Shit. I'd forgotten about that.'

47

Guido was only too thrilled to host the series wrap party at his trattoria. He had been trying to get in on the programme ever since he first heard Nessa and the Major talking about it. He had offered to cater for the television crew every single day and was horribly disappointed when they eschewed his famous gnocchi and made their own arrangements.

'It's not about you,' Nessa insisted. 'It's about mixing protein and carbs.'

But that night, even Helen, who wouldn't normally look at a wheat product, was happy to go to Tincastle's only real restaurant.

When the Prowdes' staff and the production team arrived, Guido insisted on taking a photograph of the group, with himself in the middle, arm around Timothy, to commemorate the occasion. He said that this photo would have pride of place on the wall of his restaurant, next to the photograph of Guido and Brian, winner of the second series of *Big Brother*, who had visited the trattoria while holidaying in the town.

'I'm thrilled to be among such illustrious company,' said Timothy, as he surveyed the restaurant's other celebrity pictures. Two photos of Jimmy Tarbuck, taken in the early seventies, and a signed black-and-white head shot of the actress who had played Bergerac's girlfriend. She used to have a holiday cottage in the town. Guido clapped Timothy on the back in delight, missing the sarcasm altogether.

'I will tell everybody you're my new best friend!' he said.

'Fantastic,' said Timothy, as Guido settled him into his place at the head of the table.

Guido had pulled out all the stops. He had insisted that all his staff be present that evening to make sure that the party's every need was met instantaneously. Before everyone had even taken their places, three waiters were buzzing around with trays of antipasti and glasses for the aperitif.

They toasted the programme with prosecco, the Italian answer to champagne (and the producer's answer to champagne too, given that she had blown so much of the budget on swanky London hotel bills . . .).

'Drink up!' said Faith. 'But not too much. We've got one more day of shooting, remember.'

'Well, whose stupid idea was it to have the wrap party the week before we wrap?' asked Dave, the cameraman, darkly.

'His lordship has to attend the *TV Weekly* awards on the night when we should have had it,' said Kelly, the sound girl, with a nod towards Timothy.

'Even if I win an award next week, I don't think I'll be quite so happy as I am right here, right now, with you,' said Timothy as if on cue.

With the exception of Kelly, each of the women assembled looked towards Timothy as though she was the only 'you' he was referring to. Even Nessa, who was well used to charming men, had fallen under Timothy Lauder's spell that evening, when he held out his arm to her as she exited the Major's car, and insisted that she sit next to him at the table.

'I would just like to say what a pleasure it has been working alongside you all these past six weeks,' Timothy continued. 'There's a family feeling at Prowdes Sanctuary that I haven't seen in any other animal rescue centre in the world.'

Nessa beamed.

'And this programme that we've put together is going to take that family feeling out to the whole of Great Britain. I think you can expect a bumper year for visitors next year, Nessa.'

'Thank you,' she said. 'We need one.'

That evening, Jennifer found herself sitting just about as far away from Timothy as it was possible to be on the long rectangular table. But she didn't mind. She felt a warm glow from knowing that in just over twenty-four hours' time, the television crew would be leaving Prowdes for the last time and she could tell the world the truth about herself and the love of her life. Watching him from a distance, charming Nessa and Jo-Jo and even the boys, she thought, Jennifer allowed herself a small fantasy about her future as Mrs Timothy Lauder. Not for her a white picket fence around a rose garden, though. They were going to be in Africa. They would buy a piece of land and set up their very own primate sanctuary. They would live there together far away from the temptations of the London television scene. Just Jennifer and Timothy and the apes. Perhaps they would even start a 'breeding programme' of their own one day.

At the very opposite end of the long rectangular table, Faith O'Connell was tearing a bread roll to pieces and putting none of the pieces into her mouth. On the outside she was smiley enough, but Jennifer recognised the hunger in the other woman's eyes. Faith wanted Timothy. Now Jennifer could see that Timothy had been right. Faith really was a fragile woman who would have crumbled if she knew the truth.

What a happy tableau they made. The sanctuary staff and the television crew breaking bread around Guido's big table. The food was fantastic. The sparkling prosecco flowed freely, as everyone promised Faith that a couple more bottles wouldn't inhibit their ability to use a steadicam/catch the sound/remember their lines. Guido had turned up the music and was promising to sing when everyone was on to their coffee. But only if Nessa would join him. Nessa had a fabulous voice.

'I've got a surprise for you later on,' the Major told Nessa, 'that I guarantee will make you sing.'

'Oh goodness,' Nessa grimaced. 'What on earth can that be?'

The Major tapped the side of his nose and went back to regaling Kelly with his life story. She wanted to hear more about his months in the jungle with the Matron.

'Have you heard the whole of this?' Kelly shouted across to Faith. 'Wouldn't it make a fantastic programme in its own right?'

Faith nodded.

'Well, I'd be more than happy to assist you lovely girls in putting a proposal together. That is what you do, isn't it? Put a proposal together.'

'He's been learning all the lingo,' said Jo-Jo. 'But he'll be unbearable if you give him his own show,' she teased. 'He'll demand his own hair and make-up girl!'

'I have never worn make-up in my life!' the Major said defensively.

'Come on, Major,' Jo-Jo ribbed him again. 'You're among friends here. I thought all you army types had a secret fetish for women's clothing and high heels. I can just imagine you in a nice pleated skirt. A silky blouse. Slight touch of mascara . . .'

It was a tease too far. The Major started to go red in the face, as it seemed he valiantly battled the urge to tell Jo-Jo exactly what he thought of her cheek.

Nessa shot Jo-Jo a warning look across the table.

'I'm sorry, Major,' said Jo-Jo quickly. 'I was only having a joke.'

But the Major continued to get redder.

'Major? Are you all right?' Jo-Jo asked him.

One by one, the assembled guests put down their eating utensils and looked at the old man. An apocalyptic outburst of rage directed at Jo-Jo seemed to be the only possible way to stop the Major's head from exploding. Twelve people waited with bated breath for the eruption. Jo-Jo was visibly trembling as she awaited her fate.

'I didn't mean it,' she tried again. 'Really, I don't think you'd look good in make-up at all.'

'Jo-Jo,' mouthed Guy. 'Just leave it.'

'Aaaagh!' said the Major.

Crash!

The Major fell forward. Face down in his spaghetti carbonara.

'Major!' shouted Nessa.

'Jesus!' shouted Kelly the sound girl.

'What's happening?' shouted Jo-Jo.

The Major was beginning to jerk about as though someone had attached jump leads to his toes.

Guy and Snowy were on their feet in a flash, lifting the Major out of his dinner before he suffocated in it. Jennifer shouted first aid instructions as the two men got the Major on to the floor and into a recovery position with his perfect bow-tie loosened so that he could get some air into his lungs. Guido called an ambulance from the kitchen. Jennifer got down on her knees beside the old man and tried to take his pulse.

The Major had stopped jerking now, but he wasn't coming round. Nessa stood over him, wringing her hands in desperation.

'Give him the kiss of life!' she said.

'He's still breathing,' said Jennifer. 'He doesn't need it.' She kneeled down by his head and checked that he wasn't in danger of choking on his tongue before the ambulancemen arrived. The others formed a horrified circle. All silent and staring. Except for Timothy. While the others held their breath and waited for the Major to take his next, Timothy was busy wiping carbonara sauce off his Armani jacket before it stained. The Major's swan-dive on to his plate had sent the sauce splattering right across the table.

'Can I do anything?' asked Guido. 'Anything at all?' He was desperately upset. The Major had eaten in the trattoria almost every night for the past three years. Ever since he first arrived in the town. When the restaurant was shut for the holidays, Guido even invited the Major to come and eat with him and Julia and their family at their home. He couldn't bear the idea of the Major having to eat alone. They weren't customer and proprietor any more. They were friends.

'Yes. You can do something,' said Timothy suddenly.

Everyone looked towards him expectantly.

'Have you got any soda water in the kitchen? I want to get this sauce out of my jacket before it soaks in.'

Guido stared. A few people laughed nervously. Timothy was just trying to lighten the moment. Right?

'Soda water?' Timothy repeated.

'I'll see what I can find.' Guido trotted into the kitchen obediently.

With Guido gone, the rest of the crowd drifted back to their seats but not to their fast-cooling meals. Everyone's eyes were still on the Major. Nessa cradled his head in her lap. In the kitchen, Guido turned the music off in the middle of the Three Tenors' rendition of 'Nessun Dorma'. No one would be sleeping much that night.

$\star$ $\star$ $\star$

The ambulance arrived pretty quickly. Fortunately it wasn't the weekend, when every grown man in Tincastle under the age of fifty seemed to end up in the accident unit courtesy of an alcohol-related farm machinery incident. But the Major was still unconscious as the two paramedics lifted him expertly on to the stretcher just fifteen minutes after he first collapsed. They made him seem impossibly light as they hoisted him into the ambulance with ease. Nessa was unable to hold back the tears then. The Major had always seemed such a substantial fellow. And though he was still breathing, it was as though the most important part of him had already left that old body in those smartly pressed clothes.

Nessa and Jo-Jo rode to the hospital in the back of the ambulance. Jennifer followed in her car so that she could drive the three of them back home once he was settled in.

'I'll come too,' said Guy.

'No,' Nessa told him. 'You stay here with the production people. Finish eating your dinner.'

'I don't think anybody has much of an appetite left.'

'Then get everyone a night-cap. The Major will be fine. I want you to stay here and cheer everyone up. Especially Guido and Julia. Poor people. They wanted so much to make this such a special evening for us all.'

The ambulance pulled out of the car park.

'A brandy,' said Guy, putting his arm around Faith's shoulders when they had watched it go. 'I think we all need a brandy after that.'

'I'm going back to my hotel,' said Timothy.

'No. Stay. Please,' said Faith. *Begged* Faith.

'I've got to get this jacket off. I'll be back.'

'I'll be back,' Kelly said in her best Schwarzenegger voice. She mimed a gun shot to the back of Timothy's head as he left the room. Faith stared down into her plate of cold pasta, looking even more distressed at Timothy's exit than she had done at the Major's collapse.

'He won't be back,' she said.

'Oh yes he will,' said Guy, misunderstanding her entirely. 'He spent six months in the African jungle with wild chimpanzees. The Major is far tougher than you think.'

Faith looked at Guy as though he was stupid. 'I'm not talking about the Major. I'm talking about Timothy Lauder. I don't know how you can be so cheerful. We're both in the same boat, you and me.'

'What do you mean?'

'I know what's going on beneath that smile, Guy. You're miserable. I'm miserable too. I love him and you love her.'

'Love who?'

'Jennifer. You idiot. You love her. I know you do. I've seen the way you look at her. And she doesn't even know you exist.'

Guy didn't say anything.

'They're fucking, you know. They used to go out with each other years ago at Oxford and now they're back together again. He thinks I don't know. I started to realise something was up when he told me not to be affectionate towards him in front of the staff at Prowdes. It wasn't just about professionalism. About not making other people feel embarrassed by our love. It was because of Jennifer. He told me that while she may seem a very sensible woman on the surface, underneath she's actually quite a fragile sort of person just barely holding it together from day to day. He told me that if she got an inkling that he and I were together, she might flip out and do something to sabotage the programme.'

'Such as what?' Guy asked.

'Such as damage one of the chimps! Can you believe it?'

'Frankly,' said Guy, 'I can't.'

'Neither can I. Not any more. He was just trying to make sure I didn't blow his two-timing cover. I can't believe I've got myself into this mess. You know, Guy, I was a sorted kind of woman. I'd been single for the past three years and I was getting to the stage where I just didn't care if I never dated again. It wasn't difficult. I thought I had everything I wanted in life. I've got a great job. I live in a nice flat. I've got a big gang of wonderful friends. I even enjoyed staying in on my own on a Saturday night with a DVD and a packet of Pringles. Having a boyfriend started to seem about as important as having chocolate sprinkles on my cappuccino. It really wasn't a necessity. Nice enough though probably bad for you. But then he came along.'

'Timothy Lauder,' Guy murmured.

'I knew something would happen between us the moment I first laid eyes on him. Have you ever had that experience? When you know the very first time you see someone that you're going to end up in bed?'

'I think I may have had it once.'

'Well, I had it with him. I've been in this game for a long time, Guy. I've worked in television since I left university. I've met just about every heart-throb to grace the British television screens in the last fifteen years and I've been propositioned by every single one of them. But I have always resisted. Well,' she modified, 'mostly. I have mostly resisted because I know that a TV presenter's charm is only surface deep and they can turn it on for anybody. But Timothy convinced me he was different. After all, he wasn't just some dim-witted Adonis who knew how to read an autocue. He was a respected academic before he became a presenter.'

'I know.'

'He's a professor at Oxford University. You don't get much better than that. Except Cambridge. Or London . . . And I thought that meant that he had depth. I thought that his dedication to his subject was an indication of an altogether more serious approach to life in general. And at first I did find him to be different to any other presenter I'd ever worked with. He was inspiring. I spent just about every night at home logged on to Amazon, ordering the books he'd talked about during the day. He made me feel as if there was something more to life than making television. He made me feel slightly ignorant, as well, if I'm honest.

'But he made me fall in love with him before I slept with him. He would tell me that he had been listening to an aria in his car on his way to the shoot and that it made him think of me. Now I can't help thinking that he thought of me because all opera divas are old and fat like I am.'

'You are neither of those things,' said Guy sincerely. She really wasn't.

'Then why doesn't he want me? What does he see in her?'

I'm the wrong person to be asking that question, thought Guy to himself. While Faith sobbed into his sweatshirt, Guy fancied that he could feel his own heart cracking beneath her tears the way an ice cube cracks when it comes into contact with warmer water. Was she right? Was Jennifer really screwing that joker? That posturing idiot who kept his own fragile ego afloat by making life-rafts from the splinters of the egos he tore asunder with his pomposity? Why hadn't Guy punched the fool when he corrected Snowy's pronunciation, or slapped Jo-Jo's hand when she reached out across him for a bread roll that evening rather than waiting for someone to pass the bread to her? What right did he have to make so many people feel inferior to him? What right did he have to send Guido scuttling off into the kitchen in search of a stain-removal remedy when the Major was lying on the floor fighting for his life?

'Are you all right?' Faith asked, momentarily forgetting her own misery when she saw the look on Guy's face.

'I'm fine,' he lied. 'I'm just worried about the Major. That's all.'

48

At the hospital, they had rushed the Major straight into intensive care. The doctor confirmed that the old man had suffered a stroke. It was to be expected at his age.

Nessa read a leaflet about the condition in the waiting room, while she waited for a nurse to find the forms which needed to be completed for the Major's admission to a ward. The effects of a stroke were pretty horrible but they didn't have to be permanent. The leaflet told the story of one man who had been able to get back to normality through a combination of physical therapy and a change in his diet. As she sat in the waiting room, Nessa was already planning out a wonderful new regime for the Major that would help him back to health. Guido and Julia could help her. They could make special low-fat, low-salt sauces that would lower the Major's blood pressure and make sure this didn't happen again.

'You may as well go home and get some sleep,' the nurse told Nessa when they had filled out the forms. 'The Major is comfortable now.'

'Comfortable?' Nessa tried out the word as though to check it didn't have a double meaning.

'You're sure he doesn't have any family we should call?' the nurse asked one more time when she saw 'Not known'.

'No,' said Nessa. 'I mean, I'm not entirely sure. But none that I know of. His wife passed away about five years ago, I know that much. He didn't have any children. He never spoke of any family at all. Except the one he had in Africa.'

'Africa?' The nurse put her head to one side. 'Do you have any contact details for them? A surname? A country? The name of a town?'

'Oh no. It wasn't that kind of family,' Nessa explained sadly.

257

'His family were the chimpanzees. He was rescued by a family of chimps, you see. After his regiment left him for dead.'

'Perhaps you should pop and see your own GP in the morning,' said the nurse after a moment. 'He can give you something for the shock.'

Recognising that the nurse thought Nessa was bonkers as they always suspected the Major had been, Jo-Jo put her arm around Nessa protectively. 'Come on,' she said. 'Let's go home. I'll call a taxi.'

'No. I'll drive you both,' Jennifer piped up. 'That's what I'm here for. That's why I came.'

Even at a moment like this, Jo-Jo expected a catch in Jennifer's kindness.

'It's no trouble,' Jennifer insisted.

They went back to Prowdes. Jo-Jo put Nessa to bed and rejoined Jennifer downstairs in the kitchen for a cup of hot chocolate.

'I made the Major have a stroke,' said Jo-Jo quietly.

'Don't be crazy,' said Jennifer. 'You didn't.'

'But I did. If I hadn't teased him about wearing women's clothing he wouldn't be in hospital right now.'

'He would have had that stroke even if you were talking about going to church five times a week. It wasn't anything to do with him getting angry, Jo-Jo. That blood clot just got to his brain.'

Jo-Jo shuddered. A salty tear plopped into her hot chocolate. 'He is going to be all right, isn't he?' she asked.

'I'm sure he is,' Jennifer replied as authoritatively as she could.

'Because I couldn't stand it if he died right now. Everyone I love goes away from me.' Jo-Jo sniffed dramatically.

'What do you mean?'

'I mean, everyone leaves me. My mum left when I was five. When I was seven my dad decided he couldn't cope either and sent me to live with my aunt. My aunt died when I was seventeen. Everyone I ever get close to has to leave me. It seems to be the law of the universe. Even the bloody monkeys are going now. And I know I should want the chimpanzees to be happy in Africa and I know that if you love someone you're supposed to set them free, but why does that feel like such bollocks every time?'

Jennifer smiled sadly. 'It doesn't make much sense,' she agreed.

'You know,' Jo-Jo continued, 'I hated you when you first came here because I knew you were going to take another part of my life away from me. Until you came to Prowdes, I didn't really think it was possible that the chimps could ever be released into the wild. I mean, Nessa had talked about it for ages, but she didn't really know what to do. Until you came, it was just a dream she had.'

'It'll still be a while before it happens,' said Jennifer.

'But it will happen eventually, right?'

'I've got to say, I hope so. Jo-Jo, I understand how you feel. I'm going to miss the chimps too and I've known them for a fraction of the time you have. But their release into the wild is important for the whole world. And I'll be here to be your friend when they're gone. If you'd like me to be, that is.'

Jo-Jo nodded. 'Yes,' she said. 'Yes, I'd like that very much.' She wrapped her arms around Jennifer and blubbed huge snorty tears into her jacket.

Jennifer was a little taken aback but managed not to flinch. She put her arms round Jo-Jo too until they were having a real hug. Like the friends they were going to be.

Eventually, Jennifer left Jo-Jo sleeping on the sofa at Prowdes and went back to her own cottage. The red light on the answer-machine was flashing to let her know she had a message. She leapt upon the machine hopefully, expecting to hear Timothy's voice asking what had become of her and when she was coming over to the hotel to creep into bed beside him.

It was Timothy. But he didn't want her to come over.

'Faith is very upset about the Major,' he said. 'I think I'm going to be sitting up for some time talking things through with her.'

'What about me?' Jennifer mouthed at the machine. 'I'm upset too. Oh well.'

49

Nessa was back at the hospital first thing the following morning; before she even had her breakfast. Once again, the nurse told her that the Major was comfortable. But he was still unconscious. Nessa sat with him for a while and held his hand over the sheets, wishing that she had held his hand before now.

Why hadn't she? Why hadn't she just reached out and hugged this gentle man when he first told her about the Matron and his experience in the jungle? Why hadn't she hugged him every time he turned out on a Sunday morning to man the gift shop when one of her employees fell ill? She had rolled her eyes about having to spend all those evenings with him at the trattoria, listening to stories about this war or that war, but at that moment she realised she would miss them if they ended now.

'Guido is keeping your carbonara warm,' she told the Major as he slept. 'You'll be there again by Friday, I reckon. We'll have a big celebration when you're better.'

'I'm going to give him a wash,' the nurse announced. 'You can stay if you want to.'

'I'm not sure he'd like that,' said Nessa. 'He's a very formal sort of man.' The nurse nodded understandingly. Nessa kissed the Major on the forehead and left.

The phone call came almost as soon as Nessa arrived at the office. The funny thing was, it didn't surprise her. When she pulled her car into the driveway, she was struck by how quiet everything was. It was as though the animals knew before she did.

'He passed away at about eight thirty,' said the nurse. Minutes after Nessa had left his side to drive back to the sanctuary. That was the Major. Always so thoughtful and polite. He hadn't wanted to die in front of her. He'd hung on until just after she left.

'Thank you,' Nessa said quietly.

Outside, the camera crew were setting up for the final day's shoot. Timothy had yet to arrive. But Faith was there, looking tired with big black rings around her eyes.

'I have to tell my staff that the Major has passed away,' Nessa told her. 'I don't think they're going to want to be filmed for a couple of hours.'

'I understand,' said Faith. 'We can leave you alone for the whole day, if you like. We've built a couple of spare days into the schedule in case we got rained on or something like that.'

Nessa squeezed Faith's arm. 'Then perhaps we should have a couple of days,' she said. 'You're a very understanding woman.'

Faith hoped that the rest of her team would be as understanding as she was.

Timothy called Jennifer on her mobile phone to tell her that he was going to take the opportunity to go back to Oxford and work on his latest paper.

As it was, the final day's filming was postponed for a week. After talking to her staff, Nessa decided that she didn't want to have the television crew around before the funeral which was planned for the Tuesday after the Major's death.

All that week, the weather stayed grey as slate in sympathy. Even the bright flower arrangements sent by every single one of the staff at Prowdes seemed to fade as soon as they were placed on the coffin. Nessa had at least been able to have the Major at Prowdes overnight. His coffin lay on a trestle table in the room that had once been Nessa's grandmother's salon. When the funeral cortège set out from the sanctuary, Nessa fancied that the animals had all gone quiet again, as if they too were in mourning for the man who was always willing to share the packet of Polos in his pocket.

They drove to a small grey church on the edge of the cliff and sat through a short grey service. Anglican. Though Nessa had no idea whether the Major was Anglican or Catholic or Jewish or Muslim. Or whether he believed in God at all. Probably not, given the way he used to curse when he didn't think she was listening. The vicar, who had never met the Major in his lifetime, pieced together a passable address based on what Nessa was able to tell him about the man in the box. They sang 'The Lord's My Shepherd' and 'All Things Bright and Beautiful'. Nessa herself read the story of St Francis. Francis seemed the most appropriate saint for a man who had loved the animals at Prowdes so much.

Then it was back outside for the committal to earth. The vicar sprinkled more words and dirt over a freshly dug hole with a sea view. It was in fact a plot that Nessa had expected to end up in herself; a plot in the piece of ground in the churchyard that went with the house at Prowdes. Her grandparents and parents were already resting there. Nessa was momentarily embarrassed by the grass that had grown up around their headstones, imagining her grandmother tutting at the neglect.

'You've done him proud,' said Julia, Guido's wife, when the burial was over. She had cried throughout the ceremony and now had the bright red nose of an old drunk. 'This is how he would have wanted it.'

Arlene from the Wily Fox said the same. 'This is just how he would have wanted it.' And Glenda and Marjorie, the part-time ticket booth workers. They said it too. And just about everybody else who had turned up to bid the Major goodbye, including Faith, Helen and Kelly from the television crew. And the nurse who had seen him admitted to hospital the previous week.

'It breaks my heart when there's no family,' the nurse said. 'I always try to go along in those cases. But the Major did have a family. He had you. This is how he would have wanted it,' she concluded, like all the others.

But they were wrong.

This isn't how he would have wanted it, thought Nessa, as she looked down into the hole in the cold Devon soil where the Major had found his final resting place. A handful of roses decorated the top of his coffin. Jo-Jo had thrown Polaroid pictures of Mad and Bad and Hector, the Major's favourite apes, and a small fluffy monkey from the gift shop in too. They were all gestures of the very real love that everyone at Prowdes felt for the Major. But it still wasn't right.

The Major hadn't wanted to end his days in a provincial English churchyard. The Major had wanted to end his days in

Africa. She remembered him telling her, 'Your motherland isn't always where you came from. I didn't know where I was meant to be until I nearly died there.' His heart was in Africa. It was convention and obligation that had brought his body to this dark damp soil.

After the Major's funeral, the sanctuary was closed to visitors for the rest of the day. The real work continued regardless. Just as it did on Christmas Day, the only day the sanctuary was closed in any normal year. The keepers went about their chores in silence. Jennifer didn't turn on the radio when she walked into her office and sat down at her desk. She checked her voicemail for messages. Nothing from Timothy. She tried not to be disappointed that he hadn't called to ask how the funeral went. He must have been hard at work. It was such a shame that the pressure he was under to finish his latest research had kept him from being at the funeral in person.

There was a knock at the door.

'Come in.'

It was Guy.

'Hello,' said Jennifer. She put down the red pen she had picked up to make edits on her own latest report.

'Jennifer, I need to speak to you about Timothy.' Guy went straight to the point.

'Timothy? What about him?' Jennifer asked.

'I think you're letting him unduly influence your decisions with regard to the chimps here at Prowdes. Particularly Ulysses.'

'Guy, we've talked about this already. I think that Ulysses is ready to join the others.'

'I don't think you do.'

'What?'

'I don't think you really do believe that Ulysses is ready. I think you're letting Timothy make the decision for you and I don't think he's making the decision to release Ulysses so soon for the right reasons at all.'

'And what are the wrong reasons?' Jennifer shrugged.

'He wants to make good television. And good television isn't about taking time to make the right choices regarding Ulysses' future, it's about Ulysses joining the rest of the chimps in time for the end of the series. A result, as Faith would say. Timothy is prepared to risk Ulysses' recovery, perhaps even his life, for a proper ending to the story arc.'

'That's ridiculous,' said Jennifer. 'Timothy would never put a chimpanzee at risk. The loss of one chimpanzee is equivalent to the loss of a whole city of human beings to Dr Lauder. He cares more about the survival of the species than any other man I have ever met.'

Guy allowed himself a wry smile.

'You don't think I would listen to any old idiot, do you?' Jennifer continued. 'If I have allowed myself to be influenced by his judgement, it is because I do trust it. Timothy Lauder is possibly the world authority on bonobo chimpanzees. He has written three books about pan troglodytes. What there is left to know about chimpanzees isn't worth knowing. Are you aware that when San—'

'Diego Zoo have a problem with their chimpanzees, they call Dr Timothy Lauder,' Guy parroted. 'Well, San Diego Zoo may not call me when they need advice, but I have worked with chimpanzees for the past eight years. These chimpanzees. And I have spent more time with Ulysses than anyone else at this sanctuary. Especially Dr Timothy Lauder. Jennifer, I'm begging you not to let the release go ahead too soon.'

'I know what your problem with this is,' Jennifer interrupted. 'But you can't let your personal feelings interfere with your professional life.'

'Well said. And I'm sure *I'm* not letting my feelings interfere,' said Guy. 'Are you?'

Guy left Jennifer's office before she had a chance to answer him.

'Guy,' she called. But he was already out of earshot. 'Guy! Don't walk off like that . . . Oh, bugger.' She gave up.

Jennifer tapped Timothy's mobile number into the keypad of her phone. She needed to talk to him. Get reassurance one more time that what he was asking her to do regarding Ulysses was right. But he didn't pick up. His voicemail kicked in.

Jennifer pressed her thumb down to disconnect the call without leaving a message. When she thought about it, she was secretly relieved that she hadn't given him any indication of her crisis of confidence. She could have faith in Timothy's advice, couldn't she? He wouldn't endanger Ulysses for the sake of good TV. That was a ridiculous idea.

Jennifer opened the top drawer of her desk and pulled out the tiny clipping she had secretly taken from one of Jo-Jo's old showbiz magazines. It was a picture of Timothy, promoting his first cable show. Jennifer looked into his eyes.

'I can trust you, can't I?' she asked the little photograph.

Timothy stared back. Square jaw. Blue eyes. Blond hair combed like his mother did it. He did look trustworthy.

The phone rang on Jennifer's desk. She jumped. Was Timothy returning her call? It was Dahlia.

'You're still coming over to my house tonight, aren't you? I can't believe I'm going to be watching the TV awards with someone who has actually shagged one of the nominees.'

'Great,' said Jennifer. 'It's wonderful being the nearest thing Tincastle has ever had to a celebrity.'

'Have you spoken to him today?'

'I just called him,' Jennifer admitted. 'But he didn't pick up and I didn't leave a message.'

'Why didn't you leave him a message! Call back and leave one at once. Wish him luck. And wish him luck from me, too. He does remember me, doesn't he?'

'Yes,' said Jennifer.

'Great. We'll see you at half past six. Henry is buying some champagne. I've already done the nibbles. You just need to bring your glamorous self.'

Jennifer felt far from glamorous that evening as she did her last round of the animals in her overalls and wellies.

'Where's Guy?' she asked Jo-Jo.

'Dunno,' Jo-Jo replied.

Jennifer guessed that he might be with Ulysses. But the quarantine unit was empty apart from the ape himself. Jennifer rested her forehead against the cool glass and gazed in at the chimpanzee who was causing her so much trouble.

'You're causing me a real headache, you know,' she told Ulysses. 'You do want to be with the other chimps, don't you? You do want to be released into the wild with the rest of them?'

Ulysses looked back at her with his big brown eyes, but she couldn't read what he was trying to tell her with them. If he was trying to tell her anything at all.

'It's the best thing for you,' she said. 'And it might as well happen sooner rather than later. You're bound to be a bit scared but perhaps being with the other chimps will make your recovery quicker.'

Ulysses pulled his blanket around him and shrank into its folds.

'All right,' she muttered. 'I don't believe it either. I'll talk to Timothy tonight, when he calls me after his awards shindig. I'll tell him that you're not ready to go in with the others yet and the TV people will have to be happy with what they've got so far. But I would be grateful if you could at least try to look a bit happier about it,' she added. 'I don't think Timothy's going to be very pleased at all.'

Unseen by his boss, Guy watched the exchange from the doorway. He wanted to run in and hug her when he heard her say that she was going to give Ulysses a little longer on his own. But he didn't.

'He wouldn't really put your progress on the line for his TV career, would he?' Jennifer continued. 'I can't believe he'd do that. He's got too much integrity for that. I know he has. Oh, Ulysses, do you think Guy might be right? Or Dahlia? Am I being taken for a fool?'

Ulysses couldn't answer. Jennifer shrugged and turned to leave the building.

Guy slipped around the back before Jennifer had a chance to see him.

50

Jennifer had never watched an awards show before. But Dahlia was a veteran of such things. She liked nothing better than to settle down in front of the television with a big bowl of tortilla chips and a bottle of wine, and make pronouncements on which celebrities looked fabulous and which looked as though they had covered themselves with glue and rolled around in the laundry basket.

That night, Dahlia had outdone herself. She had bought every single kind of dip Marks and Spencer had to offer and decanted them from their plastic pots into her prettiest little bowls. There were tortilla chips in every colour and bright tubes of Pringles and sausages on sticks and pineapple and cheese hedgehogs . . .

'All this for me?' Jennifer exclaimed when she saw the spread.

'Actually,' said Dahlia, 'we're going to have a few other people here as well. I didn't think you'd mind if I told some of the girls your little secret, since after you finish filming tomorrow, you'll be able to tell the whole world!'

The girls from Dahlia's office were already lined up along the sofa, scarfing sausage rolls and drinking Cava. They were saving the champagne for later. Though they had all met Jennifer at the hen night and at Dahlia and Henry's wedding, they stared at her as though they had never seen her before in their lives when she walked into the room. It was as though her brush with celebrity had rendered her something 'other'. If this was the kind of reaction that going out with a semi-celebrity could provoke, thought Jennifer, then she almost understood why the likes of Posh Spice moaned about everybody wanting a piece of them while they lounged around in their multi-million-dollar mansions.

'Hi,' said Jennifer. She waved shyly. The girls continued to gawp as though she were a speaking dog.

'Isn't this exciting? Why aren't you more excited, Jenny?' Dahlia asked. 'You're going out with one of the hottest men on the box.'

'We buried the Major today,' said Jennifer.

'I'm sorry,' said Dahlia. 'I forgot. But look, this will cheer you up. Have a Pringle. What award is he up for?'

'Best cable nature programme presenter.'

'I can't believe you're going out with a star!'

'No,' said Jennifer flatly. 'Neither can I.'

'What is he like?' asked Jane from Dahlia's office. 'Tell us how he kisses.'

'Er. . . just like ordinary men do, I suppose.'

'Don't ask such idiotic questions,' said Dahlia. 'Here, Jenny. You sit here.'

She was guided towards the super-complicated armchair that was Henry's pride and joy. Dahlia pulled a lever that set the back of the seat at an alarming angle.

'Are you comfortable?' she asked.

'Feels like being at the dentist's,' Jennifer replied.

'OK, everybody. Stop nattering. The show is about to begin.'

The opening music began.

The camera swept around the room, hesitating momentarily on familiar faces. There was Joan Collins with her son. Or was it her husband? There was David Attenborough, looking as though he would have been happier in his safari suit than his tux. And there was Timothy. Seeing Timothy in his black tie gave Jennifer a small flicker of pleasure as she remembered a ball at Oxford that seemed like a scene from a dream now with champagne and dancing till dawn. Timothy looked so good in black tie.

The camera stayed on Timothy's table for quite a while, as the voiceover reminded the great British public exactly who it was they were looking at. 'Nominated this evening for best cable nature programme . . .'

'Is that that producer bird sitting next to him?' Dahlia asked.

Jennifer nodded. Faith had scrubbed up very well. Her normally slightly dry-looking brown hair was shining thanks to a semi-permanent vegetable hair dye expertly applied at a smart

London salon just an hour before. She was wearing, Jennifer noted with a small tinge of distress, a dress that looked remarkably like the DVF wrap dress that had been lost to the baby oil on Dahlia's hen night all those months before.

'She looks good in red,' Dahlia added tactlessly. 'But look at your man. Doesn't he look amazing? You've got to get him up the aisle double-quick. You'll be able to sell your wedding to *Hello!* magazine. Or *OK!*. I think I prefer *OK!*. Perhaps you'll even have a bidding war. You've got to have me in all the pictures. I'll be your bridesmaid.'

Jennifer nodded vaguely.

An hour into the show, the nominees in the category of best cable nature programme presenter were at last announced. The camera swung round to Timothy again. It caught him whispering something to Faith. Faith inclined her head towards him and smiled. The smile spread slowly across her face as though Timothy was suggesting something naughty. Jennifer frowned. And Dahlia was frowning too.

'Darling,' she leaned across and whispered in Jennifer's ear, 'he still hasn't told that girl about you, has he?'

'No,' said Jennifer. 'No one knows except you. And all your friends . . . He didn't think it would look very professional.'

'Neither does that,' said Dahlia, referring to the way that Faith was resting her chin on Timothy's shoulder. 'I'm no scientific expert,' she added, 'but that looks like pretty intimate body language to me.'

It was.

It may not have been as obvious as seeing his big white bottom bouncing up and down but surely even Jennifer couldn't miss the signs now. Timothy wasn't trying to protect the show by not revealing his involvement with Jennifer, he was trying to save himself. Had he stayed away from the Major's funeral not because he was busy but because faced with two weeping women, he wouldn't have known which one to comfort first?

'And the winner is Dr Timothy Lauder!'

The camera swung quickly to Timothy's table. He was already getting up, but Faith was hanging on to him, her arms around his neck. He had to prise her off before he could make the walk up to the podium where last year's best presenter was waiting to hand over the trophy.

'There are so many people to thank for the fact that I am standing here tonight. Too many to single them all out but I do want to mention a couple in particular. My agent, Felicity, who saw the potential in the scruffy scientist who turned up on her doorstep one Monday afternoon. And the woman behind the scenes.'

He paused dramatically.

'He's going to mention you!' one of Dahlia's workmates squealed.

'My producer, Faith O'Connell.' Timothy raised the trophy in her direction as though it were a glass of champagne. 'I couldn't have done it without you.'

'Excuse me,' said Jennifer to Dahlia and her workmates. 'I've got to go home.'

Dahlia didn't bother to try to tempt her to stay with champagne.

Jennifer got into her house and picked up her phone right away.

She needed some answers. Was Timothy still the man she had fallen in love with? As she watched him on the television, accepting his award, he had seemed as unfamiliar to her as every other TV personality on the show. A TV personality just like Jamie Oliver and Nigella Lawson and Carol Smilie. Why then was it impossible that he wouldn't do something for the TV personality side of his life? Like put her chimpanzees in danger for a spectacular finale to his show?

'Timothy,' Jennifer said to his answer-machine, 'I need to talk to you about Ulysses. It's too early for him to join the rest of the troop . . .'

51

The camera crew had been busy since dawn. By dusk that evening they had to make sure that they had all the footage they needed to complete the series. Establishing shots of the sanctuary and the surrounding countryside, that kind of thing. And the money shot, as Timothy was calling it.

David Attenborough would always have his spectacular encounter with the mountain gorillas, where he sat among them as though he was part of the family. Now Timothy was going to have his *man meets mammal* moment too. He had decided that he wanted the crew to shoot some more footage of him inside the chimpanzee enclosure. As the rosy dawn broke over the fields behind him, Timothy would enter the enclosure alone and walk into Achilles' territory. He would hand Achilles a banana. Achilles would accept it. Alpha male to alpha male. Dr Timothy Lauder would become the 'chimpanzee man'.

When Guy arrived to take over from Snowy and Ernie at seven, he was horrified to discover that Ulysses had been moved.

'Where is he?'

'In a pen inside the main enclosure.'

'What?'

'Dr Lauder said that Jennifer said it was OK to move him this morning.'

Guy raced across to the main enclosure. Jennifer was nowhere to be seen. But Nessa was deep in conversation with Timothy and Faith.

'What the fuck is Ulysses doing in there?' Guy asked.

'Morning, Guy,' said Nessa, somewhat taken aback to hear him swear.

'Jennifer gave the instruction,' said Timothy.

'I don't believe she did.'

Timothy waved a piece of paper in front of Guy's face. It was a print-out of an e-mail.

'I agree that it's time for Ulysses to be introduced to the other chimps,' it said.

'But this is dated almost two weeks ago,' said Guy. 'What if she's changed her mind since then?'

'She isn't here to say so.'

'Nessa,' Guy appealed to her.

'I don't think there's any need to worry, Guy,' said Nessa hopefully. 'Dr Lauder has been keeping a close eye on the others. Now that those females are no longer in heat, Achilles has calmed down considerably. The sooner we can get Ulysses settled in there the better. Faith has been talking to her bosses about the possibility of a second show. It would give us all the funding we need to really take Project Africa all the way.'

'Are we going to do this?' said Dave. 'If he wants the sun coming up behind then we haven't got much longer.'

'I'll go with him,' said Guy when Faith discussed the shot with Timothy.

'There's no need,' said Timothy.

'But we never go into the enclosure alone. You'll need a prod.'

'I want to be empty-handed except for a banana.'

'Are you mad?' said Guy.

'I think I can handle a chimpanzee.'

There was more. Not only did Timothy want to have his man meets alpha male moment, he wanted to be the one who introduced Ulysses to his new troop.

'I'm going to open the door to his cage while I'm out there. He's acclimatised to the others by now.'

'He's been there for an hour.'

'And there have been no problems in that time. You know,' Timothy pontificated, 'I'm beginning to think that the traditional practice of introducing individual chimps to a larger group gradually is a nonsense. It wouldn't happen like that in the wild. A lone chimp would happen upon a troop. There'd be a skirmish. The lone chimp would find his place in the hierarchy—'

'Or be killed,' said Guy.

'You're being very dramatic.'

Guy looked around for Jennifer. She would be able to tell this egomaniac what nonsense he was talking. But Jennifer had yet to arrive. She was stuck in an incredible traffic jam just half a mile from the sanctuary.

'I'm sure Dr Niederhauser would agree with me.'

'Does our insurance cover this?' Faith asked. Guy's nervousness had infected her as well.

'I know I'd be happier if you'd just wait for Harrison to arrive,' Nessa suggested.

'What are you hesitating for?' Timothy asked Faith. 'I'm guaranteeing you a shot that will get us that Christmas Eve slot. It's this or the meerkats. If David Attenborough can hug a bloody mountain gorilla, I can share a banana with some flea-bitten chimpanzee. I'll be in make-up,' he concluded, heading for one of the vans.

'He'd better put some lipstick on,' muttered Snowy beneath his breath. 'Because Achilles is going to make a girl of that man.'

The cameras were set up on the other side of the wire. Kelly checked Timothy's microphone when he returned from make-up looking slightly orange.

'So we can hear your final words more clearly,' she said as she pinned it to his shirt.

Timothy was oblivious. The gleam of next year's *TV Weekly* award was already reflected in his eyes. He had gone over to the dark side. Kelly knew that when she looked at him. From now on, every moment in Timothy's life would be measured in TV terms. In his own mind, he was already in close-up. Everyone else was unfocused against a blurred background. He was walking up to Achilles, shaking hands with the chimp. It was the gesture of ultimate trust and strength. Audiences around the world would gasp at his daring. Chat-show hosts would ask him how he had subdued the savage beast. He would demonstrate with an arch of the eyebrow. He knew the body language required to tame a wild animal as well as James Bond knew the lines that would get the girl.

'You cannot open that door and let Ulysses out into the main enclosure,' Guy insisted one more time. 'Timothy, Dr Lauder,

I am begging you not to throw away all these months of hard work.'

'I'll take the decision when I get out there,' said Timothy. He put his safari hat on and armed himself with a banana. 'Cameras roll,' he shouted.

'That is my line,' said Faith.

'You're an idiot,' said Guy. But at Nessa's behest, he unlocked the gate to the enclosure and stood aside so that Timothy could walk in. The troop was a long way from the gate that morning. This was fairly usual. Once they had been fed, they knew there wasn't a great deal of point in hanging around the gate again until the evening meal came. Instead, they busied themselves around the dead trees in the centre of the enclosure, sunning themselves or seeking shade in the hollow trunks. It meant that Timothy had a long walk.

'He's not too far away, is he?' Faith asked nervously.

'Believe me,' said Dave. 'I have got him covered. I wouldn't miss a single frame of Dr Timothy Lauder getting his arse kicked by a monkey.'

'He's not going to get his arse kicked. He will be OK, won't he?' Faith asked Guy.

'He should be. He knows what he's doing. As he keeps telling us.'

As he approached the troop, Timothy's posture changed a little. He walked more slowly and slightly hunkered down. Achilles, who had been watching the intruder since he came in through the gate, gave him a nonchalant glance over his shoulder now. Virginia regarded Timothy more warily, but carried on picking through Achilles' hair.

Timothy began his whispered voiceover.

'It's easy to forget just how dangerous these animals can be,' he said. 'And what level of bravery it requires to step into their world. Right now, I am taking my life into my own hands, trusting in my great knowledge of these creatures that I will make all the right moves to set the alpha male at ease. Because if the alpha male is happy, the whole troop is happy.'

'Is the alpha male happy?' Faith asked Guy.

Guy shrugged somewhat unhelpfully.

274

'I wouldn't normally recommend that anyone get this close to an alpha male chimpanzee surrounded by his adoring harem,' Timothy continued. 'But today, I am here in an ambassadorial role. Ulysses, the chimp we rescued right at the start of the series, has been living in an enclosure within this enclosure for the last week . . .'

'The stinking liar!' Snowy exclaimed.

'. . . giving the chimpanzees in the troop time to get used to his presence before he is released to join them. It's a process with no real set time limit, but I've decided that today is the day. There may be a skirmish when I open the door to Ulysses' cage but that's a necessary part of establishing the hierarchy. My plan is to distract Achilles, the most dangerous ape in the troop, with this peace offering.'

Timothy waggled the banana. Achilles' attention was drawn by the movement. This time he turned to face the interloper.

'It's a tense moment.'

'You're telling me,' Faith muttered.

'Bite him,' said Dave. 'Ten pounds he loses an arm.'

'His wanking arm,' said Kelly.

'Have you got the blowpipe ready, Guy?' Nessa asked.

'Yes,' he said. 'But I won't be able to reach Achilles from here.'

Out in the enclosure, Timothy was crouching down, banana in his outstretched hand. Achilles shifted so that he was on all fours and swayed slightly in Timothy's direction to see what was being offered. Timothy shuffled forward too. Achilles took another step until the banana was within his reach. He took the fruit abruptly and sat down again just a foot away from the television star.

'It's like a meeting of minds,' Timothy continued into his microphone in a whisper. 'A gift has been exchanged. Achilles recognises that I come in peace. That we are equals.'

'I always thought he was an animal,' said Kelly.

'Alpha male to alpha male,' said Timothy. 'I'm going to sit here quietly for a while, just communing with this magnificent beast. Then, when he's used to my presence, I'm going to open the door to Ulysses' enclosure and let him out.'

'Fuck,' said Guy. 'He's really going to do it.'

'Chimp's on the move,' said Snowy nervously. Achilles had edged a little closer still to Timothy.

'This is amazing,' Timothy's breathless voice came over the microphone. 'The alpha male has chosen to groom me. It suggests to me that not only has he recognised me as an equal, he may even consider me to be his superior.'

Achilles had removed Timothy's hat and was peering closely at his straw-gold hair. Timothy's delight was written all over his face. Eat your heart out, Attenborough, he was thinking. There's a new king of the apes in town.

'I'm just going to sit here and enjoy this for a while,' he said. 'I don't think I'll have any trouble getting Achilles to accept Ulysses after this bonding experience. I'll react towards Ulysses with complete acceptance and Achilles will simply follow suit, taking his cue from me.'

Timothy got to his feet. 'Working with animals is an unpredictable business. I have to say that I didn't expect to be accepted quite so readily. While my years of experience have taught me how to behave in front of an alpha male, they have also taught me not to take for granted the kind of scene you're witnessing now. This is a very special moment. Come on, Achilles. Let's meet your new companion.'

And then Timothy Lauder made his fatal mistake. Achilles moved ever so slightly ahead of him as they walked towards Ulysses' pen. And Timothy, for reasons unknown to everyone watching from outside the perimeter, gave Achilles a brotherly slap on the rump.

Achilles stopped. His posture immediately reflected his outrage. Timothy's own suddenly knock-kneed stance let the onlookers know that he too had realised his breach in etiquette.

'Fuck,' said Dave. 'It's going to go for him.'

'Fuck,' said Faith.

'Fuck,' said Guy.

'Fuuuuuccccckkkk!' Timothy shouted down the mic.

And then they were off, like the Roadrunner and Wylie Coyote, Tom and Jerry, man and ape. All his years of chimpanzee study suddenly went out of the window. Timothy Lauder couldn't remember if he should stand his ground in front of the angered animal or lie on the floor and cover his face in submission. Neither seemed a good idea at that moment, so he ran. Possibly the worst idea of all since he failed to run in the direction of the gate and safety.

Guy raised the blowpipe and poked it through a gap in the wire, hoping that Timothy would draw Achilles in their direction soon.

'Shoot him!' Faith shouted.

'I won't reach him from here.'

Timothy and Achilles were running a circuit. They came closer. Guy chanced a shot but it fell way short.

'Run for the gate,' he shouted to Timothy but Achilles was already heading his prey back towards the trees.

'Bloody hell, he's a good runner,' said Dave. 'Did you know he could run that fast?' he asked Helen.

'No, I didn't. Did you know he could run that fast, Faith?'

'Somebody get him out of there!' Faith was screaming. She had completely forgotten that only a couple of days ago, she would have happily torn Timothy Lauder limb from limb herself.

'I think he should go up a tree,' said Kelly.

'No,' said Jo-Jo. 'That would be a real mistake. I guarantee you that Achilles can climb far better than Timothy Lauder can.'

'Jo-Jo,' asked Guy, 'where are the rest of the darts?'

'Aren't they in the pipe case?' she replied distractedly.

'No, they're not. There's just an empty case in here.'

'It's supposed to be full,' said Jo-Jo. 'For emergencies.'

'I know it is!' said Guy. And he had a pretty good idea of who had forgotten to check it. 'I haven't got any more tranquillisers at all.'

'Oh my God!' Faith clung on to the wire and wailed.

'Why doesn't he go into submission?' asked Snowy. 'I thought he was supposed to be a bloody chimpanzee expert.'

'Get me out of here. Get me the fuck out of here!' Timothy was yelling. Kelly had arranged the sound system so that everyone could hear what she had been hearing through her headphones.

'We're doing our best, Timmy!' Faith assured him. 'Where's the vet?' she asked Guy.

'He is on his way,' said Jo-Jo defensively. 'But you wouldn't wait until he arrived to start filming. That's not our fault.'

'We'll sue!' said Faith.

'For what? We advised him not to go in there,' Guy reminded her. 'He decided that he was the expert. He's in there against all our wishes.'

'Just get him out.'

In the centre of the enclosure, man and chimp were running smaller and smaller circles around the dead trees. In a moment of desperation, Timothy scrambled up the shortest tree. A pointless exercise, since the chimp could indeed climb faster. But Achilles didn't even have to bother to climb. He simply stood at the bottom of the trunk and drummed his chest aggressively. Timothy Lauder had trapped himself and his chimpanzee nemesis knew it.

52

'Help!' Timothy's plaintive voice drifted across the airwaves. 'Please help me.'

'I think he's bought us some time,' said Guy unconvincingly, as they watched Achilles stop drumming and sit down to wait for his lunch to come to him when Timothy Lauder's arms would eventually give up on holding him to the dead tree trunk. A phone call to Harrison revealed that he was still about a mile away (stuck in the same traffic jam as Jennifer) but that, yes, he did have replacement darts for the blowpipe in the back of his car.

A plan was formulated. When Harrison arrived, he would dart Achilles and hope that the rest of the chimps would be distracted and thus allow Timothy a window of time in which to escape while they pondered the fate of their leader.

'But he's got to be ready to run,' said Harrison.

'Don't think I can run any more,' said Timothy sadly when Faith relayed the plan to him over his earpiece. 'They're not still rolling the cameras, are they?' he asked then. 'I don't want this bit going into the show.'

'I think that's the least of his worries,' Guy hissed. Achilles was getting bored of waiting now. He stood on his hind legs and used his powerful forearms to give the dead tree trunk a shake. The thick trunk yielded like a bamboo shoot to Achilles' power. At the top of the tree, Timothy clung on and wailed.

'Where's Harrison?' Faith asked.

Another call to Harrison found him getting out of his car about half a mile from the sanctuary's gates. 'This bloody traffic jam is because everyone wants to see your TV star filming his last day with the chimps. I'm going to walk the rest of the way.'

'Run,' said Guy.

'If you can be bothered,' Jo-Jo added.

279

Nessa called Jennifer and advised her to abandon her car and hurry hither as well.

In the meantime, the gates to Prowdes had opened and the cars that were queuing all the way back to Tincastle began to trickle into the car park. Moments later, excited visitors were following the signs to the chimpanzee enclosure in the hope of catching a glimpse of their hero and maybe even getting an autograph.

'Who are all those people?' Timothy asked Faith over the microphone as he saw the crowd begin to gather.

'They're your fans,' she informed him.

'Get them out of here.'

'Give them a wave,' said Kelly. 'Show them what a professional you are.'

Timothy Lauder wasn't the only showman in the enclosure that day. Over his years in captivity, Achilles had got as much enjoyment from staring at the crowds as they did from staring at him. It was just as satisfying to Achilles to terrify a human family with his displaying as to frighten another chimpanzee. As he noticed the crowds gathering at the wire, Achilles seemed to sense that they wanted to see some action. He shook the tree trunk again. Timothy closed his eyes as he heard an ominous crack.

'Do you think Achilles can push that tree over?' Faith asked.

'Definitely,' came Timothy's quiet voice.

Guy felt a tap on his shoulder. It was Jamie, accompanied by his friends from school, come to get in their crowd scene as promised.

'Where's Ulysses?' Jamie signed.

'In there,' Guy signed back in dismay.

'What? But you said you'd keep him out of there. You know how frightened he is. He's not ready.'

'He was already in there when I arrived this morning,' Guy explained. 'He'll be OK.'

'He'd better be,' signed Jamie. 'I'll never trust you again. You tosser.'

Jennifer chose that moment to arrive. It took her a while to push through the crowd, shouting, 'I'm head of the chimpanzee project. Let me through.'

'What's going on?' she asked Guy.

Guy pointed towards the tree in the middle of the enclosure.
'Is that Timothy?'

'The very same.'

'What's he doing in there?'

'Consolidating his fifteen minutes of fame,' Guy snarled.
'More importantly, what is Ulysses doing in there?'

'I don't know,' Jennifer replied. 'What is Ulysses doing in
there?'

'You gave the order to have him put in with the other
chimps.'

'I did not. I was going to talk to Timothy this morning. I was
going to tell him that under no circumstances should Ulysses be
put in there yet. He's not ready.'

'Is that the bitch who put Ulysses in there?' Jamie signed.

'What's he saying?' Jennifer asked.

'He asked if you're in charge of this project,' Guy translated
loosely.

'That chimp is going to kill him!' Faith wailed. 'Somebody do
something.'

'Have you tried darting Achilles?' Jennifer asked.

'Too far away. And we ran out of darts. I'm not going in there
until Harrison turns up with some more.'

'And where is Harrison?'

Harrison was still a quarter of a mile away, doubled over on the
grass verge next to the road with a stitch from running so fast.

The TV crew and the keepers weren't the only ones who had been
watching the drama unfold from the beginning. From his holding
pen, Ulysses had regarded Timothy's overtures towards Achilles
with interest.

Ulysses had been trained by a master. The padlock on the door
to his cage presented no problem at all for a chimpanzee who had
been schooled in the art of burglary and safe-cracking by one of
southern Europe's most daring criminal gangs. The hair-grip he
had carried about under his armpit since Jennifer dropped it on
the floor of his cage a few days earlier, made the perfect lock-
picking tool. With his strong thumb, he quickly bent it into a hook
and had the padlock open within seconds. The door to the cage

swung open. Ulysses raised himself on to his back legs and bellowed.

Achilles turned to face the young pretender.

'Ulysses! No!' Guy shouted. Jamie flung himself against the wire and started to sign desperately at his friend.

'Get back into the cage,' Jamie signed. 'Get back into the cage.'

Achilles was too big for the juvenile male. He lifted Ulysses off his feet and hurled him backwards. Ulysses landed heavily on the grass. But he was soon on his feet again and rushing back at Achilles with the determination of a terrier. He leapt on to Achilles' back and started to bite at his ear. Achilles had to divert his attention from Timothy to shrug the much younger and smaller chimp off again.

Again and again, Ulysses rushed the alpha male. All the while, Timothy slid lower on the tree trunk. Achilles was merely irritated at first by Ulysses' intervention – Ulysses was less than half his size – but eventually, he started to get angry. He threw Ulysses off with increasing force each time – time after time – until, at last, Ulysses didn't get up when he fell.

Jamie uttered an unearthly scream.

By this time, Harrison had arrived. He and Guy prepared the blowpipe in double-quick time. Snowy opened the gate to the enclosure so that Harrison and Guy could go in there, but as he was doing so, Jamie slipped beneath his arm. The first anyone realised was when they saw the boy racing across the grass to Ulysses' still and silent body.

'Jamie!' Guy shouted uselessly. 'Fuck.'

Leaving Harrison standing by the fence with the blowpipe, Guy set off in pursuit of the boy. He wouldn't have risked his life for Timothy Lauder, but the safety of Jamie Grey was an altogether different matter. The boy was on his knees next to Ulysses now. And Achilles was beginning to move towards him.

'Wake up, wake up,' Jamie was signing at his simian friend. Guy couldn't attract his attention.

'Shoot him!' Faith screamed at Harrison. 'Shoot that bloody chimpanzee.'

Harrison fired off a couple of blow darts in Achilles' direction. Neither went anywhere near the mark.

'Guy, just get Jamie out of there!' shouted Nessa. 'Just pick him up and run. Don't worry about Timothy!'

'I'm sure he isn't,' said Jo-Jo.

'Oh God, Guy,' Jennifer murmured. 'What are you doing now?'

Guy had stopped about twelve feet from where Jamie sat grooming Ulysses' bleeding head. Seeing that Guy had stopped, Achilles paused in his pursuit of the young boy too. Guy gave an animalistic grunt that caused the alpha male to turn towards him.

'What is he doing?' Nessa asked Snowy, as Guy twisted his body so that his knuckles were nearer the floor. His head seemed to sink into his shoulders. His back rounded into a curve. He was transforming himself into an ape in front of their very eyes.

'Oh my God,' said Jo-Jo. 'The King of the Swingers to the rescue.'

'What is Guy doing?'

'He's turning himself into a chimp,' Jennifer explained. 'It's what he does on a Saturday night.'

Achilles narrowed his eyes as though he couldn't quite believe what he was seeing. Guy continued to display. Guy gave a loud 'wah-bark'. Achilles pulled himself up to his full height and gave a loud 'wah-bark' back. Then he bounded forward towards the new interloper, completely ignoring both Jamie and Timothy, who by now was at the bottom of the tree.

'For fuck's sake, run!' Guy shouted at Timothy. 'And grab the kid when you go past him.'

Timothy didn't need to be asked twice. He set off at top speed for the gate that Snowy and Jo-Jo were waiting to swing open as soon as he came close. As he passed Jamie, Timothy grabbed him by the hood of his sweatshirt.

Guy, meanwhile, was racing in the opposite direction with Achilles hard on his tail.

'Run, Guy, run!' everybody shouted.

Harrison managed at last to get one decent shot with his pipe. Achilles fell to the ground.

The weight of his landing seemed to shake the entire sanctuary.

53

Once again, Ulysses lay on a stretcher like nothing more than a bag of hair and bone. His eyes had fluttered up into his skull and closed.

'No!' Jennifer murmured. 'No. Don't let him die!'

But she could tell from the look on Harrison's face that it wouldn't matter how much she protested. The injuries Ulysses had received at the hands of Achilles were more than the smaller chimpanzee could be expected to bear. With every beat of his heart, more blood pumped from his fragile body and into the blanket that covered him. Harrison shouted instructions that Snowy followed quickly. Jennifer couldn't do a thing. She was paralysed by misery. And shame.

Later that morning, Jennifer found herself sitting next to Faith in the hospital waiting room while Guy had a cut on his face stitched up and Timothy was given a check-up.

'You've been seeing him, haven't you?' Jennifer asked quietly.

'Yes,' Faith confirmed in an equally quiet voice. 'You have, too.'

Jennifer simply nodded. She was surprised it didn't hurt more.

She had known for certain the second Timothy got outside the wire, collapsed on to the grass and began hyperventilating.

'Timothy!'

Faith had flown to his side. She'd thrown herself down on the grass beside him and ripped open his shirt to make sure his heart was still beating. It had been all the confirmation Jennifer needed. Faith was in love with Timothy. The tiny gestures of adoration Dahlia had picked up while watching the TV award show hadn't been media lovey-style *affectation* after all. They were genuine *affection*. Timothy was Faith O'Connell's man.

'I think I love him,' said Faith as the love rivals sat side by side in the waiting room.

'It's a good job someone does,' Jennifer smiled.

'Don't you?'

Jennifer shrugged. 'I did.'

'And you don't any more?'

'I don't think I ever loved the Timothy that you do. I was in love with someone else. The Timothy he used to be.'

'Was that better?' Faith asked.

'Different,' said Jennifer after a bit. 'Look, do you mind if I see him for a moment? There are a couple of things I need to say.'

'It's not up to me to say who he sees,' said Faith.

'But I'd perfectly understand if you'd rather I didn't go in there.'

'Go in there,' Faith reiterated.

'I really won't be long.'

Jennifer got up and walked down the row of curtained cubicles until she came to the one where Timothy lay groaning. Hearing a conversation going on behind the curtains, Jennifer paused outside. The doctor was delivering his diagnosis.

'Nothing broken. Just a few bruises. And your muscles will probably feel quite sore tomorrow after all that physical exertion you've had. But you can go home whenever you like,' the doctor said.

'Are you sure?' asked Timothy. 'You don't think I should stay the night?'

'No need whatsoever,' said the doctor. 'You're perfectly all right.'

As he opened the curtain to let himself out, the doctor let Jennifer in.

'Jennifer,' Timothy croaked in a voice designed to elicit feminine sympathy.

'I heard the doctor say you can go. You must be relieved,' said Jennifer briskly. 'Faith is waiting outside to take you home.'

'Faith?'

'Your other girlfriend.'

Now Timothy looked really sick.

'I can explain,' he began.

'Please. Don't bother.' Jennifer sat down on the end of Timothy's bed. 'There really is no need.'

'But—'

Jennifer put a finger to Timothy's lips.

'There *really* is no need. When I got to the sanctuary this morning, I was already on my way to tell you that it's all over.'

'You were?'

'Yes. And it wasn't about Faith. It was about Ulysses. I told you I didn't think he was ready to join the troop. And I know you could see that too. But you went over my head and made the decision to release Ulysses into the enclosure before he was ready so that you would have the perfect ending for your TV show. What kind of conservationist are you, Timothy? A fourteen-year-old boy might have died because of you. Ulysses may still die. Just because you wanted to be on television on Christmas Eve instead of the meerkats.'

'Jennifer!'

'The sound girl told me all about it.'

'It isn't true.'

'Forget it, Timothy. The man I fell in love with all those years ago valued the lives of the chimpanzees he worked with at least as highly as he valued the lives of the human beings who loved him too.'

'But I do value them equally highly,' he protested.

'In a funny way, you're probably right,' Jennifer agreed. 'In that you think both the chimpanzees and the people who love you are equally dispensable in the cause of furthering your career.'

'That's not true.'

Jennifer put a finger to Timothy's lips again. 'That's the way it looks to me. Now, I think you'd better go home and use some bonobo-style loving to cement what you have with Faith. Quite inexplicably, she cares very much for you.'

Jennifer stood up to leave.

But not before Timothy got up out of the bed himself and gave her an impromptu flash of his bottom through the hospital gown as he struggled to put on his trousers.

'Jennifer! Don't walk away from me now!' he said.

She was already on her way.

Jennifer couldn't help smiling. It seemed that Dr Lauder was determined to be remembered for his bottom.

*   *   *

A few cubicles down, Guy was also dressed in a hospital gown. He quickly grabbed a blanket and threw it over his crotch when Jennifer opened the curtains.

'These things are really flimsy,' he said.

'Not like you to be shy,' Jennifer commented.

'How's Timothy?' Guy asked, ignoring her attempt to lighten the moment.

'Not half as bad as he deserves to be,' said Jennifer. 'They're letting him go home now.'

'Well, hadn't you better—'

'Faith has come to take him back to Oxford,' Jennifer interrupted.

'Oh, I'm sorry. I . . .'

'Don't be sorry. I should have known how it would turn out. The thing is, I'm not actually upset at all.'

'You're not?'

'Got other things to worry about. Like Ulysses and . . .'

'What?'

'You,' Jennifer said shyly.

Guy snorted.

'No need to worry about me. I'm just glad that Jamie is safe. Just got to pray that Ulysses makes it too.'

'Guy,' Jennifer stretched out her hand to touch his on top of the blanket he had leapt beneath. 'I just want to say that I'm sorry.'

Guy withdrew his hand.

'You were right. I was letting my feeling for Timothy interfere with my professional objectivity. It's entirely my fault that this has happened. I should have stood my ground earlier on.'

Guy listened to her in silence. She longed for him to interrupt and tell her that it didn't matter. That he understood and forgave her. But Guy wasn't about to let her off the hook.

'I should have listened to you. I succumbed to all my old prejudices about qualifications mattering more than experience. I've been so very, very stupid,' she said.

Guy didn't disagree.

'Can you ever forgive me?' she asked.

'I can't even think about forgiving anybody until I know that chimp is safe,' said Guy.

54

Nessa had been fielding calls from newspaper reporters all day, wanting to know if it was true that Timothy Lauder had nearly been eaten by one of her chimps. At first, she was at great pains to tell the reporters that physical aggression is one of the risks of working with chimps and that the animals in her sanctuary were not uncontrollable beasts who should be euthanised for the good of society. But when she got the fortieth call that day, she just picked up the phone and barked, 'Yes. And he deserved it!'

'I'm sorry,' said the man on the other end of the phone. 'I think I must have dialled the wrong number.'

His apology gave Nessa just enough time to calm down. 'No. I'm sorry. It's been a difficult day. How can I help you?' she asked, a little more reasonably.

'I'm trying to contact Nessa O'Neill.'

'This is she.'

'My name is Angus Jamieson of Jamieson and Jamieson Solicitors,' said the caller. 'We're acting in the matter of Major Ronald Parkinson's last will and testament. I am calling to tell you that Prowdes Animal Sanctuary is the major beneficiary.'

'What have we got?' Nessa wanted to ask. 'A walking stick and a packet of Polos?'

'You'll have to come into the office, of course,' Mr Jamieson continued. 'But I can tell you now that the Major has left a substantial amount of money and a parcel of land . . .'

'Where is the land?' Nessa almost whispered.

'Two thousand acres in Gambia.'

For a long time after she put down the phone to the Major's solicitor, Nessa sat in contemplative silence and looked out from her office over the sanctuary she had created at her home. The wind was blowing in from the sea, carrying the evening sounds of the chimpanzee troop through her open window. Nessa smiled a little sadly as she remembered how hard it had been to tell on evenings past whether Achilles was calling out to his family or the Major was doing a damn good impression.

Two thousand acres in Gambia . . . The papers making the land the Major's own had been signed just a few days before he died. This must have been the surprise he referred to at the wrap party. The surprise he didn't have time to deliver himself. How Nessa wished she could have thanked him in person.

'Nessa O'Neill, there's no need to thank me.' Nessa could almost hear the Major's voice as she remembered a conversation they once had in the nursery, while Mad and Bad swung from the Major's well-tailored jacket like chimpy epaulettes. It was in the early days of their acquaintance. Nessa had felt obliged to tell the Major that she couldn't afford to pay him for the help he had been giving about the place.

'I'm doing this because I want to. I don't need money!'

That much had been proven to be true. The cash that came with the land he had left Prowdes was equally staggering.

'The best thanks I ever get will be to see these boys back in Africa,' the Major had concluded.

'They're on their way,' Nessa whispered now as she heard Mad's unmistakable call.

The news about the land in Gambia gave Nessa all the encouragement she needed to refuse Jennifer's resignation.

'We are going to take the chimps to Africa,' Nessa said firmly. 'And we're not going to do it without you.'

A month later, Jennifer was still at the sanctuary.

And there was more good news.

Ulysses was back as well.

Despite Harrison's initially gloomy prognosis, the little chimp seemed to have made a complete recovery. His wounds were healing nicely and a brain scan had shown no damage caused by the fall on to that rock that had knocked him out. Soon he was back in a new small enclosure at Prowdes, though the subject of reintroducing him to the rest of the troop was closed for a while.

Meanwhile, Mad and Bad were getting on very happily with their new ape family. Those fearful few weeks in the halfway-house pen seemed utterly forgotten as the chimp twins caused as much amusement and mayhem for the likes of Achilles and Virginia as they had done for Jo-Jo, Guy and Snowy. Achilles too seemed much happier now that the television cameras were gone.

'Perhaps he feels that he can relax again now he's seen off another alpha male,' Snowy suggested one lunchtime.

'What, you mean Timothy Lauder?' Jo-Jo snorted. 'Oh, save me! Save me!' Jo-Jo's impression of Timothy Lauder running away from rampaging Achilles had become her favourite party piece. 'He ran like a girl,' Jo-Jo sneered, as though that was the worst thing she could say about him.

The TV viewing public were being far less kind. Timothy's programme for the BBC hadn't been quite the hit he expected. Timothy's condescending manner proved to be popular only with insecure schoolgirls. He was edited out of *Chimpanzee Rescue*. Even Faith O'Connell eventually turned her affections to the chap who had filmed *Meerkats Forever*. Meerkats were still the British public's favourite animal. Nessa was even considering the possibility that she might build a meerkat habitat with some of the money the Major had left behind . . .

The Major's bequest had enabled lots of changes at Prowdes. Ulysses' new enclosure was the first of a series of new buildings to replace the prefabricated huts that had clustered around the main house for years. Part-time staff who had lost their jobs during the belt-tightening years were reinstated. New staff were taken on.

Among those new staff was Jamie. He could only work weekends, until he finished his GCSEs, but Nessa was confident that one day he would be as good a keeper as Guy had proved himself to be. Arlene was incredibly proud of her son. The incident in the chimpanzee enclosure that might have cost him his life had instead given him a new direction.

It was only natural that Jamie would work closely with Ulysses.

Jennifer had hoped that Ulysses' safe return to the sanctuary might be the catalyst for a defrosting in her relationship with Guy in the wake of the Timothy Lauder Incident, but though he was always polite to her, Guy chose not to spend any more time with Jennifer than he had to. In a curious reversal of the way things had been when Jennifer first came to the sanctuary, it was Snowy and Jo-Jo who found themselves defending their boss to Guy.

'She's all right,' said Jo-Jo.

'I'm not coming down the Wily Fox unless you start inviting her again too,' said Snowy.

But Guy wouldn't budge. He had not forgotten how frightened he felt when he faced Achilles to save Jamie and Ulysses. He had not forgotten whose fault it was he found himself in that position in the first place.

Jennifer gave up trying to extend the olive branch from her side of the broken friendship.

A few weeks later, the first hint that winter was on its way was in the air. It was the weekend but there had been hardly any visitors that day. Jennifer wandered into Ulysses' enclosure to check that the heating thermostat had been turned up for the night. As she pushed the door open, she could see that Jamie was already in there. Jennifer hesitated, hoping that Ulysses' reaction to her entrance would alert Jamie to the fact that he wasn't alone, before she got closer and gave him a real shock.

But Ulysses didn't seem to have noticed Jennifer walking in either. He was sitting close to the mesh, watching Jamie intently. Jamie was signing. Jennifer wondered what the young lad was saying. Until his arrival at the sanctuary, Jennifer had known only three signs, all in American sign language, learned while she was in San Diego. They had a chimpanzee language project there. Now all the staff at Prowdes were having signing classes.

'Perhaps we'll get the chimps talking too,' Snowy had joked.

Jamie obviously felt he was imparting some important knowledge to his chimp friend and Ulysses still didn't seem to have noticed the other human being. Jennifer took a couple of steps forward. And then she saw . . .

'Jamie,' she grabbed him by the shoulder. 'Jamie, did Ulysses just sign at you?'

She said it with exaggerated lip movements, hoping that Jamie would answer her question while she still searched for the symbols to ask it again in BSL.

Jamie looked terrified.

'Is he signing?' Jennifer scribbled on a piece of paper.

'Guy told me not to tell anyone,' Jamie half signed, half scribbled back.

'What does he know?' Jennifer scrawled before pointing to the chimpanzee prodigy.

'Not much,' said Jamie. 'Just a few signs. Thank you.' Jennifer recognised that one. 'Water. Hello. Am I going to get into trouble?' Jamie asked.

'It's not his fault,' said Guy. He had walked into the middle of the commotion. 'I told him not to let anyone else in on the secret. I didn't want the TV people to turn Ulysses into a freak show.'

'But,' Jennifer said sadly, 'couldn't you have at least told me?'

'I was going to. The night you didn't show up at the Boat House. After that, I didn't dare to. I was sure you would tell

Timothy and there was no way he was going to keep Ulysses' signing skills out of the show.'

'Where on earth did he learn this?'

'He must have learned it from the gang who trained him to pick a lock.'

Jennifer sat down on the bench opposite Ulysses and looked at him.

'How come he never signed to me?'

'Jamie thinks he only bothers with people he thinks might understand.'

Jennifer sank her head into her hands. Her shoulders heaved up and down as she began to cry. Jamie looked at Guy, who still regarded Jennifer somewhat stonily. Hesitantly, the teenager put his hand on Jennifer's shoulder to comfort her. Then he got up and left the adults alone.

'What are we going to do about this?' Guy asked.

Jennifer looked up and wiped her hand across her nose. 'I suppose we really ought to tell Nessa. And do some proper research.'

'I want to protect Ulysses from ruthless television people,' said Guy.

'Of course.'

Ulysses shuffled closer and brought his hands up to his mouth. He hesitated for a moment, as if to be sure he had both Guy and Jennifer's attention. Then he started to sign once again.

'What exactly is he signing?' Jennifer asked Guy.

'I think he's saying that we should be friends,' he said.

'And do you agree?' said Jennifer.

'You know what,' said Guy, 'I think I do.'

EPILOGUE

Eighteen months later. Cinderella's nightclub. Tincastle. Jennifer Niederhauser stood in the middle of the dance floor dressed in a naughty nun's habit while a stripper dressed as a chimpanzee waved his banana at her menacingly. Not that menacingly, Jennifer noted. He was pretty unimpressive beneath the monkey suit.

Jennifer submitted graciously to the monkey-man's advances. She winced at the thought of all that baby oil rubbing against her but she wasn't quite so bothered about this outfit – a nylon special from Ann Summers. From the sidelines, Dahlia clapped and shouted, 'Get 'em off! Get 'em off! Get 'em off!' She had, of course, organised the hen night. And it was the hen night of Jennifer's nightmares. Mexican restaurant, compulsory tequila slammers, a stripper.

But Jennifer didn't mind too much. Because in less than a week's time she would be getting to see chimpanzees in Africa for real. With the ape-man of her dreams.

THE END!

ACKNOWLEDGEMENTS

This book was written on location in the Hollywood Hills! And I couldn't have done it without:

Editor:	Carolyn Mays
Assistant editor:	Alex Bonham
Publicity:	Emma Longhurst
Distribution:	Hodder & Stoughton!
	Thank you all.
Business affairs:	Antony Harwood
	James Macdonald Lockhart
	Tony Gardner
	Sheryl Petersen
	Mary Stanford
	Sally Riley
	James Pusey
	Markus Hoffman
Animal experts:	Dr Kay Farmer
	Amos Courage
	Stephanie Ziebarth
	Claire Dore
Property master:	Dan Rhodes
Transportation captain:	Frank Strausser's airport limo service
Storyboard:	Louise Bagshawe, Jenny Colgan, Stella Duffy, Mike Gayle, Louise Harwood, Lauren Henderson, Lisa Jewell, Serena Mackesy, Jojo Moyes, Victoria Routledge, Matt Whyman and Madeleine Wickham.
Rigging electrics:	Chris Hobbs
Costume:	Jane Brown
Hair:	Danuta Keane

Make-up:	Jennifer Niederhauser
Focus puller:	Ryan Law
Key grip:	Jack Malvern
Special effects:	Sacha Gervasi
Still photos by:	Michael Pilkington
Best boy:	Guy Hazel

Very special thanks:
the Manbys and the Arnolds, as ever.

Find out the facts about chimpanzees and other endangered primates at The International Primate Protection League's website: www.ippl.org.

Happy ever after?
or
Right shoes, right dress,
wrong husband?
Are you...

Her new bestseller
out July 2005

Subscribe to
COSMOPOLITAN
for just HALF PRICE!

Save 50% when you treat yourself or someone special to a subscription to **Cosmopolitan** for just £17.70 by annual direct debit - saving you £17.70 a year on the full rate.

- ◆ **SAVE £17.70 a year**
- ◆ **ONLY £1.48 per copy** (new price £2.95)
- ◆ **FREE home delivery**

HURRY! This offer MUST close 31st August 2005
Simply call our hotline quoting MA07

0870 124 1050

lines open weekdays 8am-9.30pm, Saturdays 8am-4pm
You can also order securely online.
Simply visit www.subscription.co.uk/cosmo/MA07

This offer is available for UK subscriptions only (excluding BFPO addresses) when paying by annual direct debit only. All orders acknowledged within 14 days. This offer cannot be used in conjunction with any other promotion and closes 31st August 2005. All information correct at time of going to press. The full subscription rate is £35.40 for 12 issues. For subscription enquiries please call 01858 438 838.